Studies in German Literature, Linguistics, and Culture

The Last von Reckenburg

Louise von François at about age sixty.
Photograph courtesy the Kulturhistorisches Museum für Weissenfels

Louise von François

The Last von Reckenburg

With an Introduction by
Tiiu V. Laane

CAMDEN HOUSE

Introduction copyright © 1995 by
CAMDEN HOUSE, INC.

Published by Camden House, Inc.
Drawer 2025
Columbia, SC 29202 USA

Printed on acid-free paper.
Binding materials are chosen for strength and
durability.

All Rights Reserved
Printed in the United States of America
First Edition

ISBN:1-879751-96-8

Library of Congress Cataloging-in-Publication Data

François, Louise von, 1817-1893
   [Letzte Reckenburgerin. English]
   The last von Reckenburg / Louise von François ; with an
introduction by Tiiu V. Laane. -- 1st ed.
       p. cm.   -- (Studies in German literature, linguistics, and
culture)
   Includes bibliographical references.
   ISBN 1-879751-96-8 (alk. paper)
   I. Laane, Tiiu V. II. Title. III. Series: Studies in German
literature, linguistics, and culture (Unnumbered)
PT1865.F2L413   1994
833'.7--dc20   94-30482
                                                                     CIP

Acknowledgments

Louise von François was an intriguing nineteenth-century German author whose works exhibit, as the Swiss writer Conrad Ferdinand Meyer stated, a curious, yet homogeneous blend of liberal and conservative viewpoints. Her narratives, which are considerably more complex than has been recognized, deserve to be much better known today. For this reason I am especially gratified that this reprint will make her famous novel *The Last von Reckenburg* once again readily available to English speaking audiences. It is most fitting that Camden House, with its mission to restore important literary works to the reading public, has undertaken the task of publishing this translation, which in its day brought François highest acclaim in Germany. As an exciting and innovative example of nineteenth-century German literature, *The Last von Reckenburg* should serve as an important means to further arouse the interest of American and British audiences for German culture and literature. Carrying a surprisingly biting covert feminist message, the novel should also be of great interest to students and scholars working in the area of women's studies and feminist criticism.

I am grateful to the College of Liberal Arts and the Office of University Research Services at Texas A&M University for financial support for this undertaking. My special thanks go to James Hardin for his wise counsel. His quest to recover great works of literature and his love of books have been an inspiration for me during my work on this project.

TL
August 1994

Introduction

Louise von François (1817-1893), with Annette von Droste-Hülshoff and Marie von Ebner-Eschenbach, was one of three major nineteenth-century female writers in German. Her reputation rests primarily on the remarkable novel *Die letzte Reckenburgerin,* which appeared in periodical form in 1870 and in book form in 1871, (translated as *The Last von Reckenburg,* 1887). The book made her famous overnight after the noted writer and literary critic Gustav Freytag reviewed it in 1872 in the *Neues Reich* (New Reich) and praised it as one of the finest novels of the last decade. He expressed hope that this "rare gift" would endure in literature. Other well-known contemporary writers and critics joined in the accolades. The literary historian, Karl Hillebrand, surveying the novel's rich language, clear structure and original characters, pronounced *The Last von Reckenburg* a model novel in every regard. It is said that the noted man of letters, Fritz Reuter, kept a copy of *The Last von Reckenburg* on his desk at all times, while Ebner-Eschenbach proclaimed, with characteristic modesty, that she would have exchanged all her works for the honor of having written François's novel. Conrad Ferdinand Meyer (1825-1898), a celebrated Swiss poet and writer of novellas, sought François's advice for his own writings, declaring that her novel was a masterpiece. Using a complicated time structure and alternating narrators with different viewpoints, *The Last von Reckenburg* was indeed one of the most technically innovative novels of the late nineteenth century.

Freytag's heartfelt wish that the novel would maintain its prominence, however, did not come fully to pass. The work did bring François fame in the 1870s and 1880s, went through four further printings during her lifetime, and was translated into Dutch, Danish and English, appearing both in America and in England. By the time of her death, however, François had fallen into obscurity. Her numerous stories and two other novels, although praised for their careful craftsmanship and perceptive psychological detail, were no longer read, even though literary critics generally agree that François's prose rivals that of Theodor Storm and Wilhelm Raabe in artistic merit. Even *The Last von Reckenburg,* although it continued to be reprinted, was for the most part ignored by literary historians. Blame has been placed on the difficulty of François's prose and on overemphasis of nineteenth-century literary criticism on the *Bildungsroman* at the expense of sociopolitical novels. Contemporary feminist critics, until recently, have generally neglected François since they have failed to find a radical champion in her. Ultimately, recognition for François's work has suffered along with that of other nineteenth-century women writers whose literary creation has been relegated to the secondary status of the *Frauenroman* (women's novel) or to *Trivialliteratur* (ephemeral literature).

Marie Louise von François was born on 27 June 1817 in Herzberg on the Elster river. She was the eldest child of the Prussian Major Friedrich von François (1772-1818), a military nobleman of French Huguenot descent, and Amalie Henriette Hohl (1796-1871) who came from a wealthy bourgeois family in Weißenfels in the Prussian province of Saxony. When François's father died in 1818, her mother moved back to Weißenfels where she married the Judge Advocate Adolf August Herbst (1792-1874) in 1819. The family led a comfortable life in a large house on the marketplace, which François was to later describe as the home of her heroine Eberhardine in *The Last von Reckenburg*.

Not much is known about François's education, except that it was meager. She received only private tutoring in the company of a few other children. Painfully aware of the poverty of her education, François augmented her learning by reading everything she could get her hands on. A bright and mercurial child, François acquired the nickname "Fräulein Grundtext" (Miss Original Text) because of her intellectual curiosity and endless questions. Her special love was history. She often read out loud from accounts of Saxon and Prussian history to her stepfather who had poor eyesight. Notable historic events and heroic battles were to serve later as the backdrop of many of François's narratives. Furthermore, the tales of her two grandmothers, Hohl and Herbst, both avid storytellers, inspired François's interest in the late eighteenth and early nineteenth century. The historical coloring of François's works as well as her ardent love of homeland, can be traced clearly to these early influences. Her narratives repeatedly herald the glories of Prussia and call for a strong and unified German nation, brought about through the hegemony of Prussia.

During her youth, François absorbed the influence of literary figures in Weißenfels such as Johann Gottfried Seume (1763-1810) and the playwright Adolf Müllner (1774-1829), the famous author of "Schicksalstragödien" (tragedies of fate), who made his library available to her and fostered her interest in Sir Walter Scott. François's special mentor in her early years was the family physician and friend Doctor Johann Friedrich Traugott Schütze (1771-1850). Schütze was a man of science with rationalist bias who steered her away from the Romantic tendencies of her era. François's composed, unsentimental, and disciplined manner reflect this early influence. Schütze introduced François to the humanistic concepts of the Enlightenment and instilled in her a reliance on reason. Under his tutelage, François developed an inclination for critical and independent thinking along with a rationalistic stance toward religion.

Spiritual and intellectual stimulation also entered François's realm through the novelist and feminist Fanny Tarnow (1779-1862) who had moved to Weißenfels in 1828. François was invited to Tarnow's literary salon, where she participated in the discussion of the newest literary works and where she developed a love for the works of Goethe and Lord Byron. She also learned to appreciate socially critical authors like George Eliot, Heinrich Heine, Charles Dickens, and George Sand. In 1856, François was to write a probing review of Sand's *L'historie de ma vie* (Story of my Life) published in Robert Prutz's *Deutsches Museum* (German Museum). On a more personal level, Tarnow's salon became the setting where François met and fell in love with the elegant and articulate Count Alfred von Görtz, an officer stationed at the Weißenfels garrison. They met in 1834 when she was seventeen and became engaged. Unfortunately, the financial circumstances of the François family worsened significantly at this time since a guardian had squandered away the inheritance of the François children. Protracted court proceedings began that ultimately ended with the decision against the children. As litigation dragged on, Görtz became impatient and began to long for his freedom. Propelled by her sense of self-dignity, François released him from his promise in 1840. Although François was only twenty-three years old at this time, the dissolution of the engagement represented the end of her youth and she withdrew from society. Arduous and lonesome years followed as the financial circumstances of François's family continually worsened.

Relief came for François in 1848 when François's uncle, the widowed General Karl von François, called her to Minden where she was to manage his household. Here she met both Elise von Hohenhausen, a Hessian writer known for her translations of Byron and Sir Walter Scott, and her daughter Elise Rüdiger von Hohenhausen, who was to become a staunch supporter of François's literary activity. François's uncle doted on François. He had experienced a colorful career as a soldier in the Napoleonic Wars (1813-1815). The uncle's tales further stimulated François's fascination with the military and reinforced her belief in the concepts of honor and duty which she made binding to both men and women, at times to the point of self-abnegation.

The happy years in Minden ended in 1850 after the ultimate decision of the court against François and her brother. François returned to Weißenfels to arrange legal matters, returning to Minden in 1851 to care for her aging uncle. They moved first to Halberstadt and then in 1852 to

Potsdam. Here François observed first hand the profound changes in a society shifting from feudal structures to industrialism. After her uncle's death in 1855, François returned to her parent's house in Weißenfels where she was never again to leave the bedside of the sick and dying. Her mother had broken a hip and remained bedridden until she died in 1871. François's stepfather become progressively more blind. François herself was in bad health, poor, lonely, and an "old maid" — a lowly status in nineteenth-century society. On her return from Potsdam, François had brought along her first essay, "Potsdam [Weihnachten 1854]" (Potsdam, Christmas, 1854), in which she had captured her impressions of her uncle's hometown. Fanny Tarnow and Elise Rüdiger von Hohenhausen urged her to publish it. François hesitated, even though she and her family were in urgent need of money. Unknown to François, Elise Rüdiger sent François's sharply drawn sociohistorical essay to Hermann Hauff, the editor of Cotta's *Morgenblatt für gebildete Leser* (Morning Paper for Educated Readers). Impressed by the color and firmness of François's writing, Hauff published the study in 1855 under the acronym V. L. and requested further materials. François's first story "Aus dem Leben meines Urgroßvaters" (From the Life of my Great-Grandfather) appeared in 1855, based on the tales of François's grandmother Hohl. It takes up the conflict between duty and inclination that was to traverse François's narratives in leitmotif fashion, becoming later the theme of *The Last von Reckenburg*.

In becoming a writer, François, by now thirty-nine years old, was well aware that, by nineteenth-century standards, she was entering into a disreputable profession for a woman. Writers, both male and female, in fact, were considered dubious in the 1850s. She consequently kept her literary activities secret from her family, writing in the night or in the early hours of the morning. Her days were taken up by caring for her ill parents. All early works were published either anonymously or under a pseudonym. Painfully shy, François was repulsed by the thought of public scrutiny. She repeatedly denied any artistic impulse to write and did not seem to much care, in fact, if her works were mistakenly attributed to men. She claimed that if she had been able to afford a living knitting socks, indeed that would have been her preference. Her self-effacement as author led her to condemn her works with inordinate harshness, although at the same time contradictory statements point to a deeply felt authorial pride. In a letter of 1 August 1883 to Conrad Ferdinand Meyer, for example, she referred to her favorite novella, *Judith, die Kluswirtin* (Judith, the Keeper of the Klus Inn, 1862) as a piece of "old warmed-up pumpernickel" that Meyer would find hard to digest, but then proceeded to point out its best features. The majority of François's narratives appeared in the *Morgenblatt*. In all she wrote seventeen stories and six essays in the 1850s and 1860s that take up various sociopolitical themes such as class prejudice, duty to the family or fatherland, and religious intolerance. She wrote one comedy *Der Posten der Frau* (The Wife's Post), which was published in 1857.

In spite of her productivity, renown evaded François, due in large part to her anonymity. Her royalties remained meager. She began work on *The Last von Reckenburg* in the 1860s. *Morgenblatt* accepted it for publication, but due to the death of its editor Hauff, the journal failed in 1865, and the manuscript was returned to François. François's supporters began a seemingly endless search for a publisher, even in America. The manuscript went from hand to hand for years. Through efforts of the poet Otto Roquette and Dr. Julius Thümmel, the husband of François's friend Mathilde Graefe, the novel was published in 1870 by Otto Janke's *Deutsche Romanzeitung*. François received the negligible sum of 150 gulden (300 marks) for this work. A year later, Janke brought it out in book form in a two-volume edition. The novel found little recognition until the noted writer Gustav Freytag reviewed it in 1872 with highest accolades. François became famous overnight. The work was reprinted and appeared in translation.

In the years following the publication of *The Last von Reckenburg*, François continued writing stories and also published a second novel, *Frau Erdmuthens Zwillingssöhne* (Mrs. Erdmuthe's Twin Sons) in 1872. This was followed by a historical work, *Geschichte der preußischen Befreiungskriege in den Jahren 1813-1815: ein Lesebuch für Schule und Haus* (History of the Prussian Wars of Liberation in the Years 1813-1815: A Reader for School and Home) in 1874. Following the death of her parents, François moved to smaller quarters, her beloved "Mansardenstube" (attic room), overlooking the river Saale, where she enjoyed some of her happiest years, reading a great deal, especially Goethe and works of history. Frequently she lent a helping hand to those ill or in need. In this last creative decade François completed her longest novel, a "Bildungsroman" called *Die Stufenjahre eines Glücklichen* (The Steps through the Years of a Lucky Fellow), published in 1877. It received little recognition in François's day, the first edition never selling out. François remained indifferent. She characteristically took little interest in the business aspect of her own publications, at times not even knowing where her works were published and often receiving copies only as presents from relatives. After finishing her last novella, "Der Katzenjunker" (The Cat Junker) in 1879, François declared that she felt no more creative urge to write and began a life of solitude and independence in Weißenfels, taking long walks and reading voraciously.

François's final years passed quietly. After several individual grants initiated at the secret request of friends, the German "Schillerstiftung" (Schiller Foundation) awarded François a lifetime pension in 1880 which enabled her to live out her life with modest financial security. She attended concerts and exhibits and took occasional trips. As friends and relatives died, François became more and more alone. Her health began to fail. While still able to attend a meeting of the Goethe Society in 1891 in Weimar, she met well-known writers of her day, Karl Emil Franzos, Julius Rodenberg, Friedrich Spielhagen, and others, who acknowledged her work. She knew of them and was surprised that they knew her too. Her failing health took a turn for the worse in 1893. She died on 25 September 1893 in Weißenfels, all but forgotten by the reading public.

Soon after the initial excitement created by Freytag's review had subsided, the majority of nineteenth-century literary critics began to neglect François and her novel, devoting at best a line or two about its virtues in literary histories. Literary historians such as Karl Barthel, Christian Oeser and Wilhelm Pütz did not mention her at all while Franz Hirsch in his *Geschichte der deutschen Literatur* in 1883 found it sufficient to acknowledge François in one sentence and call *The Last von Reckenburg* "an important novel." Along with other women writers, François and her exceptional novel were also often relegated to the dubious section of literary histories labeled "women's novels" and dismissed with a sentence. The fact that François herself had continually denigrated her own work during her own lifetime surely must also have taken its toll. In the years following her death, a number of champions emerged who sought to breathe renewed interest in the novel. Among these, Richard M. Meyer in his *Deutsche Literatur des neunzehnten Jahrhunderts*, written in 1900, argued that the novel had such merit that if "one were to put all German novels through the narrowest of sieves, François's novel would remain behind as one of the few dozen best written after Goethe." Eduard Engel proclaimed in a similar fashion in 1906 in his *Geschichte der deutschen Literatur* that François belonged without a doubt among the great, even to the greatest writers of the nineteenth century. The majority of reviewers concentrated foremost on the high moral tone of the novel and interpreted the work as expression of Francois's "womanly nobility of spirit." They lauded the fact that it was untainted by sympathies for the growing women's movement.

François's centennial in 1917 brought a flurry of interest in *The Last von Reckenburg*, but the fame of the novel reached its zenith during the Weimar Republic (1917-1933). A five-volume collection of her works was published by Insel, and dissertations about her were written at universities. Newspapers published a flood of articles on François. Speeches and conferences were held at Weißenfels. Between 1918 and 1930 *The Last von Reckenburg* received thirty reprints or editions. The Insel edition contained a printing of forty-nine to fifty-eight thousand copies, a remarkable triumph. The sudden popularity of the novel arose not so much from the recognition of its artistic merits, but from the perception that François was an exemplary Prussian patriot. Her novel with its nationalistic message spoke to Germans recovering from the humiliating terms of the Treaty of Versailles. Accolades abounded. Paul Fechter, after praising the uniqueness of François's characters, stated in 1932 in his *Dichtung der Deutschen* (Writings by Germans) that "no woman's hand had until now produced such a novel." Indeed, few men could write such a fine one. Arthur Eloesser trumped Fechter by claiming in his *Die deutsche Literatur* (German Literature, 1931) that François had, in fact, surpassed all men around her. The greatest praise that critics seemed able to accord to the novel was that it had been written in a "manly" style and with "manly" intellect, qualities meant to laud the firm objectivity and serious thought content of the novel. *The Last von Reckenburg* was again posited as an exemplary "women's novel," a label that lowered it to a secondary literary form, even while praising it.

And yet, the popularity of *The Last von Reckenburg* fell again into decline after the fall of the Weimar Republic, although not before first being exploited by the Nazis to promote their own agenda. François's Prussian spirit, her interest in the military, her ardent patriotism, and anti-French stance, expressed not only in *The Last von Reckenburg* but also in her other narratives, appealed to the National Socialists. So also did her womanly strength of character and emphasis on the ideal of motherhood. Several new issues of the novel appeared during the Nazi years. In 1943 *The Last von Reckenburg* was retitled *Die letzte Reckenburgerin: Die Lebensgeschichte einer deutschen Frau* (The Last von Reckenburg: The Life Story of a German Woman) and was praised as an outstanding novel. After 1945, François's name disappeared, leading to renewed rescue attempts by isolated but notable literary critics such as Ernst Alker in 1950, Emil Staiger in 1954, Paul Fechter in 1960 and Werner Kohlschmidt in 1975. New editions of *The Last von Reckenburg* appeared in 1957 and 1965, but the novel did not become a part of the academic canon.

The advent of feminist criticism, with its rediscovery of women writers working on behalf of feminist causes, did not at first bring renewed interest in François. Although François had become acquainted with feminist writers in Tarnow's salon and followed the women's movement throughout her life with interest, she was never counted among writers of the nineteenth-century German women's movement nor did she excite the imagination of feminist scholars. François's stance toward women's issues was that of the moderate German feminists such as Fanny Lewald, Louise Otto-Peter, and Luise Büchner. François believed in the sacrosanct role of a woman as wife and mother, argued for the importance of the home, and affirmed the conservative view that men and women had indeed gender-based characteristics. A progressive feminist message expressing firm opinions about the inequities faced by nineteenth-century women is, however, always submerged within the broader artistic and philosophical frameworks of her narratives. Her admonition to society to redress injustices committed against women economically, psychologically, and socially is carefully balanced with a more traditional call for women to participate in "womanly" roles and to perform deeds of social service. Conrad Ferdinand Meyer described François's works as a curious, yet homogeneous blend of conservative and liberal viewpoints. It is only since the 1980s that this psychological depth of her works has begun to be discovered, bringing with it a renewed renaissance of François studies, this time with an added dimension. Thomas C. Fox took up the cause with his dissertation on François in 1983. Utilizing feminist methodology, he has sparked new interest in François's life and her famous novel with his seminal feminist reading of *The Last von Reckenburg*. Scholars are just beginning to discover the ambiguities of Louise von François's voice and have begun to use feminist literary tools to unlock the intricacies of her narratives.

The Last von Reckenburg is a complex and intriguing novel which gives voice not only to François's deeply felt humanistically rooted value system, but also to her concerns about the life of nineteenth-century women. Like other bourgeois writers of the ethically sensitive second half of the nineteenth century — Gottfried Keller, Gustav Freytag, Theodor Storm, Wilhelm Raabe and Theodor Fontane — François believed in the bourgeois ideals of duty, work, social conscience, and moral behavior, and used her works for didactic purpose to exemplify these values. *The Last von Reckenburg* is at once a social novel, a historical novel, and a fascinating study of human psychology. In a letter to Conrad Ferdinand Meyer on 17 May 1881, François claimed that the impulse for the story came by sheer accident, as if "a blind chicken had found a kernel." She had read in a newspaper or perhaps seen in Weißenfels that a vagabond had approached a fine lady on the street, claiming that she was his mother. This event had concentrated in François's mind into "a certain ideal focal point," the story of two women, one who perishes from the excesses of her inner nature, the other who must learn to augment her lacking personality. As is typical in François's writings, the theme of the novel can be summed up with a few words. It is one that transverses François's narratives. Exemplified through two contrasting women figures, the story focuses on the conflict between two opposing value systems: duty and inclination, reason and feeling, conscience and frivolity. The aristocratic Eberhardine von Reckenburg is a prototype of the strong, self-disciplined, stern and "manly" women one encounters in François's narratives. Eberhardine anchors her life in her family's motto "In Recht und Ehren" (In Right and Honor) and becomes embroiled in a moral dilemma when she is forced to evade the truth in order to protect her childhood study companion, the bourgeois Dorothee (Dorl), the daughter of a cooper. In contrast to Eberhardine, the exquisite and frivolous Dorothee, the prototype of a nineteenth-century child-woman, gives in to her every inclination, her actions leading to a scandalous pregnancy and her ultimate destruction.

François was repeatedly asked whether she herself had not served as the model for her independently-minded and highly competent Eberhardine. Verbal echoes, events and places in the novel clearly link François to her heroine and critics have persisted in drawing parallels. The studious Eberhardine, like François, is called "Fräulein Grundtext." Clear-thinking and strong in character like François herself, Eberhardine is also tall and slender, as was François who was imposingly tall and regal in bearing. François's family residence on the marketplace in Weißenfels serves as the model for the Reckenburg house, a house with an unusually high roof in relation to the building, described even today in Weißenfels as "the pug with a tall night cap." Similarly, both Eberhardine and François lose the loves of their lives in their youth, François her fiancée, and Eberhardine her intended fiancé, Prince August. François wore a white dress with blue ribbons during her engagement. Eberhardine sadly loses the opportunity, but speaks longingly of such joyous arraignment.

In spite of such correlations, François repeatedly denied that the work had autobiographical tendencies, leading her friend Marie von Ebner-Eschenbach to conclude that François must have felt embarrassed by the "too flattering" comparison. In fact, François's heroine is by no means a paragon of virtue. Although a rational girl with an iron will, Eberhardine burns with jealousy when Dorl gets the man that Eberhardine loves herself. She assesses Dorl's affair with Prince August with bitter irony and resents having to keep Dorl's secret. Eberhardine is mean-spirited toward Dorl's son and puffed up with aristocratic class-consciousness. Similarly, Dorl exhibits intriguing nuances of personality. François was impatient with black and white characters and found them uninteresting and unrealistic. The gentle and flighty Dorl can be coolly cunning if it suits her purposes. The book abounds with a rich array of secondary characters who exemplify similarly multi-faceted personalities. The most memorable among these is the Black Reckenburg, Eberhardine's aunt, a ghostly money-making machine who is at the core painfully vulnerable. Similarly, the physician Siegmund Faber is an intriguing personality. Rational and cold, he is a man of science who feels at home slicing up the dead in morgues and on the battlefield, but he is naively blind to living human beings and to their emotions.

The most innovative aspect of François's novel is its intricate structure. With her customary self-effacement, François told Conrad Ferdinand Meyer that the work had not cost her any more effort than all of her other works, although she admitted to having worked "slowly and laboriously." In fact, the novel is composed so cunningly that its structure is almost seamless. It makes use of a complicated time framework, unusual for novels of the late nineteenth century. Told by alternating narrators whose tales overlap at pivotal points of the story, the events move backward and forward in time in a complicated pattern. The unnamed narrator of the "Introduction," most likely a member of Eberhardine's Reckenburg community, an omniscient narrator, introduces the story with a "pivot," the birth of the daughter of a crippled soldier, August Müller, the "vagabond" who goes later in search of his mother. Eberhardine, speaking in the first person, functions as the second narrator of the novel. Making use of pervasive self-irony, she relates her own life's story, which makes up the body of the narrative. Eberhardine's story progresses in linear fashion, regressing at times or in other instances bringing in yet other narrative voices through the use of letters or reports. Her story intersects again and again at important junctures with the life of Dorothee. Critical scenes such as the funeral of Eberhardine's father, the meeting of "mother" and "son," repeat from the multiple viewpoints of the characters, creating intense suspense as to the truth of the happening. The novel abounds with the skillful use of foreshadowing that propels the events forward with the suspense of a mystery novel. Rich symbolism of colors — green, white, red and blue — and images of light and dark help weave the story into a dense and complicated pattern. François uses archaic language, which shimmers at times with a rococo beauty, to endow her story with a timeless sense of warmth.

While François's contemporaries were captivated by the historical content of her novel, they were similarly moved by the charm of its setting and by its social message. The work shares the ardent nationalism of German historical novels published between 1850 and 1875 and speaks of François's burning wish for a unified German nation. Written in the decade preceding the birth of the German state under the hegemony of Prussia in 1871, the novel must have appeared to François's contemporaries as a celebration of the new nation. Lauded by Werner Kohlschmidt as "a classic within the historical novel form," the work traces Eberhardine's lifetime from 1775 to 1837, and depicts the German struggle to repulse Napoleon, evoking the historical events spanning the French Revolution (1789) to the years past the Prussian Wars of Liberation (1813-1815). The novel also heralds a new social order, one without class prejudice and rigid class stratification. It was a social ideal not achieved even at François's own time, which was festering with class tensions in the 1860s in an era of growing industrialization. *The Last von Reckenburg* thus serves as an admonition to François's contemporaries to achieve more equitable social structures. At the same time, the novel recreates poetically a past era and culture which François saw disappearing. The work is tinged with a sense of nostalgia, even elegy. Peopled with colorful princes, stalwart burghers, soldiers, and aristocrats, the novel conjures up with vivid strokes the atmosphere and culture of the late eighteenth and early nineteenth century. Colorful vignettes, drawn with mellow humor and gentle irony, recreate life in a little city in the Province of Saxony with such loving accuracy that the reader feels transported. Eberhardine's clumsy attempts at learning the minuet, her acquiescence to the necessity of having her waist compressed to the size of a wasp's, her kind-hearted father's indifference to the glances of his neighbors, as he—an aristocrat!—ties up beans in his garden, such scenes linger in the mind of the reader and serve to highlight a culture bound by strict social rules and regulations. Finely developed scenes of social satire depict a society intent in keeping the different social classes in their proper places. The tone of the novel can at times be bitter as it criticizes ossified class stratification. The arrogant and aristocratic Black Reckenburg, determined to have an heir with pure aristocratic bloodlines, allows herself to be humiliated and brought to financial ruin by her noble husband, the womanizing Prince Christian, who recklessly gambles away her fortune. The bourgeoisie, on the other hand, are condemned to the life of second class citizens. Dorothee breaks all rules of eighteenth-century society when she, a burgher, dances with Prince August. Scandal erupts when he kisses her. Eberhardine sums up the momentous social implications of the occurrence pointedly: "All order was broken up." Dorothee is ostracized.

Eberhardine herself remains class conscious throughout the novel—she insists that Dorl, her childhood friend and study companion, curtsy to her after they have reached legal maturity, and address her by the formal "you" [Sie]. However, Eberhardine gradually begins to understand the harmful effects of social polarization. Significantly, she bequeaths her Reckenburg estate to a young woman of mixed class origins who is married to a capable and honest burgher. She does not adopt her heir nor pass on the aristocratic name of Reckenburg. Much like other nineteenth-century authors, Karl Immermann, Fanny Lewald and later Theodor Fontane, for whom the question of marriage across class lines also became a dominant issue, François implicitly suggests a reorganization of society based on the recognition of the inner worth of the individual. The narrative suggests the need for a healthy intermingling of the classes. At the same time, the novel appeals to the aristocrats, known for their excesses, to set their own house in order. Symbolically, Eberhardine, an aristocrat, dispatches the renovation of her estate with Faustian energy, after years of neglect by the old Black Reckenburg who let her tenants live in squalor. Eberhardine's actions affirm the universal validity of bourgeois values: the work ethos, self-reliance, and social concern for others. Ethically vigorous people like Eberhardine help forge the bridge to new, and better, times. The novel ends on a utopian note, even though François, writing in her little attic room in Weissenfels, was keenly aware that the time of social harmony was far from reality. In the end, she likens Eberhardine's story to a "fairy tale," implying with irony that the novel, which serves as an example of how people can bring about harmonious human existence, is, in fact, fiction.

A disturbing and ambiguous feminist sub-text undercuts the idealistic conclusion further. The novel makes a powerful protest against nineteenth-century patriarchal structures, but does so in such a veiled manner that *The Last von Reckenburg* has been celebrated repeatedly as the work of a "noble lady," incapable of injecting her works with a feminist message. Writing at a time when vitriolic attacks against women's causes were a norm, François recessed her incisive criticism carefully within the conservative ideological content of the story. Modern readers, sensitive to feminist methodology, however, can not miss her condemnation of the chilling abuse of the female personality. They will be engrossed by the story of the impulsive and gentle Dorl, whose collapse results as much from her own weakness as from her entrapment in the numbing constraints of patriarchal society. Significantly, the conservative philosophy of the novel is never questioned and Dorl's sins against society are never excused. Implicitly, however, François leaves the evaluation of the causes of Dorl's behavior - her economic helplessness, her lack of opportunity for self-development, and the social limitations on her life due to her class and gender - up to the reader. It is the reader who must see clearly and judge fairly. At the same time, François counters the image of female weakness with a picture of female strength portrayed through Eberhardine, who functions not only as the personification of the concepts of duty and conscience, but as a vision of the "new" woman encountered in novels of the mid-nineteenth century. Physically large, rational, and plain, she is the binary opposite of the fragile and feminine Dorl. In assuming the duties and responsibilities of caring for the estate of Reckenburg, Eberhardine steps out of the traditional role of women as caretakers of the home and enters the larger realm of men. Repeatedly, the novel underscores her "manliness," which seems to be source of her freedom and independence. Eberhardine is as "resolute and intelligent as any man" and talks with neighbors on a "man to man" basis. Her strength of character, even hardness, allows her to take charge of her life and to earn the respect of both men and women. Throughout the novel Eberhardine feels that she is "different" from other women. After losing her first love, she chooses not to marry, an unusual decision for a nineteenth-century woman. It is only late in life that she begins to feel that she has somehow neglected her "womanly nature," that something is missing in her life. The fact that Eberhardine finds fulfillment in her life through the love of a child and in motherly duties no way detracts from her accomplishments, nor lessens her desire for a life of self-fulfillment as an individual. The gentler side of women, François suggests, does not exclude them from being able to stand on their own two feet and from contributing on a broader scale to society.

Written in a strong and polished style that makes use of a rich variety of narrative techniques such as self-reflective irony, satire, symbolism and imagery, the novel reflects François's high degree of artistic self-consciousness and refutes the view of some critics that she was a "naive writer" who merely let the story slip from her pen. Her multifaceted language and nuances of expression make the novel a challenge to any translator. Publishing under the pseudonym J. M. Percival, Mary Joanna Safford was clearly up to the task. Born in Salem, Massachusetts (date unknown), she died in Washington, D.C. in 1916. Safford was a prodigious translator who transcribed seventy novels between 1879 and 1915 from German, French and Danish into English. These were mostly from German to English, with only one from Danish. All works — romances, fairy tales, mystery stories, and historical novels set in exotic settings like Greece, Egypt and Rome — were translated under her own name except four, including *The Last von Reckenburg*. Safford seems to have had an inclination for writing herself for she published two books of fairy tales and stories, and co-authored a volume, "Health and Strength for Girls," together with Mary E. Allen.

Safford's translation of *The Last von Reckenburg*, published by Cupples and Hurd in Boston in 1887, is of the third edition of the novel of 1873, which includes Gustav Freytag's review of the novel as its preface. It is an intelligent and reliable transliteration of François's unusual mix of more modern nineteenth-century German and old fashioned eighteenth-century German used to give the novel a rococo flavor. François's idiom contains intentional archaisms and traces of her own Saxon dialect. The speeches of her characters are also individualized to underscore their different personalities. Safford captures these idiosyncratic voices well and dialogue flows easily. At times, she breaks up long paragraphs, into which François incorporated dialogue, into series of short paragraphs, each beginning with a new speech, thereby adding more visual clarity to the text. Vocabulary is carefully adapted to the education, background, and personality of the speaker. Clearly, Safford gave careful thought to her choice of words. The gentle lilt of Dorl's language and Prince August's aloof speeches contrast with the language of August Müller who speaks a rough soldier's language. Faber's speeches, little pieces of oration, are accurately translated with terse sentences and more lofty vocabulary to sum up the man's rational and unemotional character:

> King Frederic William . . . has gone to the army in Silesia. There I too shall join the Weimar regiment, to whose illustrious commander I am recommended by the Jena University. Thunder clouds, like those lowering in the East and West, do not clear away. If they disperse this year, so much the better for me. I shall gain a twelvemonth for preparation. Day after tomorrow I shall be on my way to Berlin. (p. 93)

As is to be expected, some of the richness of the original German is lost in translation because the pictorial force of François's language does not permit facile translation, or simply because there is no English equivalent for some words or expressions. Eberhardine's description of the pride of the impoverished "white" line of the Reckenburgs, in not asking for financial assistance from the rich "black" Reckenburg line, serves as a ready example:

> The riches of Reckenburg were as far from my cradle as the gold mines of Peru, and the last of the "white" baronial line were not the greedy adventurers who, for the sake of mere paltry pelf, would have ventured into the domain of the "black" head of their race. (p. 74)

Safford translates the German word "Häuptling" in the passage simply as "head," missing the historical association François intended in the passage. "Häuptling" means "chieftain," specifically the head of a clan in Africa. The original passage make subtle reference to the scramble of Europeans for riches in colonies such as Africa in the mid-1800s. Eberhardine implies here that her family would not have been capable of such wanton greed. The color and cultural context of the original German is lost even though the translation is accurate otherwise.

Louise von François herself knew about the American translation of *The Last von Reckenburg* but apparently never saw it. When an Englishwoman, Mary E. Bromley, requested permission to translate *The Last von Reckenburg* into English in 1892, François replied that she had seen an announcement of an American translation in an American newspaper, but thought that the work had not had a good reception. François seems not to have known that the American translation had been reprinted by Gardner and Paisley in London in 1888, for her response to Bromley expresses genuine pleasure that someone was considering an English translation. François quickly added, of course, that the novel did not warrant translation due to its simplicity, and lack of action and suspense. François had, in fact, offered similar advice to a French translator since she felt that works of even the best writers did not endure beyond a decade.

In fact, the novel was reviewed favorably in America, although with the same subtle bias against women authors as in Germany. Writing in *The Dial* in March 1888, William Morton Payne proclaimed:

> The "Last von Reckenburg" is a strong, somber tale of sin and expiation, written with more feeling than literary art, which takes us back to the time of the Napoleonic Wars. Although in no sense a historical romance, the events of the years from Valmy to Waterloo form an effective background for the picture. The author is very evidently a woman, but a women with clean-cut ideas, and firm grasp of the scenes and situations which she describes.

Similar to critics in Germany of the period, Payne seems obliged to stress the womanliness of François's fine novel, although he does not seem to find that François's being a woman detracts from her ability to write an impressive work. The reviewer in the *New York Times* on 6 November 1887, summing up the story of Eberhardine and Dorothee, concludes in a similar manner:

> A talent of no ordinary kind has depicted these girl friends in sharp contrast, yet always connected, the one sacrificing herself in all things for her relatives and friends, the other an egoist in every particular without being in any sense depraved.

He goes on to praise the character of Siegmund Faber as a "very singular character, quite new in fiction we should say." The reviewer then lauds the psychological delineation of the characters, although he questions how the surgeon Faber could have failed to know that his wife had never had a child. Slowly masculine bias creeps into his review, not only against women writers, but *unwed* women writers:

> Where Miss von François goes somewhat beyond allowable probabilities is near the close, when she depicts remorse attacking the false mother in a way much at variance with a self-indulgent nature like that of Dorothee. In several points it is plain that she is handling subjects in a way that a married woman would not, so that it might be inferred that the clever author has not entered wedlock.

And yet, this reviewer, too, can not but appreciate the excellence of *The Last von Reckenburg* and resorts to a final compliment:

> The note struck by Fräulein von François is distinctively new, and for her strong patriotic feeling, as well as because of the comparative rarity of good work in fiction in the Fatherland, she deserves particular credit.

Modern readers, now having ready access to Louise von François's masterpiece in English translation, will not only savor the absorbing tale for its fine characters and intricate structure, but they will also appreciate its fascinating sub-text dealing with the plight of nineteenth-century women fettered by male-dominated institutions. *The Last von Reckenburg* is an important and intriguing historical and sociopolitical document of late eighteenth and early nineteenth-century German society, one characterized by deeply ingrained class tensions, a society struggling to find its self-identity as a nation. At the same time, the novel presents readers a cunningly-written critique of patriarchal structures and covertly suggests the need for a more balanced relationship between men and women. François's depiction of female self-identity, as portrayed through her heroine Eberhardine, shifts the emphasis of the novel ultimately from the representation of female weakness and subordination to a picture of female strength and dignity. The novel offers hope and encouragement to nineteenth-century women and suggests a vision of more egalitarian social patterns.

Bibliography of the Works of Louise von François

This bibliography is an expanded version of my list of François's works in the *Dictionary of Literary Biography: Nineteenth Century German Writers, 1841-1900*, volume 129. The present bibliography adds to the listing of works in book form, and presents a complete listing of her periodical publications. It also shows all dates of reprints and editions of François's novels through 1930, the peak of François's popularity, followed by dates of reprints and editions of selected modern editions. The bibliography indicates all works currently in print.

Books

Ausgewählte Novellen in 2 Bänden (Berlin: Duncker, 1868) — comprises in volume 1, "Das Jubiläum," "Der Posten der Frau," "Die Sandel"; as volume 2, "Judith, die Kluswirtin";

Erzählungen in 2 Bänden (Braunschweig: G. Westermann, 1871) — comprises in volume 1, "Die Geschichte einer Häßlichen," "Glück"; in volume 2, "Der Erbe von Saldeck," "Florentine Kaiser," "Hinter dem Dom";

Die letzte Reckenburgerin: Roman, 2 volumes (Berlin: Janke, 1871; translated by S. M. Percival (Mary Joanna Safford) as *The Last von Reckenburg* (Boston: Cupples and Hurd, 1887; London: Gardner and Paisley, 1888); reprints and editions of the German version in 1872, 1873, 1878, 1888, 1895, 1900, 1904, 1911, 1918, 1920, 1922, nine in 1924, eleven in 1925, three in 1926, three in 1927, 1928, 1929, 1930, two in 1943, 1947, 1949, 1957, 1965, 1988 (in print), edited by Enno Frandsen (Bonn: Latka);

Frau Erdmuthens Zwillingssöhne: Roman, 2 volumes (Berlin: Janke, 1873; reprinted, 1891); reprints and editions 1912, 1918, 1924, 1927, two in 1944, 1954;

Geschichte der preußischen Befreiungskriege in den Jahren 1813-1815: Ein Lesebuch für Schule und Haus (Berlin: Janke, 1874);

Hellstädt und andere Erzählungen, 3 volumes (Berlin: Janke, 1874) — comprises in volume 1, "Hellstädt," "Die Schnakenburg, erster Teil"; in volume 2, "Die Schnakenburg, Schluß," "Die goldene Hochzeit, erster Teil"; in volume 3, "Die goldene Hochzeit, Schluß," "Eine Formalität," "Die Geschichte meines Urgroßvaters";

Natur und Gnade nebst anderen Erzählungen, 3 volumes (Berlin: Janke, 1876) — comprises in volume 1, "Natur und Gnade," "Eine Gouvernante, erster Teil"; in volume 2, "Eine Gouvernante, Schluß," "Ein Kapitel aus dem Tagebuche des Schulmeisters Thomas Luft in Matzendorf," "Des Doktors Gebirgsreise, erster Teil"; in volume 3, "Des Doktors Gebirgsreise, Schluß," "Fräulein Muthchen und ihr Hausmaier," "Die Dame im Schleier";

Stufenjahre eines Glücklichen: Roman, 2 volumes (Leipzig: Breitkopf & Härtel, 1877); reprints and editions in 1877, 1917, 1918, 1924, 1926;

Der Katzenjunker (Berlin: Paetel, 1879);

Phosphorus Hollunder - Zu Füßen des Monarchen. Deutsche Hand- und Hausbibliothek, volume 1 (Berlin & Stuttgart: Spemann, 1881);

Der Posten der Frau: Lustspiel in 5 Aufzügen (Stuttgart: Spemann, 1881);

Das Jubiläum und andere Erzählungen, Deutsche Hand- und Hausbibliothek, volume 94 (Berlin & Stuttgart: Spemann, 1886) — comprises "Das Jubiläum," "Der Posten der Frau," "Die Sandel";

Gesammelte Werke in 5 Bänden (Leipzig: Insel, 1918) — comprises in volume 1, *Die letzte Reckenburgerin*; in volume 2, *Frau Erdmuthens Zwillingssöhne*; in volume 3, *Stufenjahre eines Glücklichen*; in volume 4, *Novellen*: "Judith, die Kluswirtin," "Der Posten der Frau," "Fräulein Muthchen und ihr Hausmeier," "Die goldene Hochzeit," "Phosphorus Hollunder"; in volume 5, *Novellen*: "Der Katzenjunker," "Die Geschichte meines Urgroßvaters," "Zu Füßen des Monarchen," "Hinter dem Dom"; volumes 4 and 5 published also as *Ausgewählte Novellen*, 2 volumes (Leipzig: Insel, 1918);

Gesammelte Werke in 2 Bänden (Leipzig: Minerva, 1924);

Meistererzählungen (Leipzig: Voigtländer, 1924);

Erzählungen, Langens Auswahlbändchen, 18 (Munich: Langen, 1924);

Judith, die Kluswirtin und andere Novellen (Berlin: Gesellschaft deutscher Literaturfreunde, 1927);

Aus einer kleinen Stadt: Erzählungen, edited by Albert Schröder and Karl Stork, Heimatkundliche Schriften, no. 2 (Weißenfels: Kell, 1937) — comprises "Aus einer kleinen Stadt," "Potsdam: Ein Frühlingsbrief," "Die Krippe," "Die Benneckensteiner Marlene," "Von einem lustigen Nönnlein";

Vergessene Geschichte(n): Aus der Provinz Sachsen und Thüringen, edited by Joachim Jahns (Querfurt: Dingda, 1991) (in print);

Potsdam, ein Frühlingsbrief. Und andere Prosa aus dem Brandenburgischen, introduced by Joachim Jahns (Halle: Dingsda, 1992) (in print).

Periodical Publications:

"Potsdam: Weihnachten 1854," as V. L., *Morgenblatt für gebildete Leser*, no. 3 (14 January 1855): 68-70;

"Aus dem Leben meines Urgroßvaters: eine bürgerlich-deutsche Geschichte von F. von L.," *Europa, Chronik der gebildeten Welt*, nos. 28-31, (1855);

"Der Erbe von Saldeck," as F. v. L., *Morgenblatt für gebildete Leser*, no.7 (17 February 1856): 145-150; no. 8 (24 February 1856): 181-184; no. 9 (2 March 1856): 202-208; no. 10 (9 March 1856): 226-233; no. 11 (16 March 1856): 250-257; no. 12 (23 March 1856): 269-276; no. 13 (30 March 1856): 289-296;

"Aus dem preußischen Herzogthum Sachsen," anonymous, *Morgenblatt für gebildete Leser*, no. 14 (6 April 1856): 330-333;

"Das Leben der George Sand," von einer Dame, *Deutsches Museum, Zeitschrift für Literatur, Kunst und öffentliches Leben*, 6, no. 45 (1856): 680-693;

"Aus Mitteldeutschland," anonymous, *Morgenblatt für gebildete Leser*, no. 35 (31 August 1856): 839-840; no. 36 (7 September 1856): 856-859;

"Eine Formalität," as F. von L., *Morgenblatt für gebildete Leser*, no. 8 (22 February 1857): 169-174; no. 9 (1 March 1857): 202-208; no. 10 (8 March 1857): 217-223;

"Das Jubiläum: Anekdote," anonymous, *Morgenblatt für gebildete Leser*, no. 12 (22 March 1857): 272-277; no. 13 (29 March 1857): 299-305;

"Aus dem Tagebuche des Schulmeisters Thomas Luft: eine Geistergeschichte," anonymous, *Morgenblatt für gebildete Leser*, no. 15 (12 April 1857): 344-350; no. 16 (19 April 1857): 375-379; no. 17 (26 April 1857): 390-397; no. 18 (3 May 1857): 421-426;

"Aus Thüringen," anonymous, *Morgenblatt für gebildete Leser*, no. 29 (19 July 1857): 692-695;

"Der Posten der Frau," anonymous, *Morgenblatt für gebildete Leser*, no. 42 (18 October 1857): 992-997; no. 43 (25 October, 1857): 1009-1015; no. 44 (1 November, 1857): 1041-1047; no. 45 (8 November, 1857): 1057-1063;

"Phosphorus Hollunder," as F. v. L., *Novellenzeitung, eine Wochenchronik für Literatur, Kunst, schöne Wissenschaften und Gesellschaft*, third series, nos. 4-5 (1857);

"Die Dame im Schleier," as F. von. L., *Allgemeine Modenzeitung*, 2, nos. 35-39 (1857);

"Die Sandel," *Deutsches Familienbuch zur Unterhaltung und Belehrung häuslicher Kreise*, edited by Robert Geißler (Hamburg: Seitz, 1857);

"Aus der Provinz Sachsen," anonymous, *Morgenblatt für gebildete Leser*, no. 2 (10 January 1858): 48; no. 3 (17 January 1858): 67-72;

"Geschichte einer Häßlichen," anonymous, *Morgenblatt für gebildete Leser*, no. 47 (21 November 1858): 1105-1111; no. 48 (28 November 1858): 1138-1144; no. 49 (5 December 1858): 1154-1162; no. 50 (12 December 1858): 1177-1184; no. 51 (19 December 1858): 1208-1215; no. 52 (26 December 1858): 1223-1231;

"Hinter dem Dom,", anonymous, *Morgenblatt für gebildete Leser*, no. 23 (5 June 1859): 534-541; no. 24 (12 June 1859): 560-568;

"Eine Gouvernante," anonymous, *Morgenblatt für gebildete Leser*, no. 28 (10 July 1859): 649-657; no. 29 (17 July 1859): 682-689; no. 30 (24 July 1859): 697-705; no. 31 (31 July 1859): 728-734;

"Die goldene Hochzeit," anonymous, *Morgenblatt für gebildete Leser*, no. 38 (18 September 1859): 889-894; no. 39 (25 September 1859): 924-928; no. 40 (2 October 1859): 938-945;

"Fräulein Mutchen und ihr Hausmaier," *Hausblätter von F. W. Hackländer und Edmund Hoefer*, 4 (1859): 161-194;

"Des Doktors Gebirgsreise," anonymous, *Morgenblatt für gebildete Leser*, no. 24 (10 June 1860): 553-559; no. 25 (17 June 1860): 589-593; no. 26 (24 June 1860): 610-616; no. 27 (1 July 1860): 625-632; no. 28 (8 July 1860): 660-664; no. 29 (15 July 1860): 680-684; no. 30 (22 July 1860): 707-712;

"Natur und Gnade," anonymous, *Morgenblatt für gebildete Leser*, no. 18 (30 April 1861): 409-416; no. 19 (7 May 1861): 438-443; no. 20 (14 May 1861): 457-465; no. 21 (21 May 1861): 487-494;

"Judith, die Kluswirthin," *Hausblätter von F. W. Hackländer und Edmund Hoefer*, 3 (1862): 321-390, 402-453;

"Die Schnakenburg," *Allgemeine Modenzeitung*, 1, nos. 13-25 (1865);

Die letzte Reckenburgerin, *Deutsche Romanzeitung*, 4 (1870): 581-624, 663-704, 743-784, 821-864, 905-938;

Frau Erdmuthens Zwillingssöhne, *Deutsche Romanzeitung*, 3 (1872): 513-546, 589-620, 667-696, 743-776, 825-856, 913-930; 4 (1872): 41-64, 117-140;

"Hellstädt," *Deutsche Romanzeitung*, 4 (1873);

"Teplitz," *Salon für Literatur, Kunst und Gesellschaft*, 1 (1873): 591-599;

"Ein Plauderbrief aus Chamounix," *Salon für Literatur, Kunst und Gesellschaft* (1874): 541, 712;

"Etwas von Brauch und Glauben in sächsischen Landen," *Leipziger Volkskalender*, edited by the Leipziger Zweigverein der Gesellschaft für Verbreitung von Volksbildung (Leipzig: Seemann, 1876);

Stufenjahre eines Glücklichen, *Daheim*, 13, nos. 1-26 (1877);

"Ein deutscher Bauernsohn," *Salon*, no. 11 (1878);

"Der Katzenjunker," *Deutsche Rundschau*, 19 (April-June 1879): 167-201, 335-360; 20 (July-September 1879): 21-50;

"Maria und Joseph, nach einer kalabresischen Volkssage," *Vom Fels zum Meer*, 1, no. 1 (October 1881-March 1882): 1-8;

"Schauen und Hörensagen. Aus meinen Kindertagen," *Deutsche Revue* (January 1920): 55-79.

Papers:
François's papers are located in Museum Weißenfels in Weißenfels a. d. Saale.

Works for Further Reading

Alker, Ernst, *Geschichte der deutschen Literatur*, volume 2 (Stuttgart: Cotta, 1950);

Bäumer, Gertrud, "Louise von François," in her *Gestalt und Wandel: Frauenbildnisse* (Berlin: Herbig, 1939), pp. 456-468;

Bender, Hedwig, "Louise von François. Ein Nachruf," *Neue Bahnen*, 15 January 1894, pp. 9-11;

Bettelheim, Anton, ed., "Marie von Ebner-Eschenbach und Louise von François," *Deutsche Rundschau*, 27, no. 1 (1900): 104-119; expanded and reprinted as "Marie von Ebner-Eschenbach, ein Briefwechsel mit Louise von François," *Biographische Blätter*, volume 5 (Berlin: Paetel, 1900): 102-125, 138, 213;

—, *Louise von François und Conrad Ferdinand Meyer: Ein Briefwechsel* (Berlin: Reimer, 1905);

Ebner-Eschenbach, Marie von, "Louise von François," *Neue freie Presse*, 23 February 1894, pp. 1-3;

—, "Louise von François. Erinnerungsblätter," *Velhagen und Klasings Monatshefte*, 8, no. 7 (March 1894): 18-30;

Eloesser, Arthur, *Die deutsche Literatur* (Berlin: Cassirer, 1931);

Engel, Eduard, *Geschichte der deutschen Literatur*, volume 2, second edition (Leipzig: Gustav Freytag, 1907);

Enz, Hans, *Louise von François* (Zurich: Rascher, 1918);

Fox, Thomas C., "Louise von François-Between Frauenzimmer and 'A Room of One's Own'," Ph. D. dissertation, Yale University, 1983;

—, *Louise von François and "Die letzte Reckenburgerin": A Feminist Reading* (New York: Lang, 1988);

—, "Louise von François: A Feminist Reintroduction," *Women in German Yearbook 3: Feminist Studies and German Culture* (Lanham: University Press of America, 1986), pp. 123-138;

—, "Louise von François Rediscovered," *Autoren damals und heute. Literaturgeschichtliche Beispiele veränderter Wirkungshorizonte* (Amsterdam: Rodopi, 1991), pp. 303-319;

Freytag, Gustav, "Ein Roman von Louise von François," *Im Neuen Reich*, 8, no. 2 (1872): 295-300;

"A German Authoress. The Last von Reckenburg by Louise von François," *The New York Times*, 6 November 1887;

Gregor-Dellin, Martin, "Louise von François," in his *Was ist Größe? Sieben Deutsche und ein deutsches Problem* (Munich & Zurich: Piper, 1985), pp. 175-196;

Hartwig, Otto, "Zur Erinnerung an Louise von François," *Deutsche Rundschau*, 20, no. 3 (1893): 456-461;

Hillebrand, Joseph, *Die deutsche Nationalliteratur im XVIII. und XIX. Jahrhundert*, revised by Karl Hillebrand, volume 3, third edition (Gotha: Perthes, 1875);

Hoßfeld, Hermann, "Louise von François," *Westermanns Monatshefte*, 61 (1917): 679-684;

Kohlschmidt, Werner, *Geschichte der deutschen Literatur vom Jungen Deutschland bis zum Naturalismus*, volume 4 (Stuttgart: Reclam, 1975);

Krause, Elisabeth, "Louise von François," *Mitteilungen der literarhistorischen Gesellschaft Bonn*, 10, nos. 5-6 (1915-1916): 117-155;

Laane, Tiiu V. "Critical Perspectives of Society in Louise von François's Narratives," *European Studies Journal*, 8, no. 2 (1991): 13-41;

—, "The Incest Motif in Louise von François's 'Der Katzenjunker': A Veiled yet Scathing Indictment of Patriarchal Abuse," *Orbis Litterarum*, 47 (1992): 11-30;

—, "Louise von François," *Nineteenth-Century German Writers, 1841-1900*, volume 129 of *Dictionary of Literary Biography*, edited by James Hardin and Siegfried Mews (London & Detroit: Bruccoli Clark Layman and Gale Publishers, 1993): 74-85;

—, "Die Louise von François-Rezeption in den USA," Special Issue *Louise von François. 27. Juni 1818-25. September 1893: Zum 100. Todestag am 25.9.1993* (Weißenfels: Naumberg, 1993): 47-49;

Lehmann, Gertrud, *Louise von François. Ihr Roman "Die letzte Reckenburgerin" als Ausdruck ihrer Persönlichkeit* (Greifswald: Abel, 1918);

Lerch, Eugen, "Die Dichterin der 'letzten Reckenburgerin'," *Münchner Neueste Nachrichten*, 27 June 1917, p. 2;

Marx, Leonie, "Der deutsche Frauenroman im 19. Jahrhundert," *Handbuch des deutschen Romans*, edited by Helmut Koopmann (Düsseldorf: Bagel, 1983), pp. 434-459;

Meinecke, Sigrid, "Louise von François: Die dichterischen und menschlichen Probleme in ihren Erzählungen," Ph.D. dissertation, University of Hamburg, 1948;

Méry, Marie-Claire, *Louise von François. Lecture du passé et sagesse humaniste* (Nancy: Presses universitaires, 1992);

Meyer, Richard M., *Die deutsche Literatur des neunzehnten Jahrhunderts* (Berlin: Bondi, 1900);

Payne, William Morton, "Recent Fiction," *The Dial*, 8 (March 1888): 270;

Reichle, Walter, "Studien zu den Erzählungen der Louise von François," Ph. D. dissertation, University of Freiburg, 1952;

Scheidemann, Uta, *Louise von François: Leben und Werk einer deutschen Erzählerin des 19. Jahrhunderts*, Europäische Hochschulschriften, Reihe I, volume 973 (Frankfurt: Lang, 1987);

—, *Die Wunschbiographien der Louise von François: Dichtung und prosaische Lebenswirklichkeit im 19. Jahrhundert*, Europäische Hochschulschriften, Reihe I, volume 1387 (Frankfurt: Lang, 1993);

Schoeffel, Ronald M., "The Ethical Thought of Louise von François," Ph. D. dissertation, University of Toronto, 1963;

Schroeter, Ernst, *Louise von François: Die Stufenjahre der Dichterin. Zur Erinnerung an die 100. Wiederkehr ihres Geburtstags am 27. Juni 1917* (Weißenfels: Lehmstedt, 1917);

—, "Das Modell und seine Gestaltung in den Werken der Louise von François," *Bilder aus der Weißenfelser Vergangenheit*, edited by the Weißenfelser Verein für Natur- und Altertumskunde (Weißenfels: Selbstverlag des Vereins, 1925), pp. 187-252;

Schwarzkoppen, Clotilde, "Louise von François. Ein Lebensbild," *Vom Fels zum Meer*, 2, no. 10 (1894): 193-198;

Szczepanski, Paul von, "Luise von François," *Daheim*, 30, no. 6 (1894): 92-94;

Spiero, Heinrich, *Geschichte der deutschen Frauendichtung seit 1800* (Leipzig: Teubner, 1913);

Staiger, Emil, "Vorwort," in *Frau Erdmuthens Zwillingssöhne*, by Louise von François (Zurich: Manesse, 1954), pp. 7-28;

Thomas, Lionel, "Luise von François: 'Dichterin von Gottes Gnaden,'" *Proceedings of the Leeds Philosophical and Historical Society*, 11 (1964): 7-27;

Thimme, Adolf, ed., "Aus den Briefen von Fanny Tarnow an Louise von François," *Deutsche Rundschau*, 53 (1927): 223-234;

Urech, Till, *Louise von François. Versuch einer künstlerischen Würdigung* (Zurich: Juris, 1955);

W., J. V., "Ein edeles Frauenbuch," *Der Bund*, 22 August 1911;

Wendel, Edith, "Frauengestalten und Frauenprobleme bei Louise von François," Ph.D. dissertation, University of Vienna, 1959;

Worley, Linda Kraus, "Louise von François: A Reinterpretation of Her Life and Her 'Odd-Women' Fiction," Ph. D. dissertation, University of Cincinnati, 1985;

—, "Louise von François (1817-1893): Scripting a Life" *Out of Line / Ausgefallen: The Paradox of Marginality in the Writings of Nineteenth-Century German Women* (Amsterdam: Rodopi, 1989), pp

THE LAST VON RECKENBURG

THE INTRODUCTION.

IT was about two years after the battle of Waterloo, that, in a little city on the frontiers of the Netherlands, a daughter was born to parents in very humble circumstances.

The little foreign city is not the scene of our story and the little foreign people are not its personages. This every-day event, however, will as it were form the pivot around which the latter are to move, for if this little child had not been born, or if it had not been born in a foreign land and in poverty, the wide world would have known nothing of our real heroine and we should not have revealed her secret.

The child's father was still young, perhaps scarcely twenty-one, and moreover a man of remarkable, we might say chivalrous strength and beauty of form, though traces of the rude life of camps were legible in the prematurely aged, scarred features, and the loss of an arm had made him a cripple. He had joined the Brunswick army in Saxony, when a beardless lad, shared the heroic campaigns and deeds of this corps under the British flag on the Peninsula, and afterwards in the Netherlands, where, sorely wounded and with the loss of a limb, he was discharged as *wachtmeister*. His comrades of the legion gave the handsome, merry Saxon the title of "Prince Gustel," but he modestly called himself Augustus Müller. The mother probably numbered fifteen years more than her husband and, to our great satisfaction, it is not incumbent upon us to give a detailed account of "Black Lisette's" past. Suffice it to say that she served with the legion as a female sutler, faithfully nursed her Augustus after he was wounded, had become his lawful wife, and was now industriously toiling to defray the expenses of the wretched household by sewing, to which she had long been unaccustomed.

The cradle seemed to have been an item for which no calculation had been made in her accounts. At any rate the hour of mortal conflict, which gives life to a human being, had weakened the weather-beaten, strong-limbed woman more than the twenty years of warfare, in which she had seen thousands end theirs. Her fingers trembled, and her brow was damp with perspiration as she now, in the gathering twilight, fitted together the bits of kid, which as soon as morning dawned, were to be transformed into dainty gloves, sighing when from time to time she cast a glance at the feeble creature which for three days, almost without waking, had breathed faintly by her side.

But this state of affairs in the household seemed still more uncomfortable to the crippled young soldier. He strode up and down the low dusky room like an imprisoned stag which is afraid of breaking its antlers, then, gasping for breath, threw the little window open and rudely shut it again, as he saw his wife anxiously cover the child to protect it from the draught. At last, with a muttered oath, he dashed out of the door, through which after a time he returned, holding a bottle of wine in his hand, and in a much more amiable mood.

"Put down that stuff and take a pull, Lisette," he cried, approaching the sick woman; "You're used to it and need it; poor wife!"

Frau Lisette shook her head thoughtfully, sighed and asked in a deep, but evidently weak voice, "And the payment, Augustus? Gambling again last night? Husband, husband!"

"Well, how long have you thought throwing dice and shuffling cards a sin, old girl?" replied the disabled soldier, smiling. "Drink, and don't make faces. Can I cut wood with my stump of an arm? Shall I strap a hand organ on my back and play before the houses, eh? It's bad enough that one who so bravely followed the calf's skin, must now patch miserable bits of goat's skin together. But don't groan! The idea of weeping, when we have laughed amid the thunder of cannon! One pull at the bottle and everything will look as cheery as usual. Peace can't last forever. How long will it be before Napoleon returns, and then —"

He understood the sorrowful glance with which the ex-sutleress interrupted his words, but after a short pause continued in the gayest tone: "We need but *one* arm to strike, Lisette. I've seen men fire with the left hand, and I've kept the right, the man's fist. Only let Napoleon return, have the tents pitched, and get a horse under one — bah, who'll think of lost arms and sickness *then?* Put those fiddle-faddles away and let us have a talk. Be my brave, merry old black Lisette again!"

"You are right, Augustus, let us talk to each other," replied his wife, after a pause of firm resolution, as she carefully put her sewing materials aside, uncorked the bottle, poured out some wine, and after drinking a large portion of the contents, returned the glass to the soldier. — "Stay at home with me to-night, husband. We'll tell stories as we used to do in camp; but none of the old ones, none of those we know by heart, you as well as I."

The soldier laughed. "Strange, but the very ones a man knows by heart are those he likes best to hear and tell."

"Yes, of course, of course, Augustus, as a general thing. Only to-day, by way of a joke, we'll have something extra. A still *older* one, husband. Something that happened *before* we joined the army. I mean something about the home and relatives we — "

She paused and repressed a tone which was very unusual to her voice, then casting a glance at the child, which lay like a "poor deserted creature," continued —

"To be sure, that's a long time ago to *me*. My parents are dead, I had no brothers nor sisters, and as for god-fathers or aunts, if they still lived, I should hardly recognize them, or to speak more correctly, *they* wouldn't wish to know Lisette, who — But you, Augustus, you are a boy in comparison with me. How long ago is it? Not ten years."

"Not nine, Lisette. Hardly eight. It was when the duke — "

"I know all about the duke, my friend. Eight years! In that time people are not forgotten. If you returned home, your family would receive you with pleasure, Augustus."

Augustus burst into a roar of laughter. "My family?" he said. "The forester, I suppose, from whom I ran away?"

"Well, if not the forester, those who took care of you *before* him."

"The orphans' foster father, do you mean? The good man was old; he must have died long ago, Lisette."

"But your own father, husband!"

"Oh! how stupid, wise Lisette! When I just spoke of the *orphans'* father. I have never known my *own* father."

"Or your mother —"

"I know of no mother, wife."

"No mother? But an orphan asylum is not an institution for foundlings. You must remember something *before* you entered it."

"Before? Why yes, the old nurse in the forest."

"A nurse? What was her name, husband?"

"Justine."

"And what else?"

"I know of nothing else."

"But you must have had a father. What was he, where did he live, Augustus?"

"I don't know, old interrogation point."

His wife was not at all disturbed by this complimentary epithet. "Have you no papers?" she inquired after reflecting a short time. "No certificate of your baptism, your parents' death, etc."

"Did you bring any church testimonials when you ran away from service in the night?" answered the husband in a mocking tone, but as he fancied he heard a sigh, added good-naturedly: "There, don't be angry, Lisette. Do you want papers? There is at any rate the certificate with which the Herr Provost dismissed me from the cloister."

"You have been in a cloister? Among the monks? It was Catholic I suppose?"

"No indeed, old girl. That isn't the fashion in Leipsic. The institution was only called the cloister, and the principal the provost from papal time. The old paper has been kept, I hardly know *how*. Whenever I was going to throw it away, I saw the good old man with his pale face and the tears in his eyes when he gave it to me. We called him father, and he was like a father to us, so I always put the wisp in my pocket again."

"Show me the certificate, Augustus," pleaded the wife, as she hastily prepared to strike a match and light the lamp on the table before her bed. When she had accomplished this, she unfolded the paper the soldier drew out of his breast-pocket. The blackened, bloody marks on it were an eloquent witness of the way in which he had spent his early years.

"PSALM 146TH, VERSE 9TH., — The Lord preserveth the stranger, he relieveth the fatherless and widows." Augustus Müller. Confirmed and dismissed from our institution April 4th, 1807.

CLOISTER LAURENTII   LUDWIG NORDHEIM
LEIPSIC   PROVOST

Frau Lisette read the short contents in a low tone, shaking her head. "No date of birth," she said thoughtfully, "neither the name, rank, nor residence of the parents. Was the cloister intended for children born in wedlock, Augustus?"

"For soldiers' orphans," replied the husband proudly. "Only now and then a civilian's child as a make-shift."

"And you have not the most distant recollection of any trustee, guardian, or village magistrate who took you to the institution?"

"Took me to the institution? Why, of course, Fräulein Hardine took me."

The sutleress started up with fresh animation.

"Fräulein Hardine!" she cried. "Husband, who was Fräulein Hardine?"

"A woman, tall and dark as you are Lisette," replied the soldier, roused by his wife's zeal. "If old Becker was right, my Frau or Fräulein Mamma."

"And who was old Becker?"

"The washerwoman of the institution, and a great gossip."

"Fräulein Hardine! A Fräulein, no Mamsell! Then she is of noble birth."

"Perhaps so. Her father was a major in the Elector's service."

"The name?"

"I never heard it, or perhaps have forgotten. Everybody called the daughter plain Fräulein Hardine."

Frau Lisette sat for some time absorbed in silent thought, then adopted a very cunning plan.

"Give me your pipe and let me fill it, Gustel," she said gayly; "and take another glass of wine, it will clear your head. But now tell me for once, in regular order, all that you can remember of your childhood. No matter how little it may be — one can't always tell — and we must talk about *something*, isn't that so?"

A dry text for the lover of camp stories, in spite of the pipe and bottle which were to make him loquacious. However, he had heard that people must humor a woman who has just borne a child, and he was really a kind hearted fellow. So while his wife took up her goat's skin again, he related, striding up and down the narrow space and puffing his pipe — with the exception of a few powerful expressions which a refined reader must be spared — the story of his life almost word for word as follows : —

"As I said before — where, when, and of whom I was born, I know not. So far as I can look back, I can see an old woman whom I called 'nurse' and who allowed me to suffer no want. It wasn't in any city or village, for I saw no house except the little one in which my nurse lived. I had no playmates except the lizards and squirrels in the forest behind the house, but I vied with them in running and climbing all day long. The life just suited me. My nurse I might perhaps know again and perhaps not, but the house I could still paint. It stood in the midst of a thicket; the tallest pines I have ever seen surrounded it, and on the gable was a dog's head carved in stone surmounted with a gilt crown.

"My nurse's name was Justine. At least that is

what the lady who visited her from time to time called her. 'From the castle' my nurse said, but I never saw any castle. This lady was Fräulein Hardine. Whether she was young or old, I cannot say, nor even whether she was ill or well disposed toward me. But I think she meant well at that time. I have never made anything out of her. But I noticed her, noticed her so closely that I think that I should know her again. There was something about her that is not easily forgotten. *What*, I cannot say myself.

"One day I sat with Fräulein Hardine in a little box, which moved swiftly along. That is, in a coach. At first I stared in astonishment when I saw the tall trees running past me so quickly. I can still see them run, Lisette. But I soon grew weary of this, raged, shrieked, and would have jumped out of the door and run back to my beloved forest, if Fräulein Hardine had not seized me by the ear and pinched it till I at last grew tired of howling, stretched myself on the seat, and fell asleep. I waked repeatedly and began the same noise. But Fräulein Hardine always seized me by the ear, and I fell asleep again, so I can't say whether the drive lasted hours, days, or weeks, or how I reached the end of the journey.

"From that time I remained in the orphan asylum, where I fared by no means badly. The old provost was a noble man; indeed a father of the orphans, and apparently particularly fond of *me*. There was plenty to eat, and not rods enough for us wild boys. But I had no laziness; something drew me back to the forest. Several times I took to my heels, but, of course, was caught again, and it was probably for this reason that afterwards I was never allowed, like many of the old boys, to go into the city if any extra errand was to be done."

"But Fräulein Hardine!" the listener impatiently interrupted as the narrater paused.

"Why, Fräulein Hardine," continued the latter, "Fräulein Hardine, who now and then came to visit our provost, but always looked as sour as vinegar when I was brought in to her, lectured me because I did not like to study, and called me wild stock or something of the sort. Once, in her anger, she gave me a box on the ear."

Frau Lisette started up as if electrified — "A box on the ear!" she exclaimed with an expression of the greatest satisfaction, "a box on the ear, Augustus — "

"It certainly was not undeserved, Lisette."

"Chastised you with her own hand! And must she not have been your mother?"

"Indeed? So you would rather strike your own child than a stranger's?"

The poor mother, somewhat abashed by this home question, took up her sewing again — "A young lady of noble birth and directly under the eyes of the ecclesiastical authority must have possessed some right" — she murmured, but without being heard, for her husband had already resumed the thread of his story.

"This much is certain, Lisette," said he, "if Fräulein Hardine had patted me affectionately all the days of my life, I might have forgotten her. But, as she struck me, she will remain fixed in my memory if I should live to be a hundred years old.

"I had grown to be a sturdy lad, a head taller than my comrades, and now felt but one desire. It was no longer 'the forest' as before. No, 'I wanted to have a horse under me and become a soldier.' I had seen troops for the first time in my life. Prussians and natives of the country had passed the asylum. Of course it was during the rapid movements of the soldiery, when the Austrians were to be reinforced. But the Austrians were left in the lurch and my Prussians retired. The next autumn, however, they returned. Recruits to defeat Napoleon, who was already on the march, it was said. Then I tingled from head to foot! But I had seen enough to know they would not take a half grown orphan lad in the army. So I only played soldier, and it was a pleasure to see how I drilled the other boys. I was the largest and therefore of course our Elector, whom I always imagined was a big, thick-set fellow. The larger number, but the smallest in size, were the French, and a dwarf was their Napoleon. Well, I drubbed him, as two years ago Marshal Forward and our Iron Duke drubbed the real Napoleon."

"But Fräulein Hardine?" asked the eager listener, and the *ex-wachtmeister* answered, "Have patience, she'll come directly."

"It was on the 14th of October — the date of such a day of misery is not easily forgotten, Lisette — We were ranged in order in a cross passage to get our breakfasts, when the provost came to us with his hat and cane, trembling from head to foot and as white as the wall. 'The first blood has flowed,' he said in an unsteady voice, 'precious blood, heroes' blood! You are soldiers' sons, my children. Hasten to the forest, gather the last oak leaves and make a garland for the grave of a brave gentleman, who has been the first to fall in fighting for his native land.' Then approaching me, he added in a low tone: 'Fräulein Hardine's father was brought to his house dead yesterday. I shall expect you there with the oak wreath, Augustus. The washerwoman Becker — she also did the errands in the city — will go with you and show you the way.' With these words he left me. The youngsters ran off to the forest. I climbed the trees and threw down the branches, which were gathered and fastened into a faggot by those beneath. There was enough for a cow to have feasted on till she was tired, Lisette. Scarcely an hour after I was trotting along beside old Becker on the way to the city."

"If the woman was going to the city at any rate," Frau Lisette eagerly interrupted, "why was it necessary for you to accompany her, Augustus? Why should *you* have carried the garland to Fräulein Hardine? You, rather than any one else? Husband, husband, that was a clue."

"You are taking up the old gossip of the institution, Lisette," replied the crippled soldier, who had gradually become very much excited by his story. "But listen. On the way I got very angry with the stupid woman. She said a battle had been fought in the Oberland, the very one in which Fräulein Hardine's father had fallen, and the French had won the victory. That I could not and would not believe, abused her for a shameful slanderer, and would have forced her to be silent if she, well, if she had not been a woman and an old woman into the bargain. *She*, however, stuck fast to her first statement and her fear of the 'terrible Bohnebart.' She trembled like a withered leaf whenever his name crossed her lips. She acted as if 'Bohnebart' had come into the country expressly to maltreat old Becker.

"So we reached the city in a violent rage. I had never seen one before and imagined a city to be something very different. Only the great castle, as it gradually loomed through the mist, pleased me. 'I should like to live there,' said I, and old Becker smiled mysteriously. 'Well, who knows whether you will not lodge in a prince's castle some day, Gustel. Bohnebart was only a poor boy like you, and yet he has become an emperor.' — 'And such a dwarf too,' I added contemptuously.

"Just at that moment we reached the market place. The old woman pointed to a house, saying: 'The major's family live there.' Though I only saw that dwelling *once* and have since seen thousands of others, I could still point it out exactly. It looked like a pug-nosed face on which some one had tied a tall night cap. Becker sat down on a bench beside the door to wait for me, and I went in with my wreath.

"The provost came to meet me, took me by the hand, and led me into a room on the right. The windows were darkened and I was obliged to become accustomed to the dim light, but nevertheless distinguished some person who had been standing beside the door with outstretched arms, and at a sign from the old man hastily glided into the chimney corner. I pricked up my ears; I fancied I heard some one groaning or sobbing."

"Fräulein Hardine!" cried Frau Lisette in breathless suspense. But the narrator answered:

"No, no! Fräulein Hardine wasn't one of the sort that sobs and groans. *She* was standing erect and grave, clothed in black from head to foot, in the room containing the major's body, to which the provost instantly led me. This was the first dead person I had ever seen, and I can't tell you, Lisette, how much I liked him; far better than any living man. He lay as if asleep, but his right hand was fiercely clenched; they had been obliged to use force to remove the sabre which, with the tall Hungarian cap, was now lying by his side. Then the ribbon fastening his order, the blue Hussar coat trimmed with silver lace, and the little scorched spot, through which the bullet had pierced his heart. I touched each separate article, I could not grow weary of gazing at him, put my finger into the wound to see if the bullet could be felt, raised one cold hand after the other, and should have been unable to leave the spot if the provost had not dragged me back to the other room by force.

"There he made a solemn harangue, of which, however, I understood and noticed nothing, except that he was praising the dead man, who had died like a hero for his native land — 'I, too, will die for our native land' I burst forth, and at the words Fräulein Hardine, who unnoticed by me had sat down by the window, hastily came forward and pressed my hand, as if to say : — 'Right, boy, be firm in that resolve!' — But she did not utter a word that morning, and I took no further notice of her, but gazed intently at the chimney corner; for, as I spoke, a cry which pierced my heart like a knife, came from the spot. But I could perceive nothing except a little white crouching figure, whose face was concealed by a handkerchief. The provost, moreover, now stepped directly between me and the chimney corner, so when I tried to peer behind the stove, I could see nothing but the good man's black coat and white wig.

"'You are now almost a grown man, Augustus,' he continued turning to me. 'Next Easter you will be confirmed and must decide upon some calling in life. What will you become, my son?'

"A soldier!" I cried without an instant's hesitation. And again a sound, this time like a wail, issued from the chimney corner."

"It must have been Fräulein Hardine's mother," cried Frau Lisette in breathless suspense. But her husband replied:

"I don't even know whether Fräulein Hardine had a mother at that time. But *this* I do know, it was not the voice of an old woman that was wailing behind the stove. It sounded far more like a little sorrowful child. But listen, Lisette.

"'You are still too young to be a soldier, Augustus,' said the provost. 'Besides, the fate of our native land must be decided. Would you fight *for* Napoleon, like the Germans in the kingdoms outside?'

"No," I answered "always against him." And for the second time Fräuline Hardine silently pressed my hand.

"'The time may come, my son,' replied the provost. 'At present we must wait. If we have peace and everything remains the same as of old, you must *never* think of being a soldier. You are not in a position to become an officer, and with your disposition you could not endure the life of a private. They still run the gauntlet. Would you like to be flogged, Augustus?' My only reply was to clench my fist. The old man continued :

"'You have always longed to return to the forest. How would it suit you to be a huntsman, my son'— "Very well, if I can't be a soldier, I'll become a huntsman and learn to shoot," I replied.

"I have no recollection of anything else the provost said. I was thinking of the dead major and peeping at the weeping child in the chimney corner. This almost bewildered me, and I did not know what had happened when I suddenly felt some one seize my arm and push me towards the door. It was the provost of course. He had already raised the latch and I was standing on the threshold, when I heard something behind me like the fluttering of a bird. I hastily turned and saw — well, what did I really see? It was only one glance from the light entry into the dusky room. I saw a figure with outstretched arms, a figure small and dainty as a child, with a white face and golden curls, looking in contrast to the tall, dark Hardine, who stood behind her, like a tiny white gold-edged cloud, when night has already closed in. Everything swam before my eyes as if I were dizzy. Then the provost thrust me across the threshold, the door closed, and I only heard a piercing shriek from within.

"The next instant I was standing outside the door beside the old woman. In the open air the dizziness instantly passed away, I again saw and heard as quickly as usual, and almost thought the whole affair — not the dead major, but the cloud-child — had been only an apparition.

"During the last hour the streets had become crowded with people, who buzzed up and down like a swarm of frightened bees, and my old woman was as full as a sponge of all the stories she had swallowed while sitting on the bench. The stories were true, more's the pity. The allied armies had been surprised at two points, and two scurvy battles lost. But they had just been fought. The city was three miles away from the nearest battlefield, how could people so boldly declare the wretched result? By scent, they say, as domestic cattle flee before the approaching storm. But why did not *I* have the scent? Why did you never tremble at the first cannon shot, Lisette? Because you were a man, Lisette, and those men old women like Becker, cowards who deserve nothing better than to crouch under Napoleon's lash, until at last the old Berserker fury burst forth.

"At every step the old woman peered around to see if the cruel Bohnebart was not already at her heels. But, with all her terror, curiosity to learn what I had seen at the major's was uppermost, and before we were out of the city gates, she had squeezed me like a citron and to every drop added her own mustard. I only wanted to know one thing — the name of the little girl whose shriek still rang in my ears. But just this one thing the old wisdom could not tell me — An acquaintance in the city — she thought, for the major had no relatives in this part of the country. 'But why did she sigh and weep so piteously?' I asked, and thereby set the old woman in the right track.

"'Who does not weep and wail now-a-days, Gustel?' she replied. 'Who does not in imagination see his own relatives killed or maimed, imprisoned or flying from the enemy? Bohnebart and his head-chopping machine can never be calculated upon. Yes, these times are as wild as those under the Swedish king or old Fritz himself. I shouldn't wonder, Gustel, if when we got home, we found the French had been before us and the asylum was a heap of ashes, while teachers and scholars had fled like sheep when a wolf gets among the flock. And that is why, Gustel, I will tell you now what I may not be able to reveal the next hour. Something which has never entered the head of anybody except old Becker. But when some day it is known to all the world, you must remember: 'Old Becker predicted it' and show yourself grateful to the poor old woman, that is if she has been able to save the miserable remnant of her life from the cruel Bohnebart.

"While saying these words she peeped timidly in every direction, then stood on tiptoe and putting her mouth to my ear, whispered :

"'Augustus, have you never thought what Fräulein Hardine really is to you?' I laughingly shook my head.

"'And have you no presentiment *who* the man was, to whose dead body you have been taken to-day?' "A major," said I — 'A major of course,' replied the old woman angrily, 'a major in the Elector's service, but I mean what he was to *you*, Augustus.' I shook my head again.

"'Then learn now, Augustus,' said Becker as solemnly as the witch in the old testament — 'the man was your grandfather, for Fräulein Hardine is your mother.'

"To tell the truth, at that time I was as innocent in such matters as a new born lamb. The lonely orphan asylum had a right to its title of cloister; none of us had relatives whom we visited and everything that wore an apron, unless lame and grey like Becker, was kept as far away from the institution as tinder. The teachers were unmarried tyros, fresh from college, the provost was a widower. So we knew nothing of kitchen tales and gossip, and I had no idea how injurious to Fräulein Hardine's fair fame was the rumor that had been whispered into my ear. I should, however, have prayed for any one as a mother rather than for her, if I had ever longed for father or mother. But I wanted freedom, the forest, or permission to go out into the world and nothing more. Yet I could have liked a grandfather who had fallen on the battle field, and for his sake would have accepted the stern Fräulein Hardine for a mother. So for a moment I pricked up my ears.

"But the major belonged to a noble family, and I was called plain Müller. The provost had told me, only an hour before, that I could only be a private soldier on account of my position in the world. This thought occurred to me at the right time, and without grieving much about it, I told the old witch how ridiculous her prediction was.

"But she stuck fast to what she had said and became still more positive. 'What a stupid fellow you are, Gustel,' — she said angrily, putting her arms akimbo. 'As if a noble stock could not put forth a stray shoot! As if, when people did not want a child's origin discovered, they couldn't enter it in the register as a Müller or for aught I care a Becker. Especially when a pastor is engaged in the same game. But *what*, I ask you, is our provost? An old friend of Fräulein Hardine. Who secretly smuggled you into the orphan asylum at night? Fräulein Hardine. Are you a soldier's son like the others? Does anybody know who your father was? Do you look as if you came of a common family? You look like a young nobleman, Augustus, like a prince —'

"Yes, indeed, that's as true as gospel, like a prince!' Frau Lisette interrupted, while a flush of pride suffused her emaciated face — 'You were called a prince, Prince Gustel, by the whole legion!"

Prince Gustel smiled, by no means displeased at the flattering recollection, but faithfully held fast to the thread of his story.

"'Who procured you a place at half price?' continued the old woman. 'A mother, who is a widow? A guardian, a counsellor, a magistrate? Not at all, Fräulein Hardine. Who brings the provost every six months the money to pay for your support? Who visits you in the cloister? Who scolds you? No one but Fräulein Hardine. And last of all: What did the dead major want of a wreath from the orphan asylum, unless it contained one of his own blood, who ought to pay him the last honors? Why should the provost have lectured you in the house of mourning, if you were not a quasi member of the family? One who does not plainly see this connection has no sense at all. Fräulein Hardine is your mother, that's as certain as the amen in the gospel.

"The old woman paused, she was fairly out of breath and wanted to clear her throat. I did not say a word, for I was really indifferent to the whole affair. After a while Becker began again with new energy:

'I wish to say nothing against Fräulein Hardine's character, Augustus. A lady who belongs to such an aristocratic family and with such an inheritance in prospect, of course not, of course not! To be sure Fräulein Hardine is as poor as a church mouse now, but the old black spectre, her aunt, can't bury treasures in her gold tower forever. And if she has sold herself to the Evil One ten times over, our Lord keeps him in check and the worst miser has never lived more than a hundred years. There's not another one in the whole country like our Fräulein Hardine. I mean nothing against her character, Gustel, no indeed, nothing of the sort! But there's some secret about it; I'll stake my life on that. Some princely marriage, which does not give the wife the husband's position or the children their father's name, such as the miserly old lady of the castle entered into in her time; or something of that kind, which people like us don't understand. Why does Fräulein Hardine refuse the best offers? Does a woman who could have a suitor for every finger voluntarily become an old maid? Why, I ask, except because she secretly has some one who is watching the countess' property with her. But let her once be firmly seated in the gold tower, and the concealed prince will appear. And then you'll be a young nobleman, Augustus, and a rich millionaire, then you'll remember poor old Becker, who first gave you a hint.'"

The speaker paused. "Go on, go on, husband," cried Frau Lisette in breathless suspense. "What else, what else!"

"What else — nothing!" replied the soldier laughing. "The story is ended."

"Ended?"

"Ended, I tell you. While engaged in this gossip, we had reached the door of the cloister. I made a face at my old woman, for the house had not been transformed into a heap of ashes nor its inmates scattered to the four winds. But how frightened old Becker was, when she saw how I took her wisdom. She trembled like a wet poodle, and her teeth — no they didn't chatter, for she had no teeth — but her chin shook.

"For God's sake, Gustel, keep the secret," she whimpered, "don't deprive a poor old widow of her hard earned bit of bread."

"I laughed heartily and ran into the gate, behind which my comrades were frolicking as merrily as usual. I hastily fought a battle with them, which had a totally different result from the one that was ended that self same hour. All the ghosts and gossip of the morning were completely blown away.

"The following Spring the provost took me to the forester, from whom two years after I ran away, when the duke camped in our neighborhood. But never since that time have I seen nor heard of Fräulein Hardine, and to-day, I believe, is the first time I have thought of her again."

The poor ex-sutleress was bitterly disappointed by this sudden conclusion. She silently took up her work, which in the eagerness of listening had fallen into her lap, and stitched a long time with feverish haste, until she had thought of a new plan, and obtained sufficient control over her voice to speak in the cheerful tones by which she hoped to induce her husband to be still more complaisant.

"I thank you, Augustus," she said at last, holding out her hand to him. "You know how to tell a story. And your history will always be something for our poor little baby, when I am no longer able to provide for her, I mean if Napoleon should unexpectedly return some day! And so, my friend, let us make an end of the whole matter to-day. You write a capital hand, have sent in many a report, and it surely requires only *one* hand to guide a pen as well as a sword. So write down the whole story, while it is fresh in your memory. *That* and the certificate from the orphan asylum will be the family papers Prince Gustel will leave his princess, if some day we suddenly leave this world."

While uttering these words she had carefully smoothed two of the sheets of paper in which she wrapped her gloves, and even brought out the writing materials with which she made out her bills. After sharpening the pen and stirring the ink, she began to fill her husband's pipe again and did not forget to pour the remainder of the wine into the glass.

Friend Augustus performed his due share of grumbling, but at last yielded to the sick woman's strange fancy.

"How much trouble such a little creature makes," he said, as he seated himself at his wife's work table.

Soon the pen dashed over the paper with free, bold strokes, and the story we have just heard from his own lips appeared in black and white.

Midnight had passed when he placed the last sheet on his wife's bed. She dried it with her hot breath, laid it with the certificate of confirmation in the lowest drawer of her work table, and put out the light. "Augustus," said she, as her husband removed his clothes and threw himself on the heap of straw at the foot of the bed, "Augustus, we will have our little one christened Hardine."

"I should have preferred Lisette," replied the father, yawning. "But let it be Hardine, for aught I care."

And the little girl was christened Hardine.

* * * * * * * * *

Years elapsed and Fräulein Hardine's name was never mentioned by either of the pair. Nearly six years, during which the unknown lady's little namesake wearily struggled to its feet, and of which she retained no recollection except that she was never hungry and often cold.

True the *wachtmeister* of the legion no longer waited for the return of Napoleon, since the latter was sleeping quietly and peacefully in his island grave, but he still expected some other respectable enemy, against whom a brave soldier might once more lift the sword. To be sure he rarely awaited him beside the feebly flickering hearth fire, which since the arrival of the cradle had not become more comfortable to him. He clung to the lively scenes which reminded him of the sutler's tent, where cards and dice fall, the beer circulates, and some merry soldier's jest not infrequently pays the reckoning.

But in the dull, narrow room at home his elderly wife sat sighing and stitching in such constant toil and anxiety for her child, that she did not give herself leisure for a single loving look. Week after week her cheeks grew more hollow, her fingers more tremulous, her breath shorter, but she still sighed and stitched all day and half the night.

At last the hour arrived in which all stitching and sighing comes to an end, and the careless tippler was summoned from the tavern to a death bed. Augustus Müller in his young days had seen thousands of men die, but never a woman; he had never thought before that death was a business which concerned women also, even such brave women as his Lisette had been. Now at the the unexpected sight he raved and shrieked, tore his hair, and beat his breast.

But the worthy ex-sutleress understood the gloomy comrade, whose acquaintance she had made among men. She had seen him slowly creeping nearer and looked him fearlessly in the face when he now stood close by her side. Did it grieve her to part from the creature that nature had placed in her arms so late? It did not seem so, yet she fullfilled the duty of providing for its support with her latest breath.

"Don't be a fool, Augustus," she said to her husband who, completely overcome by grief, had thrown himself down beside the bed — "There must be an end of everything *some* day. Sit down here on the side of the bed, pay attention, and do what I tell you."

As she said these words she placed the carefully treasured family papers in her husband's hand, and then continued in clear, impressive tones : —

"Keep these sheets as the only inheritance you can leave your child. I have been thinking of this matter night and day for six years, and now die in the firm conviction that Fräulein Hardine was your mother. Do what you choose, so far as you yourself are concerned. You are a man. But seek her out and take her the child, for whom you cannot provide. Sell my furniture ; the proceeds will pay the traveling expenses. I have taken care of our marriage certificate and that of the child's baptism. Do not forget the certificate of my death. Have your certificate of confirmation attested in the cloister, find out Fräulein Hardine's family name in the city, and also what has become of her. If she is still alive — whether rich, or poor as before — she must be an old woman now, and will be ashamed of the sin of disowning her own flesh and blood. If she is dead, relatives can probably be found. Perhaps the provost is still alive, or the forester. In short, you will be in your home and your child must and will find a support, if you do your duty. But let it be soon, husband, for the path you have taken is leading you swiftly downward. Carry the child to Fräulein Hardine. Give me your hand upon it, Augustus, the right hand that wields the sword."

Sobbing bitterly he held out his hand, which she cordially pressed. "Mother–Hardine;" she faltered, then turned on her side, drew her handkerchief over her eyes, and expired.

The crippled soldier — to be faithful to our former comparison — the crippled soldier raged like a wounded stag. He felt his old wounds smart more painfully than in the days when black Lisette had bandaged them up on the battle-field, and would not stir a step from the dark room so long as it contained her body.

But now the earth covered her. He had not been able to pay her the last honors with song and music, but he was accustomed to follow a brave comrade to the grave with a funeral march and return home to some merry tune. In the evening he sat in the tavern from which he had been summoned to the deathbed three days before. The beer circulated, the dice rolled as usual. The wife and mother had disappeared, and soon the merry ex-sutleress was only a prominent figure in the scenes which unrolled before his eyes under the banner of the Black or Iron Duke.

Once more years elapsed, of which little Hardine retained no recollection except that she was often hungry and always cold. A shy, trembling, sad little creature, she glided in the morning out of the cold room which constantly became more and more empty, and sat lonely and silent before the door until some compassionate neighbor gave her a bit of bread or led her into her own warm room. Her father she rarely saw. When he returned home late at night, she was already asleep, and when he departed early in the morning she still slept. The man's path led constantly downward, as his dying wife had predicted — from the tavern to the gin shop, from the circle of beer drinking citizens to a crowd of rough fellows. His curly hair grew bristly, red spots appeared on his bloated cheeks, the veins beside the scars on his forehead swelled, and a wild fire burned in his large blue eyes when he shouted for the horse he was to mount, the sword with which he wanted to cut down the still expected enemy. The old soldier's heart throbbed as before, but Prince Gustel had perished, and the man had never felt any fatherly love. The promise he had given his dying wife was the same as forgotten.

Fortunately for him the day came when the last piece of furniture, the last pillow from Frau Lisette's bridal store was pawned, when the landlord demanded his rent, and the keeper of the gin shop his reckoning, and the homeless man and his child were threatened with being driven across the frontier. Necessity required a resolution, and necessity also gave the strength to keep it.

It was again a time when a cry of vengeance against a sworn enemy rang through the world — the time of the Greek rebellion, in which many a brave foreigner sacrificed his life, although no christian government lent its aid. The sword of Vittoria and Waterloo quivered in the hand of our veteran. "Come, Hardine," he said one morning in the spring of 1825, "I'll take you to Fräulein Hardine and then go fight the Turks." And, leading his child by the hand and carrying in his pocket the "family papers" and not much more he passed through the gate of the little city in the Netherlands.

To be sure his road lay far from the Meuse into the district of the Elbe; his purse was empty, his breath and strength were feeble. The old neighbors and fellow tipplers shook their heads and said this traveler would neither fight against Ali Pacha nor reach his home, but end his days on the highway. Indeed months elapsed before he neared the goal of his journey. But it was summer time, the road lay directly through a rich native country, and the cross of honor, the powder-blackened, bullet-pierced cloak, the arm mutilated at Waterloo, were warm mediators for the poor soldier and his pale-faced child. There was many a carter or boatman who carried both a portion of the way for a God bless you, many an inn keeper who did not charge for the lodging, and many a hand that extended money or provisions unasked. If they were sometimes obliged to spend the night in the open air, it was an old habit to the soldier of the legion — the hours of darkness were short, and he woke feeling far more vigorous than he had done for years in the close room after a night's debauch.

All things considered, this time of wayfaring was not the worst in Augustus Müller's life. He would have liked to walk still farther, nay all his days if the war with the Turks had not had a still more powerful attraction. If his little companion cowered in her rags under a sudden shower of rain, or with sore feet sat silently by the road side, he had a spell which always gave her fresh strength. Her father only needed to say "Fräulein Hardine! On to Fräulein Hardine," or "we shall soon get to Fräulein Hardine," and the little one dragged herself on till they found a shelter. Fräulein Hardine's name was all she had noticed or softly repeated during the long journey. Perhaps some echo of the mother's sighs and consolations had lingered in the child's heart.

It is said that failing eyes see clearly, and there is certainly something startling in the confidence with which statements, whether relating to this world or the next, are made on the death-bed. Even Augustus Müller had been deceived for a moment by the belief his wife had cherished for years, and with which she had consoled herself in her last hours. But in the depths of his heart, now as well as before, he had never thought Fräulein Hardine a blood relation, and set out on his way home with no intention of claiming the rights of a son. He hoped to obtain a provision for his motherless child from the lady, who for some reason had watched over his own orphaned childhood. If in the course of time she had obtained luxury and wealth — an idea which his cheerful disposition readily adopted — and would moreover give him a horse and uniform for his Turkish campaign, he would be all the more grateful. So much or so little was what he had in his mind, when he said to his exhausted child: "We are going to Fräulein Hardine!"

Midsummer had arrived, when one morning he paused before a lonely old building, in a highly cultivated valley, and exclaiming joyously: "the cloister!" darted through the open gate. He passed through the courtyard, the corridor, the garden, the schoolroom, the provost's house, he recognized every nook and corner — the play ground where the boys were frolicking as they used to do in the old days; the well at which they still filled their cups; the pewter dishes that covered the tables; the wood-shed in which troublesome fellows of *his* stamp were shut up for punishment. But he knew none of the people, old and young, who crowded curiously around the excited stranger. He asked for Ludwig Nordheim, the provost and director; he had been dead and forgotten many years. He asked for old Becker. No one had ever heard of an old Becker. No one recollected any of the former teachers and fellow pupils, whose names he could remember, The Prussians, who had taken charge of this part of the country, had put strangers who knew nothing of the neighborhood in the old places. He would have been ashamed even to mention Fräulein Hardine.

Greatly disappointed, he was about to continue his journey, when he thought of the certificate, an attestation of which he had promised his Lisette to secure. Wise Lisette! The name, date, verse from the Bible, and handwriting agreed with that in the school register, the new director could confidently add his *fiat*, and the poor vagrant obtained a legitimation which made his travels far easier. Now, too, there was no lack of hospitable entertainment, since the ex-pupil's scars and cross of honor added to the fame of an institution for soldiers' orphans. The grey, quiet cloister wall once more resounded with bold pranks and merry tales, adventurous expeditions over land and sea, and stories of the Black Duke and Black Lisette. The Frau Directorin set forth all that the kitchen and cellar contained, the provost made a collection among the employees and teachers for the invalid hero. Refreshed, loaded with gifts, and happy as a king, Augustus Müller left the walls, within which twenty years before he had so unwillingly remained.

He now turned towards the city, and the sun was setting as he saw the castle, glittering in its rays, rising above the houses in the valley. He came out of the long, narrow street into the market place, and his first glance fell upon the house, which still bore a towering roof on a low foundation. The pug-nosed face with the high night-cap! "Here, here!" he shouted to his little girl, "here is where Fräulein Hardine lives!"

He passed through the door, and entered the room on the right. It had been transformed into a tailor's shop. The deep chimney corner — to which the man's first glance was turned — had disappeared, together with the huge stove of Dutch tiles. In the adjoining apartment, the spot where the major's coffin had stood was now occupied by a cradle. Gestures of alarm and angry words greeted the intruder, who was taken for a drunkard or madman.

Meantime the neighbors, who were sitting before their doors enjoying the twilight, had noticed the stranger's singular conduct. The noise attracted children from their play, maid servants from the wells; a crowd collected before the door. The women approached the emaciated little girl, who had cowered wearily down beside it. "What is your name, child?" asked a neighbor.

"Hardine," murmured the little one faintly.

"Is the man your father?"

The child nodded.

"What is his name?"

She shook her head.

"What does he want? Whom is he looking for in this house?"

"Fräulein Hardine."

"Fräulein Hardine!" The neighbors put their heads together at the name. But when the father, followed by the tailor's family, the journeymen, and apprentices, now came out of the house and repeated the same name, a bustle arose, a confusion of questions and answers, from which at last the following information was obtained.

The older inhabitants of the little city had really known a young lady called Hardine, the only person in the place who had ever borne that name. Fräulein Hardine was born and grew up in this house, the body of her father, who had fallen in the battle of Saalfeld, was buried in the city cemetery, and his daughter had had a monument erected to his memory, which was considered one of the greatest curiosities of the place. The name of Fräulein Hardine had a proud sound in her native city. The magistrates were reflecting upon the feasibility of making her an honorary citizen of the place, in return for which distinction they confidently expected a legacy to found some institution, as the much praised lady, the richest land owner in the province, had no legal heirs, and had attained an age when people usually set their houses in order. That Fräulein Hardine should ever have provided for a stranger's child — of course there was no suggestion that it was her own — in an orphan asylum, did not harmonize in the least with their recollections or ideas of her. Fräulein Hardine bore the reputation of being a noble and prudent lady, but not a good Samaritan.

Augustus Müller's memory, however, was too clear to permit a doubt that such a case was possible, and moreover the scars and decorations of their former fellow citizen's protégé were a strong recommendation, so every one was ready to give him a hospitable reception in her native city. Little Hardine, after having had plenty to eat, slept more sweetly than she had ever done throughout the whole journey in the little bed the tailor's wife had made up beside the cradle. But Father Müller had no idea of going to bed; he caroused all through the short summer night at the tavern keeper's table, and paid the generous public with the choicest humor of his Spanish recollections and the perils he expected to encounter in his Turkish campaign. Such a brave countryman, who had already travelled about the world so much, and expected to go still farther, a cripple, who in spite of his poverty could tell such merry tales, was not allowed to leave the birthplace of their chosen honorary citizen without a considerable sum of money. So the day of rest in Fräulein Hardine's native city ended as a day of joy and harvest for the orphan boy, who had once had Fräulein Hardine's protection.

Things had a very promising aspect when, with

well filled pockets, he went to the neighboring house for his little girl, pressed in token of gratitude and farewell, the hands of the nearest bystanders, and — now for the first time remembered that he had forgotten to ask the name and residence of the lady whose benefits he had enjoyed and expected to claim again! It was possible that in his intoxication of joy he had heard both yesterday without heeding them, but no matter! He did not know the name of "von Reckenburg," or that of the family seat, the richest estate in the country, the pride of the whole province! Who could describe the angry surprise of our generous citizens! Was this man with his honest face, his orders and scars, his jests and stories, his appeal to Fräulein Hardine, a hot headed adventurer, who had taken advantage of their credulity to fill his pouch? It was weeks before our worthy citizens calmed down, but only to fall from one surprise into another.

Meantime Augustus Müller proceeded on his way very cheerfully. She was called Fräulein von Reckenburg, she lived scarcely twelve miles away at Castle Reckenburg, and every child could show him the way. He could pay his expenses on the road, and had time to rest and drink when he chose, and he chose to stop and drink at a great many places. So it was a week before he reached the stream on whose opposite bank the Reckenburg estate began.

But the nearer he approached the goal of his journey, the more attractive became the information he received about the lady of Castle Reckenburg. Of course he could only question common people, whom he saw at inns or happened to meet on the road, farmers, foresters, cattle dealers, etc., but they all spoke of Fräulein von Reckenburg with the greatest respect, not only as a very rich woman, but one as wise and resolute as a man, whose agricultural regulations were a pattern to the whole neighborhood. Equally unanimous were the suppositions about the disposal of the great property after the lady's death. Many pitied the lonely woman, others envied in anticipation the laughing heirs.

Our crippled soldier, who was ignorant both of the country and agriculture, of course understood none of these details. But strangely enough the more he heard of the wealth of the Reckenburg estate, the more he flattered his mind with hopes and wishes of which hitherto he had not entertained a thought. During his poverty and hopelessness, he had laughed at the suppositions first of the old cloister gossip and afterward of his own wife. Now, while wandering through a peaceful, thriving country, with a few thalers in his pocket, something warm in his stomach, and a mug always ready filled to quench his thirst, in short in a position far more comfortable than any he had ever known, he willingly yielded to the doubt whether the two women, and especially his wise Lisette on her death-bed, had not after all formed a more correct opinion of his relation to Fräulein Hardine. than the simple boy and frivolous man.

He repeatedly read his written recollections, and even allowed strangers to cast a glance at them, without considering what germs of suspicion he was sowing. True, even now he did not firmly believe in his rights as a son, but he eagerly desired them, and from wishing to claiming, as we know, is but a step. The asylum for his child and an equipment for his Turkish campaign no longer satisfied him; above all he was no longer content to obtain these things as a favor. At every mile he travelled his castle in the air rose higher, and when his little girl grew weary, more than once the exclamation escaped him: "Forward, child! We shall soon get to your grandmother Hardine!"

It was a bright August morning when he reached the first post bearing the inscription: "Reckenburg!" The country differed in no respect from that which he had traversed for several days, but our stranger was far from belonging to the class of way-farers who notice agriculture. Yet notwithstanding this, he felt as if he had entered a new region. Was it the glimmering light of home that dazzled him or were the meadows really so much more luxuriant, the fields so much richer and better tilled? Did the trees in the forest really grow so much taller, the orchards bear fruit so much more generously? How evenly all the cross roads were paved, as if regularly laid out! "No cannon would stick on these, it would be like Quatrebras!" exclaimed the old soldier. He could not help thinking of the care the old sportsman to whom he was apprenticed took of woods and game, as he saw the stately dappled bucks and powerful stags in the ancient pine forests, while here and there the animals were lying around a spring, and the fawns gambolled merrily about. "Yes, it is pleasant here!" cried the poor vagabond. "Look around, you stupid child. All this belongs to your grandmother Hardine!"

The people on the Reckenburg estate, however, seemed less attractive than the land. It was harvest season and the fields were full of active life. There he saw a race, not tall and stately, as Prince Gustel remained in his own memory, but healthy and muscular, short and neatly dressed, eager to work and sparing in pleasure. This was ceaseless labor, each for himself, yet thereby helping one another. But meantime not a word was spoken, no looks wandered from the work — there was no laughing and jesting among the young men and maidens, while the fields were mowed, the sheaves bound, and the wagons loaded. An ant heap could not have been more silent and busy. Even those who sat by the road side taking their noon-day rest, ate their black bread and emptied their mugs of thin beer silently and more hastily than peasants elsewhere usually do. No one invited the crippled soldier and his tired child to rest and take some refreshments, nay they scarcely answered his greeting; but when he asked about Castle Reckenburg and Fräulein Hardine made no reply and stared at the poverty stricken pair with surprised, almost contemptuous glances, as if they wanted to say: "What do you lazy vagabonds want in busy, blessed Reckenburg, and why do you ask for our proud, rich Fräulein Hardine?"

The wanderer had followed the road to Castle Reckenburg for hours through many changes of forest, field, and meadow, and at last entered another game preserve of still greater extent than the first, of park like appearance, and intersected with numerous winding paths. Here, too, a busy activity prevailed. Children much smaller than little Hardine were plucking the first red bilberries of the summer, and old women went to and fro with bundles of weeds on sticks, and baskets of fragrant mushrooms. Everybody on the Reckenburg estate seemed to work from the cradle to the grave. But the children toiled as silently as the grown people had done, and the old women were as mute as the children; they, too, gazed in astonishment at the two pedestrians, while a military cavalcade and several elegant equipages which dashed past them at the same moment did not attract the slightest attention. The crippled soldier vainly asked the meaning of this brilliant display of magnificently dressed ladies and gentlemen. They silently shrugged their shoulders and stooped still more busily over their work. "My Reckenburg tenants are queer people," said Augustus Müller, "but I'll teach them better manners."

The densely shaded forest path was just leading into the open fields again, when the wayfarer's steps were suddenly arrested by the sight of a group of ancient pines. He gazed intently at the slender shafts and blackish green foliage, which had grown together in a dense mass like an arbor. "Pshaw, trees are trees!" he said at last, as he tore himself away from the spot and emerged into the open country. Hitherto he had perceived no village, only in the distance a few scattered houses which he took for farm houses, mills, or brick kilns. He was tormented with thirst. There must be a tavern somewhere. So, on leaving the forest, he looked around in every direction. To the left the road to the castle continued in a broad avenue shaded by limes; directly in front was a row of fields where vegetables were growing. He now turned towards the right and stood still as if a thunderbolt had struck him when, just before the thicket of pines, he perceived a little house of very old fashioned architecture. He stared at the gable, which was adorned with a dog's head carved in stone bearing a count's coronet, breathlessly walked round the three remaining sides of the little house, struck his forehead with his clenched fist, and at last with the cry: " Nurse, nurse Justine!" darted through the open door.

But it was not the old nurse, but a family of young children whom he found seated in the neat room at their noonday meal. The table was spotlessly clean, although the food consisted only of butter, milk, and water gruel. Herr Augustus would have felt no appetite for this fare, if he had been invited to sit down.

But he was not invited, on the contrary everyone rose and gradually pressed him back to the door. It was with visible reluctance that they told him the house, formerly occupied by the keeper of the Count's hounds, was now the dwelling of the head shepherd. Then, with suspicious glances, the door was locked and the whole family went towards the sheep-fold, a new building.

Only a grey haired grandfather was left behind to warm his stiff limbs in the sunlight on a bench before the door. Our soldier remained with him to request more particular information about nurse Justine and Fräulein Hardine, and whether because in the old man's time there had been less work and more talking in Reckenburg, or whether, according to the custom of old age, the name of one well known in his youth strengthened his memory and loosened his tongue, Augustus Müller received from him information, which as it were formed the connecting link in the chain of his recollections and hopes.

Frau Müller or, to speak more familiarly, nurse Justine, had come to Reckenburg with the young Fräulein Hardine, whose nurse she had been, and was kept there by the old black countess; she was the only person who had ever seen her in her gold tower. She usually lived in the empty dog house and practiced the business of midwife in the village. When she died, many, many years ago, the Fräulein ordered a cross to be erected over her grave, on which was the inscription: "The most faithful of servants." To be sure, the old man could not remember whether nurse Justine ever had a foster child, perhaps it was during the time he served as a soldier in the Rhine campaign.

But nurse Justine had had such a child; Augustus Müller remembered it only too well, and the church register must give some information about where, when, and of whom this child had been born. With rapid strides, far in advance of his daughter, he hurried towards the parsonage.

The house, a new, handsome dwelling, stood at the foot of the church which, being built on slightly rising ground, towered above the village. At the back, on the eastern slope of the hill, was the churchyard, while the parish school house had been erected opposite at the entrance of the village street, and like the parsonage was surrounded by neat, spacious grounds. The breathless man who rushed towards it from the forest, however, had no look of interest to bestow on all which thus appeared before him with such blissful promise.

He was in the act of opening the door, when a half grown boy, wearing a gay little school cap, came forward to meet him. For the first time he saw on the Reckenburg estate a frank, happy face, which won our wayfarer's heart at the first glance.

His father, so the lad answered Augustus Müller's inquiry for the Herr Pastor, was at the castle, where to-day, the third of August, the Fräulein was giving an entertainment in honor of the king. He, the boy, was also on his way there, not as a guest, as he smilingly added, such an honor did not yet fall to his share, only to look at the beautiful horses and carriages a little while. If the matter was urgent, he would call his father.

The soldier now hastily faltered his desire to obtain his baptismal certificate, presenting as a recommendation the signatures of the two provosts of the cloister, which he had already taken from his pocketbook.

"Ludwig Nordheim," said the boy after glancing at the paper. "My grandfather's name and handwriting."

"Your grandfather's!" cried Augustus Müller in the greatest delight. "Young sir — your name?"

"My name is Ludwig Nordheim, like his," replied the boy frankly. "The Nordheims are a fixture in the parish of Reckenburg. First my grandfather, the Fräulein's old friend, then my father, also her friend and, if his wishes were gratified, I should some day be the third. But the pulpit is too narrow for me," he joyously continued. "I should rather be a farmer, like our Fräulein Hardine. To be sure, she says, 'I must study first.'"

The soldier's head grew confused with its chaos of thoughts as the boy uttered these words, and he stood still a moment as if blinded by the light of this new revelation. "Did I understand you," he said, seizing the boy's hand and pressing it violently, "did I understand you, young sir, to say that your grandfather, before he became provost of the cloister, was pastor *here*, here in Reckenburg! Can you tell me the date?"

"Not the exact year he became pastor, but it was a long time before,—towards the close of the last century,—he was appointed to his position in the cloister."

"Then he must have been here at the time I was born. He, he undoubtedly baptised me; *his* hand entered my name in the church register. *That* is why he loved me better than any of the others. Let your father remain at the castle in peace, my dear young sir. One glance at the church register, and the whole affair will be settled."

"I am sorry I cannot gratify your wish, even if I dared," replied the boy. "There is no register of that date. The books were burned in the year '97, I think, when a flash of lightning struck the vestry and destroyed the larger portion of the old church. The one you see yonder has been newly erected by Fräulein Hardine, as everything in Reckenburg has been renovated by her — the soil, the village, and even the people. But the fire fell from heaven, my father says, that even in the registers no one might be reminded of the old evil disorderly times. But I'll tell you what, my good man," he continued after a few moments reflection, "wait until the guests have left the castle, towards evening, and then ask Fräulein Hardine herself. She was often here at that time to visit the old Countess, and she, who never forgets anything, will certainly remember every child who was born in the village, especially if her old nurse brought it up."

With these words the boy sprang gaily forward, as he saw an elegant carriage drawn by four horses turn into the village street. Augustus Müller followed with a haughty step, holding his head proudly erect. The disclosures in the forest and at the parsonage had raised what an hour before had been a mere wish, into an actual certainty. What was the necessity of any testimony in black and white, when the connection of events was so palpable?

A boy is born in a lonely house in the forest. He is reared by the parish nurse, who occupies this house and who has been his mother's most faithful servant. The village pastor, his mother's most confidential friend, baptizes the boy and enters him under the servant's name in the parish register. Undoubtedly it was *he*, who secretly blessed the lady's marriage, a marriage with some person who stood too far above or beneath her. Under the protection of this ecclesiastical friend, who meantime has been promoted to the charge of a prominent charitable institution, the mother afterwards places her boy. She takes him to him in person, but secretly. She is still poor and dependent, she dares not acknowledge him publicly; but she secretly watches his progress, provides for him, punishes him, strives to arouse a brave, soldierly spirit in him, places him in the calling he has chosen, and when at last, having obtained wealth and freedom, she can venture to acknowledge him — the boy has disappeared; his name has been unheard for many, many years. But the mother remains alone, waits for him to return, keeps the inheritance that rightfully belongs to him, increases it to a princely property. And *he*, he is this fortunate boy, *he* is the son of the last von Reckenburg, the heir of the magnificent Reckenburg estates.

Such was the romance our hot-blooded friend quickly erected. The dates which would not agree with his calculations, the numerous gaps, the contradictions in the character of the heroine, the problematical part of the unknown husband did not disturb him in the least. Although perfectly sober, he felt as if he were intoxicated. If he had had a neat uniform, he would have gone straight to the castle and appeared before Fräulein Hardine and her aristocratic guests without the slightest embarrassment. "Mother!" he would have exclaimed, "mother, your son has returned, and look, this is his daughter, who in memory of you bears the name of Hardine!"

But, unfortunately, the heirs of Reckenburg could

not present themselves before their future equal in their present attire. They must go to some tavern and wait till evening.

So our friend again took the hand of the little girl, who crept wearily after him, and walked through the long, wide village street. But, strangely enough, as the farm-houses appeared on the right and left, all new, silent, neat, and soberly solid, it seemed as if the stern Hardine's eyes were gazing at him from every window, as she had once looked at the unruly orphan boy; again the words "wild stock" buzzed in his ears, and he passed his hand over his burning cheek as he had done when he felt her blow upon it. A fit of despairing weakness attacked him; he could not now have appeared before the resolute lady without some strengthening drink. And how singular! All down the long village street there seemed to be no place where such refreshment could be obtained. "Do people never feel thirsty under Fräulein Hardine's rule?" he said, sulkily. "Or do they drink water like the cattle?"

Finally in the very last house he found what he sought, although no sign nor any of the usual marks of an inn, no bowling alley, arbor, nor dancing-room invitingly proclaimed it. No, this was not the place where a pupil of the bivouac could forget the sutler's tent, where cards and dice are thrown and the beer circulates among tippling comrades. Far less was it a shelter which offered food and rest to the weary beggar, the wandering vagrant. It was a quiet, sober farm-house, like all the others in the village, only the carriages of the castle guests and a liveried servant standing before the door announced that orderly people and animals might remain here an hour to rest, in consideration of immediate payment.

Forbidding as was the place, our veteran assumed a very consequential air, sat down on a bench, and called for wine. But, the veins on his scarred forehead swelled with anger, when the host, without moving, eyed him from head to foot with anything but a welcoming glance. What marvel if to-day Prince Gustel's splendid soldierly nature had again awaked in our poor devil! He sternly repeated his order, and at the same time, with the air of a Crœsus, threw his last thaler on the table.

Vain demand! A shrug of the host's shoulders was his only reply; the merry little word wine seemed an unknown sound in the Reckenburg inn.

Meantime, however, the attention of the liveried servants was attracted by the strange wayfarer, who was clothed in rags and threw thalers about so recklessly. They approached, gave him pleasant answers, and if scarcely an hour ago **our** friend had boldly dreamed of being at the magnates' table in the castle, he now sat very contentedly among their liveried lackeys. Cumin brandy and beer loosen the tongue as well as the denied juice of the vine. Augustus talked of his old warlike recollections, but conversed still more eagerly of the memories of the still older days of peace, which had been aroused by his walk through the Reckenburg estate, and felt encouraged when other elever people made a verse that rhymed with his. Half in earnest, half in jest, his plan of attack was supported, and the mugs clinked together as they drank to a successful result.

Now and then a native of Reckenburg, who had gone home to dinner, passed the inn, loaded harvest wagons lumbered heavily into the village and returned to the fields empty. However rarely the peasants of Reckenburg might visit this place, it was worth the price of a mug of thin beer to look at the strangers' horses, and thus the strange tidings of the Reckenburg child, who had suddenly sprung up as the heir of the estates spread also among them. Shaking their heads silently, as they had listened to the story, they walked away one after another, the liveried Round Table also broke up to prepare the carriages for the drive home. But, before evening closed in, Fräulein Hardine's long treasured secret had spread far beyond the Reckenburg estate into the surrounding country.

He who rose last was the now doubly intoxicated heir. He paid for the last glass with his last groschen, roused his child, who had fallen asleep in a sunny corner, and hastily exclaimed: "Wake up, sleepy head. Now you shall go to your grandmother Hardine!"

"To my grandmother Hardine!" faltered the child, as if still in a dream.

So they walked away hand in hand. The soldier's feet wavered and his chest heaved painfully. Why? He had often drunk twice as much without any perceptible effect. To be sure, the day had been warm, the walk long, and the excitement violent. It was sometime before he reached the trellised gate, on which a gilded coat of arms glittered in the last rays of the setting sun. At the end of a long, wide avenue of elms appeared the castle, erected on a high terrace; on each side of the avenue to the edge of the forest extended the garden, divided according to line and rule by lofty hedges. Paths yellow as gold wound among the curiously formed beds, in which, surrounded by borders of box, grew trees artificially trained into various figures instead of flowers. White marble statues, which harmonized very well with the plants in this pleasure garden, were ranged along the hedges, alternating with singular monsters, from whose open jaws flowed a slender stream of water. Little Hardine clung trembling to her father whenever she saw one of these shapes, but her father who had passed through many similar pleasure grounds in foreign countries without heeding these strange forms, found them here in his ancestral home almost terribly grand and imposing.

As he approached the castle, he saw the company in their rich dresses and uniforms descending the terrace to wander in the garden. For the first time the soldier of the legion felt ashamed of the blackened, tattered cloak he had worn at Waterloo. He turned out of the main avenue into a path between the hedges, and thus unobserved reached an arbor of gilded trellis work, which opened on either side towards the terrace. He intended to wait in this dusky hiding place until the carriages had borne away the last guests and then, plucking up fresh courage, appear before Fräulein Hardine.

In spite of his slow pace, the trembling of his limbs and the oppression of his chest increased. His heart heaved as if one of the old wounds had opened. He pressed his arm upon his throbbing heart and was obliged to lean on the railing, when from the entrance of the arbor he looked toward the castle, whose lofty windows and glass doors fronting upon the terrace stood wide open. Old servants in elegant livery, with powdered hair, walked gravely to and fro carrying coffee on silver waiters; others were removing the glittering silver ware and the dainty remains of the feast from the table in the great dining room on the ground floor. How the poor vagabond's veins swelled, and what a feverish light sparkled in his eyes at this heretofore unimagined picture of luxury and splendor!

By degrees the terrace was deserted by guests and servants. Only one couple walked slowly from the opposite direction toward the arbor, where the crippled soldier was breathlessly listening. A stately gentleman in the uniform of an official of high rank, with a star on his breast, and by his side a lady of the same height, with a majestic bearing, who wore the order so thoughtfully established for the female patriots of the war of deliverance. Rich jewels glittered amid the laces that veiled the voluminous trailing dress, and the rays of the setting sun were reflected from the diadem on the thick black hair. The gentleman was talking eagerly, the lady listened gravely and thoughtfully.

Near the entrance of the arbor they stood still. She seemed to be seeking for a reply, rested her arm on a vase in which an aloe was dragging out a crippled old age, and by this movement turned her face towards the eaves-dropper.

All intentions of reserve, all oppressive timidity

suddenly disappeared. "Fräulein Hardine!" he suddenly exclaimed, "it is she! Yes, it is Fräulein Hardine!" He rushed out of the arbor and with outstretched hand hurried towards the lady.

Thus we have seen what we first called a secret, rising mist-like from vague recollections at the mention of a name, and growing denser and denser by hasty, selfish hints, until it hung like a threatening thunder cloud over Fräulein Hardine's head. Over the head of a lady whom we honored as the creator of the prosperity of our native village, who implanted in the young colony founded with masculine strength and endurance, the motto of her house. "In right and honor" and guarded it from every demoralizing contact, like a mirror which the faintest breath of decay might sully.

And we people of Reckenburg had known her almost from childhood; her life lay before us transparent and smooth as crystal. There was no shadow, no gap, not even a tender emotion which might have allowed the existence of a secret to be suspected. The contrast between our last two mistresses, the ghostly old woman in the gold tower, with whose name the mothers still frighten their children to sleep, and Fräulein Hardine, who in her fiftieth year was almost as fresh, vigorous, and active as at fifteen, was as great as between day and night.

No one was held in greater esteem by high and low; she stood amid the most prominent persons in the neighborhood, by the side of the man who was considered her only confidant, and whom of late many had chosen for her heir, when a wandering beggar, the first of his species who ventured to enter her presence, dared to make an accusation, a charge against her, at which the cheeks of the lowliest woman would have burned with shame and anger.

The conversation with the count, her companion, seemed to have engrossed her attention so entirely that she had not noticed the presence of the two strangers till Augustus Müller pronounced her name close at her feet. In his disordered condition, with every token of the drunkard, her first feeling was that of repugnance and indignation. "Go!" she said, as she motioned to the servant to drive away the intruder.

"Go!" cried the soldier, still in the same agitation, "do you bid me go, Fräulein Hardine? I suppose you do not know me, and yet I recognized you at the first glance, though you wore no crown twenty years ago."

While uttering these words, he had ascended the steps and now boldly seized the lady's hand. She involuntarily pushed the intruder away, while several servants sprang forward, the guests from the garden crowded towards the terrace, and the count made a movement as if to throw the dissolute fellow down the steps. Whether it was in consequence of his intoxication, his previous weakness, or merely the powerful repulse given by Fräulein von Reckenburg, suffice it to say that the man staggered and fell down the steps, the ground was stained with blood, the ragged cloak dropped off, the cross of honor, the mutilated arm appeared; Fräulein Hardine turned pale.

The slight injury had suddenly sobered the intoxicated man. He hastily started up and stood for a moment in a threatening attitude with clenched hand, looking the lady steadily in the face. Then he let his arm fall, and said with a pride that formed a strange contrast to his previous roughness: "This is not the first time, Fräulein Hardine, that you have raised your hand against me; but God is my witness that it will be the last. You shall never see Augustus Müller again. I might have known that one whose existence has been concealed in an orphan asylum would now, when poverty drives him to seek a shelter for his motherless child, be turned away like a criminal from the threshold of your proud home."

During these insulting words the eyes of the speechless lady fell upon the child, who had glided near her behind her father and was now surrounded by a group of compassionate or curious guests.

"What is your name?" asked a lady. "Hardine," murmured the little one. Farther questions followed, to which she shook her head with stolid indifference. At last some one inquired: "What do you want, whom do you seek here?"

"My grandmother Hardine," said the child.

This, too, the proud lady heard; she saw the bewildered looks of the noble company, and was—silent. She seemed petrified or lost in distant memories.

"Hush, Hardine," the soldier now said to his daughter, dragging her forcibly away from the group. "Hush, and come! God is a father of the orphans. There will be more charitable souls elsewhere."

So saying he turned to go. After a few steps,

however, a leaden hue overspread his face. He shivered and clung trembling to the railing of the arbor. At a sign from Fräulein Hardine the pastor hurried to his assistance; his son, whose acquaintance we have already made, sprang from between the hedges and took little Hardine by the hand. The count also followed in evident astonishment, and they disappeared in the arbor. But Fräulein Hardine, without taking any notice of her guests, turned with an agitated face towards the castle.

How can we describe the amazement of the guests at this conduct on the part of the reserved, self-possessed lady of the house? A portion, and certainly the wisest, entered their carriages without a farewell. Others did not venture, while still in their hostess' grounds, to listen to the tales their servants had heard in the afternoon. The remainder strolled up and down the garden walks, waiting for the lady's re-appearance or some solution of the mystery.

After a short time Ludwig Nordheim came running back, panting for breath, to summon the district physician, who was among the guests, to the stranger, who had suddenly been taken sick at the inn. Afterwards the pastor and the count returned, the latter with a countenance that betrayed the greatest agitation. "The vagabond has had an attack of delirium tremens," he said in reply to the questions of his acquaintances. The pastor silently shrugged his shoulders. Both went to the castle.

A few minutes later a servant hurried to the inn, and was soon followed by the pastor. The guests learned that Fräulein von Reckenburg had ordered the sick man to be nursed with the utmost care, and even wished him to be removed to the castle in case the physician thought it prudent. They had not yet recovered from their astonishment at these directions, when the count appeared, looking deadly pale and gnawing his under lip in the most violent excitement. Without vouchsafing a word of explanation, he entered his carriage and drove off at full speed.

The last remaining guests now took their departure. Scarcely an hour after the exciting event, the pleasure grounds of Reckenburg were as quiet as usual. On the following morning, however, some returned — it was noticed that the count was not among them — in order, out of the purest kindness, of course, to inquire about the health of the lady and the mysterious stranger. The latter was still seriously ill at the inn, not with delirium tremens but inflammation of the lungs, as the doctor declared. Fräulein Hardine had gone away on a journey. She who was always on her own estate, who had never been seen beyond her own domain except when paying a visit to some acquaintance in the neighborhood, and then always in the legendary gilt coach and almost immortal greys, with two powdered lackeys,— all legacies from the black countess,— had driven in a light hunting carriage to the nearest town, and from there proceeded on her journey with post horses. In spite of the most diligent inquiries no one was able to learn whither or for what purpose. When at the end of two days she returned in the same mysterious manner, her first visit was to the inn and Augustus Müller's sick bed. Perplexing as this conduct was, it really contained nothing which ought to have been permitted to shadow a character so stainless as Fräulein Hardine's. True, she thereby admitted that Augustus Müller's memories were correct, but the conclusion a covetous nature had drawn from them might, nay, must be erroneous. Fräulein Hardine had never sought to pass for a good Samaritan and, as we already know, was not considered one. But would it have been unnatural, even for Fräulein Hardine, to place a helpless orphan in an asylum and watch over him there? Or was it so difficult to understand, that even Fräulein Hardine would experience an emotion of compassion, perhaps remorse, at the sudden appearance of one who had been a protégé in her youth, in the guise of such a ruined creature? She only needed to mention a name, explain the origin of the orphan boy, and the storm would subides.

But Fräulein Hardine did not utter this name nor give this explanation. Her friends languished for the solace of one word,— of course out of the purest anxiety for the fair fame of the noble lady,— and she did not afford them this solace. True Fräulein Hardine had no compassionate nature, not even to herself. Neither now nor afterwards did she mention to any human being the mysterious incident that occurred at the festival given on the king's birthday.

After many years, however, and for a certain purpose, or to speak more correctly, for a certain person, she wrote the story of her life and in it disclosed "her secret," as she herself called it. The task was evidently a labor of love, nay even performed with cheerfulness, and we are probably not mistaken when, in the publication of this confession, we venture to expect the interest of a wider circle than that of the personal friends. For even if the picture of characters and customs, which we unroll before our readers, is somewhat antiquated, there is a truthfulness about it totally independent of any time and fashion. Yes, God's ways are wonderful, and so are the laws that govern human hearts!

MY SECRET.

CHAPTER I.

THE ROSE AND ITS LEAF.

THE riches of Reckenburg were as far from my cradle as the gold mines of Peru, and the last of the "white" baronial line were not the greedy adventurers who, for the sake of mere paltry pelf, would have ventured into the domain of the "black" head of their race. They had for generations found an asylum that honorably sheltered the poverty of a noble family, and were content and happy under the flag;— no one, however, was probably more satisfied than the last of the line who, when a lieutenant, had married a little cousin, also a descendant of the "white" branch, as poor and noble in lineage as he himself.

Eberhard and Adelheid von Reckenburg had grown up together like a brother and sister, and I doubt whether in any stage of their acquaintance the great word *love* had ever been exchanged between them. Large words were as rare among the von Reckenburgs as little tokens of tenderness, from which observation, however, it should by no means be inferred that the members of the family were not devotedly attached to each other. On the contrary, I could scarcely imagine a happier marriage than that, which for more than thirty years had united Eberhard and Adelheid so closely that their hearts seemed to throb with the same pulsation. *He*; tall, ruddy, robust,—as he called himself, "an original Saxon"—whom some mischievous kobold had enrolled among the light cavalry. *She*; small, delicate, pale, and agile. *He*; good-natured, careless, cool, ready as soon as things became too serious for him to dismiss them with a jesting word. *She*; circumspect, clever, practical, and therefore, to their mutual satisfaction, the prompter and secret machinist of the household stage. *Both*; thoroughly honorable people of noble blood. That the heroine and writer of this story, the only child of the happy couple, resembled her father in the structure of her body, her mother in that of her mind, will be seen from her life.

I received the name Eberhardine, as my father had formerly received his, in honor of the head of the family. Both generations *per procura*, and without lender or receiver ever having seen each other. As, however, the aristocratic godmother in her turn was named for the Electress Eberhardine, that Brandenburg who, in spite of her youth and Protestant faith, knew how to maintain her right to her Augustus and the Polish crown, I am of the humble opinion that a vein of this foreign tenacity of purpose was transmitted by means of the baptismal register through the Saxon succession of godmothers in the female line. Papa smoothed "the uncouth beast"* in the beginning,

---

* Eber signifies wild-boar.

and his daughter also afterwards, *ex officio*, willingly contented herself with the Hardine, though she lacked the sanction of the calendar.

The young couple had commenced housekeeping — *nota bene;* in the times of scarcity of the Seven Years' War,— on a monthly salary of twelve thalers, and an income from inherited property of about the same amount. So far, however, as my own memory extends, my father commanded the squadron, a post which to many of his equals in rank yielded the revenues of a knight's manor, and by those not particularly desirous of honor was preferred to a major's epaulettes. But as Captain von Reckenburg was a man who did not understand how to be niggardly with pig-tail ties and made every horse-shoe a matter of conscience, the "honor of his house" kept the household purse from enlarging according to the scale of the office. With the utmost economy in management. there was very little prosperity, though the soldier's life in those electoral times can *not* have been called one of ruinous campaigning and wandering. My father, during the whole period of his military service, was attached to the same regiment and remained with it in the same garrison. We had taken deep root in the little provincial city, and considered it fortunate for our household comfort that a younger branch of the electoral family, which had formerly resided in the place, had become extinct a short time before, and we were therefore not obliged to regulate our daily life according to the demands of our rank.

Yet we rejoiced in many a brilliant memento of

those ducal times. On the heights overlooking the city stood the magnificently furnished castle, and, though unoccupied, its terraces, vineyards, and gardens, sloping downward to the houses of the citizens, afforded pleasant walks. We still had the widow of the marshal of the household, a pensioned page, a titular court huntsman, court tailor, court chaplain, and court — cellarage. The latter was even in the immediate vicinity. A cooper, Müller by name, had leased it, together with the right to sell liquor in and out of the castle pavilion, so from our house and garden we could amuse ourselves by watching the revels of our fellow citizens or feel indignant with them, according as mood and occasion prompted.

The house in which my parents lived from their marriage to their death also boasted of an aristocratic origin. A duke had ordered it to be built for his barber, but died when only the first story was completed. The office of barber was stricken from the new prince's household and the second story from the architect's design. The ridge-lead was put directly on the ground floor but, according to the necessities of later occupants, was raised story after story until, at last, the roof was three times as high as the building.

How glad I am, my friends, that I can introduce you into a house of such natural growth. For nothing so refreshes the monotony of age as a curiosity from our earliest youth. "The pug-nosed face with a high night cap" appears before my eyes like a living creature; but what should I have to describe about an ordinary suite of rooms like those in a city?

The house was called the barber's shop, or even the Faberei, for, together with its builder's trade, it had been inherited by his posterity, and "Faber" was the name of the barber who had been excluded from the prince's household, and whose high office still possessed a memento in the shape of the little gate that opened from the terrace of our garden into the castle square.

This house, with all its appurtenances, had now in consideration of a yearly rental of thirty French dollars become the same as the independent possession of the von Reckenburg family. Herr Faber, a widower, was rarely at home. His barber's shop, in a habitable room in the story under the roof, adjoined the little chamber which had been assigned me at a very early age for my private use, and the three enticing brass basins rattled in the wind and glittered in the sunlight between the windows that divided us. The rooms over our heads were occupied by the servants of the von Reckenburg family — I mean the maid and the soldier who was always called "Purzel." Higher up were store rooms for provisions and fodder, drying lofts, smoking chambers, etc., etc.

Now comes the aristocratic ground floor. From the entry which divided it in halves opened the spacious family sitting-room, whose walls were yellow washed; adjoining this was the sleeping room and council chamber of the married pair. Behind these two, overlooking the courtyard, were the kitchen and offices of the squadron. There were the baronial apartments!

But what an aristocratic harmony existed between

the sitting room and its appointments! The high sofa with its blue plaid cover, spun by Frau Adelheid's own hands, the curtains of the same material, the great oak extension table, and the leathern arm chair, in which the master of the house took his afternoon nap, the spinning wheel and the roughly made foot stool; in the chimney corner, behind the monstrous stove of Dutch tiles, the washstand where the different members of the family washed their hands after eating; over it, as drapery, the home spun spotless towels — children, look respectfully at the old furniture in the new tower at Reckenburg: *good* people lived happily amid these surroundings!

And now for the trifling details of housekeeping — the brown coffee-pot and pewter table service; the brass candlestick with the long-wicked tallow candle, the copper foot stove that honest Purzel carried after his mistress to church on Sundays — to you of the present day, these things probably seem like relics from the giants' graves; but ask a grey headed bachelor, a lonely old maid, who has never had to provide any toys for a nursery, ask them how it feels when such a far reaching thread is torn from the network of their habits?

But what would be the importance of these simple surroundings without the quiet dignity with which the occupants moved among them? No offence, my young friends, but the consciousness of having noble blood lends an ease which the majority of those who have grown rich in counting-houses and offices must still acquire, and those whose armorial bearings possessed two and thirty quarterings first *un*learned when the manners of court life had varnished them. You can take lessons from Eberhard and Adelheid von Reckenburg, if you wish to walk before high and low with head erect and unfaltering step, as every honest person ought.

If the Baroness von Reckenburg, in compliance with the demands of her position, went to call upon a member of the prince's family in the same dress she wore when, as a young girl, she was presented to the same aristocratic personage, she moved, bowed, and spoke, though with all due respect, as if she were herself an Electress, for she knew that her lineage was as ancient and as pure as that of the House of Wettin. If the wife of the grasping Herr Amtmann or the head forester came to visit her in a carriage, with a footman or huntsman behind, she received them in her yellow-washed sitting room with the towels in the chimney corner, went forward one step less and made a curtsey a shade less deep than these ladies did when they welcomed her in their magnificent rooms, for the rich magistrate's wife had no noble blood at all, and the other lady's nobility was of more recent date than that of the Baroness von Reckenburg. The Baroness von Reckenburg, without the least mortification, returned the constant entertainments of the dignitaries of the city by inviting them all once a year to take a cup of coffee, and Captain von Reckenburg tied up the beans in his garden, indifferent whether the customers of his neighbor, the tavern keeper, witnessed this homely occupation. Captain von Reckenburg, with his short clay pipe in his mouth, and before him the earthen tankard of thin beer which he had poured out with his own hands, strung on a long thread the apples "his lady" had pared, and was no more disturbed by the announcement of a visitor than when, at the head of his Hussars, he passed before the General-in-Chief. Do the same thing now in the same way, and the thirty-two or even the sixty-four quarterings of the von Reckenburgs would become a jest or a soap-bubble.

But in my time and in our little provincial city with the relics of the extinct ducal branch, they were neither a jest nor a soap-bubble, but a firm pedestal, on which, even in the movement *downward*, one might to-day allow a patriarchal mixture of society, and to-morrow without offence draw the line of caste. It would never have entered the head of the most opulent merchant or tradesman to force himself into the aristocratic circle that assembled on Thursday afternoons in the castle-garden rented by the tavern keeper. No matter how poor in pleasures and rich in daughters a widow of noble blood might be, she would never have sought an hour's amusement or a husband for one of the young ladies in the plebeian society, which on Mondays took their pleasure under the self-same arbors. The plebeian dignitaries, magistrates, pastors, doctors, belonged it is true to both circles, but without forming a link between them or being looked upon by the habitués of the Thursday assemblies in any other light than as so much unavoidable stuffing. Culture and taste were essentially the same, and thus the material for entertainment on Thursday and Monday was similar. The gentlemen played ninepins, cards, talked politics, and sipped the tavern keeper's sour wine ; the fair sex knitted, dipped home-made cakes in thin coffee, and gossipped — the Monday visitors about the Thursday ones, and vice versa. On winter evenings the young people played forfeits and occasionally danced.

We, on the contrary, did not sit apart during the twilight hour in the garden behind our house, but socially on the bench before the street door. The men both of plebeian and noble birth, soldiers and civilians, walked up and down smoking, the women talked from house to house, called to the passers by, examined one another's spinning, and asked each other to taste their supper, in which it must not be concealed that we and others of the same rank probably had the nicest morsels. Moreover, there was no festival, no wine or fruit harvest celebration at our neighbor, the tavern keeper's on one side, or our neighbor, the cloth maker's on the other, that Frau von Reckenburg did not receive a sample to try. Frau von Reckenburg thanked them by a pleasant reception and praised the palatable present, but I never knew her to return it from her own table.

Among such views I had reached an age, when it was necessary to take into serious consideration the duty of securing an education suitable to my rank. As a French woman, I mean a governess, would not have suited the economy of the household, my careful mamma from my very cradle had laid the foundation of the main point of a good education — she always spoke to me in French, and thus taught me the grammar also, which she understood more thoroughly than that of her native tongue. When I was in my eighth year a tutor was engaged to teach me the other branches, a young man fresh from the university, gentle and tender as his name, Christlieb Taube.* For seven years this pattern youth literally wrung himself dry, in order not to withhold from the pupil entrusted to his care a single drop of the precious material so lately absorbed; moreover, "for practice" he made many a correction and kept many an account in the office of the squadron — duties in which Captain von Reckenburg did not always show himself a faultless hero, and "for amusement" took charge of the garden and built an arbor on the terrace, besides painting with his own hands garlands of roses and forget-me-nots on the white walls of his little room between the ones occupied by the maidservant and Purzel; in short, he made himself useful and avoided injuring anything, in a way no one else would have done for a salary of twenty-five French dollars a year. Afterwards he gave me a proof of the most touching loyalty to friendship, and with all this in his last letter, written a short time ago, spoke of "the years he had spent as a scholar rather than a teacher in this noble family as the happiest of his happy life." Therefore let my happy tutor, Christlieb Taube, be held in all gratitude and honor.

As mamma did not think it proper for me to be alone in the schoolroom, and papa declared it quite too tiresome, the choice of a companion for my studies fell as a matter of course upon our neighbor,

---

* Christ-love Dove.

the tavern keeper's Dörtchen, who had hitherto been my only friend. This was also one of those allowable condescensions to the lower classes, since even in princely households it is quite customary to have a "Prügel-kind,"* a condescension, however, which in our case was caused by a kindly feeling; for the little one was motherless, and her father, the tavern keeper, a poor guardian for *this* child.

Yes, for *this* child! If I could conjure her up before your eyes in colors as vivid as even after the lapse of half a century, she still appears before mine! As she was in those days and almost imperceptibly grew up through each succeeding year: as girl, wife, matron, the lovely child, Dorothee!

But who can describe that charming creature, whose cradle, as the saying goes, was surrounded by the Goddess of Love and the three Graces? And even if I understood how to use the brush instead of the pen, you might perhaps see the delicate figure, which looked as if moulded from wax, the softly rounded limbs, the luxuriant golden hair that framed the rose-bud face and floated like a veil down to her knees, the dimples in the cheeks and chin. But could you see the rich blood under the flower-white blue-veined skin, the changeful color of the eyes, when like a transparent crystal they were laughingly or inquiringly raised one instant, and the next, deeply shadowed, meekly sought the ground? Could you see the graceful bending of the figure, the quick transition from passing gravity to jesting and playfulness? Could you hear the silvery

---

* A child who is punished for the young prince's faults.

little voice glide up and down the scale, the merry laughter like the carolling of the thrush on a sunny May day?

But what would it avail if I had continued to talk in such flowery language from that time to this? You will understand the charm of our little "Dörl" from its influence upon others, the only way in which any charm can be described or understood. First of all in its effect upon myself.

In those childish days I imagined the little angels under God's canopy looked like her, and the puff-cheeked trumpeters in our old church seemed to me very clumsy heavenly creatures beside my dainty, earthly little Dörl. Year after year the spell physical beauty has always exercised over me — perhaps because I missed it so entirely when I looked into my mirror — increased. The young girl became the delight of my eyes, pleasure became love, and I should probably have a story to tell you of sisterly friendship, if — yes, if —

Almost from the cradle we had spent all our time together; we were of the same age, of equal education, both poor; she was beautiful and I was not — but she was a cooper's daughter and I a Baroness von Reckenburg; there was a gulf between us, whose depths I had learned to measure almost with my mother's milk. I might receive her confidences, but not return them, and in spite of her charms or perhaps precisely because of her charms, which rendered any less delightful society distasteful, I was and remained in heart a lonely creature.

"The rose and the leaf that protectingly encircles

it" honest Taube had once called us — intending to compliment me — in a New Year's poem, and the piece of grass green serge my mother had purchased at a fair at a great bargain, since it supplied material enough to clothe me all through my childhood, undoubtedly suggested the second part of his metaphor. Let us go back to Christlieb Taube's school-room with these two — the rose and its leaf.

It would be audacious to assert that no scholar was ever more eager and attentive than the tavern keeper's active little Dörl. But there was certainly never one, with whom even a more quick-tempered instructor would have so willingly been patient. On the contrary, it may be stated without exaggeration that a pupil has rarely existed who was so anxious to learn and so persistent as the tall, quiet Hardine von Reckenburg, but also rarely one who could sometimes drive even a dove-like nature to despair. Fräulein "Original-text," her father called her, when he sometimes happened to hear the unwearied How? Where? Why? with which she pumped the well of knowledge at her command to the very dregs.

Learn what you can, is an old saying! Well, at the end of her seven years study pupil number one, let it be mentioned with all due modesty, *could* write German in a tolerably legible hand and also repeat the four tables of arithmetic from memory, as well as put them down on her slate. She *could* recite the genealogical table of the House of Wettin and the succession of German emperors down to Leopold II. who reigned a short time ago, and especially Doctor Martin Luther's long and short catechism. It is possible that she also knew the earth turned on its axis, although this seems to me to be one of the things which our teacher acknowledged with a sigh: "That we really cannot say," and drew a long breath of relief, when his patron, the baron, added laughing, "And it is very foolish to ask."

But it was a great grief to our conscientious Christlieb Taube that, with all this, there was one vein, and indeed a principal vein in his fountain of knowledge, which he was obliged to close without any exhaustive effusion. The baronial possessions did not extend to a piano, and as Fräulein "Original-text" had very little ear and a by no means pliant voice, while skill without talent was not absolutely demanded by the education of those times, the noble art of music was omitted from the plan of instruction. Only the usual church hymns were practised to the notes of the tutor's violin, and a few secular tunes now and then added for the benefit of the lark-like voice of pupil number two.

After these manifold performances there was, it is true, one last categorical necessity of a suitable education, in which the training of the university was deficient, and for which the ex-ducal capital offered no reliable substitute. However, as for the alpha of French, so for this omega a worthy amateur was found in the bosom of the family. Had not Captain von Reckenburg been trained in the Dresden cadet corps, the best nursery of that knightly art which gives the most unlicked bear grace, ease, and irresistibility in society. Had he not been praised as a pattern scholar and practised the art *con amore* at all the Thursday assemblies as the best dancer, till increasing corpulency rendered the ball-room somewhat distasteful? But in the freedom of home, without the oppressive uniform, the rules of rythmical movement might be comfortably explained to bless a rising generation, and thus we see the family sitting-room of the von Reckenburgs, already used for so many different purposes, finally transformed into a temple of Terpsichore.

Three times a week, during three winters, the heavy dining table was pushed into the entry, Christlieb Taube's violin resounded from the window as an orchestra, and the baroness, playing the part of a critical chaperon, sat in the chimney corner behind her spinning wheel. But Captain von Reckenburg in soft felt slippers and a yellow calico dressing-gown lined with flannel, his thick queue swinging to and fro on his neck like a pendulum, stood opposite to his daughter Hardine and her partner, to conscientiously put them through the whole high school of his favorite art, from the first positions through all the turns and curtseys of the minuet, the *chassés* and *entrechats* of the *Anglaise*, to the gay roundelay with the three stamps of the heel.

Many things, which in the present seem like lead, turn to gold in the memory. I now look back to those dancing lessons as the merriest hours of my childhood; then I endured them as a torturing fate. My father's *rôle* of teacher offended my sense of the Reckenburg dignity, and the inherited Reckenburg limbs showed themselves by no means skilful in the agile dance.

But my companion, oh ! what a graceful vision she was, what a pure ceaseless delight ! With a pink flush suffusing her face to the roots of her golden hair, and her lips half parted, she circled around as if in her element, laughing and joyous, hovering up and down the room in the shawl dance, the climax of skill, like a butterfly, now hiding her head behind the muslin scarf, then roguishly peering out from its folds, rising and bending and swaying, an undulating billow from head to foot. The musician in the window sighed between the soft notes he drew from his violin, her partner in the green serge forgot fatigue and anger, and her teacher clapped his hands with the enthusiasm of a connoisseur.

"*She* will make a furore !" he exclaimed one evening when the family were alone.

"A furore, where?" asked the feminine critic, in the tone her husband was wont to call the wisdom of Solomon.

"Do you think of putting her in the *corps de ballet*, Eberhard?"

"A pity, a pity," sighed my father. But Frau Adelheid continued :

"The ball room is closed to Herr Müller's daughter, and I think it is quite as well for those who frequent it."

"A pity, a pity!" sighed my father a second time.

"But, aside from that, Eberhard, she has not caught the idea of the minuet, she could not on account of her parentage. How she lifts the skirt of her dress, as if she were toying with her apron in a pastoral dialogue ! Do you call that bow a curtsey ?

There I must praise our daughter. Without moving a muscle of the upper portion of her body, she bends her knees to the ground and then gradually rises again. Without entangling herself in her dress or making a false step, she moves backward with dignity, as she advanced. Exactly the demeanor with which a von Reckenburg kisses her sovereign's hand."

"Why, of course, of course, our good, dignified Eberhardine!" my father assented, patting me kindly on the cheek. But he again sighed for the third time: "It's a pity, a pity about little Dörl!"

I had only happened to catch this effusion, and knew I must be silent on such occasions. But my mother's wisdom had fallen on fruitful soil. Poor little Dörl was denied an entrance to every place where she would have shone. Eberhardine von Reckenburg had a right to a position, from which she could offer her homage to the highest of the earth.

We were in our fifteenth year, and were educated, one in accordance with the demands of her station, the other far above it; we spoke French and danced the *gavotte*, we had had our own tutor and knew our catechism thoroughly; we were ready to be received into the ranks of grown people and Christians. So on Palm Sunday of the year 1790 we knelt side by side before the altar, to renew our baptismal vows and for the first time take the holy communion.

The first communion! A confession for two from *one* mouth; the priestly hand laid in blessing on the heads of both; the same motto for both lives — that is, or at least was in my time a powerful bond. And I certainly felt this bond to be as firm and strong as an oath, while warm hearted Dörothee, in those days, would joyfully have sacrificed her life for me. And if not her life, the dear little goose was eager to sacrifice for me on this solemn occasion something that enters largely into the composition of a young girl's existence. She had received from her godmother the present of a heavy black material for her confirmation dress, while I had only the one my own mother had worn at her confirmation. I in a shabby, pieced dress, *she* clad in new garments from head to foot; the child almost died of shame at the bare idea, and did not rest until she had discovered some compensation. She dared not give me the valuable present, for what right had she to aspire to such a happiness! But she wanted to put on her old black serge, that she might stand by my side in an attire suited to the difference in rank. Her mind was fixed upon it, she returned again and again with her humble petition. Of course in vain. I wore a pearl necklace which my mother bestowed upon me as her own confirmation gift. But I had not needed the jewels. Eberhardine von Reckenburg would have felt no embarrassment, if she had gone in tinsel and Dörothee Müller in brocade.

Moreover the rustling *gros de Tours*, to my just indignation, disturbed the devotion of my companion; she passed her hand over it and smiled at the sharp crackling sound, touched me during the singing, and looked at me to call my attention to the glances the congregation cast at her. The dear, innocent child thought her magnificent dress was the cause of the attention her beauty attracted. I myself, on the contrary, apart from that vexation, entered with absorbing earnestness into the solemn ceremonial, and the verse from the Bible which was given to us as the motto of our lives, has constantly occupied Fräulein "Original-text's" most profound thoughts. It was one of those which sound as if they were very easily understood, and yet are rarely correctly interpreted by us children of the world : "For as many as are led by the Spirit of God, they are the sons of God."

Yes, but what was the spirit that must lead us into the Father's kingdom ? Was it that which hovers over the waters, the spirit of creation and development, the metamorphosis of the natural powers, which strives to bring the vanished Garden of Eden back to earth ? Or was it that which stands recorded on the tables of the law, the spirit of veneration, justice, and faith ? I would willingly have allowed these two spirits to lead me from this world into the next.

Only I had been told of a third spirit, which often seemed to draw me in a direction exactly opposite to these two. Of the spirit that condemns taking care for the morrow, forgives the adulterous woman, and turns the other cheek to the assailant. *This spirit* did not harmonize with my natural character, and the sevenfold blessing the Saviour pronounced over redeemed humanity was an empty sound to my heart. Ought, could this incomprehensible spirit be the spirit of sonship?

Absorbed in such reflections about the mysterious verse, I paced up and down our garden on Easter morning after the early service. I did not heed the golden sunlight, the voices of the birds, or the swelling buds of spring. I felt no pleasure in the resurrection going on around me. Just at that moment I heard Dorothee's light step, hastily turned, and gravely asked what meaning *she* had given to our confirmation verse.

She raised her large eyes in astonishment and then looked down with a burning blush. She had not heard or had forgotten the verse, and had not even read her certificate. I repressed my indignation, repeated the words, and then asked: "What do you call being led by the Spirit of God, Dörothee?"

She thought a moment, then suddenly turned as pale as she had before been red, raised herself on tiptoe and whispered in my ear: "To be good, to be good, Hardine."

But the next moment, with a loud exclamation of delight, she sprang towards a flower bed in which she had discovered the first violet, plucked it, twisted a few sprigs of green around it, and fastened the little nosegay to my neck handkerchief. Then she glided as lightly as a bird through a hole in the hedge which separated our gardens, smilingly kissed her hand to me, and darted towards the house.

"To be good!" she had said, and a voice in my heart cried that the child in her simplicity had hit the truth. Yet the old mystery was only solved by a new one. Was it being good to act according to rule and precept, *as* I understood them? Or was it to feel in that beatific state, which I did *not* understand?

At last I forcibly turned my mind away from the difficult verse, and this was the first time I practised a self-denial, which in after life I made a rule. I acted according to my natural disposition, with which my education, faithful to the motto of our family, harmonized perfectly, and did not doubt that all was well, when I acted in "right and honor."

It was not until I had reached an age when others had grey hair, that that second life motto again echoed in my soul, and by a simple incident the enigma gained a meaning. Probably I am not now one of those whom the Saviour calls blessed here on earth. But if we should some day begin in the other world where we stop in this, I would console myself with the hope that I have advanced one stage nearer to the Father's kingdom.

CHAPTER II.

MOSJÖ PER–SÉ.

Our relations of course changed, after we ceased to be children. Dorothee helped her father in his tavern keeping; I was introduced as a young lady to the magnates of the city and neighborhood, received their visits, now and then attended a coffee party, and always went to the Thursday assemblies in the ducal pavilion. I found no pleasant society among my equals in rank of the same age, but neither did I miss it.

Dorothee never entered the von Reckenburg sitting-room unless she had invented some request or pretext; the use of the familiar "Du" ceased; I mean in the case of Dörl. *I* still addressed her as Du and Dorothee; *she* called me You and Fräulein, like all the others in her rank of life, only she was permitted to omit the "Gnädige." She no longer hugged and caressed me as before, but curtsied and, if her heart overflowed, kissed my hand.

Yet the new forms did not wholly destroy the old intercourse, and by no means interrupted the relation between the rose and its leaf. Not a day passed that the young girl did not slip through the gap in the hedge or enter my little attic room. I continued to be her confidante in every joy, her adviser in every danger; nay, I saw the latter more plainly and felt them more anxiously than the child herself.

Her father had abandoned his productive trade and, following the usual course of tavern keepers, become almost a drunkard. The man was in a bad position; the lease of the ducal cellar would probably be taken from him as soon as it expired; his future was the almshouse.

These things, however, careless Dörl overlooked or did not heed. Her daily vexation was the business of the tavern, for which her father required her assistance. The beautiful waitress smiled upon the guests, and the guests were not select. Then there were jests and gossiping tales, which were unendurable to the child, who was naturally refined and moreover accustomed to the tone that prevailed in the von Reckenburg sitting-room.

My father saw his favorite in imminent danger. "The child is too handsome for a bar-maid," I heard him say to my mother one day in the privacy of the sleeping-room. "Far too beautiful and too much above her position. She does not know how to help herself. Adelheid, Adelheid, little Dörl will be ruined!"

"You are forgetting Faber, Eberhard," replied my mother very positively. "True, we should have cause to reproach ourselves for having removed the young girl from her natural sphere, if we had not for years anticipated this issue. The man is ambitious, and success is written on his brow; he will appreciate her greater refinement, he knows her critical position as well as we do ourselves, and rely upon it, Eberhard, now that his father's death has made him independent, the marriage will not long be delayed."

"God grant it, God grant it!" replied my father, joyously rubbing his hands.

But while these words were uttered, I fairly gasped for breath and at the conclusion it seemed as if I must protest loudly against the hopeful "God grant it!" Why? I knew that since our confirmation we had become marriageable, and that the fifteen year old Dorothee would not have been the first child I had seen go directly from her first communion table to the marriage altar. Why did the words "God forbid" sound in my ears like the croaking of a frog?

How one after another the few people with whom I have really lived enter into my confession! Faber, Siegmund Faber! When in after years this man's name was so often mentioned before me with gratitude and admiration, only a short time ago, my friends, when you asked me if I remembered him as one of the acquaintances of my youth — you did not suspect, no one has ever suspected that this man was my earliest acquaintance, my next door neighbor, the *first* and almost the only person who gave me cause to think, and between this man and myself a fate had come, a secret which for long years I called a crime.

Siegmund Faber was the only child of our landlord, the barber, and was motherless from the first hour of his birth. As he was about six years older than I, he must have been already attending school at the time of my earliest recollections.

But Siegmund Faber had long since chosen something wiser than moving up and down on the schoolroom bench. As soon as he had quickly and surely appropriated the first elements, he objected to beginning the course again every year with a crowd of new pupils, and the clear sighted old principal was far from reproving him for it. "Faber goes his own way," he said, "Faber is a genius!" But Faber senior, who thought the art of the razor the pleasantest in the world, and believed it more profitable to invest his spare money in fields and meadows than in the education of his son, Faber senior, had turned the wise old schoolmaster's remark to his own advantage. If, as often happened, he was urged to send the remarkable boy to a higher school, his answer was invariably; "My son goes his own way, my son is a genius."

The genius, however, among Faber's customers became very much like the usual stamp of barbers' sons. But Papa von Reckenburg, who did not allow anyone he liked to escape without some innocent nickname so easily, could not deny himself the pleasure of re-modelling the "genius" a little. Mosjö Per-sé was the title the landlord's son bore within the old Faber house.

And with good reason. Siegmund Faber was an original; that is, he was one of those rare individuals, who undismayed force a way through the crowd. Nature had prepared him for a ruling passion by giving him an imperious will, and the outward form was moulded by the spirit within.

Imagine a man scarcely tall enough for a soldier,

as Captain von Reckenburg declared. No matter, strangely enough, you looked up to him. He was like his house — his principal growth was above the shoulders. There must have been several more than the usual number of joints in his neck, joints which aided the constant movement in every direction. The head was still longer than the neck, and sloped sharply away at the back, but the brow was massive and nobly formed. Beneath this high, broad forehead was a long, broad nose, with large, wide-open nostrils, and below the nose, so exactly adapted to scent out everything, was a wide, thin mouth, closed as firmly as a dash, while from the sides of the head projected two huge ears, which — heads were constantly shaken at it — moved to and fro like those of a hare.

I have sketched no Adonis for you, have I? But now look at his eyes. You cannot distinguish the color, they are so deeply sunken beneath the overhanging brows and wander from one direction to another with such a restless glitter. Yet let them once discover the object already scented, and they will pierce to the very marrow of his bones. You would not escape their questioning gaze, nor dare to resist their bidding.

In short he evidently had a doctor's skull and a doctor's physiognomy. Now imagine this face suffused with the uniform flush of healthy blood, and animated with quenchless zeal, imagine limbs delicate as those of a woman, but with muscles of iron; the hands by instinctive grasping, stretching, and pulling, transformed into steel springs; imagine the man always looking as fresh as if he had just stepped out of a bandbox, without a wrinkle in his faultless cravat, a speck of dust on his grey suit, a single hair escaping from the thin queue which was always tied with a black ribbon, or the smallest vestige of beard on his chin — whether denied by mother Nature or removed by his father's skill I won't venture to determine — and you will have a rude sketch of our "genius."

He never seemed in a hurry, and was always in motion. I have scarcely ever seen him sit down, and five hours rest at night was enough for him even in the days of sleep-requiring boyhood. Even after midnight I have noticed the reflection of his lamp on the polished basins that hung between our windows, and at daybreak heard him glide down stairs with cat-like tread and leave the house. That he took some nourishment must be supposed, but I never saw him. Perhaps he carried food in his pocket and ate it as he walked along, or had his meals standing at neighbor Müller's, where his father boarded. At any rate he was not at all regular, and you may be sure that this "genius" had not even *once* in his life sat down to a comfortable meal nor drank a mug of beer. He did not smoke, he did not take snuff, he did not know how to play any game, to dance or join in merry conversation, he had no intimate friend. His words were quick and curt, his voice was slightly falsetto; he economized his pronouns as much as possible, and paused after each sentence. He anticipated contradiction and harshly cut short all opposition. Yet he did not irritate nor offend. His self-consciousness awed others, because he only spoke of subjects he had mastered. Even the Baroness von Reckenburg dared not address him as she did his father, nor call him anything but "Herr," though he was sparing of titles and evidently studious not to recall the manners of the barber's shop by any unusual civility.

I have described the adult Per-sé; but he was precisely the same when, as a little boy, he went with his father to visit patients, carried his case of instruments, or held the basin for him when cupping or bleeding was necessary. Moreover, he also operated at that time on his own account. He could not see a wart without twisting it off, a blister without opening it. Corns disappeared painlessly under his little knife. He drew out his schoolfellows' aching teeth, and, by means of the pennies he had saved, induced many to submit sound ones to the same operation. He even surpassed his father in all the higher branches of his profession. Everybody wanted to be relieved quickly and gently by Faber junior, and Faber senior willingly gave up lancet and pincers, contenting himself with razors and the oversight of his fields and meadows.

In the leisure time, of which the indefatigable boy had sufficient in the intervals between his books and practice, he sat in the apothecary's laboratory or went to the slaughter-house or the flayer, who, like many of his craft, passed for a magician. No dead body was ever examined or dissected unseen by Siegmund Faber. But when at last he finally left school, he often remained absent from home for days and weeks, and if Father Faber had inquired for a man who always went his own way, he would have found him in the clinical institutions and anatomical cabinets of our two neighboring universities, or even in more distant Jena. Professors, attracted by the strange eagerness of the self-taught young man, willingly received him into their classes and gave him instruction, which led to still closer investigation. At the age when most youths are at the university, Siegmund Faber was already a well-known personage, and had established a certain reputation for miles around.

There was consequently no hesitation in accepting him as an assistant to our old regimental surgeon. In those days few questions were asked about what an army surgeon knew or did *not* know; people were satisfied with what he could or at all events could *not* do. But as Siegmund Faber undoubtedly *could* do something, it was considered a settled thing that he should have the old surgeon's place as soon as the latter at last became convinced that he could do *nothing*. During this period old Faber died; his son had reached his majority, that is, was twenty-one, a man of property, and entirely independent. And this was the time when my parents expected little Dörl to be saved by him.

For in such contracts, or compensations, nature delights; this man, who seemed to have no appreciation of anything except physical ailments; no desires except to cure them; no passion save that of becoming a master in his profession; this very man, as if his organs needed some refreshment, felt drawn with an eager, exclusive longing towards the most healthful and beautiful creature in his whole circle of vision. This creature was his little neighbor, Dorothee.

Even when she was an infant in the cradle, he is said to have watched her with delight; he, the ever-restless boy, often lingered for hours gazing at her; and she afterwards became, not his playmate, but the only plaything he ever cherished. He brought her sweetmeats, flowers, all sorts of toys and ornaments; called her his Dörtchen, his child, his betrothed; spoke of her as his future wife with the same confidence that he expressed the belief that he should some day become a famous doctor. And strangely enough, no one laughed at the grave little man.

Afterwards he appeared as the protector of the charming girl. He guarded her as if he had a sort of right of possession; his keen eyes flashed with a vengeful, angry light at any token of admiration from a stranger, his hands clenched at any unseemly jest about the pretty bar-maid; he would undoubtedly have killed the offender who profaned his flower. That this man, in addition to his proud, speculative mind, possessed a soul, a tender, love-thirsting soul, was disclosed exclusively in his conduct towards the child, whom, like his profession, he had seized by his own absolute will.

You may imagine that Mosjö Per-sé witnessed Dörl's introduction into our family circle with great satisfaction. Here she was safe, here she was trained for a social position which he *a priori* claimed for himself. He, who so rarely smiled, was radiant with delight when, during the dancing lessons I have described, he beheld the dainty butterfly floating up and down, or heard the silvery little voice chattering readily and fluently in a language which he himself did not understand.

The longing for the delight of his eyes, therefore, brought him more frequently to the von Reckenburg sitting-room than would probably have been the case under other circumstances, and in this way he became a sort of companion of Dörtchen's friend.

"You understand it, Fräulein Hardine," he used to say, when he confided to me, and me alone, new discoveries and conclusions in his practice, or the purpose and goal of his expeditions. And "Fräulein Original-text's" thoughts would be guided by these aphorisms into paths honest Christlieb Taube did not understand how to open. So it was a barber's son and assistant who, at a dangerous age, offered salt and spice to my youthful longings. I did not exert myself to please, but to understand him. Mosjö Per-sé was the man who, at fifteen, more than at any later period in life, *interested* me, as it is called.

But the slightest allusion to his profession ceased as soon as his Dörtchen approached us, — not because he had perhaps seen her turn pale or stop her ears at the mere mention of blood and wounds, but merely because in her presence he forgot his career, since his pulses began to beat to another tune, and the burden of aspiration yielded to a heart-felt joy.

And Dorothee? you will ask. Did the thoughtless child suspect the importance of such a nature, value the place she had obtained in its love? Did she exclaim with the experienced friend: "God grant it?" or with the inexperienced companion of her girlhood: "God forbid!"

See and hear her in the hour which decided her fate.

It was probably the first or second day after that on which I overheard the conversation between my parents, which still occupied my thoughts. It was the first of the month of July, and our landlord had been absent a week on one of his scientific expeditions. He had learned to ride a short time before and Captain von Reckenburg, an expert in the art said: "This Mosjö Per-sé is a devil of a fellow! He never had a horse under him except at the flaying place, but he rides like the deuce."

My parents were dining with a neighboring landowner, to whom I had not yet been formally presented. I was alone in the house, and in the afternoon went into the garden to pick some beans for the next day's dinner. I had just commenced the troublesome work of cutting them in the grape arbor on the terrace, when Dörtchen, her face radiant with smiles, fluttered through the gap in the hedge.

"No, Fräulein Hardine!" she cried, when a long way off, "no, there is no more curious customer than this Mosjö Per-sé."

"Has Herr Faber returned?" I asked.

Dörl nodded. "He has just put up his horse in our stable. I was standing at the door with father. Did he shake hands with me as usual? No, indeed. He just bowed so"—she bent quickly forward from the waist, as we close a pocket knife—"and sent me away without ceremony, because he wanted to speak to my father alone. Besides, he did not call me 'Du' and 'Dörtchen' as usual, but very formally said 'you' and 'Jungfer Dorothee.'"

"I think it is only proper, Dorothee," I answered wisely, "for a young man to cease such familiarities with a girl who may be married any day."

"Married!" cried Dorothee, greatly amused. "Yes, but to whom, Fräulein Hardine?"

"Why, perhaps to this very Siegmund Faber."

The child looked disappointed. "To him?" she pouted. "To him? No, indeed. He thinks of cripples and dead bodies, but not of a wife."

"My parents hope and wish the contrary, Dorothee. They call this marriage your deliverance, your happiness."

She turned pale and her eyes filled with tears. "But I am afraid of him," she whispered, trembling.

"Have you forgotten the explanation of the sixth commandment in our confirmation lectures?" I asked in the pedantic manner which had become a second nature with me towards my little Dörl, and fortunately *only* towards her. "A woman must fear, love, and trust her God in Heaven and her husband on earth."

Dorothee looked at me with her large blue eyes, as she had done on the Easter morning when by one word she explained the meaning of the bible verse. "Fear *him*," she said softly, "no, but I am afraid *of* him. Are you afraid *of* God, Fräulein Hardine?"

"But why are you afraid of Faber? He is a genius, unlike everybody else—"

"That is the very reason," she eagerly interrupted. "I don't want a 'genius'; I want a husband like other people; a person like myself, only much nicer and better."

The child had again hit the right mark. True, at that time I shook my head. Ten years after I attained the same wisdom. Singular people are not fit to live with others. Marriage and home life cannot tolerate originals.

"No, no, Fräulein Hardine," Dorothee repeated. "He does not think of me, thank God, for I have a dread of him."

So the matter was settled, and my secret protest against my parents' plan explained. Dorothee did not love him, and Siegmund Faber was too good for a woman who could not give him her heart.

I invited my little neighbor to spend the afternoon with me; we sat in the arbor and under her small plump fingers the beans soon fell rapidly into the dish on her lap. She chatted gaily and laughed at my awkwardness; the impending suitor was forgotten.

About an hour had elapsed in this way, when a hasty footstep on the terrace announced the unusual event of a visitor in the garden. The next moment Siegmund Faber stood before us: he wore his Sunday suit, and made the quick, low bow the child had imitated, The bright smile fled from her lips, she blushed scarlet and cut the beans with feverish haste.

I looked up at the young man in still greater suspense. The most powerful agitation was visible on the brow usually so calm; the ruddy hue had left his face, the quick throbbing of his heart was apparent under the silver embroidered vest, and his hands were clenched to conceal their trembling.

This was probably the way he looked when he had

made up his mind to undertake a very critical operation.

Yet he did not hesitate to declare the object of his visit. "My request for an interview is made with your father's knowledge, Jungfer Dorothee!" he burst forth.

The inn-keeper was master in his own house, and had a right to grant an interview between the young man and my little visitor; so, in spite of the latter's imploring glances, I rose to leave the arbor. But Faber stepped before me, seized my hand, and said; "You will oblige me if you will remain, Fräulein Hardine."

So I took my seat again and motioned to Faber to sit down on a bench opposite to us. He did not do so, but drawing a long breath, turned to *me*, and began at once:

"You know the goal I have set before my eyes, Fräulein Hardine. The usual years of study are lost, I must try to replace them by practical means. And I *shall* replace them. But not in my little native city, nor in the peaceful condition of Saxony. I have ample recommendations. My preparations are made, I am going to Prussia. In a few weeks, perhaps, I shall stand on a field where wounds are dealt and must be healed."

You know I am writing of the year '90, and for twenty-seven years Prussia had been at peace. To be sure, I had heard my father and his comrades discussing a difference of opinion between the emperor and the king in regard to the affair of the Grand Turk; but no one understood the jumble and no one seriously thought of danger to an out of the way province, where there was nothing digestible for Prussia to swallow. Siegmund Faber, therefore, probably noticed the astonished glance with which I answered his prediction of blood and corpses.

"King Frederic William," he continued without a pause, "has gone to the army in Silesia. There I too shall join the Weimar regiment, to whose illustrious commander I am recommended by the Jena University. Thunder clouds, like those lowering in the East and West, do not clear away. If they disperse this year, so much the better for me. I shall gain a twelvemonth for preparation. Day after tomorrow I shall be on my way to Berlin."

The orator paused, and I heard a sigh of relief by my side. Dorothee had dropped the knife and was looking roguishly up at me. Everything had resulted differently from what I had prophesied. Mösjo Per-sé was going to the war, to become a famous doctor ; he was not thinking of his Dörtchen and a home of his own.

But Mosjö had only stopped to take breath ; he was by no means at the end of what he wanted to say. The blood suddenly rushed to his face, only to subside again as rapidly ; he sat down, for his knees were trembling. What could so agitate this resolute nature ?

He now turned to my neighbor, and his voice was so tremulous with emotion that I could scarcely believe it to be his. "I do not know, Jungfer Dorothee, whether you have ever suspected the aspiration which has filled my soul for years. You smiled as if it were a jest, when I called you mine. But it was no boyish whim, Dorothee. I am not in more solemn earnest to-day, than in every former hour since I first knew how to understand myself. You are still very young, Dorothee, and I should have liked to delay the binding words. But I am pressed for the time you need. I have your father's consent; will you give me yours, will you become mine, Dorothee?"

With all my confidence in the man, this sudden proposal after the warlike preface seemed rather too blunt. To marry, to marry a half child, when one is in the act of going to the battlefield or entering a chirurgical institute as a preliminary to doing so! I was beginning to doubt the common sense of the genius, and preparing as a quasi patroness of my little Dörl, who clung to me trembling like a May flower, for a bold refusal.

But, ere I could speak, the singular candidate for matrimony cut short my protest by hastily adding: "It is a matter of course that I cannot expect the fulfilment of my wishes to-day nor to-morrow. Years may, nay must elapse, years of hard struggle, perhaps a decade. Have you the courage, Dorothee, to wait these years in faith and honor, as my betrothed bride? Are you sure of me, of yourself? You will never see me again, if I should be overcome in my progress towards the goal. But I *shall not* be overcome. And when I, sooner or later, return a famous man, will you then become mine? I have never desired the love of any human being save yourself. Do you wish me to continue to love you, Dorothee?"

The man's agitation had seized upon me. The

daring of his offer harmonized perfectly with my fifteen year old temperament. I would joyfully — of course supposing that my name had been Dorothee Müller and not Eberhardine von Reckenburg — joyfully have clasped Siegmund Faber's hand, and said: "Break a path for yourself, seek your goal. A man like you is worthy to have a woman wait for him for years, for a decade, if God wills."

But the real Dorothee, who had no mother and no father's protection, who was surrounded by temptation and vulgarity, who looked up to me with such helpless, pleading eyes, unable to say no, and still more unable to say yes; but my poor, beautiful, bright little Dörl?

Once more I endeavored to speak in her name, and again Siegmund Faber interrupted me. "I know that I am asking something unusual," he continued in a much firmer voice than before, "and I feel what you wish to answer, Fräulein Hardine. But do not suppose that I shall leave the girl I love in her present helpless position, that I shall consent to lead my betrothed bride from the tavern to the altar. I am going to follow the natural path of man, the path of action. It will be an easy matter for me to keep the feelings of this hour loyally to the end. But she, Dorothee! If I am to accept the sacrifice of her freedom, she must give her future husband the right to provide for her in the present. I would gladly place her in the charge of a cultivated family in a large city. But her father lives, and the duty of a child is paramount, so long as the wife does not follow her husband. Moreover, among strangers she would inevitably feel herself a dependent, and I want her to be free and untrammelled, to act without control. So let her take care of her father, help him so far as he personally needs her, without mixing in the business of the tavern. I have his promise that he will make no demands of that kind on my betrothed bride. All the preparations are made. Say yes, Dorothee, and to-morrow, by legal transfer, you will enter into possession of all the property my father has left. You will have the use of it until you attain your majority without any guardianship, and as it has recently been leased, without any trouble. If I do not return, you will have the entire disposal of it. This is no sacrifice I am making for you, it is a burden from which you will relieve me, my dear child. I still have more than I need to begin my career, and shall soon be entirely independent. You will move into my father's house and furnish it according to your delicate taste. Busily occupied, as mistress in your own domain, in the room where my cradle stood, where I was so long happy in hope, I shall see you in anticipation as mine, see you with confidence henceforward under the eyes of the honored family in which you have grown up, under your eyes, Fräulein Hardine, for you will not withhold your counsel and sympathy from Siegmund Faber's betrothed bride."

During the last explanation I had not looked up, for I was ashamed of the tears in my eyes. Now, when the speaker closed with an appeal to my friendship, I glanced at him in honest acquiescence, and then looked anxiously at the child, who was so suddenly called to decide upon a most unexpected change in her life. What would she say, how extricate herself from this dilemma, she, who scarcely an hour ago had said: "I am afraid of this man!" who had uttered a sigh of relief, when he spoke of his departure, perhaps forever?

And now? Oh! little, variable Dörl? Oh! the wonderful changes of a young girl's heart! Her eyes glittered like a lake that has lain grey and dreary under a cloudy sky, when a sunbeam suddenly bursts through the mist, her cheeks were suffused with a flush of joy. To be a betrothed bride and yet free, to be rich, to act without control in her own house, be permitted to adorn herself and idle as she pleased — all this joy — and not a spark of anything *more* did I read in *one* glance at those smiling features. My heart burned with a sense of shame.

Did Siegmund Faber ascribe this sudden delight to any deeper feelings? I do not think so. He knew her to be a child, loved her as a child. Nay, he trusted to the very innocence of a child's soul, the bond that gratitude weaves, the faithfulness to duty that exists in an unprofaned mind. And he felt himself a man to win a woman's heart, as soon as he was permitted to claim it for his own.

Be this as it may, Siegmund Faber no longer looked troubled, but as bright and happy as his little Dörl. He held out his hand to her, and asked smiling: "Well, dear Dorothee?"

She placed hers within it and bowed her little head in happy acquiescence.

"Say amen, Fräulein Hardine, as witness and security for our contract," exclaimed the young man turning to me.

I did not say amen, but I pressed Siegmund Faber's hand and embraced—God knows with a heavy heart—his radiant betrothed.

Siegmund Faber also—that none of the forms of betrothal might be omitted—pressed his lips to Dorothee's brow, but hesitatingly, as if he feared to rouse a dangerous feeling in the child or in himself. Then again becoming as grave and earnest as he was at the beginning of this singular scene, he drew two gold rings from his hand, put one on his own ring finger, the other on that of his betrothed bride, and said:

"My parents' wedding rings? If some day I stand before you with this ring on my finger, Dorothee you will know, without a word, that I can lead my wife to the altar in faith and honor."

At this moment my parents' carriage drove up. I walked slowly to the house, and the two others, arm in arm, moved quickly and joyously towards the home of the betrothed bride.

An almost beardless youth, a regimental surgeon's assistant, who goes wandering into the world and gives away his inheritance to buy the heart of an unfledged girl; a betrothal as sudden as a thunderbolt, a second half fledged girl summoned as a witness of the strange bond—my friends, as I draw this picture from the portfolio of the memories of almost half a century, it may well seem very foolish, perhaps childish in your eyes. But I assure you if you had known Siegmund Faber, you would not have smiled at my emotion. And not only the inexperienced daughter, but the experienced parents saw no child's play in Siegmund Faber's hasty act.

"Our little Dörl is a Sunday child!" exclaimed my father. "A Sunday child, into whose lap fortune falls as it does in dreams. And this Mosjö Per-sé is a clever fellow to bind his bird by a gold chain." But my cautious mamma, who probably felt a pang of maternal envy when she saw the tavern keeper's little daughter become rich and a betrothed bride before her Hardine, answered: "No lawyer could have managed more cleverly than this young physician. Well or ill, the deed of gift binds the butterfly till her majority, that is till the dangerous season of youth is over, and at the marriage altar the generous giver receives his present back again."

The next day the legal document was executed exactly according to Faber's promise, and in the grey dawn of the following morning the strange suitor mounted his horse and rode away. The last farewell to home was waved to Fräulein Hardine's attic window and answered from there.

"Did you bid Herr Faber farewell last night?" I asked Dorothee, when soon after she entered my room.

"No, Fräulein Hardine," she stammered in evident embarrassment, "I meant to do so early this morning, but — I overslept myself."

So even the tears that it would have been decorous to shed at parting were spared our happy little betrothed.

But how rapidly she worked that very day at cleaning and moving. Everything was turned topsy-turvy in the room, before whose window Herr Faber's barber's basins had glittered in the winter; it was washed, scoured, the old furniture varnished and freshly covered. Soon a dainty canopied bed stood in the spot where Siegmund Faber had allowed himself a few hours rest on a hard straw mattrass. In the corner formerly occupied by his rough book shelves, was a dainty cupboard filled with dolls which had delighted little Dörl's childhood; bright colored curtains and freshly gathered flowers adorned the window seat, a pair of finches kissed each other in a cage twined with green vines. No citizen's daughter had a prettier little room, and how bare and plain Fräulein Hardine's sober chamber looked beside it!

But the little house-owner, in her short skirts and high heeled shoes embroidered with spangles, fluttered joyously up and down stairs. In one pocket was the paper horn of candies and sweetmeats which the child never allowed to be empty; in the other the little purse from which a penny or kreuzer was thrown to every beggar. Then she went across to the tavern, where a stout maid servant had been engaged to attend to the work; then through the gap in the hedge into the garden; up to the arbor where she had been betrothed; next to take a walk in the neighborhood; then to peep into Fräulein Hardine's chamber, or curtsey and kiss Baroness von Reckenburg's hand in the sitting-room, smiling and dancing and singing from morning till night, good, happy, tireless little Dörl.

CHAPTER III.

THE BLACK COUNTESS VON RECKENBURG.

I HAD but a short time to watch the happy activity of our new house owner, for during these summer weeks an unexpected change occurred in my life.

I have already mentioned that the old countess was godmother to both my father and myself and added that neither of us had ever received any token of remembrance from the noble namesake nor, to tell the truth, missed any such proof of regard. Perhaps she would have taken a different course if the last scion of the old race had been a man. But a girl, the daughter of an impoverished side branch, how should the "black head of the house," in her princely splendor, remember one in whom the name might be expected to vanish in obscurity? Whoever the strange old woman's heirs might be, we knew that the unassuming Captain von Reckenburg and his plainly educated daughter were not.

Great, great beyond all expression therefore was the wonder when, during the latter part of the summer, a letter was received from the countess, written by her own hand, the first of its kind with which her white cousins had been honored. The words, translated from the French, ran as follows:

"If the Baroness and Baron von Reckenburg should feel disposed to permit their daughter Eberhardine to become the Countess von Reckenburg's guest during the next winter, her carriage will be in waiting (here the date and place were specified) to convey the young lady to Castle Reckenburg."

Unattractive as was the wording of this expression of interest, and difficult as it probably was for my parents to trust their only child, even for a short time to the care of a perfect stranger, the possibility of a refusal was not even taken into consideration. The countess was — well, she was simply the wealthy Countess von Reckenburg, and almost eighty years old. Fräulein von Reckenburg, on the contrary, was miserably poor, possessed few attractions to win a husband and, if she lost her father, would be thrown helpless upon the world. Many a motherly sigh of anxiety had probably been uttered in words within the private council chamber. A dowry, a legacy from the superabundance of her only relative, who to-day for the first time showed a certain degree of interest, could put an end to all sighs and anxieties.

My father therefore accepted the invitation, though in the most dignified manner. Friendship and confidence would be given rather than received; it was not the rich relative, but the godmother, who had a right to make the request, to whose wishes he yielded.

The manner of gratifying them required longer consideration. The young lady could not travel *alone*, nor go in the yellow post chaise; her father could not accompany her, as he would have thought most suitable, for the time fixed in the invitation was the same as that appointed for a review, and my mother had been in delicate health for some time and was strictly forbidden by the physician to undertake the journey.

The difficulty, however, was speedily solved, when "Nurse Justine" voluntarily offered her services as duenna and protector on the journey. For had it been necessary to travel hundreds of miles, instead of twelve, and spend twenty nights on the road instead of one, there was no one in the world to whom my mother would have entrusted her child with so much confidence as to our nurse Justine.

Nurse Justine, most faithful of the faithful, you appear on this journey for the first time within the frame of my story, though it was your due to have been mentioned at the first step of the journey of life. You carried me in your hands to the light, rocked me when my mother's arms were too weak to hold the "huge child," and never was nursling watched with more loving glances than the last von Reckenburg by her nurse Justine.

Justine had entered my parents' service as a *wacht-meister's* widow, and with the assistance of the soldier, performed all the work, even when the care of a new born infant raised her to the rank of nurse. She had fulfilled all the duties of this worthy class, without claiming any of the corresponding privileges. Not until her "Dinchen" had outgrown the rod of a child's nurse, did she exchange her laborious office for the at least more lucrative one of a mid-wife, but even then without losing sight of her nursling, for she shared the new maid-servant's chamber between the rooms occupied by the tutor and Purzel.

She had no child of her own and was alone in the wide world; so the *little* Hardine was her all in all, and may God forgive the *great* Hardine if the love she could not return, in equal measure, oppressed her in after years as a burden. Little Hardine was the apple of her eye, her one object in life, her hope, her pride. She saw her with prophetic eyes among the great of the earth, and in the future as an angel with golden wings before the throne of God. She may sometimes have seemed a little fierce and envious and quarrelsome to the rest of mankind; but she was only fierce and envious and quarrelsome for the rights and privileges of her Fräulein Hardine; for her Fräulein Hardine she thought and spun, saved and starved; Fräulein Hardine became the heiress of the few hundred thalers she had accumulated by kreuzers.

Nurse Justine was pious and well versed in the Bible, but the divine promise did not satisfy her where her darling's earthly fate was concerned. The most mysterious hints must be explained for her, obscure oracles questioned, and the conclusion of every investigation always resulted in good fortune, nothing but good fortune. Already the baptismal day, the third of the child's life, had promised blessings; the infant had sneezed violently three times while its little cap was being untied — that is, she was a wonder of intellect and talent; she had struggled and screamed ungovernably under the baptismal water — that is, the treasures and gifts of the world awaited her. Since that hour Nurse Justine's faith in the inheritance of the von Reckenburg property was as strong as her belief in the gospel, and a day rarely passed without her having discovered something wonderful for her darling in her dreams or the shuffling of cards. A letter bringing good news was announced weeks before the countess' invitation so greatly astonished the inmates of the barber's house.

In one point alone, strangely enough, the mysterious oracles would never harmonize with the wish dearest to my old nurse's heart. Whenever the highly important question about the "future husband" was raised, the prophetess looked dejected but gave her young lady the significant warning to beware of "flayers and jokers." After many an anxious trial my nurse seemed to have given up a victory over the king of hearts, but even the most promising combinations of kings was always at the last moment crossed by an insolent low diamond.

But who was this inevitable low diamond, that so cruelly disturbed my old nurse's rest? For a long time she had fixed an angry gaze upon our landlord's silent, ambitious son, but since the latter's sudden departure and the fortunate change in the circumstances of his betrothed bride, her thoughts had been directed into another channel. The fatal low diamond need not be a man, nay it was far more probably a woman, and this woman no other than — our new house owner, Dorothee.

Nurse Justine was not related to little Dörl, but nevertheless had the same name. Both bore the surname of Müller, but as nurse Justine was even prouder than the von Reckenburgs, she had watched the kindness shown the little plebeian with ungracious eyes. "Was there no child of noble blood who could be Dinchen's companion?" she muttered at first, and in later years grumbled: "Must it need be one with a better complexion, though not half so aristocratic and noble looking as Fräulein Hardine?" The gift of Faber's property, and the sparkling engagement ring of course did not dispose her to any more kindly feeling, but since the threatening low diamond was discovered under the mask of the tavern keeper's daughter, my nurse — even without the increased prospect of inheriting the Reckenburg estates — would have thought nothing more desirable than my temporary absence from home.

Therefore she no sooner heard of my parents' anxiety about the journey, than she declared that she would be my companion and not allow a hair of her young lady's head to be ruffled on the way. Her proposal was accepted, and the weeks passed swiftly in all sorts of preparations.

On Dorothee's birthday, the 29th of September, the first tidings came from the distant lover; a letter and a small box. She hastily opened the latter and uttered a cry of delight at the sight of the valuable garnet ear-rings sent as a birthday present.

"And what does he write?" I asked, after she had put the jewels in her little ears before the mirror. She hurriedly glanced over the letter and then handed it to me, saying, "There is not much in it."

And in fact there was not much. The usual congratulations and vows of eternal love and constancy expressed in somewhat old fashioned language. The words did not seem to come from the writer's heart. A postscript stated that he should leave Berlin immediately to join the royal army in Silesia, and there, according to his wish, would be appointed to the Weimar regiment. As the august potentates had become reconciled, there would be no war at present but the writer had obtained beneficial employment in the chirurgical institute at Breslau, a favor he owed not only to the gracious intercession of his distinguished chief, but to the recommendation of a prominent ecclesiastical prince to whom he had had a letter of introduction from the university of Jena, and with whom he had had an extremely interesting interview about the method of instruction it would be best to adopt in the domain of surgery.

(Note that Fräulein Original-text, who had the genealogical table of the Saxon Princes at her fingers' ends, had never before heard of an "ecclesiastical prince," and vainly racked her brains about the name and nature of the person mentioned.)

After the counter-march which would soon take place, he, the field surgeon *in spe*, hoped through the influence of this same remarkable man to obtain a long leave of absence and spend it in the university town of Göttingen, in the vicinity of his regiment, which would be stationed among the Hartz mountains. Thus until war again threatened to break forth, as would inevitably be the case, the writer would occupy a position where he could employ his time to the best advantage!

"Have you answered Herr Faber's letter?" I

asked Dorothee, the day before my departure. She blushed and shook her little head.

"Then do so to-day," I replied.

"If I only knew what to say!" she murmured piteously, but obediently sat down and with tolerable rapidity began to express her thanks for the beautiful ear-rings. Then the stream ceased to flow. She bit her pen, sighed, and rubbed her forehead on which drops of perspiration were standing. "Help me a little, Fräulein Hardine," she at last said beseechingly.

But that of course I did not do. On the contrary I went away, hoping she would succeed better alone. But the whole afternoon passed in the difficult task, and not until evening was the letter placed in my hands to read. "Fräulein Hardine says this; Fräulein Hardine does that;" so ran sentence after sentence. There was not a word about her own heart and life. The most singular first love-letter from a betrothed bride! But the child thanked Heaven that it was finished, hastily sealed it with a *sechser*,* and carried the missive to the post-office at once.

The morning of departure came. A journey, even if only twelve miles long, especially a *first* journey, appeared to us dwellers in a provincial city in the year '90, almost like a death. People seemed so unattainable when they could no longer be touched with the hands, one might die and be buried before even a single cry for help had reached those left behind.

---

* German coin.

We sat around the breakfast table by candle light, no one touched a mouthful, no one spoke a word. Mamma and I bravely swallowed our tears, but my honest father gave free course to his, and little Dörl sobbed aloud. The day began to dawn, the one horse chaise drove up; the iron bound seal-skin trunk was fastened, boxes and baskets filled with provisions towered in piles, as if we were going round the world. The neighbors in slippers and night caps peeped out of their doors; maid-servants with buckets of water on their backs or baskets of bread on their arms, children who had jumped out of bed in their night gowns crowded around our house. All wanted to see the captain's daughter, who was going to visit a rich old aunt, get into the carriage.

At last nurse Justine appeared with all the dignity of a duenna, attired in a dazzlingly white cap with lappets and her holiday apron of grass green taffeta. I was already seated in the carriage, and she had her foot on the step, when the prayer bell rang. No morning, noon nor evening did the nurse hear those three solemn strokes without falling on her knees to say the Lord's prayer. Only when in the street did she content herself with thrice making the bow, with which in the house of God we paid homage to the name of our Lord and Saviour. But on this important day Nurse Justine bent her old knees in the open square. My father removed the white nightcap from his head and took from his mouth the clay pipe, from which he had hitherto convulsively puffed huge clouds of smoke; my mother, Dorothee, and I clasped our hands in silent prayer. " May God bless our going and coming!" exclaimed Nurse Justine aloud, as she rose from her knees. She climbed into the carriage and sat down, as was becoming, on the front seat opposite to her young lady. My father closed the door. Another "good-luck," and away we rattled over the rough pavement into a new, unknown world.

Thanks to the resolute woman who had charge of the travelling arrangements, the three days' journey took place without interruption. At the last stage, according to agreement, the von Reckenburg "ghost's" gilt coach, with the immortal greys and equally immortal footmen, was waiting for us.

You, my friends, have sometimes seen me make an excursion in the same heavily gilt glass box. I did it, as I have done and kept up many an inherited inconvenience, as a matter of comfort. It used to be hers, so it was good enough for me. But I also did so with the intention of gradually divesting the ugly thing of its ghostly nimbus. In this old box the countess made her entry into Reckenburg, and during the first part of her ownership of the estates was supposed to inspect her land from behind its curtains. In it I, as sole mourner, followed her corpse. That the greys and lackeys of 1750 and 1806 were not the same, but merely as much alike as possible, and only wore the silver-mounted harness and silver-laced livery of their very mortal predecessors, I need not assure you.

And the immortality of the old black countess, like that of her greys and footmen, had, together with all her peculiarities, a very natural explanation. The person who, from inclination or expediency, withdraws from the bustle of every-day life, sinks into forgetfulness or becomes a legendary character to his contemporaries.

Why yes, for nearly half a century she did not leave her inaccessible dusky hermitage, but it was because the sunlight dazzled her eyes and a badly healed broken bone made any movement painful. Yes, she spent whole nights sitting erect in her chair without sleeping, but it was because an asthmatic complaint only permitted her to take a few hours' rest in the morning. Yes, for years she lived exclusively on water gruel and acorns, but only because her stomach would not endure more solid food. It was not, in some inexplicable manner, *in spite of* her diet, but in a very intelligible way *because* of it, that she prolonged her existence far beyond the usual term allotted to mankind. The simpler the bounds within which, whether voluntarily or not, we limit our functions, the more tenacious becomes the thread of life. People who lack one or more senses usually live longer than those who have them all. Misers, that is people with ossified hearts, almost always become very old.

And so let it be granted that the singular founder and supporter of the Reckenburg estates went to the grave as such an ossified miser. But how from a splendid beginning she could come to such a miserable end, will be explained to you by a glance at her life, which was first disclosed to *my* eyes after her death through some letters.

Eberhardine von Reckenburg had received nothing

from her father except the ruins of his family castle in a marshy, out of the way corner of the forest. But on her mother's side she was an heiress. Orphaned while in the cradle, her property increased threefold under a judicious guardianship, as the Electress, her god-mother, had her educated in her own household, and afterwards appointed her maid of honor. On attaining her majority she found herself in possession of a fortune which, in her time, was considered princely.

Naturally clever and ambitious, she possessed the intelligence to measure this value according to the contrast between it and the impoverished nobility at the court. She was considered beautiful and believed herself so, but she saw many of her equals and others with still greater pretensions, after a carnival or two, vanish from the stage, crowded out of sight and forgotten, unless some other power than beauty afforded a lasting support. That there was no question of virtue as such a support in the days of Augustus III., need not be discussed here, but noble blood also afforded no security for the purest lineage, at best only procured a faded beauty admittance into an asylum for young ladies. A barrel of gold was the only firm pedestal. Among entertainments and gambling, the unscrupulous expenditure of a Brühl and his mad imitators, there was at the court of Saxony a young girl, who with secret scorn held her purse-strings firmly in her hands and understood how to increase her inheritance with the cool calculation of a man. No matter if the card houses around her did crumble, she stood firm, she might mount higher.

Day after day a suitor appeared for the hand of the best match in the country. Not one satisfied her ambition. She had reached the age of thirty without making a choice. "The right one will come!" she said to herself, when she had closed her account book and put a patch on her rouged cheek to attend her mistress — now the successor of the Brandenburg Eberhardine — to a fête given by the inexhaustibly inventive, all powerful minister.

And the right man came at the right time, before the last flower of youth had withered. What do you know, my friends, among the innumerable landless sons of the royal families of this German nation, of a Prince Christian? And what need you know of him, except that he was a handsome man, and according to the ideas of his times, a man of spirit, that is, an aristocratic libertine after the pattern of the Maréchal de Saxe — only that he could boast of no Fontenay or Rocour — that he returned to the court of Saxony, whose ruler was a kinsman, either to have a period of rest after all sorts of adventures, or to open new sources of supplies after having exhausted the patrimony he had inherited. The royal kinsman was weary of repeated bleedings, the search for an heiress of equal rank proved lost trouble. Brühl therefore thought he was performing a master piece of strategy, by directing the eyes of the troublesome protégé to the still handsome, and so far as character was concerned, faultless maid of honor, the Baroness von Reckenburg, as one of the best matches in Germany.

Whether the cautious young lady would have resisted the captivating *coqueluche* if he had been merely her equal in rank, is uncertain. But he was a prince, entitled to woo an emperor's daughter, and she could not resist the charm. You children of another century have no standard for judging opinions, which raised even the smallest hanger on of a throne far above all the rules that govern the conduct of ordinary mortals, and absolved the anointed of the Lord even from the duty of obeying the table of laws; opinions which held the nobility of the most dissolute dunce of royal blood greater than that won in the crusades. After an unexampled destruction during the devastating Thirty Years War, time in our native country had, as it were, stood still, and the period of the greatest ignorance on the part of the common people, the utmost degeneracy of the nobility, had not yet expired. The clock to make a new era was first wound up under the sword and sceptre of the Prussian Frederick.

The prince of the blood could offer no equal marriage to the rich and noble lady; she was not permitted to bear his name, her children — if he had had anything to leave — would not have been eligible to succeed him. But the position of a prince's wife, even if the marriage were only morganatic, would raise her to the position of "Reich Countess* von Reckenburg," a rank next to that of the families allied to the throne by ties of blood; her ambition saw no means of attaining a higher goal, and so the original passion became a magnetic current which kindled a quenchless flame in the heart that had so long been cold. How could

---

* Countess of the Empire.

the hand a princely husband kissed with gallant fervor continue to anxiously clutch the strings of her purse? Pride, the mistress, had attained her object; Prudence, the maid, was dismissed from service.

Soon housekeeping was commenced in the capital on a scale of splendor in accordance with the husband's rank. The young couple joined the adherents of the reigning Electress-queen, and with them became the enemies of the all-powerful favorite. Hatred kindled a spirit of rivalry, and it was perhaps the only drop of wormwood in Eberhardine's cup of honey, that she could not enable her adored prince to live in the same luxury as an upstart, who kept hundreds of footmen and a body guard of his own, who as Frederic the Great says, possessed more valuables, laces, slippers, etc., than anyone in Europe, and with the cunning of a crafty slave, carried the idle sultan's caprices of his so-called master to the verge of ruin.

If the contrast was irritating during the winter in the capital, how much more so it became when summer arrived with its rural fêtes, autumn with its one royal passion, the chase. Probably no year elapsed, that the inventive minister did not arrange some fairy entertainment or wild boar's hunt for his master in a magnificent new building, that seemed to have sprung from the earth. The parvenu numbered his pleasure castles and preserves of game by the dozen; the prince of the blood did not possess a hand's breadth of ground, and even his wife's wealth was not invested in lands.

In this dilemma ruinous old Reckenburg was remembered, and as romantic natural beauty was of as little importance as productive soil, discovered to be a most desirable possession — a navigable stream near a tract of woodland, containing such a stock of game that all the efforts of the peasants could not protect their scanty crops. They enjoyed *a priori* in imagination, the sails in gondolas, the wild boar and deer hunts, which were to be arranged on the ancient Reckenburg estates as soon as a new edifice, far more stately than any of Brühl's creations, had been erected on the site of the crumbling ruins of the old castle.

To be sure this new edifice required years of labor; years, whose summers for want of a residence in accordance with the prince's rank, were spent in traveling. But what a temptation it was to supply themselves, in the most polished countries of Europe, with all the productions of luxury and fashion to adorn their home!

At last the ardently desired palace was erected; the last marble cornice, the last piece of wainscoting inserted; stucco work and carving, Gobelin tapestry and brocade, and above all, the escutcheons containing the combined coat of arms of the prince and baroness surmounted by a count's coronet, were nowhere spared. The young hedges in the pleasure garden were growing; fauns and cupids spouted welcoming jets of water; cellars and store rooms were filled to overflowing; a succession of entertainments was to celebrate the entry of the noble pair.

Then, at the last hour, the abyss into which the beloved husband's constancy had fallen with the contents of the wife's purse was suddenly revealed. An accident raised the veil. But had the whirl of pleasure really blinded the sharp sighted woman so long? Or did she not voluntarily close her eyes, while a single drop remained in her cup of joy? I am inclined to believe the latter. She would have starved with this man, she would have starved for him, nay, she would have endured his faithlessness if he could have been detained at her side. But the fading beauty saw the gold chains with which she had bound the spoiled sensualist melting away. Another year of this boundless expenditure and she would be a deserted beggar. So she consented to a divorce, as the only way of saving, not her former splendor, but the bare means of existence. The gay gentleman rejoiced in a freedom which permitted him to seek with his divining rod a new fountain of wealth.

While he again led the changeful life of his youth in Italy and Russia, then the nurseries of both princely and plebeian adventurers, to-day a soldier and to-morrow a Celadon, the countess steadily marked out her future career. She was more than forty years old, no longer beautiful, and according to her standard, poor. What marvel that she was disgusted with the world, that it had become hateful to her? So she entered upon the inheritance bequeathed by her father, with the determination to change the soil into a mine from which to replenish her exhausted treasury.

Outwardly the rank she had obtained must be supported, the usual splendor of living maintained, the hated world, and especially her still beloved prince deceived in regard to her real penury. He should feel what pleasures he had so lightly resigned. This was the cause of the whim which, in the eyes of the world, distinguished her from a real miser, the whim of keeping and using everything she had found on entering her new residence, even if it had become useless to her personal needs, and instead of bearing interest, demanded a sacrifice. No human eye, least of all the countess', found pleasure in gazing at the extensive gardens around the castle, but the hedges and pyramids were regularly clipped, the paths and flower-beds kept in the neatest order, the injuries the statues and ornaments received from the weather and time constantly repaired. No entertainments were given, no guests received at Reckenburg, but the quantity of table furniture and also the useless valuables, which if converted into money in those times of scarcity, would have yielded a by no means insignificant capital, remained undisturbed, except when periodically taken out to be cleansed from rust and dust. Nay, even the provisions in the store rooms and cellar were restored as quickly as possible, the moment a portion was used, no matter whether the remainder hardened, grew yellow, and with the utmost care could not be protected from worms and decay. This was the cause of the immortality of the no longer used greys and majestic footmen. The revenge of this singular maintainer of grandeur was to *become* rich, and while doing so, to to keep up the semblance of wealth. The innate clever power of collecting and increasing, heightened by time into an over-mastering passion, again asserted its claims.

The work undertaken by this lonely woman, who

had grown old in the atmosphere of a luxurious court, was that performed by a colonist in a primeval forest. No one suspected how entirely her property was exhausted nor how imperatively her personal economies were demanded, and therefore no one has fully appreciated the prudence, strength, and endurance with which she performed her life task.

People now rejoice in the fruitfulness of a region, which a hundred years ago was a marshy woodland, and I often with shame hear myself praised as its creator. But I have only stepped upon my predecessor's shoulders ; the foundation, the task of overcoming the inexpressible difficulty of making the soil productive, was her work. She drained the marshes and dug the canals, marked the boundaries of the forest, laid out good roads, erected commodious buildings for husbandry, discovered new means of making wet fields productive, built the large dike that protects the land from the frequent inundations of the river. *She* had the toil, *I* the reward and gratitude, because she placed me in a position so secure that I could introduce reforms throughout the whole neighborhood ; *she* reaped mockery and fear, *I* the blessing, which, bestowed by the labor of the individual on the community, is returned by the community to the individual, that first blessing of all creating, whether great or small, which has helped even me, a lonely woman, to a contented life.

Scarcely had the dauntless pioneer struggled through the hardest toil, scarcely had her seeds put forth their first fruits, when the war broke out, a war that pressed on few portions of our native land more severely than this region. What I experienced during the summer of 1813, this woman endured seven years. Where *I* was permitted to draw from my abundance, *she* saw the best portion of her foundation destroyed, and at an age when others seek rest, again began her work undismayed.

And what courage, what resolution, the solitary woman displayed in her conduct towards the rabble of both hostile and friendly armies; how bravely she defended herself against the hordes of marauders and native robbers, who, long after peace was concluded, infested our forests. It is literally true, that the black countess, with a loaded pistol in each hand, and her two huge lackeys, also armed, behind her, defended the threshold of her home from this disorderly rabble.

This heroic deed may be considered the germ of the marvelous tales, that gradually became current about the strange countess. The ghostly form increased in size, when the bodily one suddenly vanished even from the place where it had hitherto been supposed to be — the closely curtained gilt coach, in which she made her visit of inspection around her estate. From that time our peasants saw her, attired in a Spanish costume, watching the treasures of her hermitage day and night with dragon eyes, and defending them with fiery weapons. Boundless treasures! The more the figures increased, the more dazzling they became to the starving, idle throng, who only understood how to calculate hellers* and kreuzers, and had never received heller nor kreuzer from the grasping old woman's hand.

---

* Small copper coin.

Whether the countess ever heard of the fabulous nimbus surrounding her, I do not know. But undoubtedly it would have been welcome, rather than annoying, since it offered a protection against a troublesome or threatening world. Her careful eye had selected the eastern turret of the castle for her sleeping room and treasure chamber because, while wholly inaccessible from without, it also afforded the greatest possible security from within. Workmen, ordered from a great distance, had fitted fire-proof safes, with intricate locks, into the deep niches. The "gold-tower" was connected by a secret door with the room occupied by the old, trusty maid, and through this with the corridor, in which the two footmen, who alternately kept watch, were the only means of communication between the tower and the rest of the house, while the mistress kept her accounts behind locks and bars, or concealed documents and ready money in the secret iron chests. Her health failed; her strength to work lessened, and the burden of toil increased. Soon it was no longer possible to leave the important room; for after the conclusion of peace the judicious outlay, though it did not equal the wonderful measure of popular superstition, returned a hundredfold profit on the investment.

During the war she had sent the larger portion of her jewelry to England to be converted into money, as this sacrifice of former splendor was least conspicuous in her present mode of life. The proceeds obtained, my friends, were the foundation of her supposed marvelous treasures. A modest sum, but it became a luck penny at a time when the value of land was reduced to a minimum, when communities and individuals sold their property at a nominal sum, since they could get no hands to till nor seed to sow. In ten years the area of the Reckenburg estate doubled, in twenty it increased fourfold. Even if a sum could only be paid in instalments, a regular interest was a much desired boon in those times of scarcity.

The manner in which the general poverty tended to enrich individuals, is shown among other things by the famine of the year '70, when a bushel of rye rose in price to twenty thalers. Calculate how the well-filled granaries of Reckenburg — which fixed the standard of prices in a very variable time — must have emptied, and the empty money-chests filled. Where doves build their nest, doves flutter away.

"The first hundred thousand thalers cost severe toil. But he who labors for the next nine hundred thousand is a simpleton!"

When in her last days the millionaire of Reckenburg, with sparkling eyes, made this avowal, she was really the ossified mummy whose heart only beat to guard her treasure. But at the time she wearily toiled to obtain this treasure, and even in the days when she first initiated me into the secret of her gold tower, she was not this heartless, mindless mummy, for then she was working, starving, accumulating for a purpose; or, to speak more correctly, for a person.

And this is the ground, my friends, on which I have drawn before your eyes — though for a long time not so exactly as I desired — the line between the last two women who bore the name of Reckenburg. You ought to know what the woman did, who made your home productive; what the woman *was*, who left no trace of her existence in any heart save mine, and in the tenacious imagination of the peasants passed for an avaricious fiend. You ought to see this woman in a *good* light, and in what fairer one could I have shown her to two happy lovers, than that of changeless fidelity to the faithless husband, the secret fire which had been the motive of all her acts and labors.

She had rudely broken all former ties and only maintained a correspondence with one old friend, who occupied a confidential position at the court of Saxony, in order to be constantly kept informed of the movements of the restless wanderer. She therefore knew that he was rioting and carousing, while she did not allow herself an hour's rest in her eagerness to repair what he had destroyed. She knew that he remained overloaded with debt, while she had again become the rich lady of Reckenburg. But if he had, even as a supplicant, approached the house whose splendor she had maintained by so much toil, after the triumph of this satisfaction, she would have welcomed him as master with delight, again given him the key of her treasury, and commenced her work afresh, in order, even after her death, to secure him a princely property.

For many years the hope of his return had sustained her in her solitary toil, and she had become a wrinkled matron ere it was fulfilled. At last she knew that he was in his native country — and the next news she received was of his marriage with a lady of equal birth! On the confines of old age, he had apparently obeyed the impulse of a genuine love, for the young princess was as poor as himself.

The strength which had resisted so many toils and dangers, gave way at this unexpected blow. The countess' maid found her lying senseless on the floor, with the fatal letter in her hand. A fracture of the hip, sustained during this fall, made her a cripple for the remainder of her life.

Yet, after a torturing defeat, her first clear thought was again for the faithless husband. Nay, after an interval of nearly a year, all her hopes were once more revived by the almost simultaneous intelligence that he was a father and a widower. Now he must surely come to seek with her a home and inheritance for his motherless son.

It was the last hope her beloved prince was to disappoint. The next letter brought the tidings of his second departure; the following one the news of his death. He had fallen in the Crimean campaign of '71, under the banner of his patroness, Catharine.

The countess put on mourning and never laid it aside. She was and remained the widow of a prince. She worked, starved, and accumulated as before. A reflection of the flame which had illuminated her life still lingered; she was working, starving, and accumulating for a poor, unknown, forsaken child.

What do you say now, my friends, to the ghostly old countess of Reckenburg?

CHAPTER IV.

THE HEREDITARY PRINCE.

OF course I did not know a single word of this long story of love and sorrow, when I proudly and joyously entered the gilt coach to be conveyed to the presence of the noble representative of my family, the widow of a prince. Nurse Justine's cap towered beside the long periwig of the ancient coachman on the high seat before me. The gigantic footman clung to the long tassels behind the carriage, and away rolled the magnificent equipage over the lonely road to Reckenburg.

It led over level ground through dense pine forests, occasionally touching the shore of the stream. I had grown up in a fruitful, leafy valley, between whose rocky sides a smaller river wound gracefully along, and the less romantic region through which I had passed for two days, had greatly wearied me. But now, in the gilt coach, it seemed to me the most interesting spot in the world; the calm, broad surface of water awed me, and I inhaled with delight the spicy odor of the pines, which I had not noticed before. It was the Reckenburg family estate, from which the aroma streamed.

After about an hour we approached the clearing which had been made for the new edifice. The huts in the village were fortunately concealed by the forest, for their wretchedness would have considerably lessened my proud satisfaction. It was already tempered when, near the entrance of the park, we met a group of ragged, stunted figures, who stared at me as if I had been some sea-monster. I supposed them to be beggars, whom I had always despised and avoided as sluggards. The following day, however, Nurse Justine informed me that they were peasants and socagers from the village, who had been attracted by the "evil thing" of a gilt coach, which had not appeared before for an age.

The gigantic footman sprang down to open the gate, adorned with a coat of arms, and instantly locked it again. The wide avenue leading through the neatly kept, richly ornamented pleasure grounds stretched before my eyes. In the back ground rose the castle, over whose reddish hue the setting sun cast a golden light. The white marble cornices, the lofty plate glass windows, the terrace adorned with statues and vases, before which we stopped, the pillars supporting the main entrance, did not fail to produce an impression. During this drive I understood the indifference of the owner of this princely property to her unpretending cousins in the barber's house. But it must not be inferred that I felt oppressed or intimidated in going to meet the relative who was so much more richly endowed by fortune. I, too, was a Reckenburg, and never, except as an invited guest, would I have crossed this proud threshold.

Accompanied by my footman, I mounted the broad marble staircase. Each door through which I passed was carefully bolted, as if behind a prisoner. I entered the long vestibule, upon which the suite of rooms opened. The gold framed mirrors between the window niches, the mythological reliefs and frescoes on the opposite wall — you pass these works of art with a patronizing smile, arrogant pupils of another taste, but you may imagine that they astonished the simplicity of former days.

At the end of the corridor, mounting guard, stood the footman on duty, as like my conductor as a twin brother. Silently as the former — everything was silent, still as the grave in this enchanted palace — he opened the last door. I entered an anteroom, which formed the only entrance to the far famed tower (the "eastern rotunda" as it was then called). On the right of the ante room was the dining hall. These three rooms, "Her excellency the countess' suite of apartments" were the only ones in the extensive front of the castle which had ever been occupied. Those inhabited by the household were in the western wing.

The body guard had rapped loudly three times on the door of the tower with the gold head of his cane and then retired to his post. I was alone and even now not timid, but curious to see what would happen next. I laid aside my travelling wraps, and looked over the garden to the tops of the distant pines, behind which the sunset glow was fading. Amid the fantastic shapes of the trees and sculptured stones at my feet the October mist rose and hovered to and fro in grotesque forms; and as I stood in the dim light of this dark, silent room, the first and I believe the last thrill of ghostly terror I ever experienced in my life, ran through my limbs.

Half an hour had probably elapsed in this way, I had grown heartily tired of the anteroom and the romantic view; then I heard a bolt drawn back, the tapping of a crutch; and finally a wheezing cough on the threshold of the tower chamber. My distinguished hostess had entered.

My parents, if they knew the ideas current about their only relative, had wisely kept them from me. My instructions were simply to treat a very aged, and therefore eccentric, possibly haughty, and somewhat economical lady with respect.

Yet it is true that my flesh crept at the object, which gradually developed into a human form. Oh! you wise preacher of the transitoriness of everything mortal, what is man in his majesty?

Eberhardine von Reckenburg, once celebrated as a beauty at the most critical court in Germany, and now bent like a bow, gasping for breath as she moved painfully forward on crutches, trembling with inward cold like a leaf in a November storm, her face, scarcely a hand's breadth wide, shrivelled into a thousand little wrinkles, like a yellow parchment in some old convent.

And yet! All that in those days had existed under the lovely husk, still lived beneath the wrinkled skin, and the black eyes sparkled with as bold, keen, and clear a light, as much secret passion, as in the times of Augustus. One flash of those penetrating eyes, and the inmost nook, the most private corner of her poor god-child's soul were laid bare, so far as nooks and corners existed in the said soul.

The singular little figure was clothed in black from

head to foot, in a style of costume which at masked balls we call a domino. Over a trailing underdress hung a short, full cloak, finished around the neck with a thick frill. On the widow's cap was throned a round hat with a floating plume. In after years, even when on the most familiar terms, I never saw the countess without her "Spanish" hat and cloak or her gloves. They were warm and comfortable and gave her, in her own eyes, a dignity which the hood and dressing gown would have destroyed. But I shall not be blamed, if the first impression in the dim light of the ghostly palace caused me a slight feeling of alarm.

However, I was not in the habit of yielding to vague apprehensions; and before the countess regained her breath after taking her seat in her arm-chair, had recovered my self-possession. I boldly approached her, kissed her hand, and curtsied in the correct style of a von Reckenburg in the presence of a royal personage, as I had been directed.

The countess, like many persons who live alone and are somewhat deaf, had acquired the habit of expressing her opinions or ideas aloud, and to this unconscious talking I owed many a disclosure, which she would *not* have made voluntarily. In uttering her remarks to-day, however, she was perfectly indifferent whether I heard them or not.

"Heavily moulded, but good fresh blood!" she said after a scrutinizing glance, nodding her head. "A white one! We of the black line were handsomer and more delicate. A passable figure! Where did you learn to dance?" she asked, turning to me.

"My father taught me, Your Excellency."

"A Saxon cadet. Good school!" was the countess' comment.

Second question. "Do you understand French?"

"My mother has always talked with me in French, Your Excellency!"

"Repeat a few sentences. No matter what."

Nothing occurred to me at that moment except the last thing I had committed to memory; a fable describing the blessing which comes to posterity from the labor of the aged. Without thinking whether this selection was appropriate or not, I declaimed my *octogenaire plantant* from beginning to end.

"*Ingenuité absolue!*" the countess remarked with a movement of the lips which was probably intended for a smile. "The accent is passably pure!" she added nodding. "Your mother, when a young girl, spent a great deal of her time at the court of Dresden. A judicious education! We will speak French together, Eberhardine!"

"As you desire, Your Excellency."

"You may call me aunt," said the countess.

As, to express my gratitude for this mark of favor, I kissed her hand a second time, the tall footman announced: "*Madame la comtesse est servi!*"

"A second plate for my niece, Jacques," said the countess.

Ah! Eberhard and Adelheid, wise augurs in education! But for the toil of your dancing lessons, my good father, but for your labor in teaching me a foreign language, my clever mother, Heaven knows in what corner of her ancestors' family seat the last von Reckenburg would have dined, and how entirely she might *now* feel satisfied with her reception!

So at the hour we usually ate our supper at home, I followed my new aunt to the dining hall. Its furniture corresponded with the splendor of the rest of the castle. Candles, whose brownish yellow hue proved that they belonged to the stores purchased nearly fifty years before, were burning in the candelabra. The silver, though somewhat worn, showed that it had originally been very massive, the smallest article bore the stamp of the house — the two coats of arms surmounted by the count's coronet. To be sure nothing but pure Reckenburg water was poured into the Venetian glasses, and the Japanese china contained nothing more dainty than red Reckenburg grits. As a dessert, a cup of acorn tea was handed to the older lady on a silver waiter, and to the younger an apple. But don't be anxious, children! On the journey I had helped myself liberally from the basket of provisions packed at home, and afterwards at Reckenburg always had food enough, although in those days, as well as now, I possessed an excellent appetite. If, which Heaven forbid, yours should become feeble in old age, I can recommend water gruel and acorn tea as an excellent restorative.

In this place I may be permitted to make a second remark, by way of parenthesis. If no member of the countess' household ever voluntarily left her service, which was punctiliously and silently performed according to her wishes, while the majority reached a good old age in it, I prefer instead of the old womens' stories of bewitched tongues and bowels, the common sense conclusion that the aforesaid servants, besides being paid good wages, had their stomachs and mouths well filled with food.

The meal was eaten in silence and soon finished. While I followed the countess to the antechamber, I noticed with what conscientious haste the gigantic Jacques put out the candles. The countess dismissed me with the words: "Farewell until to-morrow noon. Amuse yourself as well as you can. The anteroom will be at your service and is always warm."

I kissed the hand she extended to me, and with a low curtsey went towards the door.

"You need no assistance in your toilette, do you?" the old lady called after me. I answered in the negative. "Don't delay before going to bed, bolt the door and put out the light at once."

So saying she groped her way into her hermitage, and I heard the bolt rattle within. Then Monsieur Jacques, after locking the antechamber, conducted me along the corridor to the "new tower" or "western rotunda," as it was called in those days. A winding staircase connected it with the rooms occupied by the household, and the chamber opened for me was the only one in the front, and seemed to have originally been intended for a servant's room. The walls were only whitewashed, the floor was made of rough planks, there was no stove, and it had no furniture — except a table, a chair, a clothes press, the most necessary washing utensils, and a bed which could boast of no down pillows nor silk quilt. The contrast with my attic room at home was not too great, but I dared not think of little Dörl's pleasant chamber.

I was accustomed to strict obedience, and have always cheerfully yielded where I could not command. So I threw off my clothes, put out the tallow candle my conductor had left, and undisturbed by any ghostly vision or even a dream, slept for seven hours as quietly as I have always done all my life up to this day.

But one who goes to bed with the hens, must wake with them. The stars were shining when I awoke, and as soon as morning dawned I dressed. What should I do now? At my request the body-guard in the vestibule opened the door of the side staircase, and I went down into the garden. I soon wandered into the forest and fields, and for the first time saw the sun rise in the open country, clear and bright as the eye of God.

Methodical walks were neither a necessity nor a fashion in my time, and would even now seem a very troublesome recreation. But to wander at will over the country among the peasants, watch the quiet labor of nature, although the last before her winter rest, the alterations in men, the strength and resistance here as well as there; — and all this on an estate which had been in the family for generations — it was a *noble* taste, which dawned upon me this first morning in the fields of Reckenburg, a taste which has made me happy all my life.

Then for the first time I perceived the method of managing a large domain; saw how the wood was felled and the timber dragged to the river, saw the charcoal burning and turf cutting, the last remains of the second crop of hay, and the latest fruits carefully stored. I saw the fields newly tilled to receive the winter seeds, the herds grazing on the meadows and fallows, the free, joyous gambolling of the deer in the enclosed preserves.

I talked with shepherds, laborers, and overseers about the work allotted to each, made friends with the sensible old head-forester, and became acquainted with the other employees. The fresh young girl, who bore the name of Reckenburg and pressed so suddenly from the silent castle into the outside world with her eager curiosity, was received with friendly confidence; and though not on the first day, in time even the poor villagers lost the fear that this vigorous young life would be petrified in the death-like atmosphere of the castle.

I had never reaped a richer harvest in Christlieb Taube's school-room, never felt more at home in the barber's old house, than during this first walk over the Reckenburg estate, and when towards noon I returned to the castle, Nurse Justine met me with good news. Her Excellency the Countess had been attacked in the night by a severe illness, and as her waiting-maid's limbs proved too stiff and tremulous for the necessary manipulations, the skilled travelling duenna was called to assist. Meister Faber's pupil had had a brilliant success in applying for the first time in a castle cupping glasses and other remedies less agreeable to mention, and the noble patient — finding herself relieved more quickly than ever before — proposed that Nurse Justine should spend the winter at Reckenburg at a fixed salary. The faithful soul, without the slightest hesitation, sacrificed her certain practice at home to this doubtful offer. Her eyes sparkled with joy. She felt that through her own mediation her proudest dreams would be realized, for under such circumstances a person listens to reason and becomes as soft as wax.

So I should not lose by a pleasant exchange, and still another more substantial advantage soon resulted from it. The room in the side building assigned to the important nurse adjoined mine; it was lighted and warmed; therefore when shut out from the countess' apartments, I could occupy myself a few hours as I pleased, and was no longer compelled to go to bed with the hens.

The bill of fare for dinner was by no means limited to the grits of supper. That day, for instance, after an excellent soup, a chicken was served, which, with the exception of a small piece of the breast, fell to my share. For dessert we had apples, roasted for the countess, raw for me. Wine was also placed on the table. But the old lady could not drink any kind of liquor, and took it for granted that the young lady did not like it. The bottles were therefore removed unopened, to be replaced on the table the following day, and it is possible that the very same ones played their part at the first and last of the dinners I shared.

The time spent at the meal was also longer than at supper; perhaps because there were no wax candles to be extinguished. We sat nearly an hour over the acorn coffee, and I produced a good impression by the description of my walk through the fields.

"You have sharp Reckenburg eyes," said the countess. "Keep them open and tell me honestly what you see."

These words indicated my future office — to watch closely, make a truthful report, and moreover be the verbal means of communication between the tower and estate: this is the substance of my long agricultural apprenticeship at Reckenburg.

"However," the countess continued after a pause, "the time you can spend out of doors is growing shorter, and many an hour in the castle may seem lonely, Eberhardine. Console yourself by thinking that at least your home would have offered nothing more agreeable. Your parents are too poor to spend the season in Dresden, and the society of a provincial city would only annoy you. It is better to be lonely than in a false position. Besides, I could not answer for your success even in that modest circle, and what pleasure does society afford without success? Are you fond of reading, Eberhardine?"

I confessed that I had read nothing at all as yet, but had long desired an opportunity to obtain books.

"Then take advantage of the castle library," replied the countess. "It contains everything valuable in literature up to the middle of the century. I myself have no longer taste nor time for reading. Take care not to injure the bindings, and put the books back in their places. The arrangement must not be disturbed. The catalogue will make it easy for you to choose. Try the novels, they will not hurt *you*. *Au contraire!* If you want anything newer, or German books instead of French, apply to the pastor. I do not know him personally, but he seems — though somewhat of an enthusiast — to be a well-informed man. Seek him out, apply to him. Your mind is no soil for philanthropic fancies, but they have their value as subjects for consideration?"

So another well of life opened for me in Reckenburg, although the natural satisfaction of the first did not gush from it.

In the library I found, with the exception of genealogical and heraldic works, which I left untouched, and Italian ones which I did not understand, nothing but French books; but the productions of a great nation, at the period of its utmost splendor, would have sufficed to content a young, thirsting soul for a long time. And, moreover, the pastor now came forward with his beloved German literature. I heard him preach Sunday morning, and in the afternoon knocked at his door.

I was a mere child in the knowledge of the world and formed of sterner stuff than he, yet I brought from this first meeting the oppressive sense of a marred existence. But the longer I saw him toiling to serve a parish which had run wild both bodily and mentally, the mild, thoughtful man and Christian, the foundation of whose character was based upon a noble standard and harmonious culture, misunderstood and unloved, he, the most lovable and loving nature, the more keenly I felt in his presence actual bodily pain, and much as I personally lost, had no rest until I knew that he was appointed to a position where his lessons and example might animate more susceptible minds.

And now to the priest's inspiring words was joined the pitifully empty hand of the philanthropist. One who would fain have given, given *always*, without calculation, was forced to wrangle with a wretchedly poor parish for fees and contributions, if he wanted to have anything to bestow, even on the most needy.

To this was at last added the want of a home, his beloved wife dead, his only son absent working his way in the world. This man must surely have wasted away like a spring in the desert, if a world had not opened to his joyous gaze in our young, aspiring literature. He followed even the tangled luxuriance of those days with the glance of a humanitarian and philanthropist, and his heart throbbed with the greatest joy when he had discovered something of lasting nobility for his people, who so needed the perfecting power of beauty; but his delight was purest of all when he saw it awaken even the feeblest answering ray.

He therefore received the child who knocked at his door as a messenger from God, for to a certain extent he found that she appreciated and understood his world. Every afternoon from that first day I entered his hermitage; every evening he led me back to the threshold of that other cell, in which a female hermit of an exactly opposite stamp uttered her wisdom, and his hope never failed, although the teachings of the aged child of the world made a stronger impression on their joint pupil than those of the follower of Christ.

Thus I had entered the high school of Reckenburg in a double sense, and few pupils can boast of having so rarely heard an imprudent or useless word from their teachers. But the third member of the educational league spoke to me most loudly and encouragingly of all — Nature! — no, I will not give my instructor that proud name, but my daily more fondly beloved ancestral estate. On it I knew exactly where I was, could find each path; it was the world in which I, too, should some day become a hermit. No instinctive attraction drew me towards society or books, but to a corner of the world long owned by my ancestors, where I might establish a workshop.

Meantime I made considerable progress, and my clever aunt was not slow in turning it to account. I soon found myself diverted from academical freedom of study to the writing desk. I have already said that, from the first day of my visit, I was called upon to be the interpreter of her verbal orders. The curt, exact manner in which directions and replies were delivered, no less than the weakness that often made the pen fall from the weary old woman's hand, suggested the idea of trying my skill in the department of writing. At her dictation I soon despatched instructions and replies to employees, lawyers, etc., my rapid, distinct hand speedily accomplished what had tasked the trembling fingers for days, and after a few successful trials I was promoted to the post of secretary.

Yet it was a long time before the mysterious account books were placed before my eyes, but as in this very *alpha* and *omega* of her daily toil the fortunate accumulator most urgently required a trustworthy accountant, a virtue was finally also made of this necessity.

I will no longer occupy your time, my friends, with the period of my apprenticeship at Reckenburg, especially as I have advanced far beyond the present time in my recital. In short, in the course of a few years, I became the countess's right hand in her extensive business relations; she trained me for a steward. I worked several hours daily under her eyes in the notorious tower-room, and so it happened that both within and without I, and I alone, learned to know the value of an estate, which I had neither a right nor a prospect of ever possessing. For however completely I won the countess's confidence in the course of time, I could not deceive myself in regard to the fact that only her reason, not her heart, inclined to the relative with whom she constantly became more intimate She helped her work, nothing more. There was but one person in the world for whom she still cared, only in thinking of *one* man did the restless spirit find repose.

But with my natural reserve, how could I have become attached to a person who had so little affection for me? I valued the countess according to another standard than that of the world. I formed myself in essential points according to her experience, but this did not demand any gratitude, for I gave her more than she bestowed, and gave it without any self-interest. I had as little real love for my relative as she for me. Between the old idealist in the parsonage and the old realist in the tower, the young girl developed into a creature whose heart was as lonely, nay, more lonely than the child's had formerly been when in Christlieb Taube's school room with charming little Dörl.

When the time appointed for my return home approached, the countess proposed to my parents and myself that I should come back the following winter. She expressed herself in a less condescending manner, but still only as a favor, not as a wish. "In your position," she said, "it is best for you to be removed for a time from the provincial surroundings of your father's house and learn to move in a wider sphere."

The invitation extended to the nurse, "Madame Müller," was far more pressing. True, she might accompany me back home during the summer, a season when the countess' health was usually good, but return with me in the autumn and settle permanently at Reckenburg. A regular salary would be paid for her services at the castle, permission given for the exercise of her professional skill— which included the vacant office of midwife in the village—and also the privilege of occupying the little house in the forest, which had originally been built for the prince's master of hounds, but as the prince and his pack remained absent, need not be considered a portion of the inventory of things to be maintained. A little garden, a piece of meadow land, and all the fire-wood she needed, free of charge, offered to her tempting inducements; and so the following autumn we see Nurse Justine settled to her own satisfaction and highly respected in the castle and vicinity as a helper in every bodily ailment. The potions she understood how to brew, from herbs collected by herself, cured fevers and chills, and if they did not it was because heaven had willed otherwise; and the doctor's medicines would have been of still less benefit. An active business in drugs was maintained with the apothecary; industriously as her hands moved, they were scarcely able to satisfy the manifold wants. The old woman in the castle, and the old woman in the "dog house" vied with each other in the art of accumulating and saving. But if, in spite of all the prophecies of dreams, the rich aunt's millions should escape me, the minion of fortune, the poor nurse's hundreds would still remain.

When, a few days before my return home, I came back to the castle from a morning walk — with, I confess, a heavy heart, because I could not see the seeds whose sowing and sprouting I had watched, grow ripe and be reaped — I was surprised to find a great bustle, an unusual amount of roasting and pastry making going on in the rooms occupied by the household. A butt of wine was carried from the cellar into the servants' hall; the wives and children of the men employed on the estate went home laden with bottles of wine and baskets of cake; long tables intended for the day-laborers stood loaded with food. I asked the cause of this unusual hospitality, and received from various mouths the answer that this was the Reckenburg holiday. Whose holiday? The calendar mentioned none; the time of the countess' entry into the castle occurred in mid-summer, her birthday was passed over in silence, for she did not like to be reminded of her age. The cause of the festival was a secret, like so many things at Reckenburg.

The countess' table was also abundantly supplied. Wine was not only placed on the board, but drunk. Both footmen were in attendance. The countess wore a new velvet cloak and a superb ostrich feather in her Spanish hat; an almost contemptuous glance fell upon my everyday dress (still the same indestructible serge). When the roast meat was served, she ordered her glass to be filled with champagne, touched it to mine, and said solemnly: "To his health!"

"To whose health?" I asked in surprise.

A second more than scornful glance fell upon me What was the use of my studies in the library, if I had valued pedigrees, genealogical tables, and family documents so little as to still be ignorant of the most important date at Reckenburg?

"The twentieth of April, Prince Augustus' birthday," she said sharply, after she had emptied her glass at a single draught, and as she probably saw by my expression that she had merely solved one enigma by a new one, added: "My late husband's son, and the last of his noble house. May God preserve him!"

For the first time the countess had uttered her husband's name in my presence, and for the first time the idea dawned upon me, what heir she had chosen, perhaps already mentioned in her will.

When I afterwards told my mother of the Reckenburg holiday, she said: "I have never doubted that the countess enlarged the Reckenburg estate so extensively solely for the prince's benefit."

"For that wild fellow?" replied my father laughing; "well, God knows she won't see him squander it any faster than his father!"

Mamma rejoined:

"Not during her life time and at any rate not so far as the entail will allow; but be sure of this, Eberhard, the countess will leave her inheritance only in royal hands."

CHAPTER V.

THE LAST DANCE.

THE regular correspondence between my parents and myself had been anything but communicative. Good advice alternated with assurances of obedience, and each party expressed hopes that the other continued in good health. Confidential gossip in black and white would have been contrary to the dignity of the relation ; so there was a great deal to tell, which amply occupied the first few days after we were reunited. But I soon perceived how correct the old countess' judgment had been. The lonely freedom of her house had already estranged me from the provincial life at home.

A New Year's greeting, as formal as if it had been cut out of a "Complete Letter Writer," had been also exchanged between the "most humble servant Dorothee Müller," and the "sincere friend Eberhardine von Reckenburg." I now found my little companion unchanged in her pretty chamber and state of widowed betrothal. It was scarcely perceptible, that during these six months she had passed from childhood into maidenhood, her features and expression were still so unformed and artless. She dressed more daintily than other girls of her class, tended flowers and birds, embroidered slippers and veils, from whose proceeds she increased her money for trifles; baked savory cracknels and cakes, which found a ready sale in her father's tavern, and with all this, had ample time to devote herself to reading. I saw her devour with glowing cheeks the tales of bold knights and sweet love stories obtained at the circulating library, and heard that during the winter she had devoted herself industriously to music. Gentle Christlieb Taube came from his district village school to the city every Sunday to give her an hour's instruction in playing on the guitar, and I do not doubt that this hour seemed to him the pleasantest of the week. Then Dörl, with her lark-like voice, twittered the arias that corresponded with the fashionable novels: songs about the "boldest of robbers, who was roused by his Rosa's kiss," or "Robert, whom Elise pressed to her throbbing heart."

"Fräulein Eberhardine" wisely shook her head, for even if the little one read and sang these doubtful things with the most childish innocence, she did so, though unconsciously, from ennui, the real mother of woman's sins. She admired the composure with which I received the news that a death in the family of the reigning prince would prevent all gayety at the Thursday assemblies during the summer. "I should like to see you dance, Fräulein Hardine," she said sighing, "or dance myself just once more, as I used to do with your honored father."

Siegmund Faber had sent a beautiful garnet necklace for a Christmas present, and received in return a knit case for his bandages. "I should much rather have embroidered a tobacco pouch," said Dörl. "But he doesn't smoke at all; he has no amusements except his horrible knives and pincers." Meantime Siegmund studied and worked indefatigably, and relied just as firmly on a bloody field of practise.

"It will be a long time before we meet," said Dörl laughing, " but I can wait."

" The child behaves admirably," said my father, and my mother could not gainsay the praise. Nurse Justine, however, shook her head, saying: " The maiden's wreath must not be praised, till the matron's cap is put on."

The second parting from home was not nearly so much like a death on either side, since the first had proved so free from danger; and there is nothing new to be told about my second visit to Reckenburg. When it was drawing toward an end, the countess proposed that I should remain with her permanently. I flatly refused, for though the busy activity at Reckenburg interested me more than the quiet routine of my parents' house, I would never have voluntarily resigned my home rights and duties. The countess, however, I must say, though unwilling to give me up, was not offended by my frankness, nay it was to this very ingenuousness that I owed my rapid progress in gaining her confidence. I already went in and out unannounced, and the bolt was no longer drawn when she knew I was in the ante room.

How great this progress was, I first learned on the evening before my second departure for home, which happened this year to fall on the prince's birthday. The countess had been in better spirits than I had ever seen her. She had received one of her mysterious letters from Dresden, which she smilingly read and re-read. I noticed that she gazed at a miniature with delight and carefully locked it up "Handsome — handsome — as he!" I heard her murmur, and then again: "Youth is brave!" Nay, when I entered the room after the usual noon nap, the culpable thought occurred to me that Her Excellency the countess had drunk too much champagne. She was sitting in an arm-chair with half closed eyes, gayly humming a little love song said to have been written by the beautiful Aurora Königsmark:

"Love kindles hearts by the light of the eyes,
At first 'tis but a jest, then follow sighs."

The sight was repulsive; I made a noise and the old lady noticed me. But she still murmured:

"It inspires courage, thrills the blood,"

then opened the ledger and spent an hour in calculating accounts with me, in order to finish the current business before the journey.

After supper I followed her into her room to say farewell. "You are seventeen years old, Eberhardine," said she, "and even in your little city there might be some occasion which demanded a toilette in accordance with your rank. I have one for you, which was made for myself, but never used. It can be altered to suit you. You will find the box in your room. Don't open it until you get home, that the material may not be unnecessarily crushed."

I kissed her hand with sincere gratitude. It was always an act of heroism for her to part with any of the articles brought to Castle Reckenburg. But I could not help smiling at the thought, that a dress prepared for a lady approaching middle age could be altered nearly a half century later for a young girl, who was more than a head taller.

The countess continued: "You are neither beautiful nor impassioned enough to inflame a young man's fancy, Eberhardine. I am sure of your heart. But beware of a sensible marriage like your parents. I foresee something higher for you. Your manner is now perfectly *comme il faut*, your mind and body show the strength which is needed for the ancestress of a noble race. I repeat it — you are *not* formed to arouse and satisfy affection, but to inspire respect and confidence, after passion has died away. True, it will not be to-day nor to-morrow; but you are only seventeen, and I was thirty before I reached my goal. You, too, will attain it. Impress upon your mind the coats of arms which are united at Reckenburg, and rely upon it that they will, nay *must*, be united a second time, united forever. Be brave, Eberhardine. *Au revoir!*"

So *this* was it. *This* was the secret plan of the old head of the house, when she invited the last of her race to stand an examination under her eyes; *this* was the proof that she had successfully passed the trial; the coats of arms of the royal and baronial family surmounted by the count's coronet to remain permanently at Reckenburg! The last of the von Reckenburgs and the last of an illustrious princely family to become the founders of a new, richly endowed race.

Well, it was an old woman's fancy, worthy of the resolute supporter of the race; but also a very pleasant whim to the heart of a youthful von Reckenburg. And if it would be too much to assert that the handsome, princely husband appeared to her in a dream, he really did cost his bride *in spe* a few hours of her usual night's rest.

My traveling companion this year was the pastor, who by a little literary labor had purchased a few days' pleasure. They consisted of a visit to his son, who was studying in Leipsic; a glance at the list of new books and the antiquarian treasures of German literature. My happy friend hoped to be able to repeat these trips every six months, and we agreed to go back to Reckenburg together in the autumn.

This two days' intercourse with the dear, learned gentleman would undoubtedly have been of the greatest benefit to me, if the intrusive idea of the prince had not constantly interposed between the new Spanish heroes of Schiller, and the metrical quarrels of Lichtenberg *contra* Voss. The old countess was right; her chosen successor did not possess an inflammable imagination, and the warning about the late marriage was also not unnecessary; yet, notwithstanding all this, the plaything she had entrusted to a girl of seventeen was a dangerous one. No matter how often Dame Wisdom drove the tempter from the field, he always came smiling and whispering back again. *Chassez le naturel, il retourne au galop.*

I knew nothing about the young gentleman, except

that my father had called him a wild fellow, and the countess' hints did not contradict the epithet. My tongue fairly pricked with the desire to learn something more about him. At last I made short work of the matter, and in the midst of the idyllic society of the parsonage at Grünau, burst out with a question about the character of my aunt's stepson.

The worthy pastor of Reckenburg was startled. He did not even know the countess, and was far from supposing that her faithless husband's son would some day be his patron. Therefore it was only by the merest accident, that he had a short time before, through a newspaper article, obtained some little information.

The young, handsome prince — an Antinous rumor called him — frivolous, inclined to gallant adventures, and therefore with his scanty finances vexatiously involved in debt, had long since shown annoyance and *ennui* at the methodical routine of the Elector's court, at which he found himself in a subordinate position as relative, ward, and soldier, and being hot headed into the bargain, had burst out in open rebellion at the result of the congress of sovereigns at Pillnitz the previous autumn. He secretly left Dresden to seek more attractive society at the palace of the Elector Clemens in Coblentz. Here in the gay life of the emigrants, he became loaded with a burden of debt which neither of his royal relations felt disposed to liquidate. A short time before he was said to have received peremptory orders to return at once to Dresden, and his friends thereby hoped to secure themselves from the compromising interest taken by the princely partisan in the impending campaign against French Jacobinism.

"After a sleep of a century and a half, a violent storm has risen in the German forest," said the pastor in conclusion. "The wind roars and raves in the tree tops, while the ground, a broad, damp willow bed, still awaits the ploughshare. In the world of science, in art and poetry, everywhere we see single shoots, misunderstood or falsely interpreted, tower above the crowd. Even among our countless royal families this sudden, heterogeneous impulse makes itself known. Are there not many which have put forth a bold shoot? If these shoots are heirs to a throne, like Frederick, like Joseph, they make themselves pioneers of a new order of things, to conquer or perish in their efforts, according to strength, circumstances, or temperament, but always plant a germ which will bear fruit in the future. If they are side branches, like this young man, younger sons without land or power, but reared in princely delusions, princely seclusion, we see them only too frequently fall from the tree as dead blossoms, and perish in obedience to the law which makes every unused faculty decay. Adventurers and madcaps, sensualists and originals, dilettanti and bunglers, free-thinkers and ghost-seers jog along within the bounds which custom has hitherto hallowed, and no one of them ever breaks through the barriers for the freedom and prosperity of the others. They cannot rise higher, they will not or dare not increase in breadth or depth. They simply remain princes, that is exceptions, to whom no field of glory or action is allotted, except the bloody battlefield, which even at this hour, and God knows until *what* hour, threatens to again benumb our scarcely awakened native land."

These were certainly counsels which might well divest the Reckenburg chimera of its dazzling charm, and when I jolted homeward from Leipsic alone in my modest vehicle, the bright soap bubbles vanished from my sober eyes. Would the reckless, gallant Antinous, for the sake of paltry money and lands, consent to an alliance with a plain girl, inferior to him in rank, and whom he did not even know? I asked myself. Would the old countess insist upon this marriage, against the will of the son of a man who had been her pride and joy; the open and secret ruler of her life? And lastly, *if* she insisted upon the condition, *if* he submitted to necessity, would the plain, unknown girl allow herself to be made a condition in a bargain with a man who received her unwillingly? No, three times no! Not for the possession of a princely Antinous, not for Reckenburg and all the power in the world. Never!

With this bold stroke through all dazzling fancies and the resolution not to make myself ridiculous by any allusion to the matrimonial whim at Reckenburg, I entered my parents' house. But notwithstanding this, I shall be pardoned for a relapse into the weakness when, directly after the first greetings were exchanged, my good father asked the question: "Did the old countess know that her hereditary prince had been ordered to this place?"

My head fairly swam. "Prince Augustus here — here?" I stammered.

"Not yet," mamma replied, after a discreet hem,

which was always intended to convey a mild reproof to her husband. " Not yet. But he may be expected at any moment. He has been ordered to the regiment as major, and therefore will of course be your father's superior officer. Many people say it is done in order to have him get out of his entanglements while living in this little garrison town; but I am of the opinion that they wished to give him an independent command, and selected this place because the castle affords a residence suitable for a man of his rank."

" At any rate he will be admitted to the Thursday assemblies," my father added. " A picnic and *bal champêtre* is being arranged in his honor."

" A reception, Eberhard," my mother corrected.

"Well, a reception, for aught I care," he answered gaily. " In any case on that day the ladies will make his acquaintance, and our good Dine will at last have an hour's gayety."

"We shall be obliged to attend to your toilette without delay," my mother began, but was interrupted by the announcement of a lady visitor, who wished to consult her about the picnic. I was still in my travelling dress, and therefore permitted to retire to my room.

Was I never to have any rest from the enchanted prince? Scarcely had the dream been driven away, when he stood before me in bodily form. Had the countess known of this meeting, founded her plans upon it? Was it one of those pieces of good fortune the family seeress had predicted from cards and coffee-grounds? Had the Reckenburg conditions already been insinuated to the poor, debt-laden young gentleman?

But even a real disturber of the peace may be conquered, often more quickly than a fancied one, if only the armor of pride is well polished. I had defeated mine before the important conference below was concluded.

A light step on the stairs brought my thoughts back into the natural channels. It was Dorothee, who had not expected me until the next day, and was returning from a walk. Now for the first time I laid aside my travelling dress and then, intending to surprise her, softly opened the door and stood for some time unnoticed on the threshold.

Active, lively little Dörl was sitting by the window, with her head resting on her hand; she whom I had always heard laughing and talking — sighed; she looked paler than when I left her; her eyes were larger, had a more questioning expression, and were surrounded by blue circles. The flowers on the window-sill hung their heads; the birds in the cage fluttered restlessly about for food. Their little mistress had neglected them.

As soon as she saw me, however, the usual bright flush suffused her charming face, and with a cry of delight she threw herself into my arms. "Hardine!" she joyously exclaimed, "Fräulein Hardine, oh! all will be well again now!"

"*What* will be well?" I asked, as I sat down beside her and took her hand. "Are you in trouble, Dörothee?" She shook her head. "Or anxious? Is it anything about Siegmund Faber?"

"Siegmund Faber? Dear me, what do I know about him? He is cutting cripples and dead bodies, and will soon go to the war. He doesn't care *that* for me." She laughingly snapped her fingers.

"Doesn't he write to you?"

"Twice a year, on my birthday and at Christmas."

"And you?"

"What should I write to him? Nothing ever happens to me. I thank him for his present, send him something in return, and that ends it."

"But what is the matter with you then, dear Dorothee?"

"What is the matter with me? Nothing at all, I believe. You have no pleasure either, Fräulein Hardine."

"You don't occupy yourself enough, child," I said warningly.

"How am I to occupy myself?" she answered. "I do what I can."

I could make no reply. In fact, what was she to do in her betrothal freedom and constraint? I dimly suspected that work would not be the means of filling *this* life.

"But what would you like then, dear?" I asked after a pause.

"I should like to *live*!" she cried, with the indescribable impulse with which she had exclaimed in the garden: "To be good is to be a child of God, Hardine."

And as then, with a hasty change of mood, she had rushed after the first violets to adorn her friend, she now caught her hands, pressed them to her heart, and exclaimed exultingly: "But now I have you again, Fräulein Hardine; now I am no longer alone; now I shall be as contented and happy as ever."

Yet nevertheless I left her with a presentiment of approaching sorrow. "Dörtohen doesn't look so well as she did in the autumn," I said, when I returned to my parents, and my father replied:

"No wonder! Time hangs heavy, poor little Dörl. Handsome as a picture, seventeen years old, and always the same dull monotony."

"Has our daughter any more pleasure in her youth, Eberhard?" asked my mother sharply.

My father patted my cheeks, and I saw his eyes grow dim. "Our Dine, our good Dine!" he said sorrowfully. "Confounded old witch's nest. If I had my way —." He did not finish the sentence, for a warning hem was audible from Frau Adelheid. But after a pause he continued, rubbing his hands joyfully. "Well, thank Heaven, next Thursday Eberhardine will have an opportunity to flourish her little petticoats, as is natural at her age."

The next day our little house-owner was again the old gay Dörl, and all aglow with excitement over the great affair of the toilette. The countess' box was opened and we scanned with well satisfied eyes a dress — there was no doubt that it had been intended for the dinner to be given on the day she entered Castle Reckenburg — well, a dress which fifty years ago would have been elegant in a brilliant court circle, but even now in our little ex-capital would seem sufficiently rich and handsome. A sea-green damask interwoven with threads of silver, the neck and sleeves trimmed with delicate lace. Mamma nodded with an expression of the utmost satisfaction.

"The skirt is too short," said she, "but can be lengthened with the cloak, which will also make over the waist. I never saw finer lace. Its yellow tint will heighten your brunette complexion, especially with powdered hair and real pearls in the toupet. A princely toilette, my dear daughter!"

I assented. But Dörl pouted like a sulky child. "Don't wear powder, Fräulein Hardine!" she whispered in my ear. "No Parisian wears powder or a toupet. And for Heaven's sake don't wear that silk dress with the lace as yellow as a quince! You would certainly look like your grandmother, Fräulein Hardine. A white muslin, red bows, and a fresh rose — my bushes are in full bloom — a rose in your curling black hair, I should like to see you *so* at your first ball."

Ah! I was only seventeen! In a white dress, a rose in my curls, at the first ball, for the first time under the eyes of — children, my heart fairly trembled with delight.

But it was only a moment, for my mother, who had heard the unusual whispered opposition with visible displeasure, answered: — "It is no ball, at least that is not its principal object. It is a *cercle*, a presentation. Let the bailiff's daughters dance around a prince of the blood in dresses fit for a shepherdess; *we* are not of the stamp that enjoy preparing a dish of stewed fruit. But as for the powder; if the Jacobins in Paris have laid it aside, that is the best reason for *us* to retain it."

Farewell, bright dream of white muslin! *Noblesse oblige.* The last von Reckenburg wore powder as long as anyone, and never in her life roses.

Thursday morning dawned, and society was still in the most anxious suspense. Had the prince arrived the night before? Had he not come yet? What would become of the bailiff's turkey, or the pig's head the chief forester's wife had prepared, if the warm weather continued? Would the Baroness von Reckenburg venture to mix the pastry for the cakes?

She would venture to mix it! My father breathlessly brought the joyful message; my kind papa, who had cheerfully undertaken the troublesome post of a *maitre de plaisir* and leader of the dance to-day, when the point in question was to prepare a suitable reception for his princely commander and give his daughter the first festival of her life. The prince had arrived at night and most graciously accepted the invitation of the committee. "A man like a picture!" said my father, "if your countess should see him, Dine, she would pay his debts with sugar-plums."

Everybody was now in motion. The hair-dresser appeared at nine o'clock in the morning. Scarcely was the artistic structure properly completed, when Dörtchen came in to lace the waist of the dress and fasten the hooks. "Oh! there is time enough yet!" I said deprecatingly.

"But I must dress too, Fräulein Hardine," replied the little one, "and be there earlier than you."

"You?" I asked in surprise.

THE LAST DANCE. 159

"I am only going to help father a little; the poor man doesn't know which way to turn, Fräulein Hardine."

There was really no objection to be made to this; so I allowed my waist to be compressed to the size of a wasp's, and sat for hours in my father's armchair gasping for breath, and with a much redder face than usual. Mamma glided between the cook stove and the toilette table; papa found it hard work to force himself into the old uniform. Between each article of clothing he tried an *entrechat*, to make his limbs supple for the great task of the evening. Of all who belonged to the Thursday reunions, scarcely one thought of dinner that day.

At last, at last the clock struck four. The bailiff's carriage rolled by, and the von Reckenburg family glided through the little gate of the late barber's shop to the castle terrace, and thence to the pavilion. We were the first to reach the spot. A prince of the blood not only *ought*, but *must* find everyone waiting for him.

The weather was as mild as summer; the trees and plants were in blossom. No better day for a *fête champêtre* could have been found at the end of April, if it had been especially ordered. But as the entertainment was designed for the reception of a prince's son, the managers thought it more proper to decide in favor of the ducal summer house, as my mother had chosen the dress of *drap d'argent*. True, the summer house consisted of a single apartment, but with the assistance of drapery had been divided for the complicated arrangements of the day. The front was intended for the reception and dance, the rear for the dining hall. The dishes already sent in made a very attractive display, and also, blended with the spring odors wafted from the garden, gave out a spicy perfume. Under the drapery, between the two divisions, stood Meister Müller's buffet and his portly figure leaned against the side door which led into the kitchen and cellar. Dorothee of course, remained behind the scenes.

In this room, which in other respects had preserved its old magnificence very tolerably, the company waited *one* hour, *two* hours and more for the eagerly desired guest, who — did not come. No one sat down, no one had patience to carry on any continued conversation. All eyes rested on the open door. It was so still in the crowded hall, that the birds could be heard twittering outside. The members of the regimental band resolutely kept the trumpets to their mouths, that they might not omit the welcoming flourish. At the entrance, in the blazing sunshine, stood the committee, *chapeau bas*, and at their head, with his hand doubled into the form of a tube, Captain von Reckenburg. All were watching and listening — no prince came.

Intentional want of punctuality on the part of a blood relation of the Elector could not be supposed; some misunderstanding must have occurred or accident happened. After long deliberation the head of the committee set out to enquire, and the family of this head afterwards learned in confidence, that the discourtesy which had been thought so impossible was not entirely out of the question after all. When the ambassador appeared before the distinguished guest, the latter was extended comfortably on a couch in his dressing gown, with a long Turkish pipe in his mouth and the Hamburg newspaper in his hand. "Already?" he asked, yawning. "Are the beauties so sure of their charms, that they can expose them to the sunlight?" But he promised to appear as soon as he had dressed and finished the newspaper.

Twilight was already approaching, when the envoy returned with the message. The window shutters were hastily closed and the candles in the chandelier lighted. The company ranged themselves in two rows, between which the distinguished guest was to pass. At the head were the wives of the nobility, then those of the prominent citizens, next the young ladies, and finally the gentlemen in the same order of rank.

But it was still a long time before the expected flourish of trumpets and directly after the *maitre de plaisir's* voice echoed from the upper end of the room. I had not looked around, and held my head in the haughtiest attitude, to give the lie to my throbbing heart. Not until I heard my father utter the name: "Freifräulein Eberhardine von Reckenburg," as I sank slowly in the minuet curtsey, did I raise my eyes, as calmly as I could, to the face of the person passing.

I had been prepared for a handsome man; but *he*, who now met my eyes, my friends, was not only the handsomest man I had ever seen — for that would not mean much — but was and remained — I know of no better expression — the most fascinating youth life has ever shown me. If he had been wild, his appearance at least showed no trace of this dissipation; neither the slender, pliant figure, nor the complexion of almost girlish transparency, nor the features which would have perhaps seemed too soft and delicate but for the large deep blue eyes that flashed with so bold a light. Add to this the fair moustache above the proudly curved upper lip, the thick waving hair, which rebelled against the restraint of the queue, and finally the graceful ease of manner and bearing, natural only to those whose condescension is considered a favor. My good father, with his tight jacket and stiff dignity, presented a vexatiously comical figure in my eyes beside this darling of the graces in his comfortable, half open coat.

I received this whole impression at the *first* glance, and during this first glance understood the pleasure my eighty year old relative found in her memories of the past, if her faithless husband's son resembled his father: but strangely enough — could it have been a presentiment of the future? — during this first hasty glance there was a buzzing in my ears like the dirge of Hadrian, which the pastor had so vividly described to me, for a handsomer man than *this* Antinous could hardly have delighted the imperial eyes.

When my father mentioned my name, the prince, who had just passed my neighbor with a wave of his lace edged handkerchief, started and paused a moment with a smile on his lips, as if he had just met an old acquaintance; then passed on down the line, bowing as each was presented.

The *polonaise* began. The prince led my mother

THE LAST DANCE. 163

through the hall far too quickly and naturally for the fashion of the times. Then a pause ensued; the principal female dignitaries eagerly awaited the approach of the distinguished guest and openly shrugged their shoulders when, after having already preferred his captain's wife to Her Excellency the widow of the Marshal of the Prince's household, they now saw him turn with hasty steps towards her daughter.

"You have just come from Reckenburg, Fräulein?" he said with the same smile as before. "How is my ex-mamma? Immortal, so they say—"

"At least, not enfeebled, Your Highness, and unwearied," I replied.

"Insatiable too, is she not, and inflexible in guarding her Lydian treasures! Well, even Crœsus at last found his Solon. Will you not exert your wisdom, Fräulein, to free at least *one* poor debtor from his chains?"

I cannot say that this familiar introduction would have been particularly agreeable to my taste, but I scarcely caught the meaning of the frivolous words; I only listened to the music of the changeful voice, which wove a magical spell around my heart.

As he uttered the last words the orchestra commenced a Viennese waltz, and I read in my companions' envious glances, that they supposed the prince would be my partner. The brave *maitre de plaisir* rushed heroically toward the offended wife of the principal dignitary, to make amends to her by the best efforts of his bodily strength for this new preference shown his family. I, too, expected the prince would lead me to the dance, and awaited his invitation with delight. But as he made no movement to leave the spot, I quietly sat down in one corner of the sofa.

"Do you not dance?" said the prince, seating himself beside me. "So much the better. We will talk and make our remarks on the company."

The couples whirled past us; not one escaped a mocking comment from the prince's lips. "Not *one* marked countenance! Not *one* fresh nature!" he exclaimed at last. "And all these people boast of being created in the image of God, the Father. How, amid these masks, these smooth conventionalities, have you managed, Fräulein von Reckenburg, to remain *yourself?*"

"This is my first appearance in society," I could not help answering. But I did so with tolerable humor, for I sat opposite to a mirror and understood how many summers might be adjudged the wearer of the sea-green brocade.

"Or how will you accomplish it?" said the prince, correcting himself.

"Why, Your Highness will be obliged to accomplish it also," I answered, smiling.

"I! By Jove, no indeed!" he exclaimed. "I have been chained here. But does my worthy guardian of Saxony suppose that the first cannon shot on the Rhine will not break this chain? It will surely come to that at last. Oh! what a disgrace that Francis of Austria, following his father's example, could delay until his unhappy brother-in-law, under the torture of his Jacobin bailiffs, sends his hordes against him. What a disgrace, an eternal disgrace, that the latter, who will soon be our em-

THE LAST DANCE. 165

peror, still writhes and twists like an eel. But, thank God, King Frederick William is all eagerness to apply the thumb screw to these miscreants. Let him once place himself at the head of an army, let him shout 'forward!' and we, at least, that is the legion of landless German princes, will not delay, under Frederick's banner, to reconquer for the heir of St. Louis his royal freedom."

In this way, amid the notes of the Viennese waltz, my young hero artlessly talked in mingled jest and earnest of his future plans. I already knew his war-like disposition, but could not help being surprised that he intended to desert to the Prussian service. So I ventured to remind him that a change to that particular camp would meet with scant approval from Saxon hearts.

"Have I an army of my *own* to lead to the field?" he answered smiling. "Or must I wait until the German nation has remembered its duty — pshaw! — its need of defense? Wait until the ruler of Upper Saxony has raised his little banner? Oh! only let me have the subsidies of your Reckenburg, Fräulein," he added, with a mischievous glance, "only the subsidies of your Reckenburg, and I will lay at your feet the first laurel wreath which, like my brave father of Weimar, I have won as a Prussian soldier."

During this tirade the waltz ended, and I rose to take shelter under my mother's wing from the angry glances of the company. The prince followed me. The first bars of a minuet were just being played.

"You seem to be a virtuoso in the art of bearing

ennui with dignity," said he, "will you, like a faithful comrade, stand in this dance by the side of a poor bungler?"

I should certainly have preferred to whirl in a round dance through the hall in his arms as a merry partner, but to stand opposite to him for fifteen minutes longer, even only as a faithful comrade, seemed to me a great delight. When we reached the end of the column, my partner sighed so deeply that I could not help answering the incivility with a smile. He also laughed. "The Germans call these solemn hardships pleasure," he exclaimed. "By Jupiter! I would gladly give my hand to a Jacobin for an honest *carmagnole.*"

I took the liberty of remarking, that a gay German country dance might perhaps do the same service, and His Highness only need ask for it to compensate himself for the hardship of the decorous minuet.

"It needs at least two to be gay," he answered, glancing satirically from one to another of the proud company. Suddenly he started. "Good Heavens, who is that?" he exclaimed in delight, "who is that?"

It seemed to me as if I saw a flash of lightning enter a powder magazine, for my eyes had followed his. But if they had been struck with blindness, what spectacle could have exerted so sudden a spell as that of my beauty, of — Dorothee?

The dance music had allured her from her hiding place. She was standing one step in front of the buffet, with sparkling eyes, like a child that sees the fruit for which it longs hanging unattainably on the trees. The incarnate Eve! Her arms were slightly raised, her body bent forward; in one hand she held a little basket twined with flowers and filled with the sweet biscuits she knew how to make so daintily. The light blue edge of the white muslin dress scarcely reached to her ankles; her little feet in the spangled shoes beat time to the notes of the music; the golden curls floated down from beneath the blue ribbon that loosely confined them, and the bouquet of roses she had gathered for me trembled at the quick throbbing of her heart. Never *before* and never *after* that time did I see the charming Dörl look so charming as at that moment.

As her eyes met ours, she looked down with a deep flush and glided through the side door.

"Who is this Hebe?" repeated the prince.

"The tavern-keeper's daughter," I replied, bowed, and sat down beside my mother.

Various dances followed, through which I whirled in the arms of different partners, sighing as my prince had just done over the toil of the minuet. The latter did not dance again. Unconcerned as if in a tavern, he sat near the buffet among a group of officers, with whom he boldly drank. But it was not Meister Müller's native production, nor even the best brands the givers of the entertainment had been able to furnish, but sparkling Clicquot, which he had ordered to be brought from his own cellar, as a "trifling contribution to the picnic."

So he heaped offense upon offense. But at every cork that popped from the bottles, his eyes sought still more eagerly for the tavern-keeper's lovely daughter, who, at each new dancing tune, appeared in the doorway as if lured by Hüon's horn, glided forward to the curtains, and followed the movements of the couples with longing eyes. That during this time her eyes often met those seeking ones at the sideboard, while she understood how to avoid the reproving looks of Fräulein Hardine, undoubtedly seems far more pardonable to Fräulein Hardine to-day than it did in the year '92.

At last a flourish of trumpets gave the signal for the supper. Now this scandalous intermezzo must come to an end. The company entered the second compartment, where the ladies, seated at small tables around the large one in the centre, were to be served by the gentlemen. In each of these groups, by strategy or force, a seat had been kept unoccupied, in the hope that it would be chosen by the distinguished guest.

But the indignation caused by so many offences rose to fierce wrath, when the outrageous young gentleman gratified none of these secret expectations, and disappointed all by remaining quietly seated in the same place; when he did not even taste any of the delicacies procured with so much care and expense, but contented himself with a biscuit which Hebe Dörl, at a sign from Meister Müller, offered him in the flower-wreathed basket.

As I saw the blushing girl stand before him with drooping head, saw him start up, raise his glass to her and drain it to the dregs at a *single* draught — the food choked me, and the water with which I tried to wash it down burned like poison; but it was a picture whose artistic charm even the most indignant could not fail to perceive.

According to the programme, the entertainment was to conclude with the supper. All were preparing to depart, but our hitherto indolent hero suddenly started up and loudly demanded a last dance. Strong as the universal feeling of indignation had been, generosity to a guest of the blood-royal was stronger. Besides, even for the Thursday assemblies, there was nothing indecorous in having the customary concluding dance, for whose rustic music and motley changes no one felt in the right mood until after supper. Old and young ranged themselves in couples, only Captain von Reckenburg still stood waiting until after his aristocratic chief had chosen his partner, in order to select the most prominent of the bevy of beauties remaining. But now, as the prince unceremoniously turned his back upon the marriageable group, he went up to the Frau Amtmannin, offered her his hand, and was in the act of going to the head of the column, when — oh! horror, threefold horror to our noble circle — when he saw the prince rush up to the side board and draw the tavern-keeper's little Dörl into the ranks of dancers.

A thunder-clap could not have been more destructive. For a moment everyone stood rigid and motionless, then the flames of revolution burst forth. The Frau Amtmannin turned with an "excuse me;" all the matrons and young ladies of noble blood left their places and hurried towards the door, where, concealed behind the pillars, they awaited the result.

"Does His Highness suppose he is invited to a country wake?" I heard the widow of the Marshal of the Prince's Household ask scornfully behind me, as she rustled away.

I, with a very young nobleman whom I could have handed about on a waiter, formed the connecting link between the couples of noble birth and the citizens, who still remained firm. Did I think of following the signal of desertion given from above? Probably not, else why did I avoid my mother's glance? My eyes rested upon the offending pair, who now advanced to the gap that had been made by my side. I saw Dorothee's look of mingled fear and pleasure; saw the prince's meaning glance, which seemed to say: "You are no fool, you will stay." In short, I did stay. The bourgeoise followed my example, and the dance began.

This certainly was quite a different matter from the toil Germans usually call a pleasure! How quickly and gaily the figures changed, the couples interlaced and separated. How the rosy Hebe circled through the hall in the arms of her god-like partner, when, at the conclusion of each figure, the step changed to a galopade! Voices now mingled in the whirl, the royal leader, amid a loud clapping of hands and exulting chorus, sang the old ballad of "the grandfather who took the grandmother," and at last nothing old or new remained except — the kiss!

Yes, my friends! We are writing of the year '92, and a kiss in the dance did not seem a theft in those days. The polonaise was often introduced with it, or it was exchanged in a waltz; at any rate our worthy grandfathers never lacked it, and not only at shooting matches or country fairs. My sisters of the Monday assemblies were in the habit of offering their little cheeks to their partners, and after their partners to everyone to whom they came in the dance. Fifty kisses in a *single* turn — it was no intoxicating spice, but the flavor was very pleasant.

Our aristocratic circle, with the reminiscences of the whilom ducal court, was, it is true, too nobly constituted to endure such natural excesses. But now, on its proudest day, to see a prince of the blood press his lips to those of a tavern-keeper's daughter, and press them in *such* a way — with so much method — it never recovered from the horrible spectacle! This was its death blow.

He kissed her mouth, clasped her in his arms, pressed her to his heart, and rushed through the hall with her. The rapid movement loosened the blue ribbon from her hair; he snatched it and concealed it next his heart. The golden curls fell and floated to her knees. All order was broken up. Singing, shouting, breathless, all the couples rushed after the first. Last of all came Fräulein Hardine, after a timid kiss of the hand from her young nobleman.

Then suddenly — halt! The *maitre de danse* had given the musicians the signal to stop. I can still see how Dorothee vanished through the side door like a frightened roe; how the prince swallowed a foaming glass of champagne. Then my mother threw her own hood over my head, and all pressed in confusion towards the entrance.

Thus the festival given to the prince by the noble

Thursday assembly in the year '92, the great year of revolution, came to an end in a bacchanalian tumult, a terrible scandal. I have devoted to it a long chapter in the history of my life — it was the only time I *almost* wore roses.

CHAPTER VI.

THE BETROTHAL ARBOR.

"An extremely vexatious scandal!" said my mother, interrupting the silence, as soon as the little gate of the barber's house closed behind us. "But under the circumstances, Eberhard, I must say that our daughter behaved with a great deal of tact."

"Admirably, admirably, my Dine," said my father, as if a weight had fallen from his heart. "The child was dragged into the dance by force; she was Dine's playmate, is the owner of our house, and when Faber has married her will belong to society, as much as—"

"Your reasons will not do, Eberhard," mamma interrupted. "The girl behaved most improperly. As Siegmund Faber's betrothed, she should stay at home, or as the tavern-keeper's daughter remain in the kitchen and cellar, to say nothing of her pastoral toilette. Our daughter, however, had already taken her place in the dance, and a von Reckenburg will know how to maintain her dignity on any occasion, especially when the Herr Amtmann's wife, whose father was a miller, sets the example of retiring."

I made no reply, but kissed my parents' hands and hurried to my room. I did not think of undressing and going to rest, but sat motionless on the side of the bed, I know not how long. I felt as if I had fallen from a high tower, and confused images whirled through my bewildered brain. I heard a light step at the door, but did not move; I felt a warm breath on my cheek, but did not look up, though my hand trembled with the longing to repel the offender, who was kneeling at my feet with her head buried in my lap. "Are you angry with me, Fräulein Hardine?" she murmured in her childish voice.

Was I angry with her! I gasped for breath, my blood boiled with rage against the tavern-keeper's false, bold daughter. I turned my face away and gazed steadily into the looking-glass over my dressing table. And this glance at the mirror dissolved the spell; for what is being just except seeing clearly? But I saw in the narrow frame the Freifräulein von Reckenburg in her lofty toupet and stiff brocade, the tall figure with the flushed face, to whom the worldly wise old countess had said: "You will never inflame a young man's fancy." And at her feet, shrouded in a veil of golden hair, knelt a child with all the charms of a woman, her pulses throbbing fervently, and on her brow the stamp: "No young heart will be able to resist you."

After a long pause and a heavy sigh, I turned my eyes from the picture in the mirror to the young girl at my feet. "Be kind, be kind," whispered the siren, and her lips warm with the fervid glow another's breath had inspired, burned on my hand.

"You allowed yourself to be carried away by impulse, Dorothee," I said, raising her. "But if you are sorry—"

"Sorry?" she exclaimed, trembling with the perception of a happiness whose existence hitherto she had scarcely suspected. "Sorry! Oh, never sorry! Not if I should die for it, Hardine!"

She darted out of the room. And I? Of course I lay as if on a bed of roses and slept sweetly in peace, after the manner of magnanimous heroines and noble souls? But I tell you, I tossed on thorns and nettles, my heart seemed full of boiling lead, and if *either* prayed that night, it was the happy offending mortal, not the self-sacrificing one.

The von Reckenburg family could only approve the conduct of the abashed owner of the house, when during the following days she avoided every occasion of meeting them, shrank from the watchful eyes and bitter taunts of the neighborhood, and only glided into her father's house through the garden. Even Frau Adelheid valued the child who had grown up under her eyes too highly to fear constant repetition of a saucy freak, and the provincial gossip stimulated this proud disregard of danger.

Besides, we had enough to do to defend ourselves; for if the plebeian bolts were directed towards the little attic chamber, before which the Faber basins had glittered, the poisonous arrows of "society" were aimed at the lower story, whose inmates, infatuated by the prince's favor, had bid defiance to righteous indignation and thereby made the scandal incurable.

Of course these tale-bearers only made the baronial family hold their heads the higher and more proudly. But it must not be concealed, that a headache which confined my mother to her bed for a week, may possibly have originated in some secret affection of the bile.

So it happened that on Sunday morning the father and daughter went to church *alone*, and here they saw the beautiful offender for the first time since that terrible evening. She sat in the nave, close to the pulpit, directly opposite the portion of the congregation which could boast of noble blood, and even during the singing we could not help noticing the curious glances which the plebeians cast from her seat to the high ducal pew, behind whose curtains the prince, unfortunately without truth, was supposed to be.

But how the excitement increased, when the worthy court chaplain entered the pulpit and after giving the text: "Render therefore unto Cæsar the things which are Cæsar's, and unto God the things which are God's," impressed upon his hearers in the most powerful language, their relative duties towards the altar and the throne, as well as those of submission to established gradations of rank, and drew a horrible picture of the sinful persons who attempted to make everyone free and equal.

The lonely, somewhat deaf old gentleman had undoubtedly not heard a word about the great local question of the day. He had written his sermon early in the week, in fierce wrath against the rebels in Paris, who had forced the pious unhappy king to declare war against his Austrian kinsman, his only anchor of hope. If the carefully prepared words received personal sharpness by any momentary inspiration, at the utmost no one was responsible for it except the young prince, whose heart it had been intended to rejoice, and who in such godless times shamefully neglected his duty towards the sanctuary of God. Neither at this time nor after did the fiery orator think of the modest penitent at his feet, with any feeling save that of the most paternal affection.

But how far our worthy citizens were from expecting to hear any re-action of Dumouriez's ultimatum from their pulpit! Were they a horde of Jacobins, who required an ecclesiastical call to order? Did they not, without grumbling, give God the things which were God's, and the Elector the things which were the Elector's, always supposing that the taxes were not too high? Had any one in the parish even dreamed of freedom and equality?

Yes, there was one among them, one alone, who blinded by the demon of pride and vanity, had turned her back upon the class to which God had assigned her, since like an upstart, she had shot up in a single night to be the betrothed bride and heiress of an ambitious fellow; who had thrust herself among the nobility, sneaked into the presence of the most distinguished member of society and, clad in fantastic attire, infatuated the prince and occasioned such a scandal, that a society which had existed from the time of its duke had been broken up, and a reproof from the pulpit became necessary. It would not have required much for people to point their fingers at poor little Dörl, who with downcast eyes and cheeks wet with tears, now blushing scarlet and anon white as chalk, sat trembling violently.

When the service was over, I found her half senseless, crushed against a pillar by the pressure of the crowd at the church door. More excited than ever by their morning devotions, the patricians from the gallery and the plebeians from the nave stood talking in groups before the entrance. No one exchanged a word or greeting as usual with the pretty "Jungfer Augentrost,* no one made room for her; they stared, criticized her dress, and contemptuously turned their backs upon her. More kindly than I should have done *without* this Christian spectacle, I spoke to her, drew her arm through mine, and led her — they made way for *me* — past the Frau Amtmannin, who was just entering her handsome carriage. The soldiers were having a parade in the market-place, and the godless prince respectfully saluted us.

So the envied and slandered young girls, once more united through the declaration of war made by the National Assembly, walked home arm in arm, and even strolled up and down the garden for fifteen minutes, in order to recover from the exhausting morning service: the rose and its leaf as before! I strengthened Dorothee in her resolution to keep in the back-ground as much as possible, until the storm had subsided, and even advised her for a time to attend the quiet early service instead of the principal one. She thanked me with mingled smiles and tears, kissed my hand, and said: "Fraülein Hardine, *you* are really a great lady."

Well, we like to hear our own opinion of ourselves confirmed by others, even if we do not consider them authorities in other respects.

As we returned to the house, the prince entered

---

* Delight of the eyes.

from the street. Dorothee, with a burning blush, darted up stairs. I conducted the visitor into the sitting-room, and as my mother was ill and my father still absent at the parade, talked with him an hour alone. "You have a brave heart," said he, extending his hand, "let us be friends, Fräulein von Reckenburg."

He spoke of his war-like plans more in detail than on the evening of the ball. He had been serious in his intention of entering the Prussian service, and hoped for speedy success. The Duke of Weimar had undertaken to arrange the matter with both parties, and also expressed a desire to have him assigned to his own Prussian regiment. Under the immediate command of a Saxon relative, he said, the hated uniform of electoral guardianship would be endurable, and after all what could be better than to see the troublesome protégé enter into the battle for the oppressed royal son of a Saxon prince's daughter? He also talked with the utmost frankness about his pecuniary embarrassments, and hoped that they would be disentangled by the same hand.

After this day the prince often entered the von Reckenburg sitting-room, without taking offence at the towels in the chimney corner. He treated us like old acquaintances or even relatives, and told us the progress of his private negotiations; we knew the object and result of his secret expeditions; we petted him and concealed his faults as if he were one of the family. All the other inhabitants of the city, on the contrary, he treated with sovereign contempt, and did not, under *our* eyes, even once meet the beautiful owner of our house. She remained quietly in her little attic room, and we ourselves only saw her pass occasionally. My parents praised this modest tact, and the memory of her one transgression was forgotten in the neighborhood more quickly than might have been expected. The good court chaplain's lessons about cause and effect were moreover heard with gratitude and respect.

How that which you have doubtless already suspected, my friends, could have happened during those summer weeks, how it could have been so entirely concealed that even afterwards no searching glance detected the secret, I do not know. And even if I did know, I have promised to disclose my *own* secret, not that of other hearts.

But *my* secret during those summer weeks was, that I — I *alone* — suspected — no, knew that of the others. I saw nothing, I heard nothing, I did not track it out, did not calculate upon the tempting power of opportunity. But I inhaled the truth, as it were, with the air I breathed; I felt it almost as a necessity, that a nature accustomed to happiness like his, and one longing for happiness like hers, must meet, that they loved each other and rejoiced in their mutual love.

I felt, I knew it, and I did not prevent the sin. Whenever the warning: " Remember Siegmund Faber!" or the admonition: "She is betrothed to a man of honor," hovered upon my lips, I repressed the words, for the source from which they sprung was not pure. It was *not* Dorothee's duty, *not* Siegmund Faber's honor, *not* a strong sense of right and justice, at least these were not the *only* causes, it was my own sick longing that sharpened my suspicions. If I had been *wholly* unprejudiced, wholly free from selfishness and jealousy, I, the inexperienced girl, should have trusted to the purity of my companion's soul, as my experienced father and mother did. I did not feel innocent, was conscious of it with shame, and shame and pride bound my tongue, so I became an accomplice in the crime.

True, even the trumpet of doom would not have roused the enraptured lovers from their first delirium of joy. And why did not Siegmund Faber himself think of reminding his lonely betrothed of her duty? Why did he not write? Why did he not return to her, even if but for an hour, before his departure to the seat of war? Why, amid the pressure of study and occupation, did he blindly trust to a promise which only surprise had won from an inexperienced child, to a conventional law of faithfulness to which the heart had not given its assent? Had the man, in analyzing the nerves and ligaments of the body, neglected to examine the nerve and ligament of the soul? Or had he judged her weakness by the standard of his own, and given up the venture of faithfulness as folly? All these apologies I have often repeated to myself, and they have never exonerated me.

Yet it was not only my apprehensive mood; external signs also betrayed the secret to me. Who can describe the mysterious glow that pervades the life and acts of a happy mortal? Who can describe it, especially in the life and acts of such a joyous nature as Dorothee's? I saw the reflection of the delight that filled her soul, and perceived it still more distinctly because I saw her so seldom. We were reconciled; she had no reason to avoid me. Nor did she really avoid me, but she did not seek, did not need me as before. She, who a few weeks since had exultingly exclaimed: "All will be well again now that you are here!" had found another, who crowded me out of her heart. The child, the girl, had become a woman.

But the secret change was still more visible in the prince. His personal affairs had resulted far more favorably than could have been expected, since the kind-hearted Frederick Augustus had not discharged him from his service, but consented to his taking part in the campaign under the Prussian banner, and also generously undertaken to be his security to his creditors. He, who a year ago had deserted to the dissolute camp of the emigrants, who a short time before had raged so angrily about the hesitation of the allies, was now free; why did he not go to the field? He, who had declared the destruction of the French not to be a mere parade manœuvre, the entry into Paris a promenade, and the restoration of the throne child's play, now found a thousand scruples, which served in his own eyes to cloak his intentional delay. The dissensions in the allied cabinet, the division in the Prussian camp, the choice of the Duke of Brunswick for commander-in-chief instead of the king, the unfinished preparations, the lateness of the season for a summer campaign were all considerations which subsequent events only too plainly justified.

THE BETROTHAL ARBOR. 183

But they were artfully adopted and put forward by this fiery youth, because there was a power that held him back quite as strong as the one which urged him forward.

I shared the views of the companions of my life in regard to the nature of this war. I thought it a just, nay holy cause, to risk the welfare, perhaps the existence of our own nation, to save the crown of a foreign king. I did not doubt that the Prussian army, accustomed to victory, would make a speedy conquest, and it was a satisfactory idea to me, that Maria Theresa's daughter would be restored to her rights by Frederick's heir. Besides, I did not conceal from myself that the best school for my young friend would be the battle field, and the conflict which threatened us all could find a solution only by his departure. I therefore approved the prince's warlike impulses, strengthened him against himself, and yet, yet I uttered a sigh of relief, as if rescued from some impending misfortune, when he again found some new pretext for delay.

The Weimar regiment, to which he was ordered, started without him. "The Duke of Brunswick won't be in any great hurry," said he, "I shall reach the Rhine before him." Then the "puppet" show of the imperial coronation in Frankfort was to be allowed to take place, and at last, when the king, after his interview with Francis II. went to Mayence, he still thought he might wait until the latter had joined the army on the other side of the Rhine.

My father shook his head at this sudden inertness. "Now you see," said he, "how hard it is for a Saxon to condescend, even for the highest flight, to place himself under the talons of the Prussian eagle."

I was silent, for I understood the struggle between love and ambition in this young heart, felt it in my own. Dorothee was perfectly free from care. Once she asked anxiously if the Saxon army was also going to the war, and when I answered in the negative smiled in delight. A Siegmund Faber, who was daily approaching nearer and nearer the peril, seemed to have no existence for her.

It was on the afternoon of the second of August that the prince entered our room in great excitement, bringing the Duke of Brunswick's manifesto from his headquarters at Coblentz. All his enthusiasm was again aroused; he apologized for his doubts of the tried commander. "Heaven be praised," he exclaimed, "the king's chivalrous spirit has conquered all mean jealousy. This is the voice which will drive the unchained beast back to his cage. Only let bold actions speedily follow bold words, and on the birthday of Saint Louis we will set his imperiled crown shining with fresh lustre on his grandson's head."

He remained only a few moments, embraced my father, shook hands with my mother and myself, and rushed out again. He had not said farewell, but we knew it was a farewell — perhaps for life.

We sat silently together until late into the evening. Did my parents suspect what moved me so deeply? Had they secretly cherished more hopes than I myself? Again and again I met their anxious eyes fixed upon me.

When I went up stairs to my room, I remembered

one who must be even more unprepared for this parting than I. I turned the handle of Dorothee's door, but found it locked. She was not in the habit of remaining so late at her father's house, and never went out in the evening to pay any other visit. Where could she be? I was not calm enough to reflect upon this question. The confusion in my mind must first subside, and I sat for a long time, probably hours, motionless in my room.

Months lay behind me, months which had been more full of self sacrifice than any in my life. The fleeting hopes and dreams that had not been banished, must now disappear, disappear with him who had inflamed my imagination, disappear for ever. He was a man quick to love and awaken responsive affection, not one who after an outburst of passion can endure and bestow repose. Away with the chimæras of the old Countess von Reckenburg, away forevermore.

I wished this, wished it earnestly, and even at this hour my efforts were not without success. I saw two of us once more in the spot, from which their longings had for a moment led them; the prince battling against the the enemies of established order, I in my sphere of labor at Reckenburg. The only difficult thing was to imagine the child so recently awakened to life restored to her state of betrothed widowhood.

But where was Dorothee? Had I failed to hear her light step? A word of explanation and comfort ought not to be delayed until the morrow. Tears flow most quietly at night, and children sleep sweetly after they have wept till they are weary. She had probably gone to rest early and bolted the door inside.

It was a quiet, sultry midsummer night; the moon shone brightly through the dormer window that looked into the garden. I leaned out, and drawing a long breath, inhaled the fragrance that rose from the beds of pinks. Opposite to me towered the castle, a night lamp flickered in the room in the corner turret, where my young hero was resting for the last time or preparing for his journey. It was difficult for me to avert my eyes from the tiny flame, and they turned lingeringly towards the terrace, which the moon illuminated almost as brightly as if it were broad day.

At this moment — was it a phantom of my excited blood, or was it reality — I saw two figures glide out of the arbor, the arbor where Siegmund Faber's betrothal had taken place. They were clinging to each other; the woman's delicate outlines were clearly visible by the side of the man, whose dark form half concealed her. It was only one glance, but no, there was no deception, and whatever I had suspected my imagination had not pictured this abyss.

My head swam, I tottered and clung to the window sill. When I again slowly raised my eyes, I saw a dark figure vanish through the little gate, but at the same moment the door of the house softly opened.

I rushed into my room, whose lock I did not venture to turn. I already heard steps on the stairs and would not have betrayed my presence for the world. But perhaps it was a *first* nocturnal meeting, a first and last for an eternal farewell.

I listened breathlessly at the door. No! That elastic, gliding step, that free, calm breathing did not speak of separation and sorrow. Only the happy move and breathe in this way. She was dancing over roses and did not see the sin that approached her, the death lurking in the back ground.

And now I was sitting in the arbor. Do not ask what impulse urged me to go there, or how many hours it had bound me to the spot. I had no measure for time, had no distinct idea of it. All was confusion and darkness.

The first light of day glimmered in the east, and I saw a streak of blue at my feet. "The ribbon Dorothee wore at the spring festival," I murmured, picked it up and mechanically twisted it around one finger.

Then I again heard the little gate close and a man's hasty steps. I did not stir. They came nearer and nearer. "Hardine!" cried a voice at the entrance of the arbor. I still sat as if paralyzed.

The prince was in his travelling dress and deadly pale; but he looked me steadily in the face and quietly took the ribbon from my hand. Had he been looking for *that*; a first and last memento? Had he seen me in the arbor from his room?

"You know all," said he, "and it is well. Now I shall go calmly. If I return, I call God to witness — she will be mine. If I fall, she will have *only you*, Hardine — *only you*!"

The rolling of a carriage echoed on the silence. He cast a glance towards the dormer window, where I had listened at night. A tear rolled down his cheek and fell on my hand, which he held clasped in his. "Protect the innocent child, protect my wife, my beloved wife. Guard her for me, for my sake, sister Hardine," he whispered, pressed me to his heart — and I was again alone.

A few minutes more and a post horn sounded. The last note died away in the west. Soon the sun rose, not to-day as on that morning at Reckenburg, like an eye of God: a shining ball which, bright and soulless, mechanically glided over despair and happiness, treason and love.

On the spot where I sat, a few years ago a friend had sued for the hand of the companion of my childhood, and made me the security for the faith of his promised wife. On the same spot which had heard the vow of loyalty, the faith had been broken, and to-day another friend, who was secretly the idol of my own soul, had commended the faithless girl to me as a sister.

There are fatalities, which spring from our own souls and still seem to mock at any legitimate solution. The wheel of destiny rolls over our bungling wills, and in the decisive hour it is not the light of every day, but a spark from unfathomed depths which guides us either to destruction or fulfilment.

And with such a fatality I was confronted at this hour.

CHAPTER VII.

THE BATTLE OF VALMY.

OUR breakfast hour struck. For this length of time I had sat in the arbor, absorbed in fruitless meditations. Now I rose and went to the house. My parents were already aware of the prince's departure. The long cherished secret had run through the city like a conflagration.

"He is on the right path, may God be with him!" exclaimed my father, pressing my hand. But my mother said: "You look pale and chilled, my dear daughter. Go and rest a few hours."

But I dared not rest; I was obliged to prepare Dorothee, who must need strength and courage more than I. Even while on the stairs I heard her piteous sobs. The thunderbolt had struck her from a cloudless sky.

She was lying already dressed on the floor. Her arms, which were thrown across the bed, quivered convulsively, her eyes were fixed upon the door, but did not notice my entrance. "Gone, gone!" was the only sound that escaped her heaving breast.

I lifted her on to the bed and sat down beside her. The convulsive sobbing lasted some time; at last she saw me and passionately waved me off.

"You are ill, Dorothee," I said, "I will send for the doctor."

The word made her fairly beside herself. "No, no!" she shrieked. "No doctor! I am well. Oh! only leave me alone, entirely alone!"

I drew the bed curtains together and pretended to go away, but sat down in the back ground. She gradually became calmer; a flood of tears afforded relief; I heard her sob, and at last only gently wail and sigh.

At the end of an hour she started up, re-arranged her disordered dress, dried her eyes, and looked timidly around the room. When she perceived me, another shudder ran through her frame. "Go, Fräulein Hardine," she pleaded. "For God's sake, leave me alone!"

I now really went away; but from time to time glanced into the next room. Dorothee sat on the bed weeping and wringing her hands. She did not say a word, but was perfectly well.

Weeks passed in mechanical daily occupation. News of the tardy advance of the allied armies was slowly brought by the newspapers, more rapidly from time to time by a mounted courier. On Saint Louis' birthday, when our young hero had expected to join the triumphal entry into Paris, the longed for deliverers were still on this side of the Ardennes, and the grandson of the sainted Louis was a prisoner in the temple.

Yet we did not despair. Verdun had surrendered as well as Longwy, and if from that time all news ceased for weeks, we confidently believed that the hitherto always victorious army, unheeding the despised enemy on its flank, would have reached the Marne by means of forced marches, and though later than we hoped, already restored freedom to the imprisoned monarch in his capital.

On the contrary, however, the silence of our friends who had joined the army was both incomprehensible and alarming; for though we did not expect the excited prince to be in any communicative mood, a young comrade in the regiment, who had been appointed his adjutant and was warmly attached to my father, had promised to send regular news, and now not a word had been heard for nearly two months. And Faber, who by a strange coincidence must have met the friends under a foreign flag, on foreign soil, in the same regiment, Faber also sent no word of consolation in these anxious times.

"I had a better opinion of this Mosjö Per-sé" said my father angrily. "I did not even think to give the prince a letter to take him. Poor little Dörl is completely changed, since affairs have become serious. She grieves and is ashamed to be so forgotten in her anxiety."

Yes indeed the unfortunate Dorothee was grieving and ashamed, though from a very different feeling than her old friend supposed. She avoided us with evident fear, sat in her room with the door bolted, and glided silently and timidly past us in the garden. If we spoke to her, even on the most indifferent subjects, she gave confused, evasive answers. I saw she was trembling at the thought of a discussion, which I too deferred day after day. Why? It must inevitably take place before my departure for Reckenburg. Yes, why do we dread to cut a knot, why rely upon the most improbable things that might effect a solution? For instance I depended upon a conversation and perhaps explanation between the prince and Faber, which would spare me the pain of interfering.

At last, at last the adjutant's long expected letter arrived. The prince had ordered him to delay it, on account of an accident, that his friends might not be unnecessarily alarmed. While hurrying forward to join the Weimar regiment, which was in the front, he had met and joined a Prussian mounted picket, and with it attacked a division of the enemy greatly superior in numbers. After an obstinate conflict they were cut down and taken prisoners; but during the pursuit the prince, who did not wish to let even *one* fugitive escape, was thrown from his horse and received a sprain which, in consequence of bad care, inflamed and detained him for weeks in a miserable hut.

"How he gnashed his teeth and swore at being forced to remain behind, while the army captured the fortifications in the Ardennes," wrote the adjutant, "you can easily imagine, for you know him. But how he foamed at the incomprehensible delay of a week before the weakly guarded passes of Argonne; no, that you cannot imagine, although you know him! If the king were only in command! However, God be praised, his gallant nature has triumphed over the old school wisdom, and our easy victory at Croix au bois and Grandpré, where these heroes of freedom ran like hares, will have lighted a torch for our 'Serenissimus Cunctator,' which will show the road to Paris. The army is on the march towards Chalons. If Dumouriez, that boaster *par excellence*, falls back: very well. We do not fear *such* an enemy on our flank. If he succeeds in joining his forces to those of Kellermann, who is said to be coming to his assistance from Metz: so much the better. We shall then get rid of the rabble at *one* blow. But the best of all is that our prince, now well and cheerful, will set out to-morrow to join his regiment. We expect to reach Menehould — accursed remembrance — in the evening."

The impetuosity of our prince spoke from every word of this report, but a postscript revealed the far more subdued mood of his companion. The roads and weather were abominable; there was no systematic care; epidemic diseases were decimating the army; but what was most surprising of all, the population seemed by no means so well disposed towards this expedition to free the royal prisoner, as every one had expected from the accounts of the emigrants. Several cautious hints about the divided opinions of the leaders of the army closed the letter.

We dismissed the postscript from our thoughts and relied on the good faith and good news of our hero, in which we certainly forgot the dangers which fill every moment between the sending and reception of such news.

The letter, which was written on the 19th of September, reached us on the 28th. The following day, Michaelmas, was Dorothee's birthday. I tried to enter her room early in the morning. The good news about the prince, I hoped, would pave the way to an explanation which could no longer be deferred. But again the attempt failed. She had gone to her father's house before breakfast, and did not return all the morning.

In the afternoon we were sitting round the tea-table, which was adorned with a birthday cake, surrounded with a garland of bright-hued asters. Eighteen tiny tapers, one for each year, and the large life-candle in the centre, were to be lighted as soon as honest Purzel, who was posted on the stairs, succeeded in catching the child. I had deeply felt the inappropriateness of this little yearly festival, but could think of no pretext for preventing my parents' kind intention. We waited in vain. Dorothee did not come. The Frankfort mail had also brought no letter from the betrothed bridegroom, who hitherto had written regularly at least twice a year. Papa shamefully abused his negligent Mosjö Per-sé.

Twilight was already closing in, when a courier's signal was heard from the west. At any sound from this direction officers and citizens assembled before the post house, to collect the true or false news the couriers dispensed at the stations. My father hurried out, and even we women could not rest, but stood in the doorway awaiting his return.

The courier dashed on along the Leipsic road. My father came back. "A battle is said to have taken place," he called, shaking his head; "an unusual cannonading has been heard not far from St. Menehould. But who obtained the victory, and whether at the departure of the courier the next day the armies really occupied the same positions, let him decide who can; I—"

Just at that moment he perceived Dorothee, who had glided noiselessly in from the garden and was listening to his words in breathless suspense. He laughingly handed her a letter, which he had received from the courier: "Wonderful, my dear Dörl, how he remembers dates!"

Dorothee snatched the letter and darted upstairs. My father held another in his hand. "From the adjutant," he said, after we had entered the sitting-room. "It will probably solve the mystery."

I hastily lighted the life-candle on the birthday cake, and stood waiting in breathless anxiety till my father had unsealed the letter. But he had scarcely glanced at it, when I saw him sink back into his chair, while the sheet fell from his hand. "Dead, dead!" he groaned, as if overwhelmed.

"Who is dead?" shrieked my mother. She raised the letter, glanced at the first words, and then looked at me with the deepest anxiety. I was not lying in a fainting fit or convulsions, but standing as stiff as a candle. She quietly placed the letter in my hand. It was hastily written in pencil, and dated on the 21st of September.

"Our noble prince is dead! The victim of a battle, which I have no words to describe. We set out in the middle of the night. The road was abominable, but the news that the king had yesterday given orders for an attack on the hostile army lent the prince wings. We rode our horses to death. At seven o'clock we heard the first cannon fired. A dense fog covered the whole country. The firing momentarily increased. The earth groaned. The prince was literally in a fever; the battle, the long desired battle! All the bodies of troops which we passed showed the utmost confidence, nay exuberant gayety. Our regiment was in the advanced guard, which had commenced the attack. We dashed onward. It was past noon, and the fog had lifted. We now perceived the enemy's forces on the heights of Valmy. A favorable position, and the numbers were, at least, one third larger than ours. But what an enemy! The confusion is said to have been boundless, when Hohenlohe attacked their left wing, that is, Kellermann, and Dumouriez was too far away on the right to aid him. The victory seemed to be in our grasp, and — we delayed our assault. We fired across and the enemy returned the fire, without any perceptible object or result. Forty thousand cannon balls are said to have been wasted in this cannonade.

"The prince foamed with rage, when on the opposite side of the road to St. Menehould, he met his regiment retreating. Curses and imprecations fell from his lips, and his face by turns flushed crimson and grew pale. He openly and loudly declared that Hohenlohe ought to defy the unfortunate order to retreat, and dashed madly down the hill to the position the troops had occupied in the morning. He believed that an attack from this side might even now be made with safety. He *can* have intended nothing more than to reconnoitre. The balls whistled around his head. I dashed after him, to stop the fatal act. Several officers belonging to the regiment followed me. When close at his heels, we saw him reel and fall from his horse. I caught him in my arms. Amid a hail of bullets we carried him to the farm of la Lune, the headquarters of our commander. He was shot through the heart; and in a few moments — a corpse.

"And this illustrious victim is the price of no victory, is not even the cost of the consciousness of satisfied honor.

The enemy is directly opposite to us to-day as well as yesterday. We do not advance to the assault, and even the artillery is silent. There are whispers of negotiations, of a retreat. Nothing is incredible to me after yesterday. But can, will a king of Prussia submit to this disgrace? The officers cry out against the Duke of Brunswick. The men who yesterday marched forth as proudly and firmly as if on parade, now pass each other with averted faces. I have seen them weep with rage and anger. 'If you were a Prussian like me,' said an old major, 'if you had served under Frederick's banners, you would envy your dead prince.' "

What more shall I say? Outwardly I remained unmoved, and without a word returned the letter to my father. He was sobbing like a child, and the tears rolled down his cheeks on his grey beard. My mother sat in silence for a long time with clasped hands. At last she arose.

"We all need time to regain our composure. Go to rest, my dear daughter," she said, kissing me on the forehead.

My father led me to the door, pressed my hands, and said: " God must know best, my dear child."

"God must know best." How often, in calmer hours, I have thought of those words, which seemed so commonplace, and yet are the only ones that can console us in incomprehensible dispensation. Would this pleasure-loving nature, destitute of support from without or within, have stood its ground during the twenty years of deterioration, which followed the sham fight of Valmy, to the deepest disgrace and verge of destruction? Would it have retained its strength for the act of expiation, or in what direction would it have rushed to ruin? God knew best, my dear father!

True, in *this* hour your consoling words were an empty sound, and I only heard that the *one* who had been the light of my eyes and the pride of my heart, was dead, lost to me forever. All firmness gave way, as soon as — at last alone — I reached the stairs. I sank down and the candle fell from my hand. There I lay, I know not how long; life seemed to me a night as impenetrable as that which surrounded me.

At last I hastily rose and groped my way to the door of my room. Just at that moment I saw a ray of light fall through a chink in the next chamber, and, fool that I had been, saw myself snatched from the grave to the active flood of life. I remembered one, whose light of life had been even more utterly extinguished than mine.

It was news of death her old friend had given her as a message of joy, and deadly seemed to be the blow that had so suddenly fallen upon her. She was lying cold and rigid on the floor, with Siegmund Faber's letter in her clenched hand. The long wick of the candle showed the length of time she had been in this unconscious condition, and I well knew the misery of the life to which I must rouse her.

A secret voice warned me not to call my parents or the servants to my assistance. I carried her to her bed, unfastened her clothing, and —

And what did the reserved girl of eighteen feel at the revelation she had not suspected, and yet understood with the speed of lightning? Pity, indignation, hatred? Did she cry out against the sinner? She was unconscious of any of these emotions, but even now she feels the thrill which ran through her frame at that moment, the thrill of re-awakening life after the piercing death shriek. No, he was not dead, not wholly dead; one memento of him still existed, and I envied, yes envied the happy woman who possessed a token of his love.

I opened the window, sprinkled the fainting girl with cologne, breathed into her mouth, felt her pulse in deadly anxiety, and could have screamed with delight when I felt the first feeble throb. At last she opened her eyes and looked around in bewilderment, as if awaking from a horrible dream. Then her eyes rested upon me, and a terrible cry announced the return of consciousness. She sprang from her bed like a maniac, and with uncovered bosom and dishevelled hair, writhed upon the floor. "Kill me, kill me, Hardine!" screamed the despairing woman.

But the hour of anguish passed away. A bright fire crackled in the stove, the lamp burned quietly on the table. Dorothee lay in her bed, the tears streamed down her pale cheeks, and from time to time a childish voice moaned: "Save me, save me, Fräulein Hardine!"

And the heavy lids closed; her chest rose and fell in calm, regular breathing; she was asleep. I, too, wanted to seek rest, but just at that moment I saw the letter which had fallen from her hand, and which I thought I had a right to read. My first glance fell on the following postscript:

"Yesterday an incident occurred, which moved me strangely, and will arouse the sympathy of the honored inmates of your house. Be cautious in telling them the news, dear Dorothee. I was with the outposts of our regiment, when I was hastily summoned by my distinguished commander. A noble relative of his, who had joined the troops only a quarter of an hour before as a volunteer, had been severely wounded in a hazardous reconnoitering expedition, and carried to a neighboring farm-house. I had seen the unfortunate event, and was already on the way to lend my aid. 'Thank God, here is Faber,' cried the duke. At the name the wounded man opened his already glazing eyes. Some hope of life probably awakened. 'Faber,' he faltered, 'Faber!' He groped for my hand, and with his last strength pressed it to his breast; a shudder ran through his frame, the death sweat stood on his brow. 'Mercy, Faber, mercy!' he murmured, and sank back in my arms — dead.

"How strangely I felt, as I loosened the uniform of my old regiment and in memory of home was doubly eager to help, where all help was vain. The prince was not wounded, as we had supposed, the bullet had merely grazed him, but a blood-vessel in the heart had been broken, either by the excitement, the mad ride, or the fall from the horse. I never saw a man of more superb physical beauty. On his heart I found a ribbon wrapped in a sheet of paper, which in well-known characters bore an honored name. I will not venture to draw any inferences. But with the utmost respect I place this relic, which, perhaps, will prove a consoling memento, in the hands of her friend, the only gift I have to offer you to-day, Dorothee."

And now I again wrapped the blue hair ribbon from the spring festival around my finger, looked at the piece of paper, which bore only the name "Hardine von Reckenburg," the signature torn from one of my few letters to Dorothee, and which had perhaps never been noticed by the person to whom on some occasion it was given. But was it not a singular coincidence that it should be Siegmund Faber who took the memento from the breast of the man who had destroyed the happiness of his life, and placed it in the hands of his faithless betrothed as the love-token of another?

Yet in that hour how could it have failed to touch me, that the name and handwriting of the friend he had called *his* sister, when with his last words he entrusted his beloved to her care, had rested on his dying heart? How in that hour could I have blamed myself that the dead friend's legacy appealed to me more strongly than my duty to the living?

I went to my room and, without undressing, threw myself upon the bed. Dorothee slept; I found no repose! The events of this evening mingled like tangible apparitions in my half confused mind with memories of that holiday when I had heard the old Countess von Reckenburg humming Aurora von Konigsmark's love song, and the terrible vision Siegmund Faber had revealed. I was dreaming with my eyes open, and it was probably a long time ere I distinguished between the phantoms of memory and the bodily form, which in the grey dawn was kneeling beside my bed with drooping head and arms folded across her breast like a criminal.

"Will you save me, Fräulein Hardine?" she whispered, after a long pause.

Another silence followed, and instead of an answer came the question: "What do you intend to do, Dorothee?"

"Do — I?" she replied, as she sadly shook her head. "I will do whatever you say, Fräulein Hardine."

"Not what I say, what Siegmund Faber says," I answered.

But she exclaimed with a shudder: "*He — he?* What have I to do with him now?" But she understood my reproachful glance, for she hastily added: "I will give him back his property and earn my bread by the labor of my hands."

In any other mood, looking at the dainty hands, I should have smiled at this resolution. In my present one I only said: "Then write to him this very day, Dorothee, confess the truth, and receive your fate from him."

She started up with an impetuosity I had never seen in her before. "Write to him, and this very day!" she exclaimed. "Tell him all, him — *him!* No, you will not ask that, only that one thing, Fräulein Hardine, I cannot do it."

"Well then, *I* will do it for you," I replied.

"Would a letter reach him, Fräulein Hardine?" she answered. "Ten days have passed since he wrote, an equally long time must elapse; and will he then be alive? And where? And how?"

She was right. Where was the army at this time? Had it moved forward into the enemy's country? Backward to the Rhine? It would be a marvel if a letter reached its destination in such uncertain times.

And dared I venture to expose such a secret to the risk of discovery by strangers? No. We must wait for further news *of* or *from* Faber.

"Very well, Dorothee," I said after a pause, taking her hand, "if not to him at once, show the world plainly that your engagement is broken. Return to your father's house, accept the humiliation as an atonement for your sin; set duty against duty —"

It was like a death sentence. A feverish shudder shook her frame and she again fell upon her knees.

"*Must* it be?" she murmured in an almost inaudible tone.

"Yes, it must be, Dorothee?"

"Now, at once, *before* the time? Oh! Fräulein Hardine, I feel that I shall die then. Ah! I shall be so glad to die. Spare my old father; do not let him go down to his grave in shame."

She probably noticed that the appeal to my compassion for the drunken old imbecile produced very little effect upon me, for she hastily continued in a trembling voice: "And he — he of whom I cannot speak, must his name be caluminated in the *same* breath with that of the outcast creature? And in the hour when tears are still flowing for him, when his poor body has not yet found repose with his fathers?"

This child, Dorothee, was an enchantress, or how should she always know how to produce an effect at the right moment! No, the secret was not to be kept by *halves*, and the accusation against the seducer must not be permitted to mingle with the death wail for our hero. Before my parents, who had loved him, the comrades who admired him, nay, even before Dorothee's little-valued fellow citizens, the last of his race must rest in his ancestral tomb with no stain on his character.

"So be it then, Dorothee, I will keep and guard your secret till Siegmund Faber has decided your future fate."

The agitating conversation closed with this promise. Difficult as was the decision, the plan was quickly formed and easily executed. Dorothee accompanied me to Reckenburg; everything else was revealed in Nurse Justine's lonely house. The tavern-keeper had no voice in the matter; my parents did not grudge the two sorrowful playmates the consolation of each other's society. Scarcely a week later they found themselves on the way to Reckenburg under the care of the pastor.

Dorothee was no stranger to my old friend; I had often told him of my bewitching schoolmate. Now I introduced her to him as a visitor to Nurse Justine, and thereby escaped an actual lie. In fact, if lying or deceiving is *only* to *say* what is untrue, and not also to conceal the truth, I need not be blamed throughout this whole affair. To be sure, the sorrowful woman who leaned timidly back in the corner of the carriage, weeping silently, by no means agreed with the picture I had drawn of my bright, active little Dörl. The pastor's eyes rested compassionately on the pale, haggard face. Yes, he suspected the truth, but the good man was one of those who hold out their hands to penitent sinners.

How often I had impatiently turned away from our

pastor's mild lessons and practice towards a disorderly parish. I remembered in particular one sermon about the adulterous woman, whose text and interpretation I repeated to the old countess at dinner. "The pastor might avoid such doubtful subjects but how do they concern *us*?" she replied, and I assented — even to the conclusion. This was on the Sunday before my departure, and to-day I myself brought a woman forgetful of right and honor into his parish as my *protégé;* I, who had thought my life so securely founded on the motto of my house.

Let no one depend upon a maxim if, like Fräulein Hardine, he does not wish some day to sit with cheeks flushed with shame. *This*, my friends, is the moral of the rose and its leaf.

CHAPTER VII.

NURSE JUSTINE'S FOSTER-CHILD.

At the station Dorothee remained behind, and the pastor and myself rolled in the gilt coach towards the goal of our journey. The countess was asleep when I reached the castle. An accident, which I guessed only too well, had taxed her strength more severely than usual.

It was Nurse Justine who gave me this information, so the matter which lay nearest my heart could be settled at once. Her silence and assent were certain, because it was I who asked. Besides the affair brought money, and the humiliating dependence of "Miss Upstart" gratification. Grave moral scruples of course were out of the question in a woman of *her* profession.

We therefore came to an agreement without haggling.

The next day the nurse brought her charge from the city, took her to board with her, and agreed if any one asked questions — which was very improbable, as "peasants are not curious like people in cities" — to say that she was a relative, who had lately become a widow. Moreover she undertook to explain everything to the pastor; who must be told the truth. That our arrangement was punctiliously executed and attended with the best success may be taken for granted.

It was not without emotion, that I now went to meet the countess. *I*, the young girl, had only lost a dream, a fleeting happiness, which I had first known since our parting. *She*, the aged woman, had seen the structure of a long life crumble into ruins. I must be prepared for a serious effect.

But what I was to perceive was the desolation of a burning flame, and God knows amid what tortures I strove for years against its consuming fire. Even at this first meeting, I found the aged form more bent — the movements more feeble, the speech more abrupt; the only trace of life was in the cold, steely glance of avarice. The mistress was dead, and the maid, who had early been formed in her service, the only ruler in the deserted house.

Now, that is since the hour when the death message from Valmy had reached her, she was and daily became more and more "the black countess," into which the imagination of the people during twenty-five years had transformed the lonely woman. Now she resembled the legendary demons, who watch and guard metals solely for the sake of their brilliancy; who grieve over the copper coins that must be sacrificed for their most pressing needs. I tell you, I have battled like a Hercules for the preservation of the most necessary things, and after all it was only the habit of eighty years, which mechanically and methodically kept up the motive power of the machinery.

The correspondence with Dresden ceased; the only

holiday at Reckenburg was omitted, and the name of the chosen and lost heir never crossed her lips. She no longer thought of dying and bequeathing her property. Did any will exist, dated at some earlier day, and in whose favor? No one knew. But the testator would not have made a stroke of the pen to recall or change it. *One* person was the same to her as another; she knew no duties. She wanted to *live*, only live. Eternity would not have seemed too long to her, *alone*, with her sparkling treasure. But if one day it came to an end, and the earth under her gold tower had then opened and swallowed her up with it; it would have been to her the most welcome death.

Fourteen years, the last of my youth, passed in dependence upon this mummy with but *one* surviving sense; and certainly not without leaving lasting traces. Probably the qualities we call womanly were originally but feebly developed in my nature; but the hours in the gold tower of Reckenburg, though but a few each day and filled with work, destroyed the last capacity, the faintest desire for a home life, such as had made the modest ground floor in the barber's house so cheerful. The influence of those hours has made the western tower of Reckenburg also a hermitage, and if, in spite of them, I have executed the fundamental bias of my nature, I owe it to the sphere of labor under God's free sky, which remained open to me.

You are still too young, my friends, thank God, too happy in yourselves, to understand how such a sphere of labor can become a world and a fate. But induce any old peasant to talk freely, and you will be amazed at the events he has experienced on his patch of land.

But in a creation like that of Reckenburg, accomplished by so much toil, increased to such an extent, so productive now, so rich in promise for the future ; every foundling of the fields becomes a medium of improvement, the smallest crop a living thing. We see the harvest in the sprouting blades, and the soil for new seeds in the dying stubble. We grieve for every tree that falls under the axe, and rejoice in each young germ ; we introduce new colonists into the narrow circle that has sprung from our clods, our knowledge increases, experience becomes more varied with each form and color.

And how we make friends with the animals ; how we inquire into their instincts, customs, and laws, learn to improve them and make them more and more valuable. Watch your herds day after day in their pastures, and you will distinguish in each individual sheep or cow a face and a destiny.

Last of all come the human inhabitants of this secluded little world. It is no Paradise, my friends. The stranger passes the stupid, degenerate beings with more indifference than the grazing herds, prizes them less than the deer in the forest with their unimpaired beauty and unbroken instinct. But step by step disgust and weariness disappear, and interest awakens. The stolid faces we meet every hour, and whose toilsome labor we follow from the cradle to the grave become familiar. We shake the rough hand that labors with us in the transformation of our home, pass from general to individual life, seek for traces of the divine image in our co-laborers, strive to make it known to them and raise them higher in the scale of beings who recognize and acknowledge a Creator.

Such a little world was subordinate to *me*, to *me* first, me *alone*. I had to protect it from the ruin to which a mad passion exposed it; preserve it for a future, no matter whether this future benefitted me or a stranger; and the more difficult was the struggle for the means, the more deeply rooted became the affection, the more obstinate the resistance. This unselfish love gives me more right to gratitude than the free, productive efficiency of after years.

In this field of labor, I endured more easily than I should have expected after the sorrowful episode of the autumn, the fatal winter of '93 with its biting insults. When the news of the 21st of January brought terror into our quiet corner of the country, I thought my young hero happy to have died in the last hour of hope, while his comrades returned as if from a fool's errand, and were forced to see the royal martyr, for whose rescue they had undertaken the crusade, perish under the axe of the executioner.

Dorothee, too, had lived as peacefully as was possible in her situation. The autumn brought bright days, which tempted her into the open air; her wounds closed in the quiet of the country; the disgrace did not oppress her, since she met no one who could have reproached her with it, and of the *sin* — if she had ever felt it a sin at all — she was the less reminded, as this year Siegmund Faber's usual Christmas letter was omitted.

If in my walks through the forest, which even in winter was full of life, I entered Nurse Justine's lonely house, I found Dorothee busily engaged on some dainty sewing, such as would be needed by the new comer. The maternal instinct awoke, she toyed with the little garments as she had formerly held up her dolls to my admiring eyes. "How charming it will be!" she would exclaim, turning a tiny cap embroidered with beads around her fingers, "when there is an angelic little head in it! Ah! how glad I am! I have always been so fond of children, Fräulein Hardine."

On one of the first days in spring, in emulation of the little storks and thrushes, I found the new mortal in the nurse's house. Too soon, as the experienced Justine said, although the little man was very sturdy and the young mother felt as bright and well as a fish in water. Tears of joy fell upon the child in her lap. "So beautiful, so beautiful!" she exclaimed in delight. "Ah! how I love it, how happy I am, Fräulein Hardine! I could never, never leave the little angel." At which rapture the worthy Justine made a wry face and whispered to me as I left the room: "It would be the first wild stock that enjoyed any lasting love! Children not born in wedlock vanish like chaff!"

But under the rubric "too soon," she managed, lest the child should die, to arrange a hasty baptism on the following day, at which she and I became sponsors. The boy received his father's name of Augustus, and was legally entered in the church register under that of his mother's family by the pastor. No one would have easily sought and found the name in the annals of our disorderly little village. But when, a few years later, the lightning destroyed the church books in the vestry, there was still one document left attesting Augustus Müller's birth, and you will find it fastened among these leaves in another part of the volume.

So long as Dorothee kept her room and bed and saw her boy lying beside her, she had no wish except to remain in Reckenburg as long as possible and afterwards live somewhere with him. "What do I care about other people?" she answered smiling, in reply to Nurse Justine's objections; "I shall have my child!" But the old woman muttered: "Nonsense about the child. She's still a child herself! She needs a husband and not a child!"

I secretly and openly scolded my faithful old nurse, especially when, even after Dorothee's restoration to health, she took the exclusive charge of the boy and made no concealment of her reasons for doing so. True, it is possible that the "half-shorn lamb, Dorte," proved too delicate for the care of the strong boy, and very probable that the presence of one who had never been a favorite at last became burdensome to the old woman. At any rate it was certain that the implacable low diamond was playing its pranks again. She certainly did not suspect that, during the previous summer, the wisdom of the oracle had proved true. It was still watching, and was doubly threatening under the cap of the shameless girl, whose patroness her young lady had become, and she did not rest until she saw the dangerous person leave the town, which, since she had herself settled in it, she considered Fräulein Hardine's real home.

But I clearly saw that when Dorothee found herself obliged to commit her child to a goat for food and the care of him to a despotic will, while herself confined to the lonely house under the contemptuous treatment of her hostess, her heart secretly began to long for the freedom and comfort of her own home. She grew weary and restless. "What is to become of me?" she sighed, "I am very unhappy, Fräulein Hardine!"

This year I had allowed the usual time of my return home to pass, as the countess' mood and the increasing labor brought by the spring made it necessary to have a constant intercourse between the tower and fields. But between seed time and harvest I intended to spend a few weeks at home, and had decided to travel there by post. I, too, was just eighteen, but since the experiences of the previous summer I felt independent enough to boldly undertake a journey round the world without companionship.

Early in May, however, I was called home by an exciting incident. My father's regiment belonged to the contingent the Elector had furnished for the war against France; but my father himself had remained at the depot, and we all, though certainly no cowards, heartily rejoiced at it. What could be expected of this campaign after the events of last autumn? Who could still hope to be in time to save the unhappy queen and her children, after the allies had quietly suffered the king to be murdered? We would, with pious joy, have seen those dearest to us sacrificed for the imperiled throne and king of a foreign country; I say *we*, my friends, and mean not only us women, but with the single exception of the pastor, all the men, the brave, daring men of our circle; yet how much trouble did it cause us that German rights were derided, German soil on this and the other side of the Rhine was laid under contribution, ravaged, and seized? Not until twenty years later, after a wonderful revolution in feeling, did we learn to know the value of our native soil beyond our own province, and thereby, not through the oppression of a conqueror, who would sooner or later have fallen a victim to his own despotic madness, but in consequence of this very appreciation, the wars for freedom first became a great and permanent blessing to our nation. With this indifference towards the object of the campaign, I felt it as a terrible misfortune when my father was suddenly removed from the peaceful service he had performed for thirty years, and after being promoted to the rank of major, ordered to the army before Mayence.

As soon as I received this news, I prepared to leave Reckenburg the following morning, and had only a few minutes in which to take leave of the inmates of Nurse Justine's house. In spite of my agitation, I painfully felt the necessity of representing at home that Dorothee had been left behind sick, and in this way being compelled to utter the first actual falsehood I had ever told in my life.

It was to be spared me, for to my inexpressible astonishment, on reaching the post-house the next morning, I found my *protége*, prepared for the journey, waiting for me, but without her child. "I could not rest, I must kiss your dear father's hand before he goes. He has been such a dear, kind father to me also from my earliest childhood, Fräulein Hardine!" she sobbed, and then added hastily with downcast eyes: "The child is well cared for; Nurse Justine understands such things far better than I, Fräulein Hardine, and in the autumn you can bring me back again."

I turned away with unconcealed indignation; for I perceived the secret joy with which she seized any pretext for deserting her post. She feared a longer absence from home, which might betray her secret, longed for her household ease, and gave up her new-born child to a stranger, while excusing herself to her own heart on the plea of gratitude towards a man bound to her by no ties of blood. I vouchsafed no reply, and we scarcely exchanged twenty words during the whole journey. She sighed and trembled as she had done on the way to Reckenburg, but it did not move me; she looked pale and her eyes were swollen with crying; for the first and only time in my life I thought her ugly. The offence against duty and honor had not estranged me from her; the weakness of her heart divided our lives. True, in after days I could not wholly escape from her influence, when I beheld her wonderful beauty; but while away I thought of her with as much contempt as did Nurse Justine. I was no longer her friend; the last tie formed in childhood was sundered, and I was scarcely eighteen years old.

The parting from my father was harder than I had anticipated. The terrible memories of the retreat, which had taken place the previous autumn and whose details I first heard at home, made us fear that we should never see each other again. My poor mother almost succumbed to the effort of conducting herself as a soldier's wife. She smiled at the consolation of honest Purzel — the last Purzel in the Reckenburg service — "Keep up your courage, my lady, I'll attend to everything. Nothing will happen to him; and if anything *does*, I'll come and tell you at once." She smiled and provided everything that could be useful to a sick or wounded man, but her delicate constitution never recovered from the sorrows and anxieties of the years of separation.

The evening before the departure of the troops I went to Dorothee, who had nestled comfortably down again in her little room, and began without any circumlocution: "I see you will never summon up courage to make a voluntary confession, Dorothee, so let me tell my father your secret. The Saxon army will join the Prussian forces before Mayence. Siegmund Faber can easily be found, and my father will be the most reliable mediator and best advocate for you."

She started as if a thunderbolt had fallen, and it was long ere she was mistress of the childish persuasions, with which she had already once defeated my convictions of right. "Oh! don't do that, Fräulein Hardine!" she exclaimed fairly beside herself. "For God's sake, don't. Let the whole world, let my own father know me as an abandoned, dishonored creature, but not that good, unsuspicious gentleman!

And would he, will he be able to conceal it from your mother? How should I appear before her and continue to live under the *same* roof? She is so strict, so proud! Besides you, too, would have to suffer, Fräulein Hardine! And when one person knows the secret, it will go like wild fire. I have deserved nothing else, I must submit. But I could not bear to see you, who have been an angel to me, also censured, blamed by your own dear parents. And why must all this be?" she continued after a pause, during which I had been reflecting upon this unexpected obstacle.

My father, as I knew, would really scarcely have been able to keep a *first* secret from his wife over night and certainly not after the first letter. Should I add this new trial to my poor mother's sorrow? The friendly relation with the owner of the house would be destroyed, her confidence in the frankness and honesty of her only daughter completely shaken. Even my more indulgent father would be unable to resist my mother's views and part with a troubled heart from his undutiful child, perhaps for life.

"And what is the use of disturbing us all?" continued Dorothee, encouraged by my evident emotion. "Is he still alive? He has not written all winter."

"Letters rarely reach their destination in such times," I replied; "but we should have received the news of his death."

"And even if he lives," replied Dorothee, "in what distant hospital or new position is he to be found? The country occupied by the troops is so extensive; God knows whether your father will ever meet him. But if he does and I know a place to which I can send my letter, I will confess all; yes, Fräulein Hardine, I promise you to confess all to him and do as he says. Only do not let any one else interpose between us."

So Fräulein Hardine was again conquered by little Dörl. My father went away *without* hearing our secret. Nay, fearing that it might be discovered, I only ventured to timidly request that he would inquire about Faber and tell us all the particulars concerning him.

Tears filled the good man's eyes, as he tried to utter some jesting words at parting. "Tell dear little Dörl, Dine, that I will make all due inquiries about her Mosjö Per-sé."

And in fact the first letter from the encampment before Castel, where the Saxons had joined a portion of the Prussian troops, contained a full account of the man of whom we had heard no tidings since the battle of Valmy. He had fortunately survived all the dangers of attending the sick during an epidemic and, promoted to the rank of surgeon-major, was now attached to the corps of besiegers. The fame of his indefatigableness, fearlessness, and great skill had spread throughout the whole camp; all praised the young man's zeal in his profession. The former inmates of the barber's house soon met, and the state of affairs at home were eagerly discussed. Had not the model betrothed's ears burned a little?

"You must on no account," my father wrote in conclusion, "imagine Dr. Faber as the stiff army surgeon's assistant, who always looked as if he had just stepped out of a bandbox, in order to let no one suspect that he had descended from a barber. He is as easy as any one, now that generals and princes, as well as common soldiers, are obliged to keep still under his knives and pincers. He has also become more agreeable and open hearted, but still remains the old Per-sé who sets about everything differently from other people, and yet on close examination is *always right*. When I pointed out the risk he incurred, by so rarely reminding his young, lonely betrothed of the relation to which she had consented, he assured me, it is true, that he had sent his regular letter at Christmas, and since he said so, it must have been lost. 'Yet'— he added —'what is the use of this unnecessary labor?'"

Just at that moment he was summoned to attend a consultation about the case of a general who was seriously ill on the left bank of the river. I had begged him to look after two of our hussars who had been wounded in a skirmish between the outposts, and the following day received a letter containing most satisfactory news. In conclusion he recurred to the subject in whose discussion we had been interrupted the day before, and for the benefit of my dear ' Fräulein Original-text' I will cut that portion from his letter and enclose it in mine."

"In regard to the risk, as you rightly call it, Herr Major, no warning words will avert the danger. And relief from anxiety—who can obtain it at the distance of hundreds of miles? Before a letter reaches its destination, the scene changes, and he over whose safety friends are rejoicing, is perhaps mouldering in the grave. In both cases the only comfort is confidence in a lucky star, or complete resignation. Letters are for idlers or moderate workers. Shall I entertain my dear child with military evolutions and diplomatic strategems, or make her flesh creep with my repulsive medical experiences? And vows, protestations of love! Is it not the most superlative folly, to send the most secret, unutterable emotions of the human heart, transformed in commonplaces and written in black and white, travelling about the world? How constrained my little Dorothee's scrawls are! How I can count the hours she has gnawed her pen! Where are her flowers and birds, her childish amusements? Where is any trace to be found of what really lives in and around her? I value the little pouches and bags she has knit. I use them hourly, and whenever I see them I also see the nimble little fingers engaged in their preparation. These are acts, womanly acts of love, Herr Major, and as I cannot requite them with similar ones, I do well not to boast of my affectionate loyalty.

"You assure *me* of the dear child's quiet patience, my honored friend, and I cannot tell you how happy it makes me to see my school boy experiment thus justified, an experiment which in later years I should not have tried. I felt that I was a *man* and saw in her the *child*, the one perhaps too *soon*, and the other possibly too *long*. But on the whole I judged according to nature and reason. For from whom, I ask, could such abstemiousness have been expected, except from the *man*, who is accustomed to stand sentry over himself, or the *child*, who slumbers dreamlessly in her peaceful little nest, until roused by him who is appointed to awake her. Well, Herr Major, the *man* will be constant. The state of affairs which I foresaw when I made this engagement, has already lasted two years, and Heaven knows when and where the confusion will end. But if I survive it, I shall take my father's wedding ring into her presence unprofaned, and if I see my mother's on her hand, shall bless the boyish faith that endured while many a man's was violated."

This experimental resignation, which my unsuspicious mother did not withhold, was grist to the mill of the sinner who so eagerly avoided making a confession. The singular man certainly requested no explanation, and until he came to obtain it in person — if he ever came at all — why could not everything remain unchanged! I was weary of explaining the incongruity to the empty air. If *she* was not ashamed to pass for the betrothed bride of the man she had betrayed, if *she* did not shrink from making her own life and that of another's child more comfortable with his property, why should I feel ashamed and shrink from it? Was she my sister, my equal? Folly of follies, to expect noble sentiments from the inn-keeper's wanton daughter. If Siegmund Faber returned, it would be incumbent upon me to exculpate *myself*, not *her*, to a man of honor.

As an excuse for Dorothee, and in order to have done with her philosophical lover, it must however be stated, that a later letter announced the mysterious disappearance of Doctor Faber. During an attack on the hostile camp at Pirmasenz in the latter part of September, he had won still greater admiration by his bold, untiring activity — but since then had vanished from all eyes. At first it was supposed that he had been transferred to the Polish province which had recently been so shamefully obtained, among the followers of the king, who had learned to feel a strong personal esteem for him; but as this opinion proved to be a mistaken one, some thought he had been wounded and fallen into the enemy's hands, others that he had been captured by the infuriated peasants. The majority believed him dead, though his body could not be found by the victors, who retained possession of the field. All, however, regretted the void made by the disappearance of the ever active surgeon. Even when, at the end of three years, my father returned safe and with a new order as a reward for his services, but sorrowful like all who took part in the fruitless campaign, he could give no tidings of the vanished man. He was soon forgotten by his fellow citizens, and no one would have blamed his betrothed bride, if she had wished to give her lovely self and the old barber's house to another.

I had not been willing to leave my mother during the anxious years of the campaign, and only at the pressing entreaties of both parents made up my mind to return to Reckenburg. "In your father's exposed situation and our poverty," said my mother, "the countess is your and my last hope. Do not trifle with it, my dear daughter. You can be of use *there*, but can do nothing for *me*. I am not sick, and if anything happens, have I not the dear child, Dorothee?"

The dear child, Dorothee! To imagine *her*, with her affectionate, somewhat bustling manner, beside a sick bed — really nothing more consoling could occur to me, as she no longer seriously thought of returning to the lonely forest house, and her father's severe illness enabled her to deceive herself about the nearer duty. "Keep an eye on my darling, Fräulein Hardine," she whispered as I bade her farewell; "I will help and serve your mother in your place."

So we parted, and when towards Christmas the first news of Faber's disappearance was received, I had already been a long time at my post at Reckenburg, and Dorothee — to my secret satisfaction — remained quietly at home in her room. There I found her, when the following year — though only for a few weeks in summer — I returned home, apparently unchanged, working industriously to enlarge her income by means of dainty embroideries, that her boy might lack no care, no finery. When in the evening she laid aside caps or spangled slippers, she drew baby faces or cut them out of black paper as silhouettes, laid them between the leaves of her hymn book and kissed them as likenesses of her beautiful boy. She made him little petticoats and dresses, wove flowers out of the light curls which I was obliged to cut from his head for her every year, twined around them a golden thread of her own hair, as well as one or two of another's, drawn from a beloved memento, and called them her sun-flowers. She embraced every child she saw, rejoiced and wept when she thought of her own; but she did not see Nurse Justine's nursling again. Even when her father died, when mine had also gone to his last home, and she was perfectly independent, she did not think that it was *she*, and not a stranger, who ought to take charge of her child.

But I could not awaken her conscience by the power of this duty. For a human being's growth, like that of a tree — as I gradually understood — may increase in width and at all events in height; but its roots cannot dig deeper to reach the nourishing spring. We must cherish or avoid each other, as nature has planted us. For the rest, I told myself that the fatherless boy would develop better under the stranger's rough hand than his mother's caressing one. And lastly, did *I* not keep an eye upon him?

As when a child I had never played with dolls, so in after years I was not what people call fond of children. But I became warmly attached to this boy. When on my walks through the village I saw the shy, dull, flaxen haired peasant children squatting on their dung heaps among the pigs and chickens, and on reaching the forest the supple little figure in its dainty dress sprang forward to meet me, I laughed aloud with delight, but sadly asked myself if his father, whom my little prince so strongly resembled, would not have accomodated himself to the usual fetters of life, if he had been responsible for the guidance of this dear child?

How early and firmly he learned to use his little feet, how boldly he frolicked in the forest, vied with hares in running, and imitated the notes of the birds long before he could speak our human language! With what a defiant laugh he copied the squirrel, climbed to the top of the gnarled ash tree, while old Nurse Justine, in mortal terror, stood at the foot shaking her clinched hand at him! So nature early became a teacher of the child of nature; but the necessity of subjecting him to a sterner discipline and the authority of a masculine will soon manifested itself. When the boy was in his fifth year, Nurse Justine declared that she could not and would not manage him after the next winter.

For there was nothing more curious, and to me nothing more annoying, than the discord in the old nurse's soul about her foster child! She liked the merry little fellow, nay was very fond of him; but as soon as she saw him approach me, such an angry mood came over her that, if there had been bears and wolves in our forest, she would have driven him out among them. "Nothing good will come to you through the 'wild stock'," she was never weary of repeating. The adage so current in the country about the soiling pitch and the spirit whose warning voice speaks mysteriously from the cards harmonized in this admonition. And, faithful old Justine, could you foresee that, forty years after, the question whether any good would come to your young lady through the wild-shoot, would form the concluding reflection of her life?

No persuasions were of any avail, the boy must go, leave Reckenburg; and another consideration gave this resolution weight with me. Our faithful friend, the pastor, had left us a short time before to accept, as principal of the Laurentius cloister, a position more in accordance with his fatherly warmth of feeling. During the vacation the pulpit was filled by the various clergymen in the neighborhood, who troubled themselves very little about the affairs of the village. But when, during the summer, the newly chosen pastor became familiar with the place, the singular circumstances connected with our *protégé* could not fail to attract his attention. If the pastor asked questions, the truth could not be concealed; one person more would know Dorothee's carefully guarded secret; curious investigations, feminine gossip, or some unaccountable accident might lead people into the right track, and the always interesting connection of events escape from our secluded nook into the mouths of the world.

All this I impressed upon Dorothee's mind, as soon as I returned to my parents' house to spend a few weeks in the autumn. I found her in a very thoughtful mood, already prepared for what I had to say by the pastor, under which name his reverence, now provost and head, is here mentioned in these pages for the last time.

Never since her misfortune had Dorothee mingled with young people, never by word or glance encouraged the attentions of the citizens' sons, when she chanced to meet them, and thus she kept at a distance the suitors of whom there would have been no lack. But she had also never mentioned to me the name of the only man she had ever loved. Yet whenever I surprised her alone, I perceived by her manner, by the dreamy or longing expression of her eyes, that the short summer rapture of happiness had not died away.

"Yet ever, wheresoe'er she turned, she saw the face of one,
 To whom, in days of childhood, her trusting heart had flown."

I was, therefore, the more surprised, when in reply to my question about what she had decided in regard to her son's future, she answered with downcast eyes: "Suppose I should marry Christlieb Taube, Fräulein Hardine?"

"Our tutor? Has he offered himself to you?"

"He has loved me ever since my childhood, and told me so a few days ago."

"And you?"

She shook back her curls with an indescribable expression of sorrow and proud remembrance.

"Love? I?" she exclaimed with a shudder. "Oh! never, never again! But," she added calmly after a pause, "but I could live peacefully with him, and he would be a good father to my boy."

"So you intended to confess your secret to him, Dorothee?"

"Why should I not, Fräulein Hardine? I should only marry him to provide for the child. Only for the child's sake."

"Will you confess it to him before he has become your husband?"

"If you think it my duty, before."

"And do you suppose that he will *still* marry you?"

"I think so, Fräulein Hardine."

I paused a moment. Dorothee was sitting opposite to me, with her hands clasped on her breast. My eyes involuntarily rested upon the betrothal ring, which she still wore on her finger. She noticed the glance and said blushingly, as she vainly endeavored to draw it off. "It has grown into my flesh."

It was eight years since Siegmund Faber had gone away, five years since he had disappeared without leaving any trace; no one doubted his death. But if he were alive — and a secret voice ever whispered "he lives!" — if he were alive and returned; *this* man could never become *this* woman's husband. But what milder disappointment could be found for him, than to see the long period of betrothal at last come to an end in a manner so natural. I therefore knew of no objection to make, if a man could really be found who did not see his own honor sullied by the dishonor of his wife.

But we decided to lay the whole case before our faithful counsellor, and went to the cloister.

"I do not deny your right to consider yourself free, my child," said the provost, "and for my own part I should not blame the man, who forgave the woman he loved a single error and, uniting himself to her, strove to turn its effect upon others into blessing. But I have reason to believe that our consistory does not share this opinion. The boy's presence would of course betray your secret, your husband would be compelled to give up his place as a teacher, the only one for which he has been educated and fitted."

"We should live quietly in the country, and — I am not without property," faltered Dorothee, her cheeks crimson with shame.

"Sufficient for yourself, and at all events for your child. But is it enough for a second, perhaps numerous family? And suppose, although the case is very improbable, that Siegmund Faber should return; he would not take back his gift, and he ought not to do so. But must it not crush a nature like that of our Taube's, to the very earth, to see the support of himself and family dependent upon the betrothal gift of the man who has been deceived? Moreover — to say nothing of these two possible cases — do you know what the life of a country teacher is, my dear Dorothee?"

This conversation took place on the way back from the cloister; but unnoticed by us our companion had turned aside into a path which led through a neighboring village, and as the last words were uttered he paused before a little house, whose purpose was announced by a multisonous, hesitating chorus, chiming in with the thundering tones of the teacher. A schoolhouse, and by no means the humblest of its kind, for the injuries sustained in the Seven Years war had been repaired, and it now stood unscathed.

Notwithstanding this, we could not deny that the sitting-room, into which we cast a glance in passing, was somewhat dull and bare for an idyllic life. Little Dörl could have touched the ceiling with her hand. The window panes looked like square slates, which had become tarnished by constant use in school, and the beets boiling on the stove for the cow sent forth an odor by no means refreshing. We continued our tour of inspection and lingered to scan the dull little human flock and their faithful bald-headed shepherd.

Unquestionably a teacher's life *has* its poetry. But it would have been no disadvantage in our eyes, if a little of the chubbiness of the children's cheeks could have been transferred to their master's; nor should we have considered it culpable vanity for him to exchange his coat, which had once been cotton velvet, for some other garment. To make amends, however, we paid the tribute of our sincere admiration to the progress in the art of mosaic work, visible in the family wash hung over the garden fence.

This work of art probably tempted our guide to enable us — after having made the acquaintance of the ruler of the *school* — to see the mistress of the *house*, surrounded by her private flock. Once more a chorus of voices tempted us across the court yard to a field, which bore the proud name of "garden." Here stood the heroine of our idyl. A classic figure, with a huge apron, her step untrammelled by shoes, her bushy hair unornamented by any art. The intruders did not disturb her in her business. With wonderful strength she quietly dug potatoes, which a party of young children picked up. The uprooted weeds were given as dainties to the goats and kids, which showed their delight by merry gambols. The small bipeds applauded the quadrupeds, the work stopped, and the pioneer displayed the power of her lungs and limbs in setting it in motion again.

But a tragic interlude now occurred in the rural scene. The oldest daughter, the family nurse, who was not yet trained to be as stoical as her mother, stood leaning against the gate of the courtyard. In staring at the strangers, the baby slipped from her arms and fell — fortunately into the mire before the pig sty. With upraised hands the mother darted forward to rescue and avenge it; the eldest daughter screamed, the infant shrieked, the sows grunted, the goats bleated, and the cow lowed in the stable. The boys quarreled over the prize of a yellow turnip ; the heroic mother dealt blows right and left; alarmed by the danger that threatened those dearest to him, the haggard teacher in his whilom cotton velvet coat appeared surrounded by his noisy flock ; but we who had caused the storm glided noiselessly away across the meadow.

"A worthy woman ! Exactly suited for her position !" said our friend, who was well versed in human nature, with a smile after a long pause. Dorothee walked silently onward with drooping head — and henceforth there was nothing said about marrying Christlieb Taube.

My approaching departure at last made it necessary to come to some decision about the boy's future, and the provost proposed that he should be placed in the cloister of which he was principal. Although it was originally intended only for soldiers' orphans, he hoped that an exception might be made in the child's favor if, when the trustees visited the institution a part of the secret, his descent on the *father's* side, was judiciously intimated.

Dorothee wept for joy at the prospect of soon having her boy under the care of this kind protector, and in her own neighborhood, without being forced to expose herself to a disgraceful disclosure. She covered her benefactor's hands with tears and kisses, implored God to bless him, and placed at his disposal the whole of the income she received from her house to defray the child's expenses as a half pensioner.

My soul, on the contrary, rebelled at the idea of seeing the prince's child who ought to have inherited the estate of Reckenburg, smuggled into a charitable institution and educated for a subordinate position in life. But what better plan had I to propose? The cloister bore an excellent reputation, like the majority of our Saxon abbeys which had been transformed into schools, was well endowed, and under the admirable care of the only man who felt a fatherly interest in the boy. Must I not, in this change of circumstances, respect the dispensation of a higher power?

So I set out on my return to Reckenburg, with the promise, that the following spring I would myself take Nurse Justine's foster-child to the orphan institution.

CHAPTER IX.

THE WEDDING.

NURSE Justine was violently opposed to the boy's concealment in the orphan asylum, as well as my plan of taking him there in person. She suddenly felt an unconquerable desire to see her own home again, and what reason could I have had for declining her companionship on the journey?

The day of our arrival had already been announced to my parents, when a violent attack of the countess' caused a delay. Her strong constitution triumphed, as had often happened before and frequently occurred after. But the faithful nurse was obliged to remain to guard the endangered post with the armor of her instruments, while her young lady, twelve miles away, was exposed without assistance to the malice of the incorrigible low diamond. She managed, however, to deprive the little plebeian of the honor of being conveyed the first stage of his journey in the Reckenburg coach, by dragging him to the station in a little hand-cart, after having, as I strongly suspect given him a sleeping potion. Her last words, as she lifted the child into the one-horse chaise beside me, were a warning not to go into his asylum on any account.

How the little hobgoblin raged when he awoke in the narrow box, you will learn from Augustus Müller's recollections. Moreover, I cannot contradict his assertions in regard to the means used to tame him. At all events, he chose the most comfortable arrangement for us both, by sleeping nearly all the tiresome journey.

The last letter of his future foster father was dated from a little mountain village in Thuringia, where he had been present at his son's installation into his first parish and, at the same time, had the pleasure of procuring the disappointed lover, Christlieb Taube, a better position. The situation of teacher and organist in a small, orderly parish, with a little house and garden comfortably fitted up by the owner of the estate, and the instruction of this owner's children in the "divine art of music," all this in a romantic mountain and woodland solitude; what fairer fate could he have desired for himself, or we for him?

As I wished the provost to enjoy the rare pleasure of a journey as long as possible, I had addressed the letter containing the news of the delay in our arrival to Jena, *poste restante;* and was surprised to find him at the hotel in Leipsic, the "Golden Lute," where I usually spent the night. I smilingly asked what other installation had brought him so hastily in the opposite direction?

"The installation of this boy into his new home," he answered gravely, as he laid the sleeping child on the bed in my room.

I perceived symptoms of Nurse Justine's feelings in the reverend gentleman, and therefore answered in a tone of vexation, that I could have taken the little monk to the Laurentius cloister in safety without any trouble on his part.

He was silent, but a shade of restless anxiety in the manner of one usually so composed did not escape my notice, and when, in answer to my inquiry whether he had anything on his mind, he shook his head with a sigh, I exclaimed: "Pray don't attempt to prepare me for bad news, my friend, my parents —"

"Are well and happy in the expectation of their beloved daughter's visit," he replied.

"And Dorothee?" I continued, as I noticed the sorrowful glance that rested on the boy. "Is Dorothee ill?"

"Not ill, only —"

"Only?"

"Married, or the same as married."

"So she has accepted Christlieb Taube?"

"Not Christlieb Taube, but —"

"Well?"

"Siegmund Faber."

Siegmund Faber! This was certainly news which made the blood recede to my heart. I had never doubted either that he was alive, or that he would return home; but so unexpectedly — I sank into a chair as if overwhelmed.

"Did you see him?" I asked after a long pause.

"No," he replied.

"Did you see Dorothee then?"

"No, I have not seen her either."

"But from whom did you learn?"—

"From your father, Fräulein Hardine."

"When, when, when — —"

"Yesterday afternoon, as soon as I returned from my journey."

"And do you know, do you think that Dorothee has confessed the truth to him — Faber?"

"I do not know. But you, my young friend, who are far better acquainted with her than I — do you think so?"

"No!" I said positively, and he also shook his head. "And yet she is married, really married?" I asked.

"The bans were to be published to-day for the last time. If the wedding has perhaps been deferred until to-morrow, it was done in expectation of your arrival, Fräulein Hardine."

"This very morning, and you learned it *yesterday*, man!" I shrieked, shaking him violently by the arm. "You had time, why did you not interfere?"

"Because my interference was not requested," he answered quietly, "and because, unasked, it would have been useless, or even dangerous, at so late an hour."

"It will, if God pleases, not be useless even at this hour, and avert, not cause, the greatest danger," I said, and rushed out of the room.

After I had told the hotel keeper to order post horses for me at once, I returned to the provost, who was sitting thoughtfully beside the sleeping boy, holding his hand in his. I paced impatiently up and down the room. Never in my life had I been so agitated. Each moment's delay seemed an eternity. I would gladly have fastened wings to my shoulders and flown away.

"Calm yourself, my dear child," said my friend at last. "You will reach your home to-night. A few minutes earlier or later will make no difference; you will be soon enough or too late."

"Then tell me the whole story," I exclaimed; and the old man, with intentional prolixity, began.

"When I found your letter in Jena, I remained there some days in the gayest spirits, engrossed in literary pleasures, whose description I will spare you to-day, Fräulein Hardine. Not until early yesterday morning did I enter the post-chaise to return to the institution. My good fortune procured me a polished and learned traveling companion, who, though I did not know his name, proved to be a distinguished physician in Berlin.

"The conversation, as it could hardly fail to do in the present condition of affairs, soon turned from our mutual peaceful interests to the disturbed state of the times, the phenomenal developments which, as it were, are whirled aloft in the confusion like a cloud of dust, only to suddenly fall back in the mud and mire. So how could we fail to mention the genius of the young commander, who is even now preparing for a campaign, in order both on land and sea to shake the foundations of the power of the last unconquered enemy of republican France.

"'I have heard some very interesting disclosures about General Bonaparte from an eye-witness of his Italian campaign,' said the Prussian gentleman in the course of our conversation. 'This eye-witness, with whom a short time ago I set out on my little tour of recreation, is a man in my own profession, who has for some weeks roused a perfect fever of excitement among the inhabitants of Berlin, who have such a longing for novelties, and although a dangerous rival of mine, really deserves to be held up as a notable example how a superior nature can make even the rude, bloody scenes of the present time valuable as material for acquiring greater skill in a peaceful profession.

"'Imagine, sir, a young Saxon barber, whose only training was that obtained in a practice sought with the utmost toil, who saw in the Prussian preparations for war a favorable field for his efforts, and by a series of fortunate accidents obtained it. The unfortunate campaigns of '92 and '93 gave him an opportunity to display his zeal and talent in the brightest colors. He, who has been matriculated by no faculty, passed no examination, came forth from the plague-stricken hospital as surgeon-major; men of high rank owed him relief and healing, the widest sphere of influence opened before him even in peaceful times. During the attack on the camp of Neuhornbach, where he had been in attendance on the king, he delayed to attend to the wants of a severely wounded enemy, and fell into the hands of the French. He was taken to Paris; his lucky star had ordered that the person who owed his life to him should be a prominent man; through him he obtained permission to visit various institutions and hospitals. The great, excited capital, the numerous victims of the battle fields, nay, those who perished under the headsman's axe afforded a field for energetic labor. Even amid this tumultuous world a watchful glance ever and anon fell upon the stranger who was so ceaseless in investigations.

"'The peace of Basle restored all prisoners to their native land. Our doctor also had liberty to go. But he remained. 'What would you have,' he said to me, 'a physician, as such, makes no distinctions between home and a foreign land, friend or foe. He only separates the sick and well, delicate and strong as material, and seeks, so long as he is studying, the most favorable sphere for his profession and duty.' He voluntarily accompanied the army to Italy; the young German doctor entered the circle of vision of the hero of Lodi and Arcola. He remained a year, which was spent partly in exercising his skill, partly in studying in Bologna, watched the injurious or beneficial influence of a southern climate on invalids and wounded men, and when Europe had scarcely recovered its repose after the peace of Campo Formio returned from republicanized Italy to Paris.

"'Here brilliant offers were made him to join the mysterious expedition by sea, in which we now see the bold Corsican involved with the army destined to make war upon England. 'But,' said our doctor, 'I was no adventurer. While in a foreign country I had appropriated everything that could be of use at home, and I fear will be needed only too soon in a time of heavy trial.' So he appeared about a month ago in Berlin, where he was an utter stranger. A Cæsar of the knife and pincers, he came, saw, and conquered. Rumor, rapid and mysterious as the wind, sounded his praises as a prodigy. Comrades in the army, who owed him gratitude for his aid in the Rhine campaigns, welcomed him with splendid entertainments; his peaceful colleagues pricked up their ears at the tale of the champion of their profession, who, to perfect himself in his studies, had voluntarily thrust his head into the lion's mouth; the young king, remembering his self-sacrificing labors during the epidemic after the campaign in Champagne, received him and wished to see his experiences made useful in the newly established Pepinière; the crowd thronged around the witness of revolutionary horrors and dangers, the description of which made their hair stand on end. Almost before one had time to breathe, he was in everybody's mouth; his colleagues listened to his genial aphorisms; the unlearned, before trying what the man could do, were satisfied with what he had experienced; ere curiosity had passed away, a large practice was secured. In short, never has an ambitious young practitioner commenced his career under more favorable auspices. We elders shall be obliged to hide our diminished heads, for our academical wisdom is far surpassed by his daring method.'

"I need not tell you, Fräulein Hardine," the old man continued after a short pause, "*whose* image rose vividly before me during this description, and that my question as to the hero's name was an idle one. In the reply, 'Doctor, now Geheimerath Faber,' only the title surprised me.

"We had approached the place where I stopped to take the road to the institution. 'If I understand you correctly, sir,' I said, after taking leave of the stranger, 'if I understand you correctly, Doctor Faber accompanied you on your journey into this neighborhood. You will pardon my curiosity, when I tell you that I hope to meet in his native city one who has long been deemed dead.' 'Your hope will be fulfilled, sir,' replied my companion. 'We travelled together as far as Halle; there I stopped, while he continued his journey without delay. 'On family affairs,' as he said.' 'And when was this?' I asked again. 'Yesterday, a week ago Friday,' replied the stranger, and the post-chaise rolled away.

"I had returned from my visit to Thuringia that very day, so that the decision in your home must have been made within a week. Might I hope that this decision had given my expected foster child a father? Must I fear that it had robbed him of his mother? I went to the institution in the greatest suspense.

"I had scarcely reached it, when my short-sighted old housekeeper told me, that early in the morning of the day after my departure, a lady dressed in the city fashion and closely veiled, inquired for me, and on hearing of my departure, begged permission to leave her message in writing. I found the sheet without signature, but sealed, on my writing table, and read the few words: 'As soon as you return, reverend sir, pray let me know. But for God's sake, do not come near me or the family, until you have sent me word.'

"She undoubtedly desired to have an interview to determine her child's future, and feared an intentional or accidental discovery. I now knew *what* decision she had made."

"You knew it!" I cried, interrupting the narrator for the first time, "and did not hasten to avert the impending misfortune."

My friend replied: "In spite of the prohibition, I was just in the act of examining into the condition of affairs on the spot, when a visit from your father, Fräulein Hardine, spared me the necessity. He was hoping to hear through me news from Reckenburg which would explain the delay in your arrival, and as I could give him this information, I begged him not to be anxious if the longed for visitor should be delayed several days more.

"'It is by no means from anxiety that I have come, but on the contrary, out of pure joy, my friend,' he replied. 'Only I should like to have my Dine with us at a — family festival, I may almost say — as bridesmaid at the marriage of our little Dörl and — guess —'"

"'And Geheimerath Faber,' I said, completing the sentence, and then in a few words related how I had heard of the man's return, and begged him to tell me the impression the long parted lovers had made on each other, and how the affair had been brought to a conclusion so speedily.

"I will now endeavor to make the statement as nearly as possible in your father's own words, but permit you to draw your own inferences, Fräulein Hardine.

"'On Friday evening we were sitting quietly together. My wife was spinning, I smoking. Suddenly we heard the house-door hastily open and shut, then a quick, elastic step in the entry, and three raps, as if made with a small hammer, on the door of the room. The sound of the door, the step, the rap, were all familiar. I dropped my pipe, Adelheid her

THE WEDDING. 243

thread : ' Faber!' we exclaimed in *one* breath, and as we uttered the name the man stood before us. No longer the surgeon, the doctor from the redoubts before Mayence: a distinguished man, a man of the world at the first glance ; but also at the first glance the old Mosjö Per-sé. He shook my hand and kissed my wife's with the air of one of the poor marquises, whose heads he has seen roll off by the dozen. Imagine it, my old barber's son and assistant!

"'I have come as a bride-groom, Herr Major,' said he, showing me his father's wedding ring on his finger. 'A little late, you will say, but the man has been true to his colors.' 'Oho!' I replied, ' the child is all safe!'

"'Meantime my wife had recovered from her astonishment. 'First of all,' she began, 'Herr Doctor, are you not?' He smiled and answered bowing. 'To my oldest friends, Siegmund Faber, as before, Mosjö Persé if you choose. To others : Geheimerath Faber, practising physician in Berlin.'

"'Then first of all, Herr Geheimerath,' said Adelheid, as she also bowed, 'accept the assurance that the demoiselle Müller has awaited your return under our eyes in perfect health and patient faithfulness.'

"'As a nun waits for the Heavenly Bridegroom,' I interrupted. Adelheid hemmed, and you know, Provost, when Adelheid hems she always means : '*Mal apropos*, Eberhard!' 'Yet it might be well,' she continued, 'to prepare the dear child for your unexpected appearance.'

"'She turned to leave the room. But here the Herr Geheimerath proved himself the same old Persé.

'After this gratifying assurance,' he said, 'he would beg permission to accompany Frau von Reckenburg and ascertain, from the first impression, the decision of the darling wish of his heart.' While saying these words, he lighted the candle which stood on the table, and thus, by leading the way, was the first to enter the chamber of his betrothed bride.

"'Poor little Dörl was sitting alone as usual. She had been cutting children's faces out of paper and was overcome by fatigue. Her arms were outstretched on the table and her head had drooped upon them. As the door suddenly opened, she raised it, as if roused from a dream. 'I cannot describe to you, Eberhard,' said Adelheid, for of course I had remained down stairs, 'I cannot describe to you the delight that sparkled in Faber's eyes at this picture. The dainty furniture of his old room, the little one's unchanged beauty, her childish occupation, and the gold ring on her finger, all this he had seen at a single glance. No words were needed, he knew all that he desired to know.'

"'But Dorothee now saw him, and shrieking like a child that has been stung by a bee, turned deadly pale and covered her face with both hands.

"'I have startled you, my dear Dorothee,' said Faber as he hurried towards her, drew her little hands away from her eyes, and pressed a kiss upon the finger that wore the ring. 'But this surprise is my compensation for long years of renunciation. My whole life shall be one expression of gratitude for the happiness it afforded me.'

"'But this second experiment — you know, Provost,

he called his betrothal an experiment—this surprise proved almost too great for our little Dörl. A shudder ran through her limbs, a feverish flush drove the death like pallor from her face. 'You are ill, Dorothee,' cried Faber anxiously, as he led her to the couch, sat down in a chair beside her and took her hand, not like a lover, Adelheid said, but like a physician who is counting the pulse. She shook her little head, roused herself, gradually regained her self possession, and when after a pause Faber asked if she felt strong enough to endure his presence, answered with a nod.

"'The goal I set before me is attained,' said Faber, 'later than I hoped, but it is securely and honorably won. A large practice awaits me in Berlin, ample means are at my—our disposal, dear Dorothee. True, my time is short. But what need have we to delay? In a week, I think, we can get to our new home together—'

"As Adelheid, who had hitherto remained unnoticed in the back ground, saw everything progressing so favorably, she thought it time to retire. At this movement the child perceived her. She started up, rushed towards my wife with a look, she declares, like that of a maniac, and the words, the first she had uttered: 'Hardine, Hardine! When will Fräulein Hardine come?' 'We are expecting her the middle of next week, dear Dorothee,' replied Adelheid soothingly, and left the betrothed couple alone.

"On coming down stairs, she said to me: 'The poor girl is completely bewildered, Eberhard. Even in a tête-à-tête, he won't be able to coax anything more out of her than a shake of the head and a shiver. But what marvel is it? The man has become a stranger during these eight years, nay, he was nothing but a stranger before. Now everything comes at once: the meeting, the marriage, the departure, an entirely new world, and all this without her faithful adviser, our daughter Hardine.'

"I am of the opinion that nothing helps a person out of an embarrassing situation more pleasantly than a merry supper among intimate friends, and Adelheid and I therefore instantly agreed to hastily get out the best the kitchen and cellar afforded for a welcoming feast. Scarcely an hour had elapsed, when I went up stairs to invite the guests to our extempore entertainment. I congratulated the betrothed bride, who did not yet seem to have recovered the use of her tongue, and again offered my best wishes to the radiant bridegroom. All four of us were soon seated comfortably around the table; the first bottle of wine was uncorked, and never have I heard a more joyful toast than that given to our faithful lovers.

"But our guest was now obliged to speak and describe as best he could the adventures and perils, amid which the prisoner of Pirmasenz had so fortunately reached the position of Geheimerath. The man knows how to tell a story; his language was simple and clear, his manner modest, and yet not without a proper degree of ease.

"It gave one a curious thrill of admiration and horror, to see in imagination the lonely stranger moving about so calmly with his knives and pincers, to-day under the flash of the guillotine, to-morrow amid the thunder of artillery; past men who yesterday were gold and to-day dross, who yesterday were overlooked as dross and to-morrow will be idolized as gold.

"What such a revolution means first became clear to me through the description of Mosjö-Persé. Adelheid and I could have listened all night.

"But to be sure, an old couple who are really connected by no ties of blood, are very different from a timid young betrothed bride. Poor little Dörl sat pale and silent, with downcast eyes and hands resting in her lap, and neither touched a mouthful of food nor drank a drop of wine. It really seemed to me, as if she had not heard a word of all the stories of murder, but had been thinking of something entirely different. But Faber was grateful for this stupor of alarm at the retrospect of the dangers through which he had passed when far away from her. He pressed her hand, and skillfully turned the conversation to a topic which always revives the weakest woman. The subject of the fashions adopted by the ladies during the revolution was introduced; the social gayeties, first of Paris then of Berlin; names were mentioned as those of his patrons and friends, the sound of which might well make the heart of the ex-barmaid leap with delight; and when at last their own home was mentioned as a second floor on the Unter den Linden, servants, carriage, and horses were spoken of as matters of course, my friend, you ought to have seen how the little betrothed melted. How the ears were pricked, how the eyes sparkled, how the flush deepened on the pale cheeks. Little Dörl already saw herself the Frau Geheimerathin, probably even a "gnädige Frau," *with her hair dressed à la Titus and a Greek tunic, nestling among silken cushions in a room adorned with clocks and vases, while generals and counts waited in the anteroom for an interview with her famous husband. Now she ventured to raise her eyes to his, nodded, smiled, and allowed her hitherto reluctant hand to remain in his clasp. Yes, women, women, they are all true daughters of Eve!

"'The fire is blazing on the hearth to welcome the mistress of the house,' said the clever man in conclusion — 'and God willing, the mistress will be absent only a few days longer. We are both orphans, you are also of age, my Dorothee; the necessary witnesses can be procured here. The bans must be published for the first time day after to-morrow, and I do not doubt we shall be exempted from all other observances, if I apply to the consistory at Leipsic, where I intend to seek out several old friends and patrons to-morrow. At any rate everything can be despatched by a week from next Sunday, and then, too, the witness of our betrothal, Fräulein Hardine, will be present, and I should be delighted to have her as a guest at our quiet wedding.'

"Adelheid is right, it is strange how fondly little Dörl loves our Dine. Anyone but Mosjö Persé would object to such friendship! But *he*; women's affairs — pshaw! But if it were a man who encroached on his preserves, Heaven help him!

"The child had listened to his plan with perfect composure; but at the name of Hardine she started

---

* Gnädige is used only in addressing the nobility.

up, trembling from head to foot and as white as the wall. 'Hardine!' she murmured. 'When will Fräulein Hardine come?' 'She shall not be absent from your wedding, darling,' I said soothingly, 'I will write to her to-morrow, and she will reach here in a week at latest.'

"Dorothee sat leaning back in her chair and did not stir. The betrothed bridegroom emptied the last glass to our dear daughter's health. The bride was also obliged to touch glasses and sip, but she did so with a shudder, as if death had walked over her grave. We all saw how much the dear child needed rest. My wife rose from the table, and the guest took his leave to seek quarters for the night at the inn. Our festival was over.

"'Pray do not write to Fräulein Hardine, dear Herr Major,' said kind little Dörl, as I accompanied her up stairs. 'It might be inconvenient for her. She will certainly come without it. Or we will wait till she does arrive.'

"Well, I did not write, as a letter came the following morning, fixing her arrival for the next Thursday. And now she has not come yet, and after all will not get home in time."

"As your father uttered the last words, he rose to return to the city. I accompanied him, and begged him to continue his story.

"'What more shall I say?' he asked. 'Everything has come to pass as our doctor arranged. On Sunday their bans were published from the pulpit for the first time. To-morrow it will be done for the second and third at once. In the afternoon, or early Monday morning at latest, a quiet wedding will take place in the country, witnessed only by Adelheid, myself, and of course our daughter, if she arrives. If she would only come! The child is literally wasting away under the influence of this fixed idea. At every carriage that rolls along the street, she rushes to the window and looks out. "Hardine, Fräulein Hardine!" are almost the only words that escape her lips. Day before yesterday, when we positively expected her, I was really angry with the little goose. During this one week she has grown as thin as a skeleton; the betrothal ring, that fitted her finger so tightly, rolls into her lap at the slightest movement of her hand. She does not even think of her wedding finery. 'Nothing will come of it,' she murmured, when Adelheid spoke to her about the matter a short time ago. I suppose these whims women take are called hysteria. Thank God, our Dine has no symptoms of them."

"And does the future bridegroom show no anxiety about this certainly singular state of mind," I ventured to ask; a doubt which the chivalrous major repelled almost as an insult. 'What do you mean by that, Provost?' he indignantly exclaimed. 'Has not the man my own testimony and Adelheid's for the girl's faultless conduct? Would our daughter, under any other circumstances, be her friend? Does not the whole city praise her actually timid reserve, since that horrible Thursday evening, for whose extravagances the child was really less to blame than the rest of us? That she has hitherto felt no overmastering love for her future husband, he is himself perfectly well aware, for our Mosjö Per-sé is no Apollo! But let her once be married and in her own home, and Faber feels himself man enough to win a woman's heart. With his usual cleverness, he compassionates her nervous anxiety during the short interval before the wedding, appears only in hurried visits, is attentive without being tender, and is illuminated by the halo that surrounds a distinguished man. Everyone presses forward to see the famous fellow-citizen. The news of his return has spread through the neighborhood like wildfire. People come from miles around to have diseases of old and new standing cured by the wonderful doctor. Several very difficult operations have been performed. But he is now obliged to greet and bid farewell to all his old acquaintances down to the flayer, whom he calls his first professor. In short, a whirlwind has risen around the man, and he conducts himself with the utmost tact and propriety. These qualities are particularly shown in his behavior towards us. His father's old house, his 'citadel of faith,' as he calls it, will remain at our disposal, the rent is to be given to Hardine to distribute among the poor. Not a piece of furniture will be removed from Dorothee's room, nor any luggage taken with them on the journey. In their wedding garments, as untrammelled as the summer birds, they will fly to the nest that has been prepared, where all sorts of new articles never seen before will surround and delight the young wife.'

" During this last conversation we had reached the city and your home, Fräulein Hardine. Your mother was sitting at her spinning-wheel before the door.

'The post-chaise from Leipsic has arrived, and once more without our daughter, Eberhard,' said she. 'The countess has had an attack of illness,' replied her husband, the provost has heard from Reckenburg. But what does Dörl say, Adelheid?' 'Why, since the last hope has almost disappeared, she seems to try to dismiss her childish longing from her mind. Look around you, Eberhard, there is a face at every door and window. Dorothee has just turned the corner, leaning on her betrothed husband's arm; it is the first time she has left the house since his return home. They want to bid farewell to their parents' graves. This Faber has a noble, refined nature; you ought to make his acquaintance, Herr Provost. I should have liked to have my daughter see him again too. But I cannot try to defer the wedding longer than to-morrow. Dorothee will be calmer *without* a a farewell, and if Hardine arrived to-morrow evening, what would she care for the mere *rôle* of bridesmaid?'"

The provost paused; he seemed to have finished his story. "And did you not wait for Dorothee's return and decision?" I hastily asked.

"No," he answered quietly. "I requested your mother to inform her of my return from my journey, and went back to the institution. When, as I almost expected, no message reached me after the morning service, I set off for Leipsic to receive my charge."

At this moment the post-chaise drove up. I had not laid aside my traveling dress, and had already ordered the baggage to be carried down stairs again. When I now attempted to rouse the boy and hurry on with him, my companion stopped me. "I think it will be better," said he, "for me to spend the night here with the little one, and to-morrow—"

"The child will sleep just as well in the carriage as here in bed," I angrily interrupted. "Let us go on as fast as possible." He hesitated a moment, then followed me with the sleeping boy in his arms.

My friend's circumstantial explanation had only increased my excitement. It was intentional on his part; the agitation needed to subside *before* the actual impressions were received. For the first, and thank God the only time in my life, I felt in a condition of — out with it — a condition of fury; fury directed first of all against myself. I could have torn my hair out by the roots, or broken the windows of the carriage. I could have shrieked, or like a wild horse bitten my own veins to open a valve for the seething blood. I — I was to blame for this event; *I* had covered the sin, concealed the breach of faith; I had deceived my unsuspicious parents, trusting to whose good faith an honorable man had been most shamefully betrayed. I — I had destroyed the proud confidence of my own soul.

In such a mood there is no greater relief than to cast a portion of our burden upon others, and therefore as soon as the post-chaise had entered the smoother highway, I turned upon my companion, whose mild composure enraged me.

"If we come too late, Provost," I exclaimed, "if the wedding is over, you will have taken a heavy responsibility upon yourself. You might have prevented the crime, and for the sake of ease neglected to make the accusation."

"Ought the confessional to be turned into a seat of judgment, Fräulein Hardine?" he replied, "and was I not in the situation of the confessor, who has to guard a secret intrusted to his care?"

"You did not have the secret from a penitent, at least not *at first*. Besides, in taking this view of the matter, you condemn yourself. Delicacy of feeling might bind the tongue of the man, the friend; it was the priest's duty to keep his penitent from committing a crime."

"And what was I to do, Fräulein Hardine?"

"Advise, warn, threaten; awaken the dull conscience to the first christian and human virtue, truth."

"And have not you, my brave young friend, advised, warned, awakened her conscience to the truth, you who have always had the strongest influence over this child, and at a time when she felt more than indifferent towards this man, to whom she owed the truth? And what was the result? But to-day, at the last hour, on the eve of the wedding, when all the feelings and efforts of the variable heart are directed solely against the danger of opposition—"

"In an extreme case you ought not to have avoided the most extreme measures."

After a short pause, my friend gently took my hand and said: "My dear child, do not ask an old man to perform an act which is beyond his powers, and for which, should it fail, he has no remedy to offer himself or others. And suppose matters had proceeded to extremities. If the weak creature—for she is very weak, Fräulein Hardine—disgraced before the

THE WEDDING. 255

world and before the man who is now the object of all her desires, should be seized by some fatal illness, or go mad? If she should lay desperate hands upon herself —"

"Well," I passionately exclaimed, "*I*, if there is still time, will defy these dangers and let the truth be heard, if they are standing before the altar. I stepped beyond the limits of my powers, my education, the motto of my ancestors, my own character, when I endured dishonor and palliated wrong. In right and honor, at *any* cost, I shall know how to atone for this error."

"You *will* do so, my friend," replied the reverend gentleman with marked emphasis. "You will atone for that error, sooner or later, though with other factors than those which now occupy your mind. To err in *this* manner is to live, and our development is rooted in the secret instincts that mock human logic. The showers of rain, which beat down our crops, filter through the hard surface of the earth and collect in a spring, which fertilizes the land. *This* is the logic of nature. And therefore let me believe that that, which now oppresses your conscience, will at some future time refresh your soul like a fountain. I am an old man. *My* task is, so far as lies in my power, to supply a father's place to this child, who has perhaps lost his mother also."

The old man was silent. But if you suppose that his simile of the spring of water, in my state of excitement, extinguished my anger, you are mistaken. It was pouring oil on the flames. I turned my back on the sentimental weakling who, without moving, saw his neighbor's house burn down and then kindly collected the stones to build a hut to shelter him in future.

We did not exchange another word till we reached the next station. The old man sat opposite to me in silence, with the head of the sleeping child resting in his lap. A confusion of thoughts whirled through my brain. *What* would happen, if I came in time, *what* would become of me, if I arrived too late — I did not know.

I was roused from this tumult of feeling by a movement on the part of my companion, who during the change of horses was preparing to get out of the post chaise, to take the side road to the institution with the sleeping boy. I noticed the intention and said scornfully, "You swallow camels and strain at gnats, dear friend!" Upon which he answered smiling: "I shall be glad if I can avert the poisonous sting of a gnat from you, Fräulein Hardine!"

This provocation was all that was lacking. "I think, Herr Provost," I burst forth, "that the name and reputation of Fräulein von Reckenburg —"

"The *best* name and reputation," he interrupted, "the peace of the noblest human beings may be destroyed, if a chain of casualties plays into the hands of foolish or malicious persons. If Dorothee Müller's marriage forces her to disown this boy, he will have neither father nor mother. He has grown up in Reckenburg, under the eyes of *your* trusted servant, and been placed by you in the charge of an old friend. It will be *your* person to which his memories, perhaps his expectations will cling, especially if some day a

THE WEDDING. 257

change in your circumstances should fix the eyes of a larger circle upon you. Your only witnesses, Justine and myself, are old; the church registers are destroyed and the complications of chance incalculable. I must therefore consider it a dispensation of Providence, that at least *one* irrefutable document in regard to Augustus Müller's descent has been preserved. Shortly before my departure from Reckenburg and the burning of the church, I took a copy of the baptismal certificate in order, at the first opportunity, to place it in the mother's hands without attracting the attention of any third person. I thoughtlessly delayed carrying out my original intention, and now confide it to you, instead of the mother, Fräulein Hardine. Do not reject it, keep it out of regard for a faithful friend, much as he may have sunk in your estimation to-day."

To cut short any further discussions, I took the document, and in a cooler mood saw the duty of preserving it, if not for myself, for the orphaned boy, and I have already mentioned that you will find it fastened to this manuscript.

After this concession, however, the reverend gentleman was obliged to permit me to accompany him to the institution. The cloister clock was just striking midnight, when I saw him disappear through the doorway with the child in his arms.

Half an hour later the post horn sounded before the barber's house. The dwelling and the whole city were shrouded in slumbers; everybody was asleep, and it seemed an eternity before the door opened and my father appeared in his dressing gown and night-cap. "Dorothee!" I shrieked, clinging to his shoulders with both hands.

"You come *post festum*, my poor Dine," replied my father, attempting a pun, "the Frau Geheimerath left her kindest remembrances for you!"

And now do not ask me how I reached my mother's bed and exchanged the first words. Do not ask how long I sat opposite to her and in partial bewilderment saw the concluding scene of our household drama pass before me like a dissolving view. Not until after the account had been frequently repeated during the ensuing days, was it impressed upon my mind with the sharpness of a personal experience.

The betrothed lovers had returned from their evening walk with the determination to have the wedding take place the following noon, in the manner already agreed. My father and mother made no opposition. Dorothee received the message from her old friend at the cloister with a flood of tears, which seemed to relieve her mind.

When on Sunday morning the service was drawing to a close, my mother went up to Dorothee's room to give her her little wedding present. It was a silhouette of her daughter, with a lock of her hair, which she had had enclosed in a locket set with pearls.

She found the bride already attired in her communion dress, the neck and sleeves trimmed with white lace, a gift from Faber. The dark picture fastened with a black ribbon, which was her only ornament, made the costume appear still more like mourning. But in this gloomy frame, with the flowerlike whiteness of the face, the downcast eyes, the hands folded on the breast as if in humble pleading, and the morning sunlight gilding the luxuriant wealth of curls, my mother confessed that she had never suspected this ideal beauty under the child's pink cheeks, and lingered a moment on the threshold, spell bound by the sight.

But it was only for a moment. The next instant a thrill of horror ran through her limbs and a "merciful Heaven!" escaped her lips. A bride, Siegmund Faber's bride, her charge — and without the maiden's wreath! No one had provided the indispensable symbol, which up to the last moment all had expected the bridesmaid to bestow. And now how was it to be procured in this haste, and with the shops closed for Sunday?

Dorothee had heard the exclamation and saw my mother's anxiety. At the same moment she distinguished the sound of a carriage, which came nearer and nearer. It stopped before the door. "Hardine!" she shrieked, "mercy, Hardine!" and sank on her knees.

But it was not the longed for bridesmaid, but the coaches for the wedding party, that drove up to the house. The bridegroom and my father entered just as the trembling bride rose from the floor.

Only the wreath, the wreath! All looked confounded — all, with the exception of the rigid bride. The happy bridegroom was the first to collect his thoughts. "It need not be myrtle," said he. "In Southern countries white flowers are chosen from preference, mingled with any other delicate green." He looked around the room, which the day before had resembled a garden, but all the pots had been carried to the cemetery early that morning to adorn the graves of the lovers' parents. In a glass of water, however, he saw a few green sprigs, which he thoughtlessly grasped and handed to Dorothee. My mother with difficulty repressed a shudder; then, smiling sadly, wound them in Dörl's golden hair: the sprays were a bunch of rosemary, plucked yesterday by the daughter's hand as a memento from those very graves.

But at the same moment my kind father, who in his zeal had rushed down to the garden, triumphantly brought in a handful of white amaranths, on which the morning dew was still glittering. They were twisted among the rosemary, and thus with spring flowers and green sprays from a grave-yard the bridal wreath was finished. Siegmund Faber wrapped a costly Turkish shawl around Dorothee's shoulders and led her to the carriage. My parents followed. Amid the greetings of her fellow citizens, who were just streaming out of the church, the beautiful child of the city drove from her dark home into the dazzling splendor of the world.

At the end of an hour the carriage stopped before a church in the first village on the road to Berlin. The inhabitants were at dinner, no one except the pastor and sexton was waiting in the little deserted house of God. Faber, out of consideration for his bride, had requested that the ceremony should be short, so it was limited almost entirely to the old Lutheran formula and the benediction. Without any singing or music from the organ, the betrothed lovers were speedily made man and wife. When the rings they had worn eight years were again exchanged, the bride's slipped from her hand. Faber caught it and placed it on her finger, which he henceforth held firmly clasped in his. His assent rang through the church in a clear, joyous tone. Dorothee's lips did not move.

Siegmund Faber silently led his young wife to the churchyard gate, motioned for the carriage to drive up and hurried back to the vestry to attend to the business arrangements. My parents took leave of the child, whom from her very cradle they had cherished with their own.

"May God's blessing be upon you, dear Dorothee, in the name of our dear Hardine also," said my father, after embracing his favorite, and then walked quickly towards the young husband to conceal his tears.

It seemed as if at the name of Hardine a fit of insanity suddenly seized the young wife. Shuddering convulsively, she threw herself on the ground and clung to my mother's knees.

"Mercy, Hardine!" she shrieked, "mercy! I did not *wish* to do it, but was *compelled*! I *wanted* to speak, but I *could* not. The child, the poor orphaned child! Mercy, Hardine, mercy for the sake of the dead!"

The last words were faltered in almost inaudible tones. Her eyes grew dim and she staggered backwards over a freshly made grave. Faber rushed forward and lifted his unconscious wife into the carriage. A moment after they were rolling along the highway towards their new home.

CHAPTER X.

"1806."

THE secret is revealed. You now know, my friends, *who* Augustus Müller's mother was and what sealed my lips, when the world gave that name to me. What outside events afterwards happened *to* me and *through* me are perfectly clear, so the story might come to an end.

But since every story should have a point, that is, since every fate comes to a point, not according to outside events but the spirit within, and since when the first beginning is made, it affords us peculiar pleasure to disclose to those we love the ground plan of the edifice of our lives, I will continue mine from story to story, to the summit, which will at last be revealed.

The weakness with which for years I had tolerated and kept Dorothee's secret, had not disturbed my conscience. But now, when an inextinguishable crime towards another had sprung from it, it weighed upon me like a mountain. There was now one man, whose honorable name I could not hear without turning pale; one man, at the thought of whom I cast down my eyes; whom I must either deceive or utterly crush, if he ever stood before me with the question: "Did you act honestly and honorably towards him who trusted you?" I now learned to know the demons of life — anxiety, doubt, fear, and shame — which I had dreaded more than poverty and abandonment. The pride of innocence was destroyed, all independence of feeling crushed, since by yielding to Dorothee I had been led so far away from the original principles of my character.

Of Dorothee I heard nothing. I had not expected her to write to me, and should not have answered her. I did not know whether she maintained any communication with the provost, but doubted it. We had done with each other.

The tie that bound me to the provost had also weakened, since his laxness, as I termed it, had burdened my conscience with a heavy load. I went to see him whenever I visited my parents, maintained a sort of connection between him and his old parish, and watched his labors in his present sphere with interest; but we never exchanged a word about our mutual secret. Yet no matter how often I visited him, he never omitted to bring forward his *special protégé* and attempt to arouse my former interest in him, for — and this was probably the worst change in my mood — the boy, for whom I had felt so much affection, and who was now developing into a strong, handsome lad, had inspired me with a feeling of horror ever since the night I had seen him disappear in the cloister. I no longer beheld in him the living image of his father, who had been the joy and sorrow of my short spring; no longer the offspring of his mother, the sole companion of my childhood; he reminded me only of the man who, through my participation in guilt, had been robbed of the happiness of ever pressing to his heart the pledge of a *pure* love. Unjust as I was — even towards myself — I was angry with the boy for his impetuous nature, which was so difficult to curb; he became to me Nurse Justine's "wild stock," the lost child of sin, and my old friend vainly tried to explain and apologize. "He never tells a lie and is braver than any of the others," said the old man, but I replied: — "He is a worse boy than any of the others," and when twenty years after Augustus Müller said that Fräulein Hardine's image had been impressed upon his mind by a severe blow, I probably do not remember the fact simply because my fingers had twitched, not once, but a hundred times to give the correction.

Everything disgusted, everything embittered me, especially my stay in my parents' house. For the house was the scene of the treachery which had cost me my self-respect, and I could not endure the honest eyes of my parents, who had become accomplices in it solely through my fault. The household life, in whose duties I had no share, wearied me, and the free country occupations of Reckenburg had completely estranged me from the insipid society of the little city; for nature, even in her simplest aspect, speaks an ever new and intellectual language to one who has assumed the position, not of a mere looker on, but a worker in her domain.

My visits home, therefore, grew shorter year by year, and at last were limited to a few days. I became more and more indispensable at Reckenburg, though my situation continually grew more unpleasant and constrained. Everything was stagnant, everything threatened to go to ruin under the old woman's mad thirst for gold. The old servants and employees refused to work for her; I was obliged to fight for every thaler I kept back from the greedy hands, nay, was compelled to take refuge in deception, in open fraud; to secretly sell corn, in order to pay the laborers, that the fields might not lie fallow; to secretly order wood to be felled, to pay the foresters, that the increased numbers of game might not destroy the crops.

When I saw this diabolical self-destruction, this degeneration of the most admirable natural qualities, or the constantly increasing dissoluteness of the parish, which, since the fire, did not even have a roof over the house of God; when I heard the people talking about the Beelzebub to whom the ghost in the gold tower had sold her soul, sayings before whose logic contradiction died away like the empty wind, I often asked myself with scornful indignation why a place was not reserved for misers in every mad-house? Still more often I struggled against the temptation of placing my relative under legal guardianship.

But I battled it down. The woman, who had led such a vigorous life only to pine away so miserably, was already in her tenth decade, and she should not be inscribed on the records of her country as a simpleton through the testimony of the last who bore her name. I was still strong enough to stand my ground against the destruction, until in the course of nature the stewardess became mistress of her ancestors' estates, or was compelled to leave them forever.

Year after year glided away in this condition of external and internal lassitude, which resembled a paralysing, oppressive chronic disease, in which the physician awaits the crisis that is to release his patient, either by death or rejuvenated life.

And the lonely girl in secluded Reckenburg felt this secret, lurking distress in the whole state of affairs in her native country, even more than in herself. With the sharpened powers of an unoccupied mind, she looked beyond the void in her own life and beheld the tottering steps from weakness to guilt, saw the strength of her nation overstrained, here failing, there approaching a catastrophe which must destroy or rouse it to fresh energy.

I know what you will say, my friends, or at least what you might say: there may have been a lurking disease in the German nation, though you have perhaps described the results of later experience, or the contrast between the rude population of Reckenburg and the refined friends of literature in the cloister as signs of the times, to the advantage of your penetration. Be it so. But as to the pathos of your personal sorrow, Fräulein Hardine, it was probably nothing more than the uncomfortable state of mind of every girl who is gradually passing from the twenties into the thirties. Why did you not marry? You were not beautiful and bewitching; but you were clever and sensible, and what is more, the prospective heiress of the "green robe" of your Reckenburg fields. Such a robe is comfortable, even without the girdle of Venus. Did you lack suitors, or did you play the Amazon?

Neither, my young friends. Fräulein Eberhardine was practical enough to think a sensible, suitable marriage, even without affection, a better corrective of her malady than the inheritance of Reckenburg itself. But as regards her host of suitors, oh! she might have filled her father's squadron with her cavaliers. Old and young, acquaintances and strangers, they came from far and near, attracted by the charms and virtues of the last von Reckenburg. But as soon as the latter, from due regard for the truth, represented these charms and virtues as her only certain inheritance, she saw this condition of torpor suddenly spread over the rapidly advancing army of knights. They manfully smothered their passion to a *rythmic tempo* like that of the minuet in Eberhardine von Reckenburg's dancing lessons. *Cavaliers à droite, à gauche, en arrière!* not a *whole* step, scarcely a *half* one, and always with low bows and graceful *portebras*, but as long-winded as the life in the gold tower of Reckenburg.

But when — to close the matrimonial chapter at once — when that long-winded life finally breathed its last, and the charms and virtues of the last von Reckenburg glittered in the green robe of her home, she knew something better to do than to conceal the indigence of some waiting knight under its folds. *En arrière, cavaliers!* it was now her turn to say; *en arrière au galop.*

And her heart had not throbbed while thus driving suiters away; for to her good or evil fortune she had early learned to judge by large standards, and no attractive Antinous, no character like Mosjö Per-sé was numbered among her later wooers.

The events of the autumn of 1806 drove me hurriedly to my parents' house, with the expectation of making a much longer stay than usual. The Elector, at the last moment, had decided in favor of war, and my old father was compelled to take the field under the Prussian flag a second time.

My mother, whose health had never recovered from the anxiety of those years of separation, utterly broke down at this second parting. Now she *foresaw* the fatal blow, which she had then only *feared*, and when honest Purzel repeated his former words of consolation, "Nothing will happen to him, and if anything *does*, I will come and tell you at once," she did not try to smile, and her fixed eyes said: "I know you will come."

I did not share this apprehension. Napoleon's campaigns did not last so long as those on the Rhine; the present one was expected to take place in our immediate vicinity, and why should we doubt the goodness of God, when we had once experienced it with so much gratitude? I hoped to see my dear father again very soon.

But my gloomy forebodings in regard to the result of the campaign were all the more unconquerable. As solitary shepherds or huntsmen learn to understand the course of the clouds and stars, I, as I have already mentioned, in my mental isolation had become accustomed to fix my eyes intently upon the horizon of our times, and I saw threatening clouds rising above it. I now came home. Our little city resembled a Prussian camp. The larger portion of the army, fragments of which I had seen during the movements of the troops the previous year, marched through our streets on their way to the distant headquarters. With natural keenness of perception for everything practical, and, as a soldier's daughter, familiar with many military necessities, I could not fail to feel doubts, which were only too well justified by the result.

But there was a memory, which, even more than these intuitions, intruded amid the constant changes, foreboding misfortune. I saw and heard the cavalier whims among the representatives of Frederic's school of heroes, the only mood which was openly displayed and frequently offended the less hot-blooded Saxon allies; — well, one might smile at them. During short interviews I exchanged a word with the heroic prince, who so vividly reminded me of him who perished at Valmy. I bent in homage before the queen and read proud, victorious confidence in the eyes of the fairest of women — ah! her words and looks might well have inspired courage.

But I again saw at the head of the army the irresolute general of '92, under whom Frederic's victorious banner began to droop; now an old man, surrounded by grey-beards, and on the enemy's side not a horde of *sans-culottes*, but an army intoxicated with victory, under an *Emperor* — Napoleon. And to that authority of memory I again saw a King of Prussia voluntarily submit; a reserved, timid man, in whose grave eyes might be read a foreboding of the catastrophe, a premonition of all the sorrows of the time, which he learned to understand too late.

The army had moved westward, toward the river,

nearly two weeks before. No garrison remained in the city; an anxious stillness followed the noisy bustle; the stillness that precedes the storm. Hour after hour the news of a collision was expected; but no one guessed *where* the dreaded conqueror of Austerlitz, who, according to the last intelligence, received the first of October, had reached Warzburg, would seek or find this meeting. Even the army did not know, as my father's first letter informed us.

The last news about him was brought by the provost, whose son had hospitably welcomed his father's friend to his Thuringian parsonage and found him well and in good spirits. The main body of the Saxon troops was with the eastern wing of the army; one regiment of cavalry, with the vanguard, commanded by Prince Louis Ferdinand, was stationed on the Upper Saale. Every one was still ignorant whether the corps would advance up the right bank of the river, toward the enemy, or fall back nearer to the main army at Erfurt. This letter, dated the 8th of October, did not reach us until the afternoon of the eleventh. My mother listened to the encouraging contents without faith, and almost without interest. She sat brooding silently. A sudden foreboding darted through my mind, that, even without any crushing blow, she would not survive this time of trial.

The following morning alarming rumors ran through the city, rumors which, at such times, seem to whiz through the air; no one seeks or knows their origin. I read them in the faces of the people who hurried past, caught them in their half-uttered words, when I ventured to leave my mother a moment and go out into the street. Travellers were said to have met French troops the day before moving upward along the right bank of the Saale; it was rumored that the allies were surrounded, that the enemy was established in the Elector's dominions; people no longer thought themselves safe for an hour, talked of removing their property to the mountains, of securing an ample stock of provisions, of flight.

The excitement increased when, towards noon, there were rumors that several skirmishes had taken place between the out-posts, in which the allies were defeated and the cavalry badly cut up; it reached its climax, when a few hours later — how? — by whom? ah! heaven knows! the most terrible news ran from lip to lip. A battle — so it was said — had been fought, the enemy had forced a passage to the left bank of the river in the face of the Prussian prince, and consequently our own regiment of cavalry. The losses were said to be immense, and even the prince's name was mentioned among the number of killed.

In this state of watching and listening the day drew toward a close. The Frankfort stage arrived, two couriers dashed after it along the road to Halle and Leipsic, the crowd in front of the post house grew dense, their gestures more anxious; it seemed to me as if all eyes were turned toward our house. I could endure the suspense no longer.

My mother sat motionless in her arm-chair at the window, gazing fixedly at the crowd, but asked no questions. I left her in charge of the maid-servant. It was already growing dark. I ran across to the post-house; it was scarcely a hundred paces away, I could return in a few minutes.

And in a few minutes I did return, bearing in my heart the news which I knew would sound like a death-sentence to the only object of my love now left me on earth. My dear father was dead. He had fallen at the head of his regiment, during the last unfortunate cavalry attack, which also proved fatal to the illustrious commander. What a feeling of horror overpowered me as I crossed the threshold which, so long as I could remember, had always been the abode of domestic happiness. Only a few minutes had elapsed, and I found it transformed into a chamber of death.

In her chair at the window, where I had left her, lay the wretched wife, with limbs relaxed and filmy eyes, like those of a corpse. At her feet knelt the maid-servant, wringing her hands, and before her, still gasping for breath, sobbing aloud, covered with dust and blood, his arm in a sling, stood the messenger of woe, who had anticipated me.

Honest Purzel had kept his word. When the enemy's ranks grew denser and denser, while friends began to waver, and after a last, brave assault, the squadrons of his own regiment scattered; when he saw the prince, their commander, turn his horse, and at the same moment his master fall to the ground, his only thought was to save him, and when he found him dead, perfectly lifeless, conceal him under a bush, and then, poor wight, set off at full speed till his horse dropped with fatigue, and he ran, gasping for breath, almost day and night, until he had reached "his house" and the wife to whom he had promised to report at once, the first fugitive who brought the news of the terrible prelude of Saalfeld.

The murderous words had not crossed his lips; a single glance at the entering figure had broken the sick, foreboding heart. The remedies used in apoplectic paralysis were instantly applied; they prolonged the bodily life for an incalculable time, during which the soul remained dead. The unhappy wife never uttered another word, and, I trust, heard none of our lamentations.

This terrible grief held the equally great sorrow in check. All through the long night I sat mechanically counting the feeble throbs of the pulse, which might stop at any moment. At dawn sympathizing friends and curious acquaintances crowded around me; I scarcely saw or heard them. I sat rigid and silent.

I was roused from this stupefied condition by an act of friendship, which touched my heart as no other had ever done before or since. This day taught me what it is to reap faithfulness where your parents have sowed love. And yet I have reverenced them twenty years, without scattering even one kernel of the same seed. True, I knew of no heir to whom it would have borne fruit.

It was about noon, when I heard a carriage stop before our door; heard, without heeding it. A sign from the old soldier summoned me from my mother's bed-side; he was trembling and weeping like a child, and *he* to whom he led me, also trembled and wept.

"Fräulein Hardine," stammered Christlieb Taube;

"I bring you all that could be saved of the best man who ever lived."

His body. He had discovered it under the sheltering bush, when with his pastor, the provost's son, he searched the neighboring battle field for wounded men, laid it on a layer of the last oak leaves of the year, in a coffin hastily constructed of rough boards, had a benediction pronounced over it in the church, and then, alone in a light basket wagon, drove night and day, almost without rest, to bring it as a last consolation to those he called his benefactors.

And there he lay, the man with the brave heart, unchanged, as I had so often seen him sleeping in life; the kind, strong face marred by no expression of pain. He still held his sword firmly grasped in his clenched hand, and only a small singed hole marked the spot where the bullet had pierced his heart. So he died a quick, gallant death, in the consciousness of a just cause, *before* the days of ignominy which were to rest upon his country for years, and in whose final expiation he would scarcely at his age have been permitted to take part. My poor father, God knew best, even for you!

Never in my life have I wept so bitterly, realized the benefit of tears so thoroughly, as at the sight of this dead form. When I raised my head from his heart and pressed the hand of the faithful friend, who knelt in silent prayer at the foot of the coffin, I felt the old strength and my usual courage again awake. It was like a sunbeam struggling through the leaden mist of winter; the ray lasts only a second and darkness soon surrounds us again. But we have been reminded of the unfailing light above.

A sudden hope thrilled me. Might not my mother's paralyzed mind be roused by the sight of her beloved husband? The physician made no objection to the bold attempt, but also gave no hope of its success. So the coffin was carried into the sitting-room and placed where the sofa, on which the dead man had so often rested, usually stood. The cloak covered the rigid limbs, the head was turned as if in peaceful slumber.

I carried the invalid out of her chamber in my arms like a helpless child and seated her opposite to the coffin. With what eager suspense I watched her features! Alas, the staring eyes rested mechanically on the dead face, but not even the quiver of a muscle betrayed pleasure or pain, there was not the slightest token that she recognized him, that she even saw him! Her heart was dead, perhaps already in the other world with him; only the blood still flowed in the soulless machine. How long would this last, hours, years? The doctor silently shrugged his shoulders, as my despairing eyes asked the question.

We placed the invalid in my attic chamber, in order to have the lower rooms free and quiet for the dead. Sorrowful arrangements about the funeral were to be made. The old soldier had no comrades in the city, who could accompany him to his final resting place, the last von Reckenburg had no son, no blood relative to throw the first handful of earth into his grave. But his daughter should not fail him on his last journey, and that the journey might be made as quietly and unostentatiously as possible, I selected an hour in the evening and kind Christlieb

Taube made all the preparations with this object. He himself, aided by the faithful servant, dug at night the grave for which room had been found beside the Faber family lot. The old neighbors were to rest near each other under the earth.

Not until this mournful service was finished, did good Christlieb Taube set out to convey the sad news to my friend in the cloister, spend the night with him, and go back to his pupils the next day. As soon as he returned from the funeral in the evening, he intended to leave for home, accompanied by Purzel.

The poor fellow, after having conquered his first alarm, gradually arrived at a repentant realization that he had abandoned his colors.

"I didn't desert, Fräulein Hardine," he said, sobbing; "only scattered. And my wound isn't mortal, as I thought, but a mere scratch. Only let me stay to see my Herr Major buried, and then I will find the regiment and be shot like him!"

While on his way to us, Christlieb Taube had heard that the troops from Saalfeld had fallen back towards the north, upon the main body, and occupied Jena. The regiment, therefore, was to be sought there. Various rumors, however, asserted that the army had already seized upon the pass of the Saale at Kösen, and a roundabout way must, therefore, be taken. What unhappy fate threatened our army, if this hostile investment proved true, by what gross errors it had become possible, we were to learn only too soon; in those first hours of personal bereavement, we failed to appreciate the position of the nation.

Christlieb Taube had set out on his way to the

cloister, the maid-servant, after the anxiety of the previous night, went to bed early; Purzel was keeping watch, that is, the poor, exhausted soldier slept like a dead man beside his dear master's coffin. A death-like silence pervaded the house. I sat alone beside my mother's bed, whether minutes or hours I do not know. In this dreary solitude the consciousness of my orphanhood rose distinctly before me for the first time. Orphanhood! For the heart that throbbed mechanically beside me was no longer that of a mother, and no one can measure the desolation of this consciousness unless, like me, with the threads that lead back to the past, every tie of the soul is sundered. I was thirty years old, had neither brother nor sister, no hope of a coming race, — was the last of my blood and name. *Before* me, *beside* me, *behind* me, all was vacancy — yes; I was, indeed, an orphan.

And then, I was poor; whatever might happen in the future, at this moment I was terribly poor. On my own account I should scarcely have considered this a trouble. I had my post at Reckenburg, and if some day I should be compelled to leave it, "I will go to the backwoods of America, as a colonist," I had more than once smilingly answered, when the provost urged the necessity of reminding the countess of her duties towards me. In my present mood I would quickly have turned the jest into earnest, at any rate, found my place in the management of larger estates. But when I looked at my mother, whom I could not desert in her slow agony, poverty became an oppressive burden.

The change in my situation, however, was too new

and agitating, for me to realize it with any clearness of thought. Ideas glided through my soul slowly and heavily. The lamp, veiled by a shade, diffused a dim light; it was necessary to keep the sick room cool. I shivered, as even the strongest, after a great agitation, shiver in the house of death. I had not rested a moment for two days, and was now oppressed by that leaden weight, which, is half-way between sleeping and waking, and in which we vainly try to consider whether the various things we see are really visible to our waking eyes, or only glide past us in a dream.

While in this state it suddenly seemed as if I felt some living creature brush past me; I saw a muffled figure bend over the sick bed, gaze intently at my mother's face, and then fall on the floor between her and myself. The noise, the touch drove away the nightmare. It was no dream; the mysterious apparition was lying at my feet. I started up, seized the lamp, and threw the light upon the face — Dorothee! Dorothee was lying in convulsions, icy cold, with fixed, glassy eyes, clenched teeth, and hands clutching her dress above her heart — the same terrible sight my mother had witnessed on her wedding day.

All the mists that had clouded my mind vanished at the frightful spectacle; my own fate was almost forgotten. I carried her to the sofa, opened the window, and gave her some drops of a cordial that stood ready for my mother. She did not seem to have lost her consciousness, and it was only a few minutes ere the rigid muscles relaxed, the limbs began to grow warm. The pulse once more became perceptible, but it was long ere the expression of agony left the eyes.

She was still beautiful; the same pliant, youthful figure, the same transparency of complexion. The delicate hands, the arrangement of the hair and dress, everything I saw betokened elegance and comfort; everything I had heard of her social position during the recent occupation of the city by the Prussians, spoke of security and honor; she was a beloved wife, a happy woman, and how desolate, how wretched I had seemed to myself a few minutes before.

And yet — for who can describe that expression of constraint which, like an iron band, distinguishes the unhappy, or was it a sadder look than that of fear in a child's eyes? — and yet a voice within said to me: this beautiful, richly-endowed woman is more wretched, more forsaken than you!

And as if the voice had roused an echo, the pale lips whispered: "Hardine, I am more unhappy than you."

The convulsion had passed away; she breathed and moved freely, but did not start up as usual; she did not blush, her lids did not droop, she did not cling to my knees, to my arms, did not even hold out her hand to me. She fixed her weary eyes upon mine, and rose slowly, as if long accustomed to self-control.

Just as quietly obeying my mute sign, she lay down again, and after I had taken a seat beside her, explained, without any question on my part, her sudden appearance. She did this in clear, curt words, as if making a report, not relating a story. Her accent was purer, her language had become more finished, but the silvery, lark-like tone of the voice sounded muffled.

"Faber," she said, "had joined the army several weeks before in the king's train. I could without discovery, and even if discovered, without exciting any surprise, venture to take a journey home, make arrangements for the boy's future, perhaps see him. From the last station I went to the cloister on foot. Evening had closed in. The provost declined to let me see the boy to-night, just before bed time. It would attract attention, cause suspicious recollections, discoveries. The boy ought not to be reminded of a mother, who could neither tell him a father's name, nor take him to a home."

"I was forced to yield," she continued after a pause, with almost icy rigidity. "I should never have the courage to confess in my husband's presence that I was the boy's mother."

"And what would you fear, if you did?" I asked. She started, nay, I believe sighed gently at the you* I involuntarily used. Yet she seemed to quickly understand the change in our relations, and answered with an expression of the utmost sincerity: "Nothing for myself. If he cast me off, I would thank him for my freedom; if he killed me, I would bless him for the deliverance. You do not know, Fräulein von Reckenburg, what it is to have denied nature. But do you ask what I fear? I cannot explain clearly. A vague, perhaps false presentiment of hatred, vengeance — since he cannot reach the father — against the innocent boy, hostility also towards — towards—"

---

* Germans always use the word thou in familiar intercourse.

"Towards the accomplices in the guilt," I said, completing the sentence.

She bent her head. " He is a just, an unsuspicious man, and kind, oh! far too kind to me," she continued; "but when I think of *that*, it seems as if a dagger glittered before my eyes. He would never forgive, and the innocent, perhaps, still less than me, whom he has been accustomed to love. All this may be self-deception; even the fear of pouring the corroding poison into a trusting soul. Can one whose whole life has been *one* long lie, know herself? So I simply say: I have not the courage to confess the truth. And then, I have no longer the power to do so. Whenever I try to speak, I am attacked by the convulsions you have just witnessed. If I attempted to write, my hand would be paralysed. It is no disease; it will not kill me; I shall grow old with it, or — or " she pointed to her forehead with a look that made me shudder.

" Have you any children?" I asked, after a long pause.

She shook her head. "God is just," she replied at last. " No, He is merciful. I could not be a good mother to any child."

." And your husband?"

" Does not miss them, or does not show me that he misses them. He is very, *very* considerate towards me," she added, as for the first time something like a smile flitted across her features. " 'You are my child, Dorothee,' he has said more than once. 'No physician wishes the martyrdom and cares of maternity for a beloved wife. He sees suffering enough *outside* of his home.'"

"And have you learned to return his love?" I asked, after another pause. She gazed at me as if reflecting upon her answer, and then said: "I think I should have overcome my childish awe, and learned to love him, if I had become his at the time of our betrothal, when I had no reason to fear him. But now that I have — love him? oh! not even as a benefactor, as a friend. The soul dies in the slavery of sin."

"And does he not feel this lack?"

"Not that I have ever noticed. My cool reserve suits the imaginary picture he has formed of me. I think my original nature would have been burdensome to him. Either, Fräulein von Reckenburg, love is an enigma with many constructions, or this man has no idea what it is to love."

After these words we sat side by side in silence for a time, then she continued the story my question had interrupted. "The provost persuaded me to spend the night in the city in my old room. He would find some pretext to bring the boy to me the following morning. He accompanied me only to the gate of the city, as I did not wish to be seen and perhaps recognized in his company. Neither he nor I suspected the calamity which has fallen upon this house. I saw a light in the lower room and found the door unlocked. I should have liked to glide silently upstairs. But could I do so unnoticed? So I entered. The old soldier was sleeping in a chair beside the covered couch and did not awake. I raised the sheet and beheld the dead face of the man I had loved far more than my own father. I went up stairs, and again bent over one, whom I deeply honored, and whom death had already seized. I now wished to escape from the house unseen, to spare you the sight of me both now and forever. The convulsion attacked me. Pardon me, Fräulein von Reckenburg."

I cannot describe in words, how this expression of dull resignation cut me to the soul. How the impulsive child must have struggled, what must she have suffered, to acquire such entire self-control! I drew her head to my heart, pressed her hand, and said: "The dead man loved you like his own child — let all evil memories be forgotten between us, Dorothee."

A flush as bright as had ever tinged her cheeks in her happiest days suffused the pale face. She bent over my hand and warm tears fell upon it. The clock struck twelve. "Oh! Fräulein Hardine!" she exclaimed, "if you are in earnest — and you never made a promise which you did not keep — prove it now, for this is perhaps the last time we shall ever see each other in our lives. Rest, and let me watch beside this dear lady, nurse her once more as I used to do. You need strength for to-morrow, and I, could I rest while expecting it? Do not grudge me the comfort of this confidence, Fräulein Hardine!"

"Yes, watch beside my mother, Dorothee," I replied without hesitation, "I will sleep in your bed in the other room."

As if transformed by some magic spell she instantly became the old Dorl, kissed my hand, inquired about the physician's prescriptions, busily arranged everything for the night, lighted a candle, and led the way to the chamber she had occupied in her girlhood.

On the threshold she paused; she saw that the room had been kept in the neatest order, precisely as she had left it. On the window stood a clump of rosemary, which my mother had raised from the sprigs used on the wedding-day.

She burst into a flood of tears and buried her face in her hands. "Oh! if I had never, never crossed this threshold!" she sobbed. But she soon regained her composure, arranged my bed, helped me undress, mixed a glass of sugar and water for me, all with her graceful floating movements, then kissed my hand and went across to my mother's room.

But, as if the lovely creature had given me a sleeping potion, I slumbered undisturbed until morning dawned. When I entered the sick-room, Dorothee was standing at the window attired in one of the white dresses she had worn in her girlhood, as she did not wish the bright colors of her traveling costume to form too striking a contrast with our mourning. Her luxuriant hair had fallen a sacrifice to the fashion of the times, the short locks curled naturally around her delicate head. She was standing behind the curtain, watching with sparkling eyes and a feverish flush on her cheeks for the boy, whom she no longer dared to call *her* boy.

But no matter how she might strain her eyes, the dense morning mist — the fog of the 14th of October — veiled every object. She uttered no sound, a slight tremor ran through her figure, over which the passionate agony of expectation had shed a semblance of the impetuosity of her early youth.

At last she heard steps on the stairs, and I followed her to the door. But it was the provost *alone*, who had caught the sobbing woman in his arms. "My foster son will follow me immediately," he said, "This *first* hour belongs to our mourning friends, dear Dorothee."

With these words he entered the sick-room; *another* to pour balm into the sore hearts, *another* long estranged and now regained friend.

He was a counsellor and help to us all throughout the long anxious day; Dorothee, in particular, who in her excitement often forgot the caution prescribed by her friend, owed to him the preservation of her incognito. Christlieb Taube remained in the country until the evening, the old servant had left the house early in the morning to attend to the business of the funeral, the door was closed to all visitors. The maid-servant could be trusted, she knew nothing of the past history of the household and, in her dull honesty, scarcely noticed the presence of the stranger in the house of mourning.

Our friends had said farewell to the dead and left me alone in the room beside his coffin. A noise at the door roused me from my reverie; it was the provost, who led the boy to the corpse, that the concealed mother might see him, while at the same time the child's attention would be diverted from the violently agitated woman. If he also hoped to produce a discouraging impression of the perils of a soldier's life, his plan, after the manner of many wise designs, produced precisely the opposite effect; it only roused the thirst for battle, the soldier's blood, in the boy.

You have had a detailed account of this scene in Augustus Müller's recollection, my friends. Let me add only one thing. When the boy exclaimed in such a eager, joyous tone: "I, too, will die for our native land!" and that terrible cry burst forth from the mother's heart, I felt my unjust anger against the "wild stock" disappear; for I again saw in him the son of the friend who had atoned for the follies of his youth by a chivalrous death.

"I shall never see him again, never!" With this cry of agony the unhappy mother fell upon the floor, as the door closed behind her child. She was again attacked with convulsions. We carried her up to her chamber, and she revived in the arms of her old friend, whose tears were falling upon her. "God is the Father of the fatherless," he said, but she fixed her glassy eyes upon him, murmuring, "and you are God's priest on earth."

After these words I went away, leaving the two to a long conversation about the boy's future. A considerable sum, to pay the expenses of tuition and defray the first cost of apprenticing the boy to the forester, was placed in his guardian's hands on this occasion. Dorothee did not exchange another word with me until she took her departure; she remained in the sick room and humbly obeyed every sign from her friend. The iron band, from which she had been released for a few hours, again pressed upon her brow. She had again bowed under the burden of her fate, and could I now venture to say — break it, or fly from him.

While these events were occurring, the first vague rumors of the terrible catastrophe of the day spread through the city. Peasants, who came from the more western villages to the market, stated that they had heard constant cannonading since early in the morning; Leipsic merchants returning from Frankfort spoke positively of Davoust's successful manœuvre and a bloody battle with the main army, which had been seen the day before on the march from Weimar. The village of Hassenhausen was even named as the point where the conflict had raged most fiercely. All our citizens who had any kind of carriage or horse, sallied forth towards the west, to ascertain the truth of these statements and their consequences.

Again a dense crowd thronged the market place; but not *one* glance was hopeful, not *one* voice spoke words of cheer. The tragic prelude of Saalfeld had aroused the darkest forebodings.

But no one felt these presentiments more sadly than *those* who, assembled in the house of mourning around the victim of the battle of Saalfeld, saw the 14th of October pass away in silent brooding. Who could describe the sorrowful emotions, which within a few hours met beneath *one* roof? Tragedy followed tragedy, personal grief was merged in the calamity of the nation, the anguish of the past in that of the future. Each individual had some peculiar sorrow, anxiety, fear, or torture, while sharing the suffering of the others, and over all the impending fate of their native land brooded like a threatening thunder cloud.

At last evening closed in, and the funeral procession moved forward. Although I had wished the burial to take place quietly, without the presence of strangers, I could not nor did I desire to prevent the citizens, almost without an exception, from walking at the head of the train, bearing torches in their hands. If they honored the brave soldier who died for his native land, they likewise mourned an old and valued friend.

I walked behind the coffin with the provost, followed by Christlieb Taube and the old servant. And so we lowered the beloved form to its last repose, all in tears, all oppressed with grief, at the very hour when, routed at the same time in two battles, the German armies, neither suspecting the fate of the other, dispersed in wild confusion.

The first and still vague report of the defeat of Hassenhausen — it was not called Auerstädt until afterwards — reached us when we returned from the funeral. Christlieb Taube, with his "scattered" companion, therefore hastily departed in the direction agreed upon the day before by way of Freiburg. The provost also urged Dorothee to set out on her return by the night coach, for who could be sure that on the morrow the whole country would not be flooded with a disorderly rabble of friends and foes. So the first eternal farewell was now followed by one parting after another, and each probably with a foreboding that it might be the last.

The former tutor and lover did not suspect that he had been under the *same* roof with Siegmund Faber's wife. "The faithful heart has hardly found repose, do not let us disturb him again," said our old friend, and Dorothee remained concealed until the little carriage rolled away. But I must bear witness that the faithful heart had by no means found repose. After the worthy man had said farewell to us, I found him on the threshold of Dorothee's room wiping his eyes. "No one who has ever loved *her*, can forget," he said in a broken voice. A sorrowful little interlude amid so many scenes of horror!

Dorothee had put on her travelling dress, and I held her hand for a last farewell. It had been a day of silence for us both; now something which she vainly strove to express in words evidently oppressed her heart. "May I speak?" she asked at last with downcast eyes, and when I cordially assented, said hastily:

"You will be rich, very rich, Fräulein Hardine, some day — perhaps soon — But at present, during the unsettled state of affairs in the country, if you would perhaps — perhaps — "

I shook my head.

"You need not take the loan from *me*, Fräulein Hardine; you *would* not, I know; but — from *him*. He makes so much money, and values it so little. He uses so little. You would give him a great pleasure, Fräulein Hardine."

"No, Dorothee," I answered, hastily; "*no*. From *you* I might accept a loan, a support, if I needed it. From *him*, never!"

I saw her turn pale, and regretted the evil memory I had involuntarily recalled. I clasped her in my arms, kissed her for the first time in my life, and we parted without another word. A few minutes after I heard the post-chaise roll away. In the general confusion no one had recognized in the silent, closely veiled traveller, the much envied ex-fellow-citizen. Her hasty visit home remained a secret.

The provost, too, could not leave his institution any longer in such troubled times. After the two most disturbed days of my life, I again sat alone, at midnight, in the silent sick room.

How, during the next few days, the extent of the misfortune, which far exceeded all anticipation, became apparent; how the proud victors took possession of the country, half of whose troops became French allies; how the Prussian prisoners, deprived of the barest necessaries, were shut up in churches and sheds; the stately castle was converted into a hospital, plundered by friend and foe; how all crowded in admiration around the unconquerable emperor, as on the 18th of October, a day so fatal to him seven years later, he dashed through our little city toward Leipsic; how each expected safety solely from the mercy of this ambassador of God — spare me the account of these loathsome, horrible scenes. They lingered in my memory, long after the anguish of my heart had subsided into peace.

At the time, to be sure, personal necessities smothered sympathy for the nation. The hostile train, which so often follows a great sorrow, and in true tyrannical fashion takes vengeance upon pride — anxiety about the means of existence, fears for daily bread, sleepless nights beside a sick bed, shame at failing strength, humiliating hopes for aid from strangers, rose above the horizon of my life. True, it was but for a short time, perhaps *only* that I might learn to know them face to face. I did learn the lesson, but was approaching the limits of old age ere I took it to heart.

My poor mother's helpless condition might last for years, while our little store of money would scarcely suffice for a few months. The small widow's pension, if it could be granted at all in these times, would not have covered our most imperative wants, work done by my unpracticed hand would scarcely have found a purchaser. The invalid, according to the doctor's opinion, might have been removed to Reckenburg without danger; but the countess did not even vouchsafe an answer to my letter containing the news of the loss we had sustained, or the representations of our situation repeatedly made by the provost. This faithful friend, therefore, had reason to think that all my future hopes would be destroyed, if any one else should take the post of steward I had vacated, and skilfully make use of it, and how much more important, how much more alluring than I had ever acknowledged, these prospects seemed to me now. In short, I saw no escape from my trouble and the little door that at last opened to me, the door which now, wreathed with the evergreen garlands of faithfulness, shines before my memory as the portals of the gold-tower of Reckenburg, then seemed narrow and oppressive to the proud heart.

The asylum which the rich relative refused in her empty palace, the poor servant opened in her lowly hut. Nurse Justine offered to receive and take charge of her former mistress, while the daughter returned to the post which so urgently needed her services. The faithful soul urged a speedy departure, and described her little store of savings as an inexhaustible supply.

And I did not delay to grasp the outstretched hand. Preparations for the change of residence were hastily made. The invalid was to be removed to her new home before Christmas.

But God's will was more merciful. He spared me the shame of seeing my mother nursed by a stranger's hands, and gave her a resting place beside the husband she had loved so long and so tenderly. A few days before the morning appointed for the journey, I found that she had gently fallen asleep, and thus my home-life closed with a second funeral.

But this was not the last of the great year of change. When I entered Castle Reckenburg, early on Christmas morning, the countess was in her death agony. She tore her clothes and hair, clung to the nurse in mortal terror, and shrieked for help, air, and light.

I opened the window. A bright flood of sunlight was reflected from the white snow, a refreshing breeze streamed into the long-closed, airless room; the Christmas bells rang from the steeple, which still uninjured, towered above the dilapidated house of God. The countess's convulsions gradually ceased, her breathing grew calm and quiet. She turned her eyes, now bright and keen as ever — not upon the coffer of gold beside her chair, but upon me, held out her hand, seized mine in a strong clasp, and exclaimed in an almost joyous tone:

"In right and honor!"

Those were her dying words and I understood their meaning. In the last hours of the year 1806 we lowered the mysterious old woman to her rest, and the rule of the last von Reckenburg began.

CHAPTER XI.

THE NEW GOVERNMENT.

WALK through Reckenburg, if you wish to read the history of the next twenty years of my life, years in which the time that had preceded them gradually became a vague memory, and from whose commencement I have become accustomed to date the story of my real existence.

It was a period of labor, but a labor that contained within itself all the conditions of success, and, therefore, of satisfaction; for to a long-cherished plan was joined a persistent will and command of ample means for its execution.

My predecessor's wealth was not inexhaustible, as popular fables had described it; nay, for years, it had lain almost as dead capital. But it was more than sufficient for an important object, if we take into consideration the person who had the power to dispose of it at pleasure.

Money, *in itself*, had little charm or value for me, for, although I should not have relished my predecessor's porridge and acorn tea, my character and education rendered simplicity a necessity, rather than an obligation. My fields were my sphere of labor, and the hitherto unused balcony-room, made a little more comfortable and furnished with the articles brought from my former home, afforded sufficient comfort for the hours of rest. I had no æsthetic tastes, no social needs; I was destitute of family ties and free from that good-natured liberality which squanders the largest means because it is unable to say "no." *Summa summarum;* nature and fate had made the economy, required by every struggle, easy to me.

But what first gives the authority for such struggles: a place and time, were, at least, not unfavorable to mine. Amid events that shook the entire continent I had six whole years of peace, during which to lay a firm foundation. The estate was away from the main routes of the armies, and though there was no lack of recruiting and levying supplies, while people bore their burdens with sullen faces, because those who were hated as enemies styled themselves friends, my plan would not have prospered so well under the rule of the neighboring province, striving so hard to maintain the remnant of its independence, as under the quiet vassalage of our own. You know this plan; it was to extend the rich cultivation of the landed property belonging to me over the whole poor parish.

If canals and protecting dykes, good roads, reclaimed marshes, and well-guarded forests extended over the lands belonging to the village; if timber was felled for the benefit of the whole community, brick kilns built, loads of stone from the quarries hewn out; if the church and school-house rose from their ruins, and at last, instead of the loathsome, dilapidated huts, neat villages appeared, which I include under the one name of "Reckenburg"—all this, which meets the eye as a result, was only the means to an end and an easy expedient for a free, full hand. The object of my task and its difficulty was to put a renovated race in the renovated fields; a vigorous, orderly, and industrious peasantry in the parish of Reckenburg. "His Majesty Fritz in Pomerania," my kind provost jestingly called me in his encouraging letters; and in fact it was just such a starving, idle population, over which I usurped the government. Yes, usurped; for it was not hereditary submissiveness, but necessity and the charm of wealth which made them my slaves. The productive lands of even the rich peasants had been sold in times of calamity to large proprietors, scarcely anything except a few barren shreds of moorland and bogs remained in the hands of poachers, smugglers, and idle day laborers. But my certainty of cure rested upon this very foundation of misfortune. For the most luxuriant fields degenerate, and the poorest soil is improved by culture. Soil, which for a long time has borne crops of oil and sugar, sinks, exhausted, into producing oats; a forest that a century ago was devastated by a hurricane, by dint of patience and industry is converted, at the end of another century, into a pine forest, and at last stands as of old. And as with the earth, so with the lord of the soil. Not on the sluggard's bed, whether it is that of misery or luxury, but upright, by the sweat of his brow, is man formed.

I did not impress this horn-book wisdom on the minds of my colony by the blundering words of the missionary, but as mint-master, with the stamp I had found in the black countess' gold tower. He who cultivated his barren land and fed his cattle according to my directions, received from the stock on the estate tools, seed, and young animals, and in case of failure in the crops or sickness, obtained another supply; but *never* except on condition of gradual restoration after years of prosperity. He who was most industrious received an addition to his land from the estate, which, during the time of war, had been still more enlarged without any very heavy expenditure. This, too, however, was *never* done, except on condition of a moderate, but regular rent, that was accepted in payment for the land.

In making these enlargements, it had been arranged from the beginning that the pieces of ground obtained by each individual should be as near each other and his farm-house as possible. This practical beneficial arrangement was executed entirely through my arbitration, and certainly through my sacrifice. But he who is not willing to make sacrifices, ought not to attempt to institute reforms.

Everything was founded on mutual services; not the smallest article was given away, the most customary infringement upon property tolerated. Even the berries the children gathered in the woods, the twigs and gleanings collected by the women, were subjected to a trifling tax. True, the mistress of the castle, as agent, bought at the highest market prices, and in this way carried on a game of which she was well aware, by giving with *one* hand what she took with the *other;* but she saved the people time, did not divert their attention to business in general, strengthened the sense of right, which is most surely undermined by small transgressions, and a feeling of honor, which begins with the idea of profit and ends with that of toleration.

The rebuilding of the villages was gradually accomplished according to a plan previously made.

The old proprietor, who moved his ruinous house to the spot I designated, the new-comer, who built according to my design, each individual who agreed to keep his premises neat and orderly, received the ground on which to erect his house, the material, and a gratuitous support during the time required to build, to be afterwards repaid with interest; and all this without the use of a pen or an account-book. A simple clasp of the hand was sufficient; and the inexorableness with which I withdrew the assistance at any stratagem on the part of the peasants, answered to me for the faith of the contracting parties, till order and honesty had become a habit at Reckenburg. That the castle treasury could scarcely have done a worse business, if I had said: "Hinz, I will give you a piece of land," or "Kunz, you may have one of my meadows," that the joy of the receiver and giver might take the place of the uneasiness of the debtor and the watchfulness of the creditor, was not considered and ought not to have been. It was not the flower of kindly feeling, but the tree of right and honor I desired to plant in the soil of Reckenburg.

Lastly, yet not for the last time, the assistants who labored so bravely with me in establishing this colony must be remembered. I must consider it a piece of great good fortune, that shortly after the commencement of my rule, the pastor, a worthy German and father of a family, preferred the comfortable position of a city preacher to this rude parish at Reckenburg. Only one little hour of church service was given to the active citizens. The man went to the right place, and I found the right man for mine. Without wholly releasing the parish from its obligations, the salary was sufficiently enlarged by the mistress of the castle, and at my invitation Ludwig Nordheim, the second, took charge of it.

With his disposition and the later development of my character, the son could not be the friend his father had been; but the active man became a far more efficient colleague. If his father, by gentle words and acts, had tried to spread the kingdom of heaven among us, the son spared no denunciations to make hell hot for us. The former was thwarted, the latter produced an effect; for at that time there were more candidates for hell than heaven among the people of Reckenburg. Moreover, we found for the children a master who, in addition to book knowledge, understood how to use the axe and plough. I had at first thought with ardent longing of our faithful Christlieb Taube, but at last spared him immolation on a lost post. He is still living among his mountains, tending his roses and playing the organ to the honor of God. Without wife or child of his own, he is beloved as a father by the generation he has educated. The poorest and richest among the companions of my youth! The happiest also! I have not seen him since my father's funeral.

Another faithful friend, our honest Purzel, I was able to keep under my own eyes for several years. His time of enlistment had expired, and he had a horror of serving under the banner of the conqueror of Jena, whom he fiercely hated; not as a patriot, but as the servant of his dead master. He therefore entered easily into the *rôle* of footman which was always maintained at Reckenburg, under the honorary title of "Heyduc," and wore his queue till the day of his death. The most faithful of the faithful died many years *before* him. Her goal on earth was reached, when she saw her darling at the height of the grandeur pictured in her dreams, and in this proud position no longer compelled to parry the arts of any malicious low diamond.

The hardest loss was that of my only friend, the provost. I never saw him again. His delicate health and my constant occupations bound each to his or her post. His last letter was written in the summer of 1809 and contained the news of Augustus Müller's disappearance from the forester's house. Anxiety about his beloved *protégé* may have worn out the feeble body.

I did not share this anxiety. The lad's soldierly instincts could not have been forever restrained; and of what were we so greatly in need as these daring military impulses? If in a premature thirst for vengeance he had found a premature death — well! The soil, from which freedom is to spring, must, it is said, be watered with the blood of martyrs; and how could I have failed to recognize a happy coincidence in the fact, that the son of my hero of

THE NEW GOVERNMENT. 301

Valmy should rush forward under the son of the commander-in-chief, to efface the disgrace that commenced with the battle of Valmy.

When Augustus Müller suddenly appeared before me, I had almost forgotten him for many, many years. Whether Dorothee knew of his disappearance among the troops of the black duke or whether she merely suspected it, I had never discovered. Since I said farewell to her on the day of my father's funeral, she, too, had been as one dead. I was glad that we had parted in peace, but I felt the same as during the time of discord: we had done with each other. Now and then her husband's ever increasing fame reminded me of the only playmate of my childhood. Though little more than thirty years of age, my loneliness was such as rarely falls to the lot of women. A strongly rooted tree amid a quantity of low bushes.

But during my active labor I remained a sympathizing observer of the national life, whose catastrophe had occurred at the time my own new existence began. I had never doubted its recuperation. I had learned on my own estate that storms which crush *ripened* harvests, fertilize new crops; and in Prussia a strong, hardy race was struggling for development.

Through the count, our neighbor, who was then in another province, I entered into a sort of league with the patriots, who were secretly weaving their plans in Prussia and Austria, and why should I conceal the fact, that much of the income at my disposal was applied to the loftiest purposes? But when at last the holiest conflict had begun, with what delight the magnificent apartments of Reckenburg were thrown open to the wounded men, the fame of whose noble deeds filled the whole country. Yes, yes, my friends, the heroes of Bülow and York fared sumptuously on the provisions the black countess had stored in cellars and barns. So I can boast of being one of the few among my equals in rank, who from the first hour stood forth openly on the side of the struggling people, boast that no one submitted more joyfully than I to a government, which had again boldly fought its way to right and honor. For anyone who labors so industriously at the improvement of his own house as I have done, endeavors to place it under the shelter of a strong nation.

But it was now necessary to repair many damages the troops had made in my territories, and no less needful to accustom myself and my tenants to the stern, often harsh acts required by the new order of things. Then followed the famine of 1816 and 1817, which drew largely upon the stores of barns and treasuries. At last, however, a pause ensued, in which it was only necessary to keep what had been already won. A quiet survey could be taken.

Then I saw the work accomplished, which as it were, had become my existence; saw the soil bearing rich harvests, and the tree of right and honor taking deep root in a new race. I looked with confidence at the germ of the parish, which now boasts that, for nearly a generation, no law suit has been conducted nor crime committed, no gambler nor drunkard lived within its precincts, no young girl approached the altar without the myrtle wreath; a parish that sends its recruits to the army without a murmur, educates its orphans to labor without assistance, and permits no widow nor old man to suffer want.

And I say yes and amen to this boast. In fact it was an upright and honest, but also a joyless, loveless colony.

Joyless and loveless as she who founded it. For — why should it be concealed — what you call a heart, my friends, had nothing to do with my acts. I had used certain material, as every skilled workman — or artist — uses his. I had developed my energies in and for a community — I would, and this seems to me a mark of love — I would not have limited them for the sake of any individual. My pulse beat neither quicker nor slower at the fate of any individual among the peasants I called mine; I carried the new born infant to the baptismal font, accompanied the bride to the altar, the dead to their graves; but I felt less emotion while so doing, than when I saw my trees planted and felled, or my fields tilled for a new harvest. While I was trying to form a model peasantry, the true peasant spirit had developed within me, a spirit which looks upon man as a product of the soil that supports him and which he nourishes in return.

The tools clattered and the church bells rang, but there was neither singing nor talking on the Reckenburg estate. We did not dance under the May-pole, we did not rejoice at weddings and christenings. No Christmas festivals reminded us of the joyous message of God's coming as a helpless child. The girls and young men did not marry from affection and inclination, but motives of interest or in obedience to their parents' wishes; the beggar avoided Reckenburg, for he saw no crumbs fall from the tables of the rich; and "work like us, and you will probably fare as well as we, let each provide for his own," were the words that met him on the inhospitable thresholds. In fact, we were a very respectable, but a very loveless colony!

The vague consciousness of something *wanting* in my work and life dawned upon me, for the first time, in that pause when I ought to have rejoiced in my success. I felt no relaxation, but a sort of restless weariness, and there were hours when I said to myself that, if I wanted to begin to live, I ought not to commence again like a working bee. I might have sought amusement, society, change, might have travelled, cultivated artistic taste, or adopted any of the pursuits that occupy the time of wealthy people. But I knew my own nature well enough to be aware that what I lacked could not be given me from without, but must spring up within. Yet I could not find the solution of what was struggling within me for accomplishment.

According to my habit, I did not in these investigations grope after the moon but took the matter exactly as it was. I was almost fifty years old, and though I had not felt more active and vigorous at twenty, I knew that the strongest threads break most quickly, and if mine tore suddenly, what would become of my Reckenburg robe, which had almost grown to my body, or what disposal did I wish to make of it?

True I saw many a proud sail set and many a flag

of distress hoisted to run into the protecting harbor. But as in the days when pursued by suitors, so now it was repugnant to my feeling to satisfy insatiate greed, or shameless extravagance. I desired a free choice, and no instinct of the past, no interest of the present guided me into the right track.

Plans of another kind also arose in my mind. How would it do to found an asylum for invalid soldiers or their orphans, for which, unfortunately, there was no lack of candidates at that time. Or an establishment for maiden ladies, for which, unhappily, there is *never* any lack of applicants. But do you know an old peasant — and I was in part just such a person — who would not prefer to bequeath his land to the least needy of his equals, rather than to the most indigent community? The thought of a communal model government of my estate was repulsive to me; I wanted to imagine the land stamped with the impress of a certain individuality, as had been the case first in the old countess' time and afterwards in mine, I wanted an heir, and in middle life began to regret that I had not in my youth married the first young nobleman who offered himself, and thus in the most natural way spared myself the trouble of a choice.

As for my external position, since the return of peace I was no longer the hermit of the new tower. The impoverished government valued wealth, the newly won province a faithful adherent; my advice was sought in rural arrangements, in short — from the highest to the lowest, every one treated me with the utmost respect, and thus a social intercourse was established, not as it exists between man and woman, or woman and woman, but as is common between man and man; yet anything different would have excited my surprise.

From time to time I now felt obliged to do the honors of Reckenburg by giving a banquet; then all the surroundings, lackeys, gilt coach, greys, etc., lent their aid to add to the splendor of the owner of the castle. The Baroness von Reckenburg was quoted as an aristocrat of the purest water, and the remark was true.

But these obligatory entertainments only made me feel my secret ennui still more keenly. *Here* my heart was least in the work, and the desire to make the building I had erected secure, never tortured me more than after such an interruption of the course of my simple daily life. If I could only have decided upon the where and how!

As during my youth of dependence, now year after year of boundless freedom glided by, in which only the mechanism of a regular routine supported me and I was fifty years old, when a prospect suddenly opened before me, upon which I certainly should not have turned my back in the days of my girlhood.

I have already casually mentioned the count, our neighbor. You know and respect him, my friends, I therefore need say no more than that an extensive business intercourse had been maintained between us, and at that time he already enjoyed the confidence of the government to a far greater extent than any other nobleman in our province, whose posts of honor and most influential offices were nearly all conferred upon him. And no one had a better right to them.

He was and is an official of the stamp which has won a classical name in the Prussian annals, a man who labors with such unwearied and unselfish energy for the public welfare, that his private business, especially the management of his large entailed estates, perceptibly suffered.

I prized the man according to his deserts, but his wife was one of the few women whose society was not burdensome to me; for I possessed such a masculine taste that only the most feminine qualities in women attracted me. I believe, even on a desert island, I should have remained aloof from a female steward like Fräulein Hardine; while the child Dorothee, even as a sinner, had not lost her charms for me. The countess, however, was a quiet, delicate creature, the "true woman," and my first thought would undoubtedly have been to choose an heir for Reckenburg from among the children of this charming couple, three beardless youths, if they had grown up a little less dissolute and frivolous. True, I said to myself, that with the father's ceaseless labor and the mother's calm contentment, the fiery young spirits had lacked control ; but under all the circumstances it was absolutely necessary to await the result of future developments.

A year before the count had become a widower. He had loved his wife very dearly, she had made him happy, and after her death he broke off all social intercourse, even with me. It seemed as if he wished to mourn her all his life and, apart from my fifty years, I could have had no greater surprise than when he came to me one day and, without any preliminaries, made me an offer of marriage.

The man was perfectly sane and as grave as a Cato. The bold request annoyed me more than it would have done from any one else. "I am fifty years old, Count," I said curtly.

"And so am I," he replied with equal brevity.

"That is, being a man, a quarter of a century younger," I answered, and he rejoined:

"Certainly, according to the usual ideas of marriage."

His strange frankness began to amuse me. I laughed heartily; but my suitor became still more grave.

"Do you take into account only the husband, not the father?" he asked. "I have sons—"

"Who need wives rather than a mother," I interrupted. "Why do you not say plainly: 'Adopt my boys and make them your heirs, Fräulein Hardine?'"

"Simply because this arrangement would not fulfil my wishes, or only half gratify them," replied the count calmly. "I am of course the first to appreciate the advantages which would result to my children from the name and inheritance of Reckenburg; but the wants of the present are nearer to my heart than the splendor of the future. You will not expect me, Baroness, to give these wants a sentimental dress. My heart is dead, and I am far from having the vanity to suppose I can awake yours to life. But we may be friends; you can become my adviser and support, and I yours; thereby mutually satisfying an evident need.

"You, Fräulein von Reckenburg, stand before a successfully accomplished task, whose mechanical

THE NEW GOVERNMENT. 309

maintenance is not enough to satisfy you. You possess no contemplative nature, but hourly require some success won by your own efforts. You see yourself alone, and seek among strangers for one who would worthily bear and transmit a noble name. Well, I have a new sphere of usefulness and a prospect for the future to offer you, when I say: Draw from a pure, vigorous trunk the shoots you desire to graft upon the dying tree of Reckenburg.

"I, on the contrary — well, you know me; you know what I do in the province of public affairs, and neglect in my own. Life on my estates is stagnant, while my sons are running wild. I see it with the anxiety of the father and the owner, see it — and cannot change, cannot curb my wider plans, or if you choose to call it so, my ambition. I am not the first man who has neglected his family for his profession; every servant of the state does it, must do so, to a greater or less extent. Let me add, that at the present moment I am more than ever embarrassed by this conflict of duties. The government of the province, which has been confided to me as a stepping-stone to a higher office, would remove me permanently from the vicinity; or, to speak more frankly, it will remove me, for I well know what my decision will be, and the question is only whether I am to go with a light or heavy heart."

He paused a moment. I, too, was silent. Then he continued:

"Let us clasp hands upon it, noble lady. No greater trust can be offered. *You* will add to the unlimited control of your own property the entire management of mine. The task is not too heavy for you. While a lieutenant and assistant to the father, you will be to the sons the wise friend they so greatly need. There is no other woman who can so well supply to boys a father's place. You are strict and vigilant, and will be just, because you can judge a man's nature by your own. My eldest son would leave the military school, and under your animating influence, fit himself for the duties of heir. You would find for the two younger boys the positions in life which, with more moderate means, will suit their talents, and if the father, with a mind at ease, succeeds in accomplishing his plans for the benefit of his native land, the good he does and enjoys will be inscribed in the book of your benefactions."

Well, now I saw a rock for my house! Now, with a family connection, I still retained undisturbed freedom for myself, a sphere of action similar to the one in which I had already tested my powers, and a second, where new faculties could and would be developed. For although I might have been a support to which a delicate little vine would hardly cling, perhaps too harsh for the mother of daughters — I had learned among my peasantry how to train and control intractable lads, and should probably be able to manage the scions of a more aristocratic race. The count was right, I was a fit guardian, step-mother for boys. Why did I still hesitate, why did I not give my consent?

Was the habit of solitude so strong in the hermit of the new tower? Did she hold in such high esteem the opinion of the world, whose ridicule is always aroused by an old maid's marriage? Or did she listen to the voice in her heart, that whispered in tones of warning: "This is not what you need." Did she feel a secret, incomprehensible protest against a new masculine task, while the *woman* was pleading for the rights of which she had been deprived.

I requested time for consideration; and weeks elapsed, during which I did not see the count again, weeks of indecision such as I had never experienced before. But at last I could delay no longer.

The king's birthday was approaching, on which, according to a ten years' custom, a great entertainment was given at Reckenburg.

All the pomp of the household was displayed on this occasion, even my aunt's old fashioned jewels were brought out to heighten the magnificence of her heiress. Of course the count would be one of the invited guests. I expected the renewal of his offer. Reason had conquered; I was resolved to accept it.

Often as the third of August had been celebrated in this way at Reckenburg, I had never remembered, that long, long ago, in the grey dawn of this day, I had uttered an eternal farewell and seen the dream of my youth vanish. Now, in my fiftieth year, the third of August was to become the day of my betrothal.

CHAPTER XII.

MOTHER AND SON.

That was a dull meal, my friends! I broke down in the toast I proposed to His Majesty; every complimentary speech I exchanged became entangled in my throat with the yes I could not utter, and yet did not wish to leave unspoken. It was fortunate that people were not in the habit of expecting anything but aristocratic dulness at the entertainments given at Reckenburg.

After dinner the guests dispersed through the pleasure grounds. I remained alone on the terrace with the count. He had told me before dinner that his appointment had arrived, and therefore a decision could be delayed no longer. I had undergone the last struggle, bravely uttered the preliminary words and was just about to place my hand in his, when I heard a voice at my feet exclaim: "Hardine."

Although very young, you were witnesses of the scene, my friends, and have undoubtedly often heard it described since; so I need only explain the feelings aroused in my own heart, which caused so much suspicion.

Interrupted in the decisive moment, I looked up and saw a young, powerful man, with the flush of intoxication on his face; at any time the most repulsive spectacle I could behold, but doubly so on this occasion. Muttering wild, scarcely intelligible words, he ascended the steps, a terrible odor of bad liquor greeted me; with the hand I had just stretched out in pledge of my betrothal, I pushed the insolent fellow away. He staggered, fell, and drops of blood on the ground induced me to look at him more closely. Now for the first time I noticed the dilapidated uniform, the maimed arm; I gazed at the scarred features, and a terrible dread overpowered me. But when, suddenly sobered, he now confronted me with clenched hand and bold defiance, the proud carriage of the head, the angry light in the blue eyes roused a long slumbering memory; but strangely enough it was not at first that of the son, who had wished for death on the battle-field, but the father, who had so early found it there. Prince Augustus, not Augustus Müller, suddenly stood before me. The vision lasted only a moment. At the first words from the father and child I understood their singular mistake; but dared I, could I explain the error before this gaping crowd? Ere I had formed my resolution, the man had turned to go; I saw a livid hue overspread his features, saw him cling trembling to the arbor; I motioned to the pastor to support him, the count also hurried after him in visible perplexity, and they soon disappeared.

I was not in the mood to enter into any explanations with my guests; we curtsied to each other afterwards in the castle, and if any went away without a farewell,— so much the better. That anyone could seriously believe the stranger's accusations, never occurred to me. I sought the solitude of my own room.

I was really very much agitated. As if conjured up by some magic spell, a long past forgotten life rose before me, at the very moment that I was in the act of disposing of the remainder. Besides, I perceived the desolate condition of the man and his child, the error he had made, and which his and my old friend had predicted! So, after a generation, I was once more to thank this friend for his care.

While I was searching among my papers for Augustus Müller's baptismal certificate, I did not doubt my right to explain to the deluded man his origin. I would show him the certificate, conceal his father's name as well as his mother's fate, and when I had provided a suitable support for both father and daughter, the affair would be settled.

I had just found the document, when the pastor entered with the count. The latter showed an agitation which, in the usually calm man, gave me an unpleasant surprise. "He is at the inn pretending to be ill," he hastily exclaimed.

"He *is* ill, Herr Count," replied the pastor, "he is shaking with a feverish chill."

"The sickness that follows intoxication, if it is not delirium tremens," retorted the count. "It is fortunate that I was still one of the magistrates of the district and could take his papers from him. Read them, Fräulein von Reckenburg."

With these words he handed me the often mentioned childish recollections of Augustus Müller, and while I was glancing over them, poured forth a torrent of angry words about the slanders which had spread through the parish since morning and would be disseminated through the whole region before night. "I'll have the vagabond put in the hospital without delay," he concluded, "and after he recovers, transported beyond the frontiers. It is the shortest way to put a stop to the gossip. The man is mad, or a fraud of the first order."

"He is neither," I answered quietly, as I locked the papers and certificate in a drawer of my writing table. "Augustus Müller's recollections are correct, and the conclusion he has erroneously drawn may be pardoned on account of his necessity. He is a native of Reckenburg, and it is our duty to take charge of him in the parish."

With these words I rang the bell and told the servant to find the family physician and see that the sick man was properly cared for at the inn.

"A kindness which will bear bitter fruits," said the count, in what seemed to me a scornful tone. "The *first* of its kind, that has ever been known in Reckenburg."

The *first* benefit to a stranger in Reckenburg? The lesson, little as it was intended in *that* sense, would have been severe, if I had ever cared for the reputation of a sister of charity, or at least had received it in cool blood. But the count's ill-humor had infected me. I bore within me a sore spot, whose touch I had once scarcely forgiven my *first* friend, and which I would never have pardoned my *last*. In order to at least have no witnesses to impending explanations, I requested the pastor to consult with the physician and, in case he did not find the sick man sufficiently well cared for at the inn, order his removal to the castle.

As soon as I was alone with the count, I said: "Will you not more clearly point out the bitter fruits which, according to your opinion, will grow out of the care of a stranger?"

"Yes, but what stranger?" cried the count, shrugging his shoulders. "After his public accusation and the confession you have just made —"

"You mean the confession of having placed an orphaned child in an institution?" I asked.

"Have you any testimony to prove the parentage of this child?" replied the count.

"I think my word is enough," I replied, as I crushed the baptismal certificate, which I still held in my hand.

"Then speak that word. Mention the parents' names, which seem to be so intentionally concealed in the certificate of the institution."

"And if I desired to continue to conceal them?"

"Then you would have to answer for the neglect of a hitherto stainless reputation."

Until then I had maintained my self-command; now I could no longer control myself. "Do you mean to say that I placed my *own* child —"

"*I* have nothing to do with the matter," interrupted the count, who was now as calm as I was agitated. "The world judges from appearances, and it is incumbent upon me, as a magistrate and your friend, to oppose these appearances. So I ask once more; *can, will* you give me any proofs of this man's origin?"

"No!" said I, "whether I *can* not, or *will* not, is of no consequence. I need no friends who require a stranger's testimony in behalf of my reputation, and I expect the magistrate to respect the *guest* of my house."

With these words I left him. I knew that I had closed the open doors of my bridal hall, and felt as if a weight had fallen from my heart.

Nevertheless, I was trembling with secret indignation. Dorothee was living, and I had no right to disclose her secret. Even if she had desired to reveal it for my justification, I would have checked the words on her lips. Passion had suddenly enlightened my understanding; not *I*, but the *mother* had the right to decide the fate of her son.

That very night I set out with post horses for Berlin. I travelled without servants, because both for my own sake and that of the persons to whom I was hastening, I objected to have any watch kept on my movements.

Evening was closing in when I reached the goal of my journey, and without going to a hotel, went on foot to Siegmund Faber's house, to which every child could direct me. If I succeeded in speaking to Dorothee that evening alone, my task would be performed and I could go back to Reckenburg unseen the same night. The sick man's condition made me anxious. The physician, to whom I had spoken of my intended journey, and who had discouraged his removal to the castle, had declared his disease to be inflammation of the lungs, caused by an imperfectly healed wound in the breast, and which his habit of indulging in strong drinks rendered doubly perilous. I, too, after so long an interval of repose, again expected a sort of crisis in my life, which I wished at any rate to await at my post.

When we read such a story of life, in which only the principal events, following each other in rapid succession, are described at length, while the intermediate incidents, the quiet, transforming labor of time are merely superficially mentioned, we easily imagine the personages unchanged in regard to the secret relations in which they stood towards each other in the last scene. And so you, young, impetuous people, probably suppose that I went to meet these old acquaintances with the old passionate feelings, or the throbbing heart of guilt. But twenty-seven years had elapsed since I had heard of Dorothee's marriage, how many a life is completed in that period, from the cradle to the grave! And though during this time I could have mentioned no special crisis in my nature; a totally different position in life, a great epoch in the world's history, important considerations and a wide sphere of action had made me a totally different person, the friends of former days strangers. Now I could have confronted Siegmund Faber without embarrassment, and calmly discussed the condition of affairs with Dorothee, with due consideration for her temperament and position. Nay, as I walked through the streets in the dusk of evening, I repeatedly felt a doubt whether my *first* decision in regard to her son's fate had been the right one, whether the man supposed to be dead ought not to have remained dead to her?

But anger had urged me to this awaking of the mother's heart, and we are so disposed to see a dispensation of Providence behind these personal inspirations. At any rate I could try whether she was in the mood for my message, and further proceedings were wholly under my control.

As I approached the Faber house, I found the pavement covered with straw, and perceived that the passers by collected in groups, or gazed anxiously at the dimly lighted windows on the second floor. I also caught a few disconnected remarks. "Out of this window! — The husband, the poor husband!"

The door of the house was unlocked, the staircase empty, but covered with a thick carpet; all was still. At the entrance stood a servant, and an anxious moving to and fro was visible in the corridor.

"She is ill and can see no one," was the reply to my inquiry for the Frau Geheimeräthin.

"Not even an old acquaintance, who is passing through the city?"

"No one."

"Nor tomorrow?"

"Nor tomorrow either," replied the servant, but offered to inform the Herr Geheimerath of my presence.

I hesitated a moment. The object of my journey had failed, but I was anxious to learn further particulars about the condition of the invalid, which the evidently excited servant either could not or would not give. I decided, however, not to disturb his master so late, but come early the next morning to make my inquiries, gave the man my card and was in the act of going away, when a portière opposite to me was drawn aside and Siegmund Faber hastily approached.

I had not seen him for thirty-five years, and a strange expression of anxiety and grief rested upon his features; yet, even in any other place, I should have known him at the first glance. *His* outstretched hand also showed that he had instantly recognized in the matron, who stood before him, the girl of fifteen. Time had made no great changes either in him or me; a privilege of those whose hearts have little life.

Obeying his mute sign, I followed him into his own room. "A sorrowful hour for you to enter my house for the first time, Fräulein Hardine!" he said, pressing my hand with deep emotion.

"Do you still hope, Faber?" I asked, already hopeless myself.

"Hope?" he replied; "yes, I hope, but not for life," and when I softly uttered the words "brain fever," answered: "If it were, you would find me less hopeless. No, it is no fever —"

I interrupted his explanation by a hasty gesture; the horror in his eyes had confirmed my suspicion. I thought of the hour, when Dorothee had intimated this result. We stood in silence for a time, listening to the piercing cries that issued from the adjoining room. "Do I disturb you?" I asked at last.

"Unfortunately, no!" he replied. "I have no rest outside, and in that chamber, which I would not willingly leave day or night, I can only remain while unseen. My unfortunate wife apparently sees in me only the doctor she always feared, not the inconsolable husband, from whom she affectionately concealed her sufferings till they reached the climax."

" And when did the climax occur?" I asked.

" Yesterday," he replied. " The malady is an insidious, malignant one, which perhaps commenced before our marriage. All in all, it is a mystery."

I cast down my eyes and remained silent. I *alone* could have given him the clue to the mystery.

He asked me to sit down, took a chair beside me, and described the convulsions, which had attacked the blooming creature at intervals ever since her wedding day. "Sometimes," said he, " I could see the attack coming on for hours. She was troubled, restless, often approached me with her hands clasped on her breast, a gesture by which when a child she had made her requests so irresistible ; she looked at me with a heart-rending glance, tried to speak, and struggled until she became convulsed and sank, though without losing consciousness, on the floor. As this condition, however, occurred very rarely and passed away quickly, and did not disturb her general health, I supposed it to be one of those incomprehensible nervous affections to which women are subject. I attributed it to the suspense and anxiety of the long years of betrothal, the too sudden change of all the relations of life, among which she could only regain her usual composure by degrees. I fell into the error of many physicians, who judge of the physical life of their relatives according to the critical experiences of their profession, and the soul life according to their own needs. Because, after a day of toil, a pause of rest was beneficial to *me;* because I wanted *nothing*, except to see the lovely creature, still and bright as a sunbeam, relieving the shadows of my professional life; in my selfish comfort I overlooked the unchanging monotony of her existence, forgot the contradiction between it and her impulsive nature, forgot it the more easily as she herself never complained, never asked for anything, always said that she was well, and no trace of failing health belied her words. She was and remained a blooming, lovely child, Fräulein Hardine, an angel of humility; Dorothee, my gift of God, my sunbeam!"

He hid his face in his hands, and I heard a convulsive sob; for a long time he was unable to speak, and when he at last began again it was rather to himself than to me. "When nature is repressed, she always revenges herself — always — if I had made her travel, sought amusements and society for her — procured light and air amid the wilderness of the city; I have done *nothing*, nothing for her; I refreshed myself with the sight of her, egotist that I was, and am now so cruelly punished!"

A new pause ensued. After he had collected his thoughts, he hastily continued in an almost business like tone. "Her sufferings increased during the exciting events of the autumn of 1806. When, on my return from the army, I unexpectedly entered her presence, for several minutes I embraced a senseless body. Since that time attacks have returned more frequently, and lasted longer, one might say they increased with the tortures and humiliations of our native land. In the summer of 1809, when blow after

blow followed each other in the defeat of Schill and
Brunswick, and the humiliation of Austria, they
seemed to reach their climax. Then a pause ensued;
the stillness of resignation. I had followed the army,
and afterwards heard for the first time from others —
never from herself — that she had joined the band of
women who, after the battles, nursed the wounded
in the hospitals. The poor, delicate child, who could
never see a drop of blood, never even hear of a
a wound! Day after day she entered their places of
suffering, went from bed to bed, gazed anxiously into
the face of every patient, as if she were seeking some
one who was not to be found, wished to save some
one who was not to be saved, and then sank down
utterly crushed at the door, only to renew the torturing quest the following day.

"Of course, if I had been on the spot, I should have
prevented this useless torture, but when at the
end of a year I returned from France, I found the
hospital empty and Dorothee almost unchanged.
Not until the battles of Ligny and Waterloo — I was
again with Blücher's army — an event is said to have
occurred, which ought to have prepared me for that
which happened to-day. I did not witness it, and consoled myself with the thought that the impressionable
childish nature, her idiosyncrasy against everything
that is called death and suffering, had caused this
powerful emotion. Her present condition, which has
been occasioned by no external event, mocks this
consolation. I stand like a fool before this mystery
of nature.

"You may suppose, Fräulein Hardine, that where

the happiness of my whole life was at stake, I did not trust to my own judgment *alone*. I obtained the advice of all my colleagues far and near. But Dorothee rebelled against all medical treatment with a vehemence that was entirely unlike her usual manner and increased the violence of her attacks; and no one had any judicious method to propose. She herself declared that she was perfectly well, and she seemed to be so. I heard on all sides the supposition that it was mere hypochondria. At the utmost her childless state was mentioned as the cause of momentary physical or mental disturbance. But I am too experienced a physician to believe in such suppositions. Dorothee was too delicate for a martyrdom, to which my mother succumbed in giving me birth, and let me add, Fräulein Harding, Dorothee was too much of a child for the education of children, in which the father could be of so little assistance to her. She has never shown any maternal longings; nay I saw her shudder, when on one of our rare walks through the city we once met a party of orphan boys. When after the year 1806 — not on my account, but hers — I proposed to adopt a soldier's orphan, an attack of convulsions was her reply, and when speech returned she said with a gesture of the most imploring entreaty, "Pray, pray—don't."

"We become accustomed to such things, Fräulein Hardine. My professional life grew more and more absorbing. I was often away on journeys and, when in Berlin, frequently remained in the house only a few minutes a day. So I scarcely noticed that she became more and more quiet year by year, that days elapsed without hearing a sound from her lips. People naturally grow more silent with age, and what did we have to tell each other? She experienced too little and I too much, but not the events which are suitable to discuss in the household. The attacks gradually ceased, and I felt relieved — until perhaps about three months ago.

" Then I could no longer conceal from myself that the silent apathy had changed into strange agitation. She paced up and down her room all day and at night sat erect in her bed with eyes wide open, or I found her even then wandering softly to and fro. If I told her to go to bed, she obeyed, lay down and pretended to be asleep. But as soon as I returned to my room and she fancied herself unobserved, she again rose and began her wanderings anew. She did not sleep, asked no questions, answered only by mute, but perfectly intelligible gestures; and only took necessary food when it was forced upon her. Oh! that the poor brain had gently worn out in this way, but since yesterday —"

"Since yesterday?" I asked eagerly.

A piercing shriek from the next room interrupted him. He started up and listened at the half-open door. "Who can understand, Fräulein Hardine," said he, when everything had grown quiet within, "who can endure to see the most peaceful creature on earth die suffering the tortures of a murderess, be obliged to restrain her by force from laying violent hands upon herself — Oh, God! Oh, God! Yesterday at twilight, one unguarded moment, and — she was—"

He could say no more, and I, too, stood shivering

with horror. For months, during which the son had wandered through the land, seeking a mother, and yesterday, yesterday when in rage he stretched out his hand towards another — can we believe in such sympathies, in an electric communication between kindred blood?

"Can I see her?" I asked the unhappy man, after a long silence.

"She would not recognize, scarcely notice you. But you, how could you endure the sight? Fräulein Hardine — she is raving!"

"Take me to her," I said moving forward. At the door I paused. "One question more: is it a formless sorrow, or —"

"It is a fixed idea," replied Faber in a whisper, "the wildest — or could it spring from repressed maternal affection — have I been deluded a second time —? But not a new-born infant, as is a common idea of lunatics; no, she raves about a boy, an orphan boy, whom she, she herself, has murdered. About every fifteen minutes a pause ensues; then she makes a ball of pillows and handkerchiefs, presses it to her heart and caresses it as a mother does her child, but soon with the energy of madness tears it into pieces, hurls it from her, shrieks, sees herself — or whom? — surrounded by a crowd of friends she calls "the blacks," and can only be prevented by force from seeking release from this torture by violence. And yet, yet, would you believe it, Fräulein Hardine? The angelic nature is not conquered, even in this extremity. She would fain conceal her sufferings from her inconsolable husband. 'Hush!

hush!' she whispers, whenever I approach. But as the agony is stronger than her will, she always becomes more restless, writhes, tosses, and moans, until I go away and she draws a long breath as if relieved, and soon returns again to her fancy about the murdered boy."

We entered the sick room. It was brightly lighted, for the threatening spectres increased in the darkness. Two strong nurses were in attendance. Dorothee was sitting upright in bed, pushing away with one hand a soothing potion, while with the other she tore off the ice they were trying to bind on her head. The once golden hair hung over her shoulders like a veil of silver, bestrewed with melted drops of ice, her face looked like a snow-white flower, and her dilated eyes glittered with a restless light. The unfortunate woman, in her fiftieth year, in the bonds of madness, at the portal of the grave, was still beautiful; nay, it seemed to me I had never seen her look more beautiful than in this excitement.

I signed to the nurses to cease their fruitless efforts; they drew back, and I sat down on a chair beside the bed. Siegmund Faber listened intently at the door, there was not a sound in the room.

For a long time she did not notice me; it was one of her quiet moments; she busily wrapped the bandages of ice she had torn from her head in a towel and pressed the bundle to her heart. "Oh! oh! how cold!" she murmured shivering, "how cold!" I bent over her, took both her hands and fixed my eyes steadily on hers. "Do you know me, Dorothee?" I asked.

Strange! She had scarcely heard my voice and looked at me a moment, when she exclaimed, "Hardine, Fräulein Hardine!"

The husband could not repress an exclamation of surprise. Dorothee listened intently. "Hush, hush!" she whispered, hiding the bundle under her quilt. But as everything remained quiet, she drew it out again, pressed my hand upon it, and said: "Feel how cold it is, Fräulein Hardine. It is dead, oh! so cold, so cold, the poor child, dead!"

"This is no child, Dorothee," said I, "it is a cold stone, which has long rested on your heart. I will take it from you. There, now it is gone, now you will feel easier, Dorothee."

She willingly allowed me to take the bundle, but still moaned: "Dead, dead, poor child, dead!" I hesitated a moment, then in spite of the listener, dared every danger. I pressed the moaning mother's hand to my heart, and said, raising my voice: "The child is *not* dead, Dorothee. God is the Father of the fatherless, the boy lives."

"He lives, he lives!" she shrieked. "Who says he lives? Who has seen him alive?"

"Hardine says so," I replied. "Hardine has seen him. The boy is alive."

"He lives, he lives!" she exclaimed. "Hardine says so, Hardine never tells a lie, never! Hardine has seen him. He lives! Where, where? Take me to him, Hardine!"

"Yes, I will take you to him, Dorothee. I will take you with me to Reckenburg. Do you know? To Reckenburg, Dorothee—"

She reflected a moment, rubbed her forehead, and murmured, "Reckenburg! Reckenburg!" At last she obtained the clue. "In Reckenburg, yes, in Reckenburg, that was it. Not in the orphan asylum. He lives in Reckenburg. Fräulein Hardine has seen him. Fräulein Hardine will take me with her to Reckenburg; Fräulein Hardine keeps her word!" She clapped her hands like a child. "To Reckenburg!" she excalimed exultantly, "come, Fräulein Hardine."

"I will take you to Reckenburg with me," I said, "but not now, you must get well first, dear Dorothee."

"I am perfectly well," she replied, attempting to leave her bed.

I was obliged to prevent this by force. "You are ill, Dorothee," I said positively, "but you will soon be well, if you will obey me. Take these drops; lie down quietly, close your eyes, and go to sleep. Then you shall go with me to Reckenburg."

"I will obey you, Fräulein Hardine," she said and without resistance took the medicine she had so violently refused to swallow a short time before. But she suddenly grew restless again, gazed anxiously around the room, and whispered: "He! He! If he should come now! If he should notice! He will not let me go, Fräulein Hardine!"

"Be calm; I will watch beside you," I answered aloud. "And he will let you go with me, for he loves you, Dorothee."

"Fräulein Hardine will watch beside me," she murmured, her lids already closing drowsily, and then with the docility of a child, allowed me to dry her wet hair, and wrap the clothes closely around her. Both hands were clasped in mine; she looked up several times, but when she saw me sitting quietly beside the bed, with my eyes fixed upon her, gently fell asleep.

After a time I noiselessly rose and approached the man who, unobserved, had witnessed this scene. Tears, perhaps the first he had ever shed, were streaming down his cheeks. He pressed both my hands to his heart. "The blessing of one hour's rest," said he. "What a magic there is in the memories of childhood, the people whom we first knew. Oh! selfish, blinded man, who only counted by the pendulum of the hour. If I had taken her to you years, even months ago —"

"And if it should not be too late even now, my friend?" I asked.

But he shook his head and replied: "It *is* too late."

I promised him to watch with Dorothee through the night, and begged him to seek for a few hours the rest he so greatly needed.

"I, too, will obey you," he said, and with a sorrowful glance at the sleeper went to his own room. Every fifteen minutes, however, he came to the doorway until at last, resolving that he *would* sleep, a few hours undisturbed repose restored his exhausted strength.

I sat alone with the invalid, holding her hands in mine, and God only knows in what an agitated mood! What a sarcasm was contained in the happy delusion of the deceived husband! What a punishment in the horrible fancy of the deceiving wife! But she lay so calmly, breathed so quietly; was it really too late to have truth and peace reign in the place of error?

No, I still hoped, hoped when I rose at dawn to put out the lamp and draw back the window curtains. But when at the end of a few minutes I returned to my post, I perceived the sudden, indescribable change, that destroys every hope.

I would have called Siegmund Faber for a last farewell, but Dorothee now raised her eyes, no longer glittering with the light of madness, but with the old inquiring expression they had had in the days of her innocent childhood. She groped for my hand and whispered: "Do you believe that God is merciful, Hardine?"

"I do, Dorothee," I answered firmly.

"Even to me, who can no longer dare to call Him *Father*!"

"To every weak, erring creature, who longs for His fatherly love."

"And he is alive, you said he is alive?"

"He is alive, and I will keep my eyes upon him and tell him that a loving mother is waiting for his coming in the Father's kingdom."

I had scarcely uttered these words and Dorothee, with her last strength, pressed her lips to my hand, when Siegmund Faber entered the room and, with a cry of agony, threw himself on his knees beside the death-bed. She opened her glazing eyes once more, a last tremor shook the stiffening limbs. "Faber!" she gasped. "Mercy, Faber! Oh! Lord, my Saviour, mercy!"

All was over.

I went away unobserved. But when, at the end of several hours, I returned to take a last farewell of my friend, I found the husband still in the same spot, clasping the dead form, which to the last he had called his child, never once his wife. But he composed himself as soon as he saw me, and after I had taken a long look at the woman who was still so beautiful, even in death, accompanied me out of the room.

"So long as I live, Fräulein Hardine," said he, "I shall thank you for this peaceful end. She was the joy of my life, my whole happiness!"

I parted from Siegmund Faber with the resolve to keep the memory of his sunbeam pure from every stain.

My soul was filled with the awful picture of offended nature revenging itself, but also — I can see your tears flow, my child — but also of a faith, whose strength I have never seen surpassed on any death-bed. She had perceived the sin against the eternal order of God and atoned for it here below with all the tortures a human heart can feel; delusions had fled, with the prayer which she had on her lips in dying she commenced the new life, and holding her recovered son by the hand, could once more venture to say father.

In this mood it seemed an incident rich in consolation that, as soon as I returned to Reckenburg, I was summoned to another death-bed, an end as bright and composed as the brave heart had ever desired.

"Fräulein Hardine," cried Augustus Müller, "you are *not* my mother, I know it now, for death makes everything clear. Forgive me the disgrace my folly has brought upon you."

"You were seeking a mother and erred in good faith. You did not offend me, Augustus," I answered frankly, holding out my hand to him.

He pressed it firmly, lay for some time absorbed in thought, and then said: "One thing more, Fräulein Hardine; that fair woman with the yellow hair, whom I saw beside your father's corpse, *is she* — ?"

"She *was* your mother, Augustus. She has gone before you in love. But I will provide for your daughter in her place."

APPENDIX BY THE EDITOR.

YES, our brave soldier is dead! Three days after the hour when, intoxicated with hope, he recognized Nurse Justine's house, he departed this life, and it was fortunate for him, we exclaim. We would not have grudged him a death blow from a Turkish sabre; but ten years of peace had consumed his vitality. Now he died quickly as he had lived, well cared for, on his native soil, and his glazing eyes rested on the orphaned child, whom Fräulein Hardine took to her home. Augustus Müller died more happily than his brave Lisette had anticipated on her death-bed.

And three days later we saw Fräulein Hardine follow his coffin, as sole mourner, to the resting place which had been prepared for him by the side of the most faithful servant. This was a last honor which the mistress of the castle showed to each native of her parish, and we, who have read her confession, know what memories made it a duty, but her contemporaries, who will first learn the truth from these pages, cried in chorus: "A stranger, a beggarly idler! The man who has spread the most shameful rumors about her?"

So it was Fräulein Hardine's own acts and silence, which supported these rumors in such a way that her fair name was permanently blackened. We will not pause to relate how blank amazement was followed by the most contemptible prying, how suppressed envy triumphed, anger, nay revolt against such long years of hypocrisy was openly displayed. The house, admittance to which had been regarded as a great honor, found itself shunned like one where a contagious disease has broken out; the proud edifice of right and honor seemed shaken to its foundations; no hand was raised to support it, since even the count had given up his relations with Reckenburg and all future prospects, and, silently, it is true, but in a manner that spoke volumes to the eager watchers, hurried to his distant post.

Who has not seen a tottering power abandoned in a similar manner? Yet the noisy zeal that attended this catastrophe could not be understood, if the time at which it occured were forgotten. The excessive strain of all the vital energies in danger and conflict had for ten years subsided into apathetic quiet; every one obeyed the need of repose by restoring order and repairing damages within a limited circle. All desire to enter a wider sphere was repulsed, the interest of the state, even the memory of our recent triumphs, seemed forgotten. With patriarchal ease patriarchal narrow mindedness and love of gossip spread through the country. A less remarkable event than the fall of Fräulein Hardine's crown of honor, would, at such a period, have been treated as an affair of greater moment, than the loss of a monarch's diadem at another epoch.

Did Fräulein Hardine notice this fall? Did she heed it? She gave no sign, but quietly attended to her daily occupations as before, and did not hesitate to draw the doubtful creature she had taken home more and more into her society. Under all the circumstances, she could have adopted no course which would have paved the way to milder feelings more quickly than this proud indifference. But we, whom she called hers, we people of Reckenburg did not trouble ourselves at all about the gossip. We neither believed nor doubted it. Each individual attended to his own affairs, as Fräulein Hardine had taught us.

Yet the most violent storm passes away, and even the hurricane at Reckenburg subsided; not quite so suddenly as it had burst forth, but quietly and slowly, after the manner of German tempests. The hand which has a gift like Reckenburg to bestow, retains its attractions, her equals in rank remembered their former hopes, her inferiors possible favors. Soon every one only longed for an occasion to publicly deny what was secretly doubted by no one. This occasion, however, was not long delayed, and it was the place from which all the help is expected in our dear native land, the highest of all, to which Fräulein Hardine owed the preservation of her crown of honor. She received the diploma of canoness in the most aristocratic chapter in the kingdom, and with it the prerogatives of a married lady. She made no use of this position, called herself and continued to be called Fräulein von Reckenburg. It was said that she had gratefully declined the offer of quartering her coat of arms with the counts' coronet. She seemed to be determined to go down to her grave as *Fräulein* von Reckenburg. The royal favor, however, was the signal to doubt or generously cover the slander.

A brave veteran of the war of freedom, attacked by a sudden feverish delirium, had found at Reckenburg a resting place and an honorable grave, his helpless orphan a generous support. Woe betide him who, a year after the fatal banquet on the royal birthday, had ventured to utter any other version aloud! Neither this year nor ever after did Fräulein Hardine celebrate the 3d of August with a patriotic entertainment but, if she had done so, she would have missed no invited guest from her table.

And guests arrived uninvited. Visitors seeking counsel, offering homage, cherishing hopes of gain appeared with an innocent smile upon their lips, as if they had never held aloof, and were received as if their absence had never been noticed. Avoidance seemed forgotten on both sides; the old order of things at Reckenburg was restored, only that the interest of the community was more and more divided between Hardine senior and the little namesake growing up at her side.

For how the first visitors stared in amazement, to behold in the neglected vagabond, after the lapse of a year, as healthy and pretty a child as could be found. Surely Fräulein Hardine was fortunate in everything she undertook. Even her sorrowful *protégé* had prospered in the air of the new tower and on the fields, where she had become their mistress' daily companion. People were expecting an act of adoption, and already numbered the youths of noble birth, who might, without reluctance, receive the inheritance of Reckenburg from the hand of the ex-sutler's daughter. And the list was a long one.

But nothing that was expected happened. Fräulein Hardine took no steps to raise the little plebeian to her own rank. She did not even make her will. Her foster-child still remained Hardine Müller.

Besides, she was by no means educated as would have beseemed an heiress of Reckenburg, placed in charge of no boarding school, no learned tutor, no foreign governesses. The child's first teacher, Pastor Nordheim, was also her last; and of all the fashionable accomplishments of the day, only music was taught the talented girl by a competent master in the neighborhood. For the rest, she soon took charge of the domestic affairs of the household, and seemed to have the same taste for them as her patroness felt in the management of the outdoor business.

To be sure this education did not indicate any very ambitious plans for the mysterious orphan. But who could say that Fräulein Hardine, who in so many respects ventured to row against the stream, would have given her own daughter or granddaughter a more comprehensive education, that the standard of her own knowledge would not have seemed to her enough for the management of a large property?

To these well-founded doubts was added the perception of a gradual change in the mode of life at Reckenburg, so far as household affairs were concerned. This course was perfectly natural for one who did nothing by halves, like our Fräulein Hardine. For one person draws others after, and no one more than a child. The little orphan needed attendance, instruction, and society; she required rooms to live in, to play in, to see her little companions, who were not slow in coming. A pleasant room is wanted for a child's toys, and afterwards for a young girl's treasures; guest chambers and sitting-rooms must be fitted up. The new tower was too narrow and plain for more than one; the adjoining halls were too spacious and magnificent for anything less than a large assembly. So partitions were put up; stoves appeared by the marble chimney pieces; soft carpets covered the cold mosaic floors; comfortable cushioned furniture took the place of the hard gilt chairs; fragrant flowers that of the mouldering potpourris and nodding Chinese mandarins on the pier tables. Music and singing echoed through the long-silent palace, and modern table furniture, instead of the quaint silver and porcelain utensils, covered the well-spread board.

And the garden underwent the same transformation as the house. All the lifeless inhabitants of Olympus, from which little Hardine had shrunk in terror, were removed without mercy; the triangles and squares, at which she had laughed when they were called trees, made way for untrimmed shrubs and bushes; the stiff hedges and glass-bordered flower-beds, which interfered with the children's playground, disappeared, and broad lawns took their places on both sides of the stately avenue. Young girls love flowers, and therefore luxuriant blossoms extended to the edge of the forest; nurseries of fruit trees, beds of vegetables, and hot-houses surrounded the castle, for the hospitable house needed the dainties, which the lonely mistress had not missed. Seats at all the pleasant places invited passers-by to repose;

a fountain in the centre of the terrace dispensed in cooling spray the water which the monsters in the pleasure gardens had distributed in countless tiny threads, and the singing birds of the forest fluttered to the edge of the basin, where childish hands strewed food. All in all, our Reckenburg, without denying its origin, had in the course of time acquired a homely comfort; and how could a needy person have been turned from its threshold without food and care, when little Hardine uttered in his behalf her "please, please." Kind-hearted children are so fond of giving, and little Hardine was a kind-hearted child. When, during the first few years, the cholera demanded numerous victims throughout the country, and making one of its cat-like leaps, spared only Reckenburg, Fräulein Hardine erected a splendid orphan asylum, and on the day of her foster-daughter's confirmation, fifty little fatherless and motherless girls were received into it.

So little Hardine had now become a grown young lady, and an alternate intercourse with city and country had been established and extended even to circles which formerly had not been numbered among the society of Reckenburg; within this sphere, however, since the more agitating times that followed the days of July, opinions have been uttered to which in former years Fräulein Hardine would hardly have listened. In short, wherever we look, since the appearance of the little beggar child, the old has gradually become new, the antiquated young again.

So we no longer saw the gilt coach with the ancient grays, but a light carriage with a pair of fast horses conveyed the mistress of the castle and her guests to and from the nearest station; and active young servants took the place of the powdered footmen in the rejuvenated household. The periodical entertainments ceased, but in the castle and village the youths and maidens sang and danced around the May-pole and under the harvest wreath; the tavern held out its sign invitingly, the balls rolled, the mugs of beer clinked, though in moderation; we were still a respectable colony, but have become very different people from those who gazed at the wandering soldier with astonished eyes and did not vouchsafe a glance at the magnificent cavalcade. The peasants of Reckenburg were well entertained; but an all-powerful spell lured guests to the magnificent apartments of the castle, for the elder lady smiled graciously and the younger one was beautiful.

Though the young girl was still called plain Hardine Müller, she occupied a position which would have been equally suitable for the petted companion or the relative of an aristocratic family. Her education and mode of employing her time fitted her for the family life of a household in the middle ranks of society, while her grace and ease of manner rendered her by no means beneath the dignity of a man of rank. But precisely because she seemed adapted for such different positions, the hopes of each class were restrained. Suitors of plebeian birth were repelled by the title of the aristocratic foster-mother; the aristocrats shrank from the young girl's plebeian origin, unless her future prospects were assured. For a time a marriage was expected between her and the count's eldest son, a handsome, gay cavalier. But the young gentleman thought otherwise, and chose a lady who possessed countless ancestors, and though she did not, like little Hardine, have two birds in the bush, held *one* firmly in her hand. It was the doubt concerning the inheritance of Reckenburg, that kept both classes of suitors aloof, and so we must unfortunately admit the fact, that the charming, much admired little Hardine reached her twentieth year without being able to boast of a single offer of marriage.

All these doubts regarding suitors, however, found a surprising solution when, in midsummer, just twelve years after the orphan had found a home at Reckenburg, Fräulein Hardine announced the betrothal of her foster daughter. The chosen husband was the first companion of her childhood, the school boy whose acquaintance we have already made, but who did not take the hereditary ecclesiastical office at Reckenburg, and after his father's death, which had occurred a few years before, exchanged the profession of a lawyer to study that of agriculture under Fräulein Hardine's eyes, and now managed the estates of Reckenburg as her assistant.

Many a secret hope was destroyed by this marriage, many a new one kindled. It was supposed to be Fräulein Hardine's denial of any intention of adoption. Never could this prototype of a noble lady bestow the family seat of her ancestors, the inheritance which was to perpetuate their name through future generations, upon a man who received a salary from her as an employee. Every one who had noble blood in his veins applauded the old Baroness von Reckenburg.

In a few weeks Ludwig Nordheim and Hardine Müller became man and wife. But the anxious expectation increased when, on the day after the marriage, the news spread abroad that Fräulein von Reckenburg had made a will. She had prepared it without the assistance of any notary, and strictly forbade any legal interference with the persons managing her property at the time of her death until, after an interval of thirty days, it was opened. The testator was perfectly sound in mind and body, not a hair on her head had turned grey, the proud neck was not bowed a single inch. She was sixty years old, perhaps more, but she seemed likely to live to be a hundred.

Many of our contemporaries will therefore remember the universal surprise, nay stupor — the editor's hand trembles even now as he reaches this crisis — when on the 21st of September 1837 the news of the death of the last von Reckenburg spread through the country like wild fire. Much as they had held aloof from any kindly intercourse beyond their own estates, the eyes and thoughts of high and low for generations had been fixed with too eager and manifold an interest upon the two eccentric mistresses of the castle, not to feel touched, as if by some personal calamity, when the place they had occupied was now suddenly left vacant. Who would fill this place? Individuals, as well as corporations, anxiously sought for the slightest clue that could guide them to the fountain of blessing. Every one saw himself justified in cherishing a hope, the more so as no one was entitled to a claim, and only good fortune or favor could cast a great prize into his hand.

But fortune hunters were not the only persons concerned. A large community had lost a mistress who had made its prosperity the task of a long life; a vast number of employees the most just of rulers; and even poverty a kind patroness, since by the hand of a beggar's child the virtue of charity had become a habit at Reckenburg, so it is not too much to say, that thousands looked forward with anxious hearts to the hour which was to decide the choice of the heir of Reckenburg.

But no one felt this anxiety more keenly than the young pair whose happiness had been so sadly clouded by the sudden death of a benefactress.

Not until this hour had Ludwig and Hardine felt the full significance of their early orphanhood, the anxiety of homelessness. A warm, soft nest had hitherto sheltered them; but where would their future residence stand?

And it was not only the doubtful future, the sorrowful present, but also the mystery of the past, that weighed so heavily on the hearts of the two poor children. They alone of all the numbers who looked forward anxiously to the final disposal of their home, knew that, at the same time, the mystery which had opened it to the soldier's orphan would be solved.

When on that unhappy morning the young husband and wife had joyously entered their old friend's room to give her the usual greeting, they did not find her prepared to attend to the business of the estate.

The bed was untouched, and she herself, still in her night-dress, was leaning back in the large arm-chair that had been brought from her father's house. On the writing table before her lay the old family bible, open at the 8th chapter of the Epistle to the Romans, and the words of the 14th verse "for as many as are led by the spirit of God, they are the sons of God" had evidently been freshly underlined. Beside the bible they found a manuscript, on which, in the usual firm characters, were the following words:

" My secret. To be read without witnesses by Ludwig and Hardine Nordheim the evening *before* the opening of my last will."

This communication seemed to have been sealed late at night, for the wax as well as the seal bearing the Reckenburg coat of arms showed signs of recent use, and the one candle, which was still sufficient for the keen eyes and simple habits of the lady of the castle, had burned low in the candlestick. Still, she had carefully extinguished the light, and then, with clasped hands, had probably rested for a time, absorbed in memories of the past or plans for the future, and thus fallen asleep. *Not* as the children at first hoped, to wake again, no, she had fallen asleep forever. She had died of palpitation of the heart. No trace of struggle or suffering marred the calm features, a smile rested on the lips, and the last flush of life had not yet left the cheeks. The dead face looked more beautiful than the living one had ever done. It still showed the mild rapture with which she had welcomed death, the grandeur of the last hour, which transfigures the grief of the survivors into an eternal consolation. The last von Reckenburg had died *before* the loss of a single power, at peace with God, the world, and herself.

But to-day the interval of a month, which she had fixed before the disclosure of her long guarded secret, was at an end. The sun of the October day was setting, and we can imagine the solemn earnestness with which the young husband and wife, clad in deep mourning, ascended the steps of the terrace and silently walked down the avenue of elms to the edge of the forest.

An affection which had been cherished for years had united Ludwig and Hardine, and love, it is said, is blind. But even the keen eyes of their patroness could scarcely have found two human beings, who seemed so created for each other.

We might have imagined a scion of the old Reckenburg race to possess the clear eyes, powerful frame, bronzed countenance, and erect bearing of the young man. The assistant, whom Fräulein Hardine had chosen, must be thus sure of himself and prompt in action. The joyous school boy, who had won the crippled soldier's heart at the first glance, had become a noble, upright man.

But Hardine, as she now nestled closely to her only protector, whose shoulder her little head, crowned with its wealth of golden hair, scarcely reached, every glance of the large, lustrous eyes a question, every movement of the pliant limbs, every flush of color that tinged the transparent complexion the expression of a loving nature, resembled the young birch tree, whose foliage trembles at the faintest breeze, and whose slender trunk would be snapped, if the towering crest of the stately oak did not shield it from the storm.

It was one of the rare days, whose golden sunlight and shifting hues we gratefully enjoy as the last favor of the year. Ludwig and Hardine ascended a hill which, rising between the pleasure grounds and forest, afforded a view of the country for miles around. The spiders had veiled the stubble in the fields with a network of silver, the meadow saffron spread a glimmer of violet over the green grass. The bells of the grazing herds echoed softly on the air; the fragrance of late blossoms of mignonette mingled with the spicy odors of the forest, which in every shade of autumnal foliage and evergreen pines formed a frame to the landscape. The broad, calm river flowed silently along, a mirror reflecting the unclouded blue sky, till far into the west it vanished in the glow of the setting sun; but towards the east the slender sickle of the moon hung like a diadem above the dark pine forest, and from the valley rose the white mists, that remind us of the forebodings of our souls, when the brightness and joy of youth have vanished.

No coloring throughout the year enhances the beauty of the simple forms of our scenery like that of autumn, and was it in farewell or for a welcome home, that it had displayed its brightest hues to-day?

Ludwig and Hardine had gazed silently at the fair scene. Now the young husband interrupted the stillness; he clasped his wife's hand and said, with a smile, in a frank, earnest tone: "Yes, it is a dear home, and it must be delightful to obtain the right of citizenship in it by owning the land. But dry your tears, my Hardine. Do we not belong to each other? Has *she* not trained us to active labor? You will be happy elsewhere, too, my dear, gentle wife."

"Anywhere, Ludwig, anywhere with you!" she whispered, as she leaned her bright head upon his breast. But after a moment's pause a shiver ran through her frame, as she added: "It is not *that*, Ludwig, not that alone—" She hesitated, but he replied: "No, it is not *that*, and I know *what* it is, my Hardine. There is no more anxious mystery than that of our origin. If the future is concealed from us, we want to have a clear view of the past, know the ancestors to whom we owe the blessing of life. And therefore—"

"Therefore!" murmured the young wife.

"Therefore," continued Ludwig with proud confidence, as if rejecting a doubt of his own honor, "*therefore* I say to you that, whatever the immediate future may disclose, no stain will rest upon the noble image of the woman, who has been a mother to us both."

The wife stooped and kissed her husband's hand, as if in gratitude to him for confirming her own belief. But her tears still flowed. "And my father, Ludwig," she sobbed, "my poor father—"

"Your father," replied Ludwig, "in the shipwreck of his life, clung to the straw of a memory, a delusion, to save himself and his helpless child from sinking."

The young wife sobbed convulsively. Her husband kissed her on the forehead and drew her down beside him on a bench, over which an ash-tree spread its heavy foliage.

"Compose yourself, my child," said he. "We still have an hour. Let us prepare ourselves for the disclosures we expect, by recalling the memories of our childhood. I should never have allowed myself to enter upon such a subject, even with my beloved wife, so long as *her* eyes watched over us. I should have felt her secret disapproval. But now, when her own will reveals the secret, now I ask you, Hardine — did she ever speak to you of the past?"

"Never, never, Ludwig," replied the young wife.

"And to me only by a few grave words that disclosed nothing," said Nordheim, deeply moved by the recollection.

"On that happy morning, when she led me to express my long cherished wish, and granted it she asked: 'Do you know the origin of the child whom you will henceforth take under your protection, Ludwig?' And when I answered in the affirmative, she continued: 'she was born in honor; her father was a brave soldier, whose wounds cover later errors. Be a brave soldier also, and do not fear wounds in the always stern battle of life.' That is the only time she ever reminded me of Augustus Müller."

Ludwig talked a long time about those sad days. The memory of the quick, curious schoolboy had grasped and retained many things, which the little girl had not noticed or had forgotten. He did not fear to remind her of her father's neglected condition or even of her own, when, like a trembling half-fledged bird, almost stupefied with privation and suffering, she had appeared before the lady, who had hitherto never belied her aversion to every phase of ruin in favor of any human being.

"I cannot spare our hearts this retrospect, dearest," said he; "that we may understand this woman and her acts. Now ask yourself, whether such a vision, intruding itself upon her with the most unprecedented claims, and not sparing the most disgraceful insinuations, would have been likely to intimidate or strengthen our friend's previous character and principles?"

Then he spoke of the consequences of these events. Hardine now learned, for the first time, at what a sacrifice the matron, who had so long been accustomed to homage, had preserved her secret, and both bowed in reverence before the silent heroism which the young wife designated by the ready name of "love."

"No," said Ludwig, concluding his careful survey of the past; "no, it was not what you call love, Hardine, not a natural instinct, which made this woman depart from the rule that had governed her life and defy the opinion of the world. Nor was it the supernatural strength of the Christian, that accepts disgrace and persecution as a blessing."

"Then, what was it, Ludwig?" murmured the young wife; "what was it?"

"'A secret,' as she herself calls it; a secret, which, when it is revealed, will teach us that we have the power to do right, even *against* our inclination. This heavenly power is *conscience*. Fräulein Hardine fulfilled a duty. She performed it fully and entirely, according to her magnanimous nature. And if, in the course of time, the re-active blessing of love sprung from her virtue, we are *doubly* her debtors — first, for the sake of the conflict she endured, and secondly, that of the victory which made her our mother."

With these words Ludwig Nordheim rose, took his wife's hand, and after a pause, continued with deep emotion: "And, therefore, my Hardine, before we hear the last words from her lips, place your right hand in mine in token of an inviolable resolution. Whatever she may disclose, or withhold, we will respect as the revelation of a mother; whatever she may command, or forbid, we will obey as the precepts of a mother. If we are to be poor and depend upon our own exertions among strangers, we will not despair; it was a mother's wisdom that perceived we needed the spur of necessity to mature our characters. If she points out a path to us, we will walk in it; if she gives us any charge we will execute it, strong in our remembrance of *her*. But, lastly, my Hardine, if her hand should draw aside the veil from a picture that angels might revere, we will date our family from the day when this woman gave the desolate child an asylum in her heart, and hold our heads proudly, because the courageous love of a mother has interposed between us and the spectres of darkness."

He paused. The young wife had placed both hands in his, and he held them for a time in a firm clasp. Evening had closed in; the last hues of sunset faded;

the first star appeared above the horizon; the white mists rising from the meadows grew denser and denser around the dark pines. Ludwig and Hardine gave one farewell glance at the scene, and then returned to the castle silently, but more quickly than they had come. Without delay they entered the simply furnished tower chamber, which had remained undisturbed and still bore traces of the life that had fled.

During the summer Fräulein Hardine had sat to a distinguished artist for the only picture of herself in existence, and which now, according to its destination, occupies the last vacant space in the picture gallery at Reckenburg. This space had been left vacant by the childless countess for her husband, the prince, in order to close the long line of ancestors with the purple of royalty. Now the spectator stands thoughtfully before the simply attired form, which the artist has painted well and understood still better.

We have a long row of pictures behind us. First, come the dames and nobles, somewhat coarsely moulded both by nature and art, of the days of chivalry, with their coifs and helmets, bodices and shirts of mail. Next, numerously represented, appear the cavaliers and their wives, in curled perukes and queues, uniformed and covered with stars, with powder, toupets, and patches, the air of a dancing-master and the smirk of a courtier. Last is the small figure of the countess, with her sharp, bird-like profile, and a coronet, with nine points, on her towering hair, as she stands before the ruins of the old castle, holding the plan of the new edifice in her jeweled hand.

A century intervenes between *this* picture and the last, which concludes the line. And what a century! The most wonderful revolution the history of the world has known strides before our minds with seven league boots. The foot takes one step — and we stand before Fräulein Hardine's portrait.

Towering above all the women in the gallery, and even most of her masculine predecessors, she is represented standing in a forest glade, in the act of advancing, her eyes turned with an expression of calm confidence in the direction from which the light falls upon the scene. Her hair is brushed plainly back, she wears a green riding-habit, and holds in her hand an oak branch — we have met her in this guise daily on her estate. On her breast, her sole ornament, is the black and white order of the year of deliverance.

This picture had not been delivered by the artist until after the lady's death, and, surrounded with a garland of star-wort, had been placed by the children above the arm-chair in which the beloved friend had breathed her last.

They took their places opposite to the picture, before the old-fashioned oak table, on which the Bible was still open at the eighth chapter of the Epistle to the Romans. Hardine lighted the candles and placed her trembling hands in her husband's. After drawing a long breath he broke the seal of the manuscript and, without any interruption, except a loving glance at his weeping wife, or at the portrait, read the contents, which we have given the reader as far as the death of the invalid soldier.

The secret of the past was revealed, in the spirit Ludwig Nordheim had predicted to his wife. Only a few sheets remained; he suspected that they must contain the directions for the future, and after a long, long pause, read the last portion of the story of this singular romance.

THE FOUNTAIN OF YOUTH.

THE concluding chapter of my story we have lived together, dear Hardine. It will tell you little that you do not remember, and, after all, is only the sum total of what we mutually owe each other.

You think it was a loving hand that led the orphan from her father's corpse, beneath her own roof. How often I have felt, with shame, your grateful tears upon my hand. My child, I was a very cold guardian, and it was a long time before I — loved you? oh! no, even learned to endure your presence.

It was a moment in my life, when the last faint trace of interest in others threatened to become extinct. The fate I had witnessed had startled, not softened, me. Out of love, Dorothee had become a sinner; out of love, the man who had staked his whole existence upon her, an impostor; in a vague impulse of the most justifiable feeling, Augustus Müller had turned slanderer, and had not I, myself, in my youth, from an impulse of sympathy, left the safe anchorage of my life, in order, when a matron, to reap the spleen of the world as a righteous punishment? "The heart makes us fools and weaklings!" I exclaimed with a bitterness never before known.

For I felt the universal desertion all the more deeply because I did not seem to notice it, and because, up to the last, I had not believed in its possibility. No one of these people, not even the count, was a loss to my heart; my self-appreciation had not developed according to *their* valuation. But are not honor and respect like the air that keeps the breath in the body, the breath that labors the more violently, the more feebly the pulsations of the heart maintain the circulation within? All these people, I knew very well, led by vanity and selfishness, would sooner or later come back to me, wearing the semblance of respect. But I also knew that the foundation of respect was forever destroyed. And honor is not sufficient for itself, like conscience; it lives only *by* and in reflected rays. It is a lonely fire, that burns in the light-house, but it warns the sailor at its feet, and if it is extinguished, the light-house is a useless thing. I seemed to myself like such a rayless light-house.

And what had I to compensate me for having the honorable name of Reckenburg die out in mockery and derision? A task for the energetic mind? A pleasure? A great joy, or even the memory of one — for which many have hazarded fame and repose? Well, the support of a beggar's child was no heroic deed for the rich woman, who, without a sacrifice, might have maintained a hundred; but it was far less a joy.

If it had only been a boy! An active, lively boy, like Ludwig Nordheim, who might have been trained for an able laborer on my estates. But a girl! Of what use to me and my Reckenburg was this frail, weak creature, who, at the utmost, could only learn to manage knitting-needles and pot-ladles? And such a stunted, miserable child, who did not bear the slightest resemblance to the pair that had roused my youthful sense of beauty, and hitherto *alone* satisfied it. If I secured the little one a comfortable, plebian life, for which, after it had regained its strength, I would have it educated in some worthy family, my promise would be fulfilled and my task performed.

The care of restoring this physical strength I had committed to my maid, on whom I could rely as implicitly as on myself. For "like master like servant," was an axiom which had held good since the establishment of the new order of things at Reckenburg. The child was dressed, fed, bathed, and nursed exactly according to the doctor's prescription or my own orders, with the same accuracy that my linen was ironed, or my room dusted; but there was also not a spark of any other feeling than the zeal of the servant. I could be sure of this, without examining into the matter. Yet I did examine into it, whenever, before and after my inspection of the castle, I visited the servants' rooms on the ground floor. There was no lack of care, and the child was evidently healthy. But it cowered wearily, with vacant, glassy eyes, in the chimney corner, or some sunny spot on the terrace, never spoke unless questioned, and carelessly laid aside the toys that were placed in its hand. "The child is an idiot!" I said, turning my back upon it.

Months passed in this mood, the most mournful, because the most hopeless, of my life. One November morning I received the royal patent, which was to raise me to the position of a married lady. I recognized the good intention of repairing a bungled affair, wrote my thanks, and laid the document among my other papers.

In consequence of this, I set out on my way to the fields at a later hour than usual. The child was sitting on the terrace steps. Its eyes, which were usually half-closed and gazed sleepily into vacancy, were now raised to the sky, where the sun was struggling to break through the veil of mist. The expression attracted my attention; I walked silently past; but after taking a few steps turned and saw the child still in the same attitude, not heeding that the black Newfoundland dog, my constant companion, was trying to make its acquaintance by taking a bit of bread from its hand.

I could not forget the look. It was the first time that my thoughts had been occupied with the child. I shortened my morning walk, returned the same way, and paused before a picture, which, if I had been an artist, I would have sketched on the spot.

The child was still sitting in the same place, with the great black dog waiting patiently beside her. She had thrown her little arm around its neck, and buried her face in its shaggy hair. The sun, which now shone clear and bright, cast a gleam of gold over the fluttering hair. I now noticed, for the first time, that it curled prettily, that the thin limbs had grown white and rounded, and the cheeks, which at this moment were tinged with a faint color, were beginning to gain the plumpness of childhood. An air of peaceful repose was impressed upon the little figure. At my approach she raised her deep blue eyes to mine; she smiled for the first time under my roof — perhaps for the first in her life.

"The child is freezing. It needs warmth!" said I; and from that day it lived and slept in my tower-room, which received the noon and afternoon sunlight and was the only one of the long, magnificent suite of apartments, which was warm and at least comfortably furnished.

I now ate at the same table with the little one, saw her in her bed in the morning and evening, and watched the development of the tender germ. To be sure, for a long time it was not with the love of the gardener, who rears a tiny plant from a seed; but from a sort of curiosity to see whether it would really blossom. She daily grew fairer, more rounded, prettier. I often exclaimed, in surprise: "Dörl!" But she did not move like Dörl, did not laugh, did not prattle, did not play like her, and the great black dog was her only, but devoted friend.

I had agreed with the pastor upon a plan of education, which was to be commenced after New Year's Day. On the afternoon before Christmas, he came to invite the child to a Christmas tree, which his son, now at home spending his vacation, had arranged. There would be no entertainment at the castle; the servants received their usual presents in money and the customary holiday feast. In other respects the night, that was a season of rejoicing to all Christianity, resembled every other evening in the year.

Young Herr Ludwig had accompanied his father and remained with the child, while I walked to the village with the pastor to attend to some of the affairs of the parish. When we returned, the boy was sitting at the window, through which the sunlight slanted into the room, with the child in his lap, her little hands clasped in his, her head resting on his breast, and her eyes, sparkling with an eager light, raised to his; he had just finished telling her a pretty legend of the Christ-child. I had never thought of telling the little one a story; nay, I really did not know whether I could remember one.

I ordered the toys and sugar-plums I had provided to be carried to the parsonage and, though not invited, accompanied the child. Long as I had regularly spent my winters at Reckenburg, for thirty-six years I had seen no Christmas festival, and there must certainly be some spell emanating from the brilliantly lighted fir tree, a spell that awakens a sacred family joy. The most confirmed old maid has a mother's feelings, while she sees the Christmas candles burn, and the spicy odor of the fir, blended with that of the wax lights, fruits, and candies, that inimitable Christmas fragrance, salutes her nostrils.

And how joyously Herr Ludwig played on the piano and sang: "Hark! the glad sound, the Saviour comes!" How artistically he had adorned his tree, how mysteriously he divided the gifts, how charmingly the Christ-child looked in its cradle of moss. A merry party of children from the school-house had been invited to the festival, and — do you still remember it? — little Hardine vied with the whole circle in dancing round the Christmas table; she played, laughed, and twittered after her teacher "Oh! fir-tree, oh! fir-tree" more eagerly and joyously than any of the others. But when, late in the evening, holding my hand, she returned through the silent village, over the snow glittering in the moonlight, to the silent castle, she repeated word for word the story of the Christ-child, which she had heard for the first time to-day from a stranger's lips, and for the first time the aged heart perceived the likeness of God not only in the *One* gracious, but *every* helpless child.

"The little one is not an idiot," I said, as before going to sleep I saw her lying in her little bed with flushed cheeks and quick, regular breathing, "but she needs excitement and pleasure."

On the first holiday a teacher appeared at Castle Reckenburg. Nordheim junior, as proxy for his much occupied papa. And when at Epiphany Sunday the proxy laid aside his dignity, the wonderful child knew twelve fairy tales and all the letters of the alphabet, as well as the cardinal numbers. Her progress was somewhat slower under the older professor's method, but always advanced with seven league boots during Herr Ludwig's vacations, especially in the art of rhetoric. When the king's birthday came round, I no longer thought of placing the little candidate for the pot ladle in any family, but thanked God that I was permitted to keep her as the treasure of the new tower.

But it was astonishing how many unsuspected wants I daily found to satisfy, how with each gratification the hunger for new things increased, and how my sober, uniform life gradually became so bright and changeful. The child needed comfort and freedom, playmates and friends, flowers and birds, singing and music; she needed alms for the poor and shelter for the orphans, whom she had attracted to her; in a word — the child needed love!

When we glance over the lives of distinguished people, as history or poets describe them, we find in the eager struggles of their youth, in joy and sorrow, an effort to pass out of their own personality into that of others, until at last, after many an error, egotism is banished and the heroic souls, forgetting themselves, labor for the community. But it is not merely with this chosen few, among ordinary mortals a more limited, but unvarying mode of development is perceptible: joy, longing, and fulfilment in youth, and in age resignation, loneliness, modest retirement into our vocation, the mechanism of the hour, and with the happiest among us — into religion.

Nature and fate had led me by the opposite path. I had scarcely passed beyond childhood when, without dancing or amusement, friends or conflict, except the transitory one with a dream, I entered a masculine sphere of action, labored for others more than myself, and until middle life felt my existence filled by this labor. Not until the age when others begin to have white hairs, did the spirit of my lost youth, a vague longing stir within me.

And this late, almost incomprehensible longing, was stilled as if by a miracle. Out of the whole great world from which I could choose, it was the most desolate, forsaken creature, a stumbling-block thrown in my way, that crept into my heart, wove a spell around it, roused it, filled its inmost corner;

that crowded out all claims, outbid all wishes, that unconsciously transformed all my surroundings, remodelled old customs, and set the rich fulness of the present time, young faces, natural pleasures, and the rule of love in the place of inflexible axioms.

My dear Hardine, who is most indebted to the other, the helpless orphan, who took a child's place in the house of the rich old woman, or the rich old woman who, through the beggar's child, obtained youth, love, and pleasure, who through this child first became a woman and a happy mother?

Into a lonely spring, cool and transparent as crystal, a seed once fell, the germ of a flower, whose blossom no one saw. For long years it remained at the bottom, then suddenly shot upward and dimmed the clear mirror. But the sunlight was refracted in brilliant hues from the darkened surface; the first green sprig rose above it, soon a leaf unfolded, then a blue flower of the sweetest fragrance; there was life and motion in the lonely fountain, spring within and around it, color and perfume, the song of birds and vivifying sunlight. The transformation in the old spring seemed like a fairy tale.

And *therefore*, my children — *not* because a strange destiny was to be disclosed — *therefore* I have called my story a *secret*, and revered "the logic of nature" as a marvel of grace.

The little world, to which our Reckenburg had become a centre, could not fail to notice its gradual renovation, and many expected the stranger who had unconsciously caused the change to be, not only the heiress of the property, but also of the fading name of Reckenburg.

But it never entered my mind to prop up, with this new scion, the old tree which, according to God's will, was to die out. I have honored an *old* nobility as a secure support; I look upon a *new* nobility as a soap-bubble. Young races may strive after more lasting foundations. But I would never, by the sound of a name, have perpetuated a delusion which, caused by a premature hope, had been fostered by a half necessary, half defiant silence. The last von Reckenburg will not go down to her grave with even the *semblance* of dishonor.

But neither had I any intention of imposing the burden of a great property on your weak shoulders. I was not disposed to bestow my work as a source of ease, even upon the person I most fondly loved. It was a charge, a trust I transferred, and you are a woman, Hardine, whose strength is rooted in the strength of the heart to which you belong. "The child needs love," I said. "Let her love freely, according to the dictates of her own heart, without any obligations save those that spring from this heart."

Therefore it was not *unintentionally*, that I kept every one in doubt about your future relations to Reckenburg; nay, I cherished the doubt myself. You were reared and educated to suit any station, and it might have been supposed that my foster daughter would not have lacked the means to secure her a firm position in this station. A rich man, or a poor one — an old name or a new one — a contemplative or active character: the heart had a free choice, for the inheritance of Reckenburg was independent of it.

It must not be concealed, however, that a connection between the two closing acts of my life, especially an alliance with the count's family, hovered before my mind, and it is uncertain whether the sound of the ancient name did not exert a secret charm. It is certainly a difficult matter to do away with fixed mental habits called prejudices, nor is it even necessary thus to level one's little fragment of the soil of life with rake and shovel; if only in the decisive hour the judgment rises far above prejudice and the heart is in the right place.

So *secretly*, it is *possible*; the sound of the old name in which the new one was to disappear tempted me; but *openly*, I am *sure*, only the desire to fulfil a disappointed expectation spoke. I esteemed the count more than ever in his widened sphere of influence; I knew him as the *only* person among my acquaintances who, inflexible as he had been towards the appearance of evil, had not distrusted me for a moment. I saw the handsome young cavalier's regard for my Hardine, and if her heart inclined to him, why should not the advantages the parents had striven to obtain be reaped by the children? My unsuspicious Hardine, you did not see my wishes and efforts in this direction, and to-day I thank God for it. For when it became clear to me, that the count's estimation of rank was perhaps *weak* enough to bow before the inheritance of Reckenburg in my child's hand, but too strong to take this child home without a blush; when I learned to know the young gentleman as his father's son only in his weaknesses; but lastly, when I saw how Hardine's lips smiled at the unexpected desertion, and how immediately after her lids drooped before another's glance, the last bandage fell from my eyes, and at least *one* half of my last deed was arranged in secret.

Ludwig Nordheim, a native of my parish, was the grandson of my gentle friend and the son of my efficient co-worker; I had seen the best traits of both blended harmoniously in the boy, and even detected the charm that the first story-teller aroused in another heart. But they were only children, years of separation elapsed, and when he returned home it was to take leave of his father's grave and, dependent upon himself, make his own way in the world.

Energy, a cheerful temperament, a sincere love for his native soil, and — my child's blush, what more did I need to induce me to ask if he would become the elderly woman's assistant in her daily labor? And what more did *he* require to consent and introduce many a new idea into the renovating work?

Now for the first time, in the joyous intercourse of hearts, everything around me became warm and bright, fresh and gay. The present seemed so delightful, that I did not wish to think of the changes of the future. "There is still time," I said, delayed my decision day after day, and Heaven knows how long I might still have hesitated, if a ray from without — or shall I say from above — had not broken through this comfortable self-forgetfulness?

Do you remember, Ludwig, the afternoon, about

six weeks ago, when you came to me with the words: "Here is a newspaper containing the obituary of the famous Doctor Faber. I did not know that he was your countryman, perhaps might have been your contemporary. Were you acquainted with him, Fräulein von Reckenburg?"

Some business matter summoned you away at that moment, and spared me an answer which I could scarcely have found breath to utter. The first and only remaining companion of my youth had gone before me!

I took the paper in my hand and read the notice. He had died on the third of August, after a short illness. The third of August! You know what that day meant to me. Can we believe in such fatal dates? Ought we to turn from them, as a bewildering game of chance? Decide according to your own heart, but — the clock is striking one — strange — it is the twentieth of September, the anniversary of the battle of Valmy, on which I bring this record to a close.

And I read on: The man, like his wife, had died without heirs, without relatives or near connections. No point of honor would, therefore, be violated if I now told you, Hardine, and him you love: "This man's wife was your father's mother."

So the old magician, Death, once more called the old figures before me, and the sorrowful past intruded into my bright present. But, strangely enough, as vision after vision unrolled before me, your image, Hardine, suddenly appeared to me in a new light.

I had, probably, when looking at you, often been

reminded of the charming Dorothee. I saw her golden curls on your head; your features, your inquiring eyes resembled hers. But your eyes asked a different question; your figure was taller, your complexion paler, and the quiet gravity of your movements made the resemblance only an occasional one. No, it was not Dorothee's granddaughter, it was simply the child who had nestled in my longing heart.

On that evening, I now saw in my child — not Dorothee's granddaughter — but, for the first time, the granddaughter of the man, for whose heir the black countess had rebuilt the family seat of her ancestor, the man, who, if he had lived, would have prepared a home in this heritage for the beloved mother of his son. I felt as if I had only been holding a trust for the rightful owner.

Among these old recollections and new ideas I at last fell asleep and — dreamed. I have never, during my life, been much molested or blessed by dream-faces, either waking or sleeping, and I need not assure you, my children, that I consider myself anything but a visionary. I was probably agitated, but not excited, and in perfect health when I fell asleep that evening, and in perfect health I awoke the next morning, but with the distinct consciousness of a dream.

What dream? It seems to me that I might have painted it; might still paint it to-day; and yet it was something indescribable, infinite, which we only feel, not see. Shall I call it a surging sea? Or was it a dazzling cloud, which floated down before a throne and surrounded with a transparent veil four figures, kneeling hand in hand, with their eyes raised to heaven. But I saw these figures as distinctly as I ever saw them in my life, they were Siegmund Faber, Dorothee, her son, and her son's father. And a fifth was approaching them to close the chain between the last and first, but this fifth was I, myself. The shining veil floated down over me also, and voices beneath it whispered: "For as many as are led by the spirit of God, they are the sons of God."

Amid these whispers I awoke, and it was some time before I remembered that only the fountain was splashing in the morning stillness, and the shining sea that surrounded me was the morning sun, gilding the mist rising from the meadow.

I hastily rose. My pulse beat as calmly and quietly as usual, as it does at this hour. But something had awaked within, which constantly urged me on. If I had said until to-day: "There is still time enough!" I now exclaimed, "It *is* time!" and knew without reflection for *what* the time had come.

That morning, Ludwig, I induced you to utter words I had long expected to hear, and in the evening began these records. But on the day when I entrusted the darling of my heart to you, for time and eternity, I wrote my will.

You will open it — it may be in weeks, or it may be in years — on the morning after you have read these pages, and you will find in it only these few words: "The heiress of all my property is my foster daughter, Hardine Nordheim, née Müller."

I bestow the inheritance of Reckenburg upon the granddaughter, as my predecessor would have given it to her ancestor. I bestow it upon the wife of my trusted co-laborer. But I also bestow it upon the child who awoke in the lonely woman a mother's love, and *above all* I bestow it upon the orphan, with whom the spirit of love entered my domain. I do it without any conditions, for I am sure of my children's hearts.

So let this legacy crown the work of the dead race. Its motto will rule in the young tree amid the changing streams of time, and the spirit of God exert its influence to bless all future generations.

It was after midnight when the last word was uttered. Ludwig and Hardine knelt with clasped hands before the portrait of the last von Reckenburg, to renew a solemn vow. And until this hour they have been faithful to their oath.

END.